In Luc

By Julian Kitsz

In Lucem is written by Julian Kitsz, self-published via KDP Amazon. This product is a work of fiction. The views of the characters are not necessarily the views of the author. Fans of this work can keep up to date on the author and his writing via the author's website, or by following their instagram. All enquiries can be made via the author's website: juliankitsz.com.

The cover illustration and design is the work of Harry Carley. All enquiries can be emailed to: Harryoliverart@gmail.com.

Acknowledgements

The first script of *In Lucem* was finished in early 2020. Now, as 2024 draws near, with this paperback manuscript finally ready for the world, I must thank those who helped me along the way.

Firstly, I must thank my wonderful parents. They told me I would be an author long before I ever considered the idea. They have worked tirelessly to enable opportunities for me, and have supported me in all manner of ways when I fully decided to make writing my career. They are also those who have read this novel more times than they would probably have preferred, so I must thank them for their endurance. Similarly, my sister has been a steadfast supplier of words of encouragement, especially in times of crisis. My whole family has been a rock: I love you all from the bottom of my heart.

Thank you to all my friends for your ears and shoulders during my ups and downs, and for always reminding me to persevere. Those closest to me who have seen me at my lowest; words cannot express how grateful I am for your patience and support. You all know who you are, and I love you.

Thank you to Harry Carley for all the beautiful art you have created for *In Lucem*, especially the cover. Your unique mood and style seems perfect for my writing, and I look forward to an enduring creative relationship.

Thank you to all those proof-readers who took the time to read the manuscript. Firstly, Lucy, I must thank you for pointing out how the stories I fashion will be read by those with a similar lived experience to the protagonist, an especially important point where such sensitive subject matters are concerned. Though I have not experienced the grief of my protagonist first hand, I hope that any reader who has, will not feel dismayed nor disappointed by how I have represented these subjects. A writer's job is to put themselves in another's shoes, but of course, there will always be some level of disconnect. Finally, Lucy, thank you for prompting the idea of introducing scenes with Lorelei. She completely changed the entire feel of the novel.

I must thank Lisa and Gilly for their in-depth responses to the story, as well as their keen eyes for language and grammar. Thank you to Geert for engaging in questions regarding the philosophical bend of the book. Thank you to Eva and Martina for checking the French translations in this story, especially as your lives were so busy.

Thank you to John Baker at Bell Lomax Moreton. Your help with redrafting, and as literary agent, will not be forgotten.

Thank you to Mrs Weston-Betts for helping me discover my passion for literature when I was 13. Mrs Henshaw, at Sevenoaks School, your lessons still make me smile. You showed me Baudelaire and Keats – what more could an author ask for?

Finally, thank you to William Melling for letting me borrow your name in this story. It's a strong one.

Foreword

Existence is a beautiful mystery, but, at times, painful, confusing, and deeply distressing. To anyone going through a dark period, I am of the staunch belief that there is always a turn in the road, even when you cannot see it. You never know what beauty, kindness, laughter, love, and new joys await. To anyone struggling, I really hope you will find a way to keep putting one foot in front of the other to eventually fall back in love with life.

To any reader who feels alone, I urge you to seek help. I know first-hand how daunting this can be, but also how relieving. If you are ever in doubt, there are many places and resources to turn to. In the UK, for example, the Samaritans are a free 24-7 helpline on 116 123. I encourage anyone in the pits of isolation to utilise such avenues of support.

You never know just who in your life may need help. Always check on your friends and family. We're in this world together.

In Lucem

'Darkling I listen; and, for many a time
I have been half in love with easeful Death,
Call'd him soft names in many a mused rhyme,
To take into the air my quiet breath;
Now more than ever seems it rich to die,
To cease upon the midnight with no pain,'

-    John Keats, 'Ode to a Nightingale'

"Dockery was junior to you,
Wasn't he?' said the Dean. 'His son's here now.'
Death-suited, visitant, I nod. 'And do
You keep in touch with—' Or remember how
Black-gowned, unbreakfasted, and still half-tight
We used to stand before that desk, to give
'Our version' of 'these incidents last night'?
I try the door of where I used to live:

Locked.'

-    Philip Larkin, 'Dockery and Son'

I

The Unhindered Moon

May 1969

Detective Robert Melling stared at the corporeal carnage which lay sporadically across the tracks of platform one, Horsham station. West Sussex did not have abnormal suicide rates. This person, now mere fragments of his former self, was simply an average number on a national list. Then again, not everyone was reading that list. Robert Melling, inhabiting the moment of after-death, found it a sorry sight. Just hours before, Jacob Wenley, a twenty-two year old law graduate, had stood where he was now pensively standing, gazing down the linear tracks which led towards a hollowed escape through the hillside. It was almost dusk, and the detective watched as his breath fogged upwards before him, rising into the air to join the spirit of the deceased. His exhalation however, dispersed into nothing. This boy, as Melling deemed him, had wasted into symbols of his prior being, limbs hardly able to denote identity. This was a different nothingness.

The train had met Jacob at twenty-seven minutes past two, greeting him with an unfathomable velocity. Its weight alone required the mere exertion of a few miles per hour to kill him. That was unsatisfactory for Jacob. He had chosen this exact train because it didn't slow at Horsham. Yearning for its later destination, it carved through Jacob's spine with the curve of a scimitar, pushing him open, then shovelling his human shrapnel across the uncaring tracks. If indeed there was a soul, Jacob Wenley's would have had little trouble escaping his dismembered corpse. It was as though he had been pulled inside out, cracked open with his yokey blood sizzling on the warm metal brakes.

The train driver had been ordered home for the month, but Melling knew it would take far longer to process – if the man would ever fully do so. The station was closed, yet due to some egregious stupidity, the authorities had left the blended carcass to dry well into the early evening. They had been hoping to wait for Melling's authority on the matter. A picture would have sufficed.

A friend had once asked the detective what made a corpse so difficult to face, and he had instantly answered with: the smell. However, even for such a loquacious man as Melling, it would be impossible to accurately convey that sense's reaction to death. It remained an unspoken abhorrence where only those who had experienced it could authentically shudder under its wet odour. After the war he thought that every man left in England must know the smell of death. These days it seemed fewer and fewer people were acquainted with it. He was sometimes called to investigate a scene and, with one whiff of the air, Melling could declare: 'here, there is no death'. This new generation was not equipped with such a palate, and would ask him: 'how could we have known the difference?' The detective hadn't found the right adjectives for an adequate response. What he *could* convey was that the smell of death brought with it the true barrier of mortality. As soon as one's life was snuffed out and their pulse ceased, their body immediately dropped the dam of humanity. The common man was no closer to death than a medieval jouster, mid-duel. When one considered the science of it all they began to understand that mortality was a maintained mirage. One's body biologically cheated death just so long as their heart was able to thump and their brain able to send the correct orders. Too much interruption to those fundamentals permits the beginning of everyone's eventual rotting. As soon as blood cools, the smell arrives; one hadn't really passed over or away, it was simply the collapse of their wall against decay.

Melling's eye caught a severed palm dangling on a bush branch, and he stifled a retch. The boy's parents had seen the posthumous rearrangement; they had probably seen the unreadable hand reaching from the foliage. The detective pulled a cigarette from the case inside his coat-pocket and rolled a lighter in his own palm to remind himself of its presence. Striking a lonesome flame, he lit the Gitanes and took a long, slow drag.

That's suicide too… his wife used to say. She also hated the smell. He would have preferred to finish the half-smoked, seven-inch *Romeo y Julieta* in his other case, but when he worked, he moved, and it was a hindrance to always be relighting. When he worked, cigarettes were his habitual comfort. But when he could sit down and contemplate, it was Cuban cigars that he employed to soothe his mind. His wife had always ridiculed him for leaving the house with both.

His eyes went back to the semi-stumps that now passed as fingers and he pictured the boy's mother standing in his place. Had she recognised the cruel remnant? The bloodied lines of the shortened limb? Had she scorned him, herself, or God? Had the father been able to console his love, or had he struggled to stand, dropping to a knee on the hardened asphalt of platform one?

The scene conjured a polluted version of a poem he used to love. In its case, the poet had pondered what it meant for a dead father to leave behind a child, seeing life's tragic trajectories as unavoidable train tracks. Melling's literary background forced him to, as always, ponder on life's cruel ironies. The poem *he* was witnessing would be too painful for paper; hang he who would ever dare to write it! And yet he could not help but consider how universal the original poet had been. Men would always leave sons or daughters behind. Unavoidable train tracks were dreadful in their own right, but they resembled life's natural transience. There was a reason for the grief. But parents weren't meant to outlive their children, and certainly not because somebody's boy had been skewered with such unpicturable efficiency. The detective noted how much more painful poetry would be if it grappled with those rare incidences that were no less real, simply less frequent. A brutalised body and cold, uncaring train tracks, both receiving anger and tears from a mother and father. Could one neatly package such a heart-wrenching thing into writing? Then again, who would want to read such things? Shaking his head with a heavy sigh, Melling finally turned to walk away from the platform's end.

Back in the car park the local officers were chatting as the sun began to wane.

'Detective Melling?'

Melling turned to address a podgy constable who smiled, lengthening his bushy moustache and half-closing his russet eyes.

'Chief Constable Whaites.'

'Pleasure,' Melling muttered, shaking a greasy hand.

'We appreciate you coming. I trust the journey was shorter than expected?'

Robert Melling ignored the man's forced smile. He now had someone to blame for the way the boy's remains had been shamefully abandoned.

'I know you called because I was just outside the area but next time, please, Constable Whaites, make sure your team handles the human debris in a timely manner.'

Melling's irritation at their incompetence was not lost on the constable, who cringed under the disapproval.

'Apologies, sir,' the latter stuttered. 'Won't happen again, Detective Melling. I was told you had business nearby and we only wanted your expertise unspoiled.'

'Unspoiled…' Melling pondered. The notion was ludicrous. 'What spoils a body more, Constable? Fresh air or clean up?'

The man paused, russet gaze flickering in embarrassment.

'You're right, sir. That was an error.'

'The boy's parents are home now?'

'Boy, Detective? He was almost twenty-three. Hardly a lad by any means.'

'I suppose you're right, Constable,' Melling said, throwing the burned stump of his cigarette to the ground. He reached back inside his coat-pocket for one of his two beloved silver cases, but then decided against another smoke. Instead, he ran a contemplative finger over the cool metal edges as he spoke. 'I should like to see the victim's bedroom. To see if he left anything behind.'

'Certainly. I'll have my team stay on site, and I can lead the way.'

Melling began to walk to his dated Ford when the constable interrupted him. 'Detective… it's not half a mile.'

Melling sighed, desperate to avoid unnecessary conversation. Nevertheless, he joined the constable, walking away from the closing horizon.

'So, what are your thoughts, Detective?' he was asked as they wandered down a quintessentially English close, organised into red-brick, terraced units.

'I'm not quite sure one needed my expertise.'

'The Chief Inspector is an old friend?'

'We studied together.'

'Ahh, so he asked you to do him a solid?'

'A what?'

'A solid? It's what the kids say,' the man said back, but Melling cringed in the moonlight. 'Well, anyway, I'm glad he could call in the favour. Makes us feel a touch more certain about handling the process.'

'Well, as I said, though there may not be a decorum to clean-up, there is a definite in-decorum in allowing limbs to dry on the tracks. We'll be stepping into 1970 at the year's end, Constable, so we really need to handle things in a modern fashion. Never mind the parents bearing witness.'

'Apologies again, sir,' the man reiterated, staying silent as they continued walking for a few more minutes.

It's what the kids say...

Jacob Wenley didn't need the constable to understand his slang. He needed his remains cremated, not sun-bleached. *That* was doing someone a favour.

As the moon slowly waxed, they wavered by a polished white sign at waist height which read: Efrud Drive, 12.3.

'Twelve point three?'

'The area relies on lane codes,' the constable elucidated as they walked onto the lane, where Melling noted the same red-brick organisation. This time the buildings were slightly wider. The sun had now almost entirely abandoned the moon, and Chief Constable Whaites paused in front of number 116. He mumbled unintelligibly to himself.

'Pardon?'

'This is the place,' he repeated more clearly. Melling turned to the blue door and swallowed. This was the part of his job which he loathed. Fortunately, in this instance he wasn't delivering the news. Despite his experience however, the fifty-five year old had learned that there was never a way to stomach the slaughtered elephant in the room. He always found himself nauseated by the weight of grief which the family endured.

The constable walked up the dampened, stone steps and knocked thrice on the blue door as it paled in the setting horizon. Melling, as usual, yearned for a smoke to settle his unease, but instead exhaled the evening, walking up the steps as the door opened. A small boy in grey pyjamas stood expectantly below the handle, blue eyes passing between Whaites and himself. His shirt had red locomotives patterned onto it, and Melling cringed at the irony.

'Hello Tim. Are your parents in?' Whaites asked in a mournful voice. The boy ran back in, calling his mother as he disappeared. A few moments later, a woman of around forty-five met them at the door. She had greasy, dark-chestnut hair which was noticeably unwashed. Her skin was Saxon-pale, and her eyes were the same hue of blue as her son's, except hers were embedded by the racoon circles of grief, sunken in pallor and in life.

'Constable Whaites,' she said with a sniffle. Her voice had found that particular croaking which is only reached after one too many screams.

'Good evening, Mrs Wenley. I am so sorry for your loss. Jacob was truly a bright light.' He paused, waiting for a response. She snivelled, widening her empty eyes expectantly; their abyss deepened. 'We, uh, have come to try and get to the bottom of what happened.'

'It's obvious, isn't it?' she replied, somewhat aggressively, and Whaites took a step back. He looked at Melling to intervene.

'Not always, Madame,' the detective said with an injected tone of sympathy.

'Carol?' her husband asked from atop the staircase, walking down with pacing thuds. He appeared by the door to support his wife, revealing a middle-aged countenance, darker than Mrs Wenley's but no less British in nature. He had chestnut eyes that matched her hair, but his own was peppered with age and stress. More would follow. 'Whaites,' he said, seeing the constable and extending a hand which the latter shook. He turned his attention to Melling.

'This is Detective Melling from Scotland Yard. He is a specialist in tragedies such as Jacob's.'

Mr Wenley's eyes withered at the mention of his first born and first gone. Nevertheless, he remained admirably steadfast before his wife. He nodded at Melling. The latter decided to tread carefully.

'I must apologise for disturbing your home at such an hour, and so soon after your loss. I was in the area and, as Constable Whaites has said, matters such as yours are a speciality of mine. I hoped that I might be granted access into your son's room. I don't want to intrude, but it may provide some answers as to what led him to take such a drastic step.' He finished speaking and Mrs Wenley started to cry quietly, disappearing from view.

'I appreciate your help,' Wenley said, adding the word 'Detective' somewhat dubiously. 'But I can save you the trouble. He left a note.'

'A note?' Whaites asked.

'Yes,' the father responded with despondence, and Melling's heart felt all too heavy in his chest. 'He was a very serious boy. He'd been through quite a lot, you see. Well, I don't expect you to understand but...' he paused, and Melling offered a gratifying nod. He could see that there was not much more he could do for these two grievers at this time. If anything, they clearly needed time away from the likes of a constable and a detective.

'I understand completely, Mr Wenley. Please, forgive our intrusion. As this is not my jurisdiction, I'll be on my way now, but if you ever have questions, Whaites has my details. If you want to forward the note to me at any time; I understand if not, but if you do, I will offer you my perspective from all my experience.'

The father nodded and shook both of their hands, denying himself tears. His hand had betrayed him though, trembling fiercely. Melling could not imagine what it must be to witness your own son's exploded body. He imagined Mrs Wenley's wracking sobs and screams of anguish. Pain like that almost resembled the stage. He hated how they had been allowed to see it all.

As Whaites and Melling turned away, the detective felt sombre and ill. The blue door closed, separating the men from the tragedy, and closing Melling off from the Wenley family story forever, or so he thought. Occasionally, buried in the hundreds of tragedies that he witnessed, a death had the ability to make its way back to the detective when he least expected it.

'Just like that,' the constable said with a deep sigh, more in observation than in question. 'Jacob was such a smart boy too – such a dreadful shame. Where is it you went to, Detective? Somewhere posh, wasn't it?'

'Huxley College you mean?' Melling suggested, inferring that the question was academically oriented.

'That's right! He was at somewhere similar. His parents raised him well. He studied hard. He wanted to be somebody. Such a shame that he couldn't work through whatever it was that forced him to…' the man had to pause, unsure of how to finish. Eventually he settled for a repetition: 'anyway it's a bloody shame. He was such a hard-working boy.'

Melling didn't respond. When academic people died in Britain it always seemed to add to the shame of it all. That's just the way it was in the local consciousness. It was as though their snuffed, unmaterialised future prospects increased death's cruelty. He hated thinking so callously, but it was a cold truth. Even he, someone who had seen countless die in equally, perhaps more gruesome and unjust ways, felt sorrier for the lad because of who he could have been.

That thought finally saw him acquiescing to his itches and he pulled another cigarette from inside his coat pocket. Once lit, he exhaled his melancholy, trying to detach from his sickly feeling; he focused on the Gitanes between his fingers, returning to a forced state of rationality. It was hard for him to do so being the sensitive and overthinking man he was. Nevertheless, rationality had become his attempted fortress, constantly cultivated after all he had been through in his fifty-five years.

'Just like that,' the constable repeated.

'Most of them are just so, Constable. The thing with death is that it is almost always out of the blue,' he muttered. 'Anyway, this job, as you have seen, is often a therapeutic one. More one of overseeing than inferring.'

'To let them grieve in their own way.'

'Grief is universal,' Melling murmured involuntarily, dripping smoke from his upper lip. The constable watched him peer into the cloud with a disconnected gaze.

'I'm sorry?'

'Sorrow is not as individual as you think,' the detective said. His voice grew morose. 'I used to think it was but…'

'Is that what you do, sir?' Whaites asked. 'Make equations out of people?'

'Not at all, Constable,' Melling replied before releasing a repressed laugh that was void of all a laugh was meant for. 'As much as I try.'

The constable's russet eyes brimmed with pity, quickly ascertaining that the detective was far more affected by the situation than he had let on.

They both stood in silence for a minute until Melling proved unable to remain stoic. 'I feel like that's the only way through it,' he blurted out. 'What is?'

'Equations… rationality. That's the only way to handle this mess. Equations, details and probabilities. Otherwise, it won't be long until…'

'Until what?'

Melling sucked on his cigarette nervously before he spoke.

'If we don't have a means to rationalise absurdity and horror, Constable Whaites, then, well, it won't be long before it's us standing at the platform's end.'

The constable stifled a cough as he listened, and Melling's voice dropped into a despondent murmur. 'The even more vexing thing is that all we know of life is autonomous, and beyond that we can't assume that our human experience is any more unique than the experiences of the people we meet. In so many ways we are all the same. That's why whoever it is who takes Jacob's train doesn't ultimately matter. We're still forced to wrestle with the edge where subjectivity and otherness meet. On the one hand, we are ruined by the possibility of being Jacob, understanding what it would mean to *be* him.' An ironic chuckle escaped as he said: 'or not to be. To lose ourselves. Even just to know him and lose him.'

'And on the other?' the constable asked after some moments of silence.

'We can still displace him. After all, we aren't Jacob. That's the only reason why, after tossing, turning and crying: we fall asleep. If we didn't dilute and displace the world, everyone would turn a gun on themselves sooner or later. Or a train.'

The constable cringed, and Melling's mind felt like it was melting away. 'The absurdity of life is that Jacob Wenley's train could have been anyone's. It was simply him who chose the twenty-seven past two. Tomorrow, who knows? Anyone can be in front of it, just as anyone can board it.' He turned to the constable, overcome by his own analysis of everything. 'That's the underlying reason why we struggle with this.' The man shook his head, waiting for Melling to finish. 'We'll never know where Jacob is. If he even still… *is*. If, as everyone ubiquitously preaches, all we know of life is our own experience, then it is true that we cannot conceive of a life without an 'I am'. So, when we see someone else lose it, well, we feel our very own sense of self, of who we are, shattering. Someone once said that when we die, everything goes with us; that's what's so terrifying about it.' With that he gave a dry cough, signalling that he had finished talking. He had already indulged his inner sympathies too much.

The truth of the matter was that all he had just said was for Melling's own benefit. Too many things had forced him to repress his eloquence, his desire to qualify and moralise. It was just too soul twisting to fully confront the things that could, very well, one day also place him at the platform's end. Sometimes he needed a release. When it was only his own vexations and considerations, he was destined to scream at the moon. Sometimes one needed a listener. If he had gone further, however; if he had explained what happened when it wasn't a stranger, someone who wasn't disengaged from one's own inner world. If he had revealed how it felt when it was someone who had entered into one's life with a bang. When you lost more than one of the few you could claim to love. He quickly closed the doors on such thinking before even a mental articulation brought him to his knees. It quivered his lips to do so, for the dam was difficult to close after so raw an evening. He focused on the warmth of the smoke that was kissing down his windpipe.

The constable seemed to understand the detective's desire for peace, and they continued back to the car park in silence. Yet, although Melling had now promised himself an inner, apathetic speechlessness, the uncomfortable axiom he had quoted managed to reaffirm itself. It had already solidified its place in the evening: the pair were now a three, and as they walked away from the moonlight, Melling had to acknowledge what aggravated him the most: when someone died, everything went with them. How did that make sense when you left so many sufferers behind? He well knew that fact. Without you the world still rotated. Everyone in history had died and the earth kept moving. It wasn't that which was so discomforting. It was that the world would never and could never be objectified in this way. The past dead however, could be, and eventually, so could your friends and family – they had to be abstracted and distanced if you were ever to leave the house again. *Your* world was all that mattered, even if you had once called your dead wife exactly that. The world stopped turning only

when *you* left it. No one else. When someone died, everything died with
them.

II

The Supreme Drama of One's Life

Paris, October 1938

'Your views terrify me!' said the Parisienne, her coquettish giggle managing to survive the noise of shuffling feet and the clamours of conversation reverberating throughout the opera house. The man in the restrictive waistcoat beside her did not find the speaker as enjoyable as she did. Instead, he placed a protective arm on the belle's shoulder. 'So, you think there is no refinement to art then, *Monsieur?*' he asked with an interrogative scowl. Robert Melling, the addressee of the Frenchman's question, found himself smiling at the irritated inquisition, leaning back in his red-cushioned seat. With a lazy toss of the head, he requested a match from the brunette beside him. She was one of those who found a poetic danger to his idealistic arguments, all too happy to oblige as he leaned his mouth forward to light the Gitanes cigarette between his lips. The flame torched the end of his vice, and he inhaled the soily taste of fresh smoke with a sedated grin. The tobacco was like an all too tannic Pauillac from a dusty cellar, and Robert Melling was certainly a man who drank Bordeaux.

As an overeducated and overdressed Englishman, still handsomely painted by the brush of youth at twenty-four, he was indulging himself in his own opinions – especially the effect they had on others; he was spending his post-education embracing the opportunity of casting smiles on the lips of beautiful Europeans. He loved life. More accurately, he loved making a romance out of his life.

Exhaling a feigned insouciance alongside his smoke, he redirected his gaze towards his interviewer.

'I just don't think you can attach cultural prejudices to art. Or at least, you shouldn't.'

The man did not agree.

'Et pourquoi donc? Is a man not better for being cultured?'

'Comparatives only hold true for those who establish them. Your boss may consider you a better man than your colleagues. Your maidservant *en revanche*, may find you uptight.'

'And I am to weigh the opinions of who I pay?'

'Whether you do or don't, she'll still find you uptight.'

The ladies giggled at that, which only worsened the Frenchman's mood.

'This has nothing to do with art.'

'All I am saying,' Melling began, before inhaling from his cigarette, 'is that better men, as you put it, are always characterised by *types* of men. Art shouldn't be desecrated by classist presumptions. Art is for everyone. Sure, I can quote Shakespeare. Would that make me a better man? I think not. It may,' he teased, tapping a finger on his armrest, 'make me a better lover. But that is all.'

The Parisienne's cheeks blushed pink, and her suitor frowned in irritation.

'Art should be sacred. It should evolve a man,' came the thin-lipped assertion.

'Art *should* be nothing,' was Melling's easy response. 'You know, one of the greatest reasons why so few people understand themselves, is that most writers are always teaching us what we *should* be, and hardly ever trouble us with who we are.'

'*Maintenant, je suis vraiment perdue*,' murmured the husky voice of the woman beside him.

Now, I am truly lost.

'Well, my dear, I just mean that we are being forced into an age of entertainment. Books, ballet and opera. Now we have the rise of cinema too. Our quotidian is rapidly declining into something unacceptable. The coat-check lady lacks the grace or cheek that an author could otherwise have granted her, the tram conductor speaks with tones too crude for music, and the footsteps of the company we keep are never as pliant nor perfect as those wrapped in the delicate pinks of Russian academies. The realistic has become dull. Art dictates a more desirable day. Furthermore, in a world at peace, we have no means of being heroic. We have never had the chance to chase after a Helen, nor to avenge like Orestes. We, both the French and the British that is, hear of legendary battles fought by our forefathers in the name of love, lust, religion and every other absolute that humanity clings to. They rode on horses, screaming the word 'glory' as they galloped towards the arrows and swords that would signal their final breaths. Our own parents fought in trenches against the Germans,' he added with a frown, and the entire group tutted their distaste. It was a bitter memory here, especially considering the Fuhrer's current aggression elsewhere in Europe. '*Our* decisions however, bound to a life of security, lack any *real* importance. We cannot relate to heroes or villains. All we know is the meagre notion of right and wrong. We swing like a pendulum between the delights of entertainment and the bored longing of daily life.' He didn't allow himself to undermine his own loquaciousness by articulating how France was especially nervous these days, and certainly did know of villains, nor of how Europe was not as secure as politicians pretended. Nor indeed, that there were many lovers in neighbouring countries whose decisions *counted* in the manner previously idealised. Those decisions meant far more than the empty sentences said in this Parisian opera house, full of beauty and boredom.

'*Vous êtes de mauvaise influence,*' remarked the Frenchman coldly, attempting to push his lady's shoulder towards the stage.

'Not as bad an influence as entertainment, my friend. Soon enough it will truly be everywhere. We will not escape it.' He then sipped smoke from the end of his cigarette, getting lost in his own aphorisms. 'But life never follows narrative. It is predictably mundane.'

'Isn't that the point of art, though, *Monsieur?*' answered the beauty on his left whilst lighting a cigarette of her own. 'To escape ourselves?'

Melling shook his head.

'That's just it. Art has begun to suggest that life can be larger than, well, life. Life as unartistic, begins to feel further removed from art and somehow less alive. Reality starts to seem painfully unreal.'

He was at that stage in his life when the man of words realises how easily he can be perceived as brilliant, just because he is armed with enough half-true sentences. For the French belles around him, his manner of speech was enigmatic. They didn't fully understand his choice of words, making him appear more impressive than he was. Indeed, he could have used their mother tongue would that not have made him less artful in his delivery.

'So why come to the opera?' he was asked by the blonde before him, who smiled at her own question.

'I'm determined to prove myself a hypocrite, I suppose,' he said, trying to sound nonchalant.

'Or maybe you too are destined to long for art instead of life,' assured the brunette, moving another pawn towards the well-read king inside his mind. Nevertheless, before he could twist her words with further confusion, a penetrating hush cascaded down the boxes of the opera-house and into the stalls. The space was plunged into an eager silence and desirous darkness, only the poking bronze of lazy cigarettes flaring around the room with eager glow.

Given the chance to speak, he would have refuted the brunette's statement. Maybe he would have played with it or artfully misdirected her intention. That was what he did. He was a master of blurring the boundary between levity and philosophy, and yet, as they waited for the performance to start Melling, instead, considered her argument. She had dealt into his game and somehow, probably unwittingly, pierced at an inner truth. It *was* true that when the music stopped, when the ladies left, and the alcohol and smoke were all that remained, his hotel room felt void of anything other than the malodorous weight of unfulfillment. The women wrote chapters when they came, but the drama of his life remained without an all-consuming fire. As much as they sparked a piercing appeal, it dwindled with their leaving footsteps. Life never allowed him to be a hero either, merely a character. He enjoyed performing for the flirtatious smiles around him, but at what point would he find a means far greater than himself? At times he'd even settle for a tragedy if he could.

The curse of an over-read mind, his friend Harry would say. Maybe that was also true. After all, there was a reason he had applied to Scotland Yard. He had even shown a knack for analysis that was somewhat discordant to his literary studies. Perhaps studying characters had made him more attuned to characterising the criminal?

He shook his head as the spotlight bounced onto the stage, signalling the start of his next distraction. It was Berlioz's *Béatrice et Bénédict,* a comedy inspired by Shakespeare. For Melling it was another chance to flee the world. However, when the figure of Béatrice glided onto the stage, it was not comedy which Melling felt. Instead, a tragic pang of sorrow pierced his heart. He felt all too heavy in his seat, awash with a feeling he had never felt before. The usual lines of literature that helped him diagnose reality, now escaped him as he sat there, hopelessly enthralled. Her entire being was enchanting: from the raven curls that cascaded down her olive shoulders, to the rose petal lips that refused the light. Every pupil within the building seemed destined to trace the twitch of her movements, or so Melling assumed. Inside him an inner cord, hitherto untouched, began to throb, and he squirmed in his seat whilst wrestling with confusion. The orchestra was well underway with its thundering cacophony, but Melling couldn't hear it. Nor could he recall the faces of the ladies previously speaking to him. Not the rigid waistcoat of the unhappy Frenchman, nor the scent of tobacco reached his senses. This Béatrice became an all-encompassing and focalised event, flittering back and forth in her white dress. Then, she began to sing.

All at once the chorus and orchestra found his ears, but these vibrated like a lapping wavefront next to the tsunami of her voice. It plunged into him like the cannonball of revolution, struck backwards as though he were a sailor thrown overboard. Flailing in ferocious foam, he was tethered by the seduction of her siren calls, stuck in some diachronous dystopia. This was how French was *meant* to be heard. She possessed the language. She guided the words with strong inhalations, playing with each syllable as it rolled along her tongue.

His cigarette fell from stupefied fingertips and still he could not find reality. Indeed, she *became* his reality. The outside world throbbed into a numbing black as she took center stage. He tried to formulate an inner dialogue with the sensations she conjured, but for a man who was always armed with a quotation, the inner havoc she wrought seemed to wash every sentence away. He could do nothing but drink her in and watch Berlioz's art come to life through this maddening medium.

One focal understanding pulsated from within: this was the supreme drama of his life. This Béatrice was no heroine; she was the bridge between art and reality. He finally knew that he knew nothing – not armed with his preferred social constructs, at least. Here he was throwing language at the world, building things up within intricate designs, and in turn, he was met by someone who could smite these castles down with a rising octave. She simply sang. True art echoed an effortlessness that the well-read lacked by the very virtue of their need to speak artistically. Beauty and art. In their purest forms these phenomena could not be encapsulated by eloquence, no matter how loquacious the speaker. He abandoned his words. Language could no longer serve him. Only she could.

III

A Streetcar Named Death

'That's suicide too, you know?' a voice soothed from over his shoulder, as Melling struck a tall match by the chestnut-filled fireplace of his two-night hotel room. He knew the room's wide, crimson interior without looking behind him, but his mind wouldn't allow him to face the sonorous speaker. He lit his dry *Gitanes*, wetting its tip on his unplaceable lips. He drowsily inhaled its lethe-ward expulsion, and staggered slightly. 'Careful,' the voice repeated.

'Careful,' came an echo, landing familiarly on the nape of his neck. He coughed into the fireplace, adding cancerous smoke into the burning chestnuts.

'Air,' the voice offered confidently, and Melling staggered onto the balcony, pushing the white framed door as he lunged outside into the uncaring dark. He ventured slightly onwards, finding the stone edge with his hands. It iced against his fingers, and he fumbled, dropping his cigarette over the edge. His mind told him that this was a street, identifiable with the sounds of cars and peopled chaos. He, however, was detached from the humans and machines, seeing only the final sparks of his French cigarette disappear into an obscurity. The mouthless embers sailed downwards into nonexistence. 'That's where you're going anyway,' said the voice.

'Falling,' Melling mumbled in anaesthetised intoxication.

'Falling,' beckoned the voice.

'I ca… can't…'

He heard people scream below him, gradually losing feeling in his limbs at the speed at which ice melts. The horn of a distant tram grew closer.

'Melt,' the voice said in instruction. He was to dissolve.

'No,' Melling croaked, whose face numbed against a single tear. It ventured towards his chin, pausing mournfully where it found the oxygen, hanging there in trepidation.

'Melt,' someone said, almost questioningly.

'Orders,' Melling slurred. He licked his lips, and they tasted like chaos. The voice grew in comprehension.

'Solve the equation, Detective,' it mouthed from behind him.

'Everything goes with them!' yelled Constable Whaites from below.

'Yes, everything goes with you,' cooed the voice.

'So, do you,' Melling said, his intended determination coming out as a mumble. He now felt nothing but the smell of chestnuts. As he faded into obscurity, his eyes bronzed into embers. The tear droplet fell, and a woman screamed.

'Auf Wiedersehen,' murmured a familiar voice from above him.

*

London, May 1969

Sunlight sprang earnestly through the window of 13, Thurloe Place, South Kensington. It was a Spring late-morning, Sunday the 9th of May. Detective Robert Melling lay asleep in the master bedroom of the family's historic, white-painted home. Thurloe Place arranged these terraced buildings in a quadrant fashion, just thirty metres away from the underground railway that had opened almost a century ago.

Outside of the curtain-drawn bedroom, the Irish housekeeper, Mrs Dryad, whose original employment had begun with the detective's father, was standing in apprehension, holding the detective's breakfast on a silver tray with the morning's paper folded next to his toast. The reason for her apprehension? Melling's old friend had called, or so she had claimed to be, asking for a favour, and Mrs Dryad had recognised a peculiar sense of mourning in her voice. Despite the nature of Melling's work, she felt an ominous foreboding in this particular favour. She stood perturbed, postponing the day.

'This is ludicrous,' she finally scoffed to herself. 'Mr Melling!' She knocked twice as accustomed, then opened the door. Striding in, she dropped the tray onto his Venetian bed, noting the sunken eyes of a poor-night's sleep.

'Morning Gladys,' he said lazily with an unthinking yawn. Mrs Dryad ignored his first-name assumptions. She was old-fashioned that way.

'Mr Melling, I'm not sure you've slept,' she said. Though she had not returned to the Republic of Ireland for at least twenty years, her homeland accent was as strong as ever.

'Is it my eyes again?'

'Quite disturbingly.'

'Well, contrary to the wisdoms of poets: eyes lie.'

'If I hadn't heard the ivories last night, I might believe you.'

'I'm sorry Gladys, you know how it reminds me of her.'

'That's quite alright, Mr Melling. Though I do wish you would take the medication the doctor gave.' She perched on the end of his chocolate sheets. 'They really might do you some good.'

'I'm afraid,' Melling sighed, 'it'll remain Scotch therapy. Well, Scotch and Debussy.'

'And I suppose a long, dry *Romeo y Julieta?*'

'The holy trinity,' Melling agreed, lying back in relish. Mrs Dryad scoffed, crossing herself. She unfolded his paper and pondered the recent phone call. 'What's on your mind, dear Gladys?'

She had clenched her jaw in thought, and her employer well knew when something was bothering her. 'Well, spit it out.'

'Mr Melling, I know you don't care much for my premonitions but, well, I received the most uncanny phone call.'

'Gladys,' he groaned.

'No, no, please, Robert,' she said quickly. 'You must listen to me now.' She then regretted her informal outburst and Melling noted that she straightened her clothing before speaking, as though she could restore convention that way. '*Mr Melling,* last night, when you played at that lonesome hour, I can't explain it, but as I lay listening.'

'Gladys…'

'No, you really must listen to me for once. You see, I felt the most distressing calm wash over me. Your lullaby faded away and only a coldness remained. Even though I was so cold, so fearful, I couldn't quite place myself in the room. I felt… distant.'

'As much as –'

'And then the call. The call this morning. That lady's voice sounded like the lullaby. It really did take me back. It was the most peculiar thing, but I felt myself back in my bedroom, freezing in death.'

Used to her histrionics, Melling replied through deflection.

'We ought to sort the upstairs draught.'

'Mr Melling!'

'I'll make sure to mute the piano. About that call?'

'Oh, I beg of you. Do not ask me to elaborate on such wickedness.'

'Wickedness!' he repeated with a laugh, eyes wandering to the breakfast tray.

'Mr Melling,' she continued flatly, earning a loud exhale from the detective.

'Mrs Dryad?' he said in playful echo, but her response was only to pause in reservation, hesitating by the door.

'No, I won't do it!' Then, with a huff, she sprinted from the room, leaving him sprawling in his bed.

He had not slept well. In fact, he had not experienced a refreshing night for some months now. The continuity of it all was really starting to irritate the detective, who ironically, remained unable to detect the cause of his own condition. His melancholy, as the doctor had termed it, resulted from the loss of his wife. His sleep deprivation and unrecollectable nightmares however, these remained a perplexing mystery for the doctor, leaving Melling with medication instead of answers. Lately, whenever he awoke with the flight of fear, chasing the escaping memory of a dream, he took to his Steinway, haunting the halls of his Kensington abode.

He dug his knife into a pot of butter, dwelling on the incredulous Gladys Dryad. How that lady fashioned such absurd sensitivities was almost amusing. Opening the paper, he glanced over the morning's headlines, ignoring almost everything political. By the time he made it to the commentary on yesterday's wickets however, Mrs Dryad had returned.

'Okay, I *will* tell you her name, but only on one condition,' she said, patently distressed. Robert Melling dropped the paper onto his tray and lowered his brows.

'And who is this unnamed madame?'

'The lady on the phone. Please pay attention, Mr Melling.'

Melling chuckled at her semi-comedic attitude and sat-up.

'So, what is your condition?'

Mrs Dryad found the end of his bed, again, and nervously played with the sheets.

'I beg of you, whatever she needs, to politely decline.' She looked up at the detective in earnest, and Melling couldn't help but laugh. 'Please, don't laugh like that. I really feel some foul play about this whole affair.'

'Foul play? You inferred all of this from the lady's voice?'

'Just something about it makes me… well…'

'Alright,' Melling said with a mutter of defeat. 'What's the hag's name?'

'She is no hag. In fact, you're the same age.'

'What makes her so unappealing then?'

'Oh, to hell with it,' Gladys sighed. 'It's a Miss Olivia Rosewood.'

'Rosewood?' Melling shouted involuntarily. 'My God, it's been years. What was this all about, then?'

'Call her yourself,' she replied, going to the door. 'Just remember, *not* to take the favour.' With that, she left his room with a final huff.

'Livia Rosewood asking me for a favour,' the detective mused. He recalled her English beauty: raven eyes against blonde hair, mixing with paling dimples. Her charm and sarcasm were Melling's twin favourites, however. They had gone toe to toe in wit on many occasion, for they had studied together at Huxley College, the historic namesake of the medieval Baron Huxley in the Midlands. Revisiting the university in his mind, he remembered his father's pride at seeing his son graduate from one of Europe's top institutions. Robert had been standing next to the son of the French Ambassador which had truly been the cherry on the cake for his father, William Melling. But Livia, what had happened to her? He hadn't seen her in years, not since her engagement to the Duke. Then again, hadn't Gladys referred to her as a Miss? A thousand questions danced inside Robert Melling's mind as he finished his tea. So dear a past acquaintance, no, a close friend, despite the years, should certainly not be refused. Yet what a state Gladys was in!

Fuelled by these new perplexities, Melling ventured to his bathroom and washed himself in his silver tub, scrubbing away his fatigue and watching as it disappeared down the drain. In his dressing room he cringed, as he always did, at the suits, custom-made by the gentlemen from Savile Row. His eyes fell on the untouched oak drawers, wherein lay one hundred handkerchiefs of every colour under the sun; none would ever again find his coat pocket. There *had* been a time when his appearance was a critical factor behind his morning routine. How many times had he sported his days in Tuscan greens, London greys and threads the tone of Arabian sands? It used to mean so much to him: to be overdressed as well as overeducated. Now, as he caught a glimpse of his aging frame in the dress-mirror, his face seemed paler than he last recalled, and it hardly bothered him. He cared little for how the world perceived him, neither in image nor in intellect. Some of the arrogant axioms he used to pronounce now buried him in shame.

Once dressed, he returned to find the bed made and breakfast cleared away. On his desk, Gladys had written Olivia's number and address. Feeling giddy, he took the writing downstairs to the phone, waiting through four rings before the melodious whisper of a woman he recognised intervened.

'Rosewood residence.'

'Still that name after all this time Livia. You were so determined to be married off at Huxley, I have to say I'm a little surprised.'

'Robert?' came an uncertain whisper. Then, with recognition came a laughing candour. 'Oh my, I can't believe it! Still teasing me as always. It is so wonderful to hear from you! I shouldn't have waited so long. How *did* we let it get to this?'

'How did we, indeed?' Melling said as he smiled. 'Though, that's partly because I was led to believe that you had left for Austria in order to join your Duke.'

'Oh, strapping Luca! How funny! Well, Robert, you were right about him after all. Turns out, despite his lands, he was ultimately ruled by his mother.'

'Welcome to the masculine race, my dear.'

She laughed into his ear.

'I've missed your wit. I really have.'

'And I yours. I was delighted when I heard you'd called.'

He was met by silence, and he cursed himself for not, perhaps, having had the forethought of exercising some sensitivity. What a state Gladys had been in, after all!

'Robert, you weren't to have known but…'

As he waited for clarity, he felt an overwhelming sense of pity.

'Olivia, I'm so sorry. Whatever has happened. Whatever I can do to make you happier, I will do it in a heartbeat.'

He heard her sniffle.

'Thank you, Robert. Hearing you say that makes me regret not having you back in my life sooner.' Her voice had cracked, and Melling debated whether to take the train down and visit her.

'Livia, what happened?'

After a few moments of dreadful silence, Miss Rosewood answered.

'It's Lucy, my daughter.'

'A daughter?' Melling said, wondering where the time had gone. His voice was a cautious whisper.

'Yes,' Olivia whispered back. 'A beautiful, intelligent and clumsy daughter.'

Melling beamed through tears that had just started to form in light of the agony on the other end of the line.

'How wonderful. Does she have her mother's eyes?'

'She did,' was the reply. Detective Melling was accustomed to the past tense, but to be reunited with an old friend in the light of death seemed to be the cruellest discordance that life could muster.

'What happened?'

'Evidently, she wasn't happy,' Miss Rosewood said with a tear-choked stutter. 'She was always a sensitive girl, but I never dreamed she would feel such dreadful things.'

Melling now understood that this call involved his work, and he pledged himself to Olivia in that moment. Hearing her voice forced a blind devotion which only nostalgia could leverage.

'What can I do?'

'I knew you would help,' Olivia cried out between her actual crying. 'I knew you would.'

'It's alright, my dear. Just tell me what to do.'

'She was at Huxley, just like us.'

Recollections swam in his half-smiles, and he cried silently from his end of the phone, completely overwhelmed by her wretched tones. 'She was in her final year when it all happened.'

'I'm so sorry,' Melling offered, painfully. 'I'm so incredibly sorry for losing Lucy.'

Olivia cried anew into his ear, and Melling then found himself pacing nervously in indignation. 'That Huxley can fail with this! They don't care one bit for a child's happiness. There's always someone who falls through the cracks.'

'My friends keep saying she was delicate –'

'Nonsense! The place was as much a physical prison as an intellectual one. How we managed the pressure was pure luck. I mean, we didn't know any better. These days, children know an awful lot better.'

'The professors are telling me it's a classic case but Robert, she should never have wound up in such a position as to take… take her…'

She couldn't finish that sentence; 'Robert,' she managed. 'Robert. I'm not calling for the reasons that you think. You see, I know your profession, and well, with your mind back then there's no surprise as to why you are the man you are now. I was going to ask you the most awful of favours.'

'But of course I'm going to say yes to whatever it is that you need, my dear.'

'Oh Robert Melling, your heart hasn't changed since Huxley, though I fear it will now.'

He paused at the remark, turning rational.

'What do you mean?'

He waited for a reply as Olivia sniffled.

'Robert. I know my Lucy was sensitive, and perhaps susceptible to what I keep being told is melancholy. However, Lucy... Oh please, Robert. Please don't think less of me for saying it. But she wasn't herself. I cannot explain it, but something about my poor girl's last moments doesn't make sense. She was reading things too serious... too morbid. Nothing about this makes sense, not even the reasons she gave to...' She couldn't finish the sentence. Her daughter's suicide note had cut her off, and Melling wouldn't allow her to relive the words.

'You don't need to finish.'

'Please don't think less of me,' came a fearful whisper.

'Less of you? Olivia, I can only see you as braver by the second,' he said, fully understanding just why she had called. She wanted an investigation. 'If something tells you I need to ask certain questions on behalf of your daughter, then I will go to Huxley and do exactly that.'

'Oh Robert, I... I'm not sure how to react to such a beautiful man. I knew, I knew in my heart that you were the one to call!' Then her voice croaked: 'Thank you.'

Melling heard a man scold her quietly. 'Robert?'

'Olivia?'

'I'm afraid I must go. I'm so sorry for being so flighty, but I have a lot to work through over here!'

The voice spoke again, and Olivia grew louder. 'She shares her mother's family name. Please keep me in your heart Robert, as you are in mine. I must go.' With that, she hung-up the phone, leaving Detective Melling trembling in his kitchen. The call was over sooner than it had started.

So, Olivia Rosewood had a daughter, but that daughter had tragically taken her own life. Melling felt his heart cruelly whetted.

What a disgraceful sensation: to be presented with the joy of learning that his old friend had birthed an intelligent girl, only to learn of this wonderful creation's demise all at once. He felt sickened, slamming the phone down in hopeless anger. When would the heartbreak stop?

Wiping his eyes, he hurried for his front door. He heard Gladys call after him but he bolted, running away from Thurloe Place; he heard nothing in the busy street save his black shoes clapping against the grey stones in a pacing hysteria. His lips quivered for Scotch and an ear to offload onto.

'Harry's,' he said to himself, sprinting over the street and narrowly avoiding a car as it honked past. The sound plunged the detective into remembrance, sucking his daze away. He watched after the car as a familiar voice called out from somewhere inside his hysterical thoughts. For the briefest of moments, he felt the vaguest sense of recognition tearing through his mind as he climbed over questions – questions which seemed rooted in a faraway place he knew not how to control. For but the slice of a second, he didn't even feel awake. Caught somewhere between *déjà vu* and the pushing pinprick of memory, the car's horn had rooted him. But the sensation fled as soon as it arrived, and the horn of the vehicle died away in the distance, as did whatever memory had been struggling to the surface. He shook his head and carried on over the main road, sprinting towards *Saturn's Bespoke Tailors.*

IV

Huxley's Ghosts Always Meet

Paris, October 1938

He had been too overcome to act. The curtain had closed and everyone around him had left him in his state. In his mind's eye, he had ripped the velvet from the stage ceiling and hunted for an audience with that person who seemed to blend art and reality until neither binary sufficed. Then he decided that such behavior was not realistic, and that one couldn't simply demand to speak to the main performer. Besides, a part of him was too anxious of what would ensue. Surely, he could keep watching, keep enjoying, never breaking the invisible barrier that kept her as an entertainer and him as spectator?

'*Monsieur?*' he was finally prompted by a half-giant with a long moustache. The man had just checked his pocket watch, and was as rain-soaked as Melling.

'About bloody time.'

The black-suited, balding Frenchman was the gateway between the raining of droplets and the raining of sensations; Melling was standing outside one of Paris' hidden dens for his sort. For those bored intellectuals with money in their wallets and quotations in their heads, the city housed some well-kept secrets which only those with copious curiosity and craziness lusted after. This haunt was named *Le Lapin Blanc*, and Melling was too often prepared to follow the white rabbit down into wonderland, trading glasses and wit with his fellow hedonists. Tonight however, he lusted after details rather than delicacies.

Melling left the giant behind, finding a familiar darkness. He traced the downwardly winding way by keeping one hand trailing along the wall. The deeper he went, the more he felt the rowdiness that awaited as it vibrated from below. Soon enough, he was among the horde of hilarity, hope and hopelessness; it was maddening from the start. *In media res*, one was flung into a gold-painted ballroom, marble-top bars on either side, the trumpets of an up-tempo jazz band shrilling the eardrums. Melling narrowly avoided a hurrying waiter, tray blooming with slender cocktails. He watched the man tiptoe around the sweat-glinting ankles of all those dancing. Many elites preferred the other cocktail haunts littered around Paris for their greater tranquility, softer jazz and desirous, cavern-tavern appeal. For those who had been overstimulated most of their lives however, it was necessary to always be chasing a subsequent sensation. *Le Lapin Blanc* threw as many at you as they could, all at once.

Tonight, he had chosen *Le Lapin Blanc* because he knew of a certain someone who had a penchant for the swinging drumbeat. Melling also knew where he would find her: couched with fellow *culturati*, sharing a bottle of champagne but ignoring all their witticisms. Looking at the far left of the sweating dancefloor, Melling already espied the purple bow that would decorate her hair. He cut through the crowd and walked up to the emerald cushions on the platform.

'Patty!' he shouted, but the fifty-two year old music journalist stared straight at the stage, smoking slowly from a lapiz pipe. All he managed was the attention of Albert Lenchen, whose thirty-something face was already wrinkling from the copious cocaine lines he had sniffed his way through. The brown in his eyes could not be darker than the poison he preferred, but one could spot the twinkle of sharp wit.

'Robert bloody Melling!' he shouted, shooting to his feet with a clap of the hands. 'Huxley's ghosts always meet!' He rushed over and clasped the younger man on the shoulder. 'How are you, chap?'

'Just fine, Bertie. Didn't realise you were back from Capri.'

'Oh, stuff Capri! There's nothing good to dance to, and no one speaks French. Have you noticed how awfully whiney Italian women sound?' Melling choked a laugh.

'I've never been to Capri. But I'm sure they have adjectives for how *we* sound.'

The man laughed, running a hand through sweaty dark-blonde curls.

'You're too democratic. You know women love a man who's slightly mean.'

'Oh yes,' Melling laughed before his sarcastic rejoinder. 'I believe it was the Buddha who said something similar.'

'Oh, don't be *too* good! Patty's already a dullard when the music is the most alive. Imagine it, Melling, to shrivel up more into concentration the faster the drums go! I'd imagine she practically gyrates when the violins come out!' With that he boomed his characteristic laugh.

Patty hailed from New York but was *the* worldwide authority on all things Opera. At six years old, she could play Tchaikovsky on her father's dated piano with her eyes closed. She had the ear, the passion, and as it turned out, the prose to keep things avant-garde. She kept her journalism where the money was, but her heart was always on pushing boundaries, for flare. She loved the orgiastic nature of the screams and sweat… of the unrelenting drum. That's why she went silent under the aggression of the band; she was inhaling the performance, millisecond by millisecond. She was a good contrast to the superficial yet oddly charming Bertie, a classic English gentry with too much money, boredom and enthusiasm. Some of their comrades in Paris found him distasteful, but they always allowed him to pick up the bill. Melling enjoyed his transparency.

'Ironies are everywhere, my friend,' he offered in conclusion.

'The man speaks truth,' the fun-lover shouted, now turning back to the final three guests seated behind him. '*Permettez-moi de vous présenter un homme capable de réciter Hamlet à l'envers!*'

'*Qu'est-ce un Hamlet?*' an auburn belle dressed in gold asked her friend. *What is a Hamlet?*

Said friend, with northern-blonde hair, scowled, not even dignifying a response.

'It is hardly important what a Hamlet is,' Melling offered both with a smile. 'What's more important is that I cannot cite Shakespeare backwards.'

'As if the alternative would have seduced them,' Patty said with a laugh, finally joining the conversation. She kissed Melling's cheek as he sat beside her.

'How are you, darling?' she asked with her classic, old-money, North American honey. Her voice was lower and far raspier than it had been in her youth.

'Here for you, actually,' Melling replied, earning a raised brow, just as the jazz singer called up all lovers for a swing.

'That's our cue,' Bertie shouted, re-leaping to his feet and escorting the two girls onward. He held a seductive stare with the blonde as she passed, then he darted back to Melling with an embarrassingly obvious grin.

'That one's trouble. Isn't she gorgeous?'

'A very fair beauty.'

'Fair, but let's hope unjust!' Bertie finished with a cackle before chasing after the ladies.

'*Votre ami est fascinant*,' the man seated opposite complimented.

Your friend is fascinating.

He had bushy brows that matched his marron hair, with a round face that templated kindness.

'You think so?' Melling replied with a laugh. 'Whenever I see him, I think: God, why am I not drunk already?'

That brought a laugh from the gentleman. Melling noted that he was rather underdressed for *Le Lapin Blanc*, but Melling was also jealous of the fact that he didn't seem out of place. Someone who carried themselves comfortably could wear anything.

'Before you showed up, he was just telling us that foreplay could never go on for *too* long. That it had no limits,' Patty said. The Frenchman laughed in recollection.

'He was at the limits of his French too, I believe,' he proposed in his thick Parisian accent, and now both Melling and Patty were laughing. Bertie's laugh returned too, for he was staggering before the three of them, slightly out of breath.

'I have no limits!' he roared with a drunken grin. 'Now Pierre,' he said, putting a hand on the Frenchman's shoulder. 'You've been requested for a dance.'

'*Bon*,' the gentleman acquiesced, though probably in his late sixties, getting to his feet. 'One must always dance if a lady asks.' Then, with a wink, he was following Bertie back into the sweating throng.

'He is going to give that man a heart attack,' Patty said with a giggle.

'Who is he?' Melling asked, finally turning to his friend. Her usual purple-bow was there, and he smiled under the constancy. Patty's eyes were a common brown, but the sharpness of her stare was far from typical. Her white skin had freckled slightly with age, and her lips were stained by too much tobacco. Tonight, she seemed worn.

'A dear friend of mine: *Pierre Veilleux*,' she pronounced with mellifluence. 'He was the first man to rent me a room in Paris all that time ago. He used to stay up for me when I was out late, just to make sure I wouldn't have trouble.'

Melling nodded slowly.

'And what's with you, my dear? You seem tired.'

'You aren't supposed to say that, Robert! What would your mother say?'

Melling chuckled but held her gaze. She frowned.

'What's the matter?'

Patty looked away, her fingers tapping nervously on the table. 'Patty?'

'Oh, to hell with it,' she said, voice dulling with a metallic melancholy. 'I'm dying, Robert.'

Melling was stupefied. Not quite allowing her words to actualise. 'What?'

'Oh, don't look at me like that!'

'Like what?'

'Like… that… *that*. With pity. I'm still me, and I refuse to be a pitied version.'

'What happened?'

'Cancer,' she said with futility.

'But the battle isn't over!'

'There is no battle, Robert. That implies it is up to me to win. That's like telling a baby to try harder not to drown. There are no losers and winners in this death.'

Melling released a heavy exhalation. She *was* right. He had reached for the first defence at his disposal, but her realism was too sharp for such hollow statements. He wasn't sure what to say.

'Bloody hell,' he managed. 'How long?'

'Not much left for old Patty,' she said with dampening eyes. She was steadfast, however. Melling's heart was turning.

'Hence your old friend, Pierre?'

She nodded.

'It is time to be around kindness and music.'

'I'll drink to that,' he said, raising his glass. 'And to a worldwide musical authority. Someone who changed the scene, someone you cannot meet twice, and… to a bloody good friend.' His eyes were watering.

'That's much better than saying I look tired,' Patty laughed, and they took a sip of their drinks. The champagne tasted flat in Melling's mouth.

'If anyone could be more stubborn than death, it's you, you know?' he said in earnest.

'That's sweet of you, darling. But what's even the point? We are all destined for it, right? Better it takes me now before I become one of those ladies whom society forgets. I see them all the time and I don't have words to say how I feel. They cling to their handbags, they crawl around, alone. They used to be dancers like the rest of us: singers, lovers, haters, writers. Now they are forgotten, but still living. Are you even alive when that happens? If the world rejects you, do you truly live?' She pointed at the stage. 'That singer is nothing without us sitting here.'

'You have given many people a spotlight,' Melling complimented. 'Under your logic you have kept so many alive. Besides, *you* will never be forgotten.'

'You're a man of words, Robert,' Patty said, smiling slowly. 'But they *are* always well-meaning words.'

'I haven't had the chance to offer anyone much else,' Melling said, turning introspective.

'You will at some point. You are still trapped by your education and money.'

'That's not –'

'No, no. Don't make it personal. You're still a diamond to me, but you're also still green, darling.' Then a thought struck her. 'Anyway, you wanted to ask me something?'

'Well, I'm embarrassed to tell you why I came now.' He looked at his hands. 'To discuss something superficial after…'

'Let us not remind ourselves! By all means: keep matters superficial. Though don't think I will go easy on you.' She wagged her finger with a smile, and Melling realised she wanted him to carry her from her reality.

'When do you ever?' he said with a playful wink. 'Well then, I wanted you to tell me all there is to know about the Béatrice I saw last night.'

'You mean from the Berlioz?'

Melling nodded. 'Oh, for goodness sake,' she said with a big huff. 'Is art ever separate from women for you?' Her shoulders had raised to an almost hyperbolic level.

'Now come on, Patty!'

Patty just burst into laughter, then pointed at the singer once again.

'It is too easy for me to see that singer as nothing other than the bridge between me and the dizzying notes he knows how to sing. I don't sexualise him for doing so!'

'But there is a tension within him as medium too!' Melling flustered.

'This is true, darling. But you seem a little too preoccupied with the latter than the former. Art doesn't come before romance for you. They arrive together. Which, well, is fine. It is beautiful in a way because it's the perfect example of subjectivity – the art unfolds in your mind. Not mine.'

Melling felt uncomfortable.

'Do you really think I am too concerned with women?'

Patty's brown eyes widened with a mother's sympathy, and her voice was soft.

'It isn't your fault. You haven't really felt what it means to properly exist amongst others yet, but you will. For now, Shakespeare and seduction is your prerogative, and there is nothing false in that.'

'There's *more* to it.'

'Oh Robert,' she began, placating him with a hand on the shoulder. 'Don't intellectualise it. Just because you use bigger words than the women who listen to you, doesn't mean you're any different from Bertie! At least he is to the point with them. You make a game of it!' She was laughing again. 'And both you and these women are pretending it's real. It is a mutual romance. They make you the foreign gentleman, and you make them the foreign belle. In time you will realise that men and women can mean many other… *simpler* things to one another. But you hate simplicity. You want the existential. You are always after what is *too much*. That is dangerous too. You would have been happier an illiterate labourer, believe me.'

Melling was grated by her words because the mirror she held up was too obvious to refute.

'Perhaps you're right,' he relented, shifting uncomfortably. It *was* true that he was playing an intellectual game. It wasn't as though he was unaware of what he was doing, but he was only now beginning to feel childish under her reasonable brown eyes. Those same eyes filled with greater empathy.

'Now, now, Robert. It isn't all so serious.' Then she chuckled. 'I am *dying*, remember?'

'Not a laughing matter.'

'I am beginning to realise how straightforward it all is. When I'm not afraid, I'm humorous. Strange, no? Well besides,' she continued. 'I suppose I could tell you something about that Berlioz performer.'

'You would?' Melling started, heart lifting excitedly.

'Goodness me,' Patty toyed. 'She really left an impact. Well, I'm glad,' she said, almost to herself. 'Glad that you give her the credit she deserves. She has all the misery, love, hope and anger of a world war. In all my career I have scarce been so astonished as I was by her performance. So young too.'

Melling was silent under the weight of memory. 'I will be honest with you, Robert. I don't know her name, because, well, perhaps it is nonsense, but I have avoided finding out who she is for as long as possible.'

'Then it is not cupid's arrow that struck me, but something else entirely that has struck us both,' Melling said in an energetic prophecy. 'I did not want to meet her because I was afraid it would ruin everything I felt.'

'Then you are finally learning how to experience art,' Patty aphorised. 'You are fully accepting it. Well then, if any woman deserves your narratives, it is certainly that singer. She deserves to fill many more too. She has a rare gift.'

'About who are we talking?' a warm, aged voice interrupted. Pierre had returned and he looked at Melling with a cheeky grin. 'Whoever she is, and however beautiful she is, I can assure you she is someone else's nightmare.'

Melling laughed outright at that.

'*Elle est déjà mon pire cauchemar*,' he replied. She was already his nightmare.

'Don't be too dramatic,' Patty said.

'What do you do?' Pierre asked Melling.

'That question is too loaded,' Melling replied all too honestly. 'Literally speaking, I spend money that isn't mine to live a life that belongs to poetry.'

'You don't work?' The question was asked without judgement, and Melling shook his head. '*Bon.* But you *are* smart?'

'Incredibly,' Patty asserted.

'Smart enough to know that I should be working.'

That made them all laugh.

'Who's the girl?'

'Someone I saw last night.'

'*Et... c'est tout?* You saw this girl?' He sighed before continuing. '*Donc*, you're saying that you spend your day doing nothing and you don't have time to talk to this girl?'

'I didn't say I do nothing.'

'It was implied.'

'Look, it wasn't like I didn't want to meet her... I just. Have you ever seen something so beautiful, to engage with it would be a crime?'

The man paused, running podgy fingers through his moustache.

'You're a reader, *non?*'

'*Oui.*'

'*J'en étais certain, ça saute aux yeux,*' he replied flatly.

That is all too clear.

That earned a snigger from Patty. She was enjoying the conversation more than the music. Pierre worked his mouth as if fighting to capture the correct words in translation. Eventually he found them. 'Keep the heroines for the books, *mon ami.*' Then he grew animated, talking to both of them now. 'Once, I was playing guitar behind the Odeon *avec mes amis.* During my performance there was the most beautiful woman...' He paused for a moment, a lonely smile twisting the edge of his ruddy lips. 'I will always remember the way she looked.'

'How *did* she look?' Patty asked.

'*Non*,' came the smiling denial. 'I could never share her!'

Melling chuckled at the man as he continued. 'She smiled at *me*, you see? That smile: we will always have shared it. There was something there and I know we both felt it.'

'And *you* didn't talk to her?' Melling asked.

'It is as Baudelaire wrote: *J'ignore où tu fuis, tu ne sais où je vais.*'

'I ignore your direction, while you don't know mine,' Melling murmured in translation.

'There is a beauty in that, *non?* That distance? *Ne te verrai-je plus que dans l'éternité?* We are destined to share only a few seconds. Had we met, maybe she would have been the love of my life. *Mais,* maybe she would have been *la femme la plus ennuyante!'* He laughed again, loudly. 'Still, we will always share that magical moment. She and I can always look back to it wherever we end up. I'll probably feel that look when I take my final breath. *Mais,*' he continued, motioning to the room around him. 'No matter where I am now, with moments like this, one can always imagine another life, *non?'* The man had seemed mentally elsewhere as he spoke, but now, awfully, he was all-too present, and Melling felt an eerie tug in his chest. It was like he was listening to his own internal monologue.

'That's exactly my problem.'

'*Quoi?'* Pierre asked with an investigative look.

'I seem determined to keep women inside some narrative.'

'As if I didn't just tell you that,' Patty said with a self-righteous laugh.

'*Bon.* So, it's as I thought. You imagine what women could be rather than seeing who they are. You were as I was.'

'Hold on just one moment,' Melling began, but was interrupted.

'*Mon ami.* Take it from me. It is better to leave women out of dreams and nightmares.'

'I fear I may have —'

'Forget the books. Forget them! Whoever that woman was —' he paused, looking for the end of the sentence. Melling was about to answer when the man became enlivened once more. 'Do you not think I regret my woman? If I could go back, I would settle for more than just a smile. *Oui* there is a romance to the separation *mais...* if I was young once more.'

'You're saying you would gamble meeting her and losing all the poetry, in favour of the poetry of never meeting her?'

Pierre smiled warmly.

'You still have youth, *Monsieur.* You cannot leave it up to *you* to decide who she is! You must learn to discover her. Maybe not her, *mais* the next. If you spend your whole life making romances...'

'You will keep pushing real ones away,' Patty finished for him.

'*Exactement.*' The sagacity ended with a kind smile. '*Compris?*'

'You know,' Patty continued, brown eyes becoming parental once again. 'Though I too was struck by that desire for distance, clearly Cupid still fired a shot. It was clearly reserved for you. Pierre is right. You cannot fall in love from a distance. You would only be imagining something that doesn't happen. You know what,' she paused, growing excited. 'I don't think you should wait for the next. You should meet the singer!'

'*Oui, oui.*' Pierre added with a grin. 'I agree with Patty. Find the girl! Then tell us everything!'

'Everything!' Patty chimed, raising her glass.

'I'll bloody drink to that,' Melling said, heart stirring with anticipation.

'Oh good, we're drinking again!' Bertie shouted, surprising all three of them. He was alone and drenched in sweat.

'Where are your friends?' Patty asked with a smirk, clearly knowing the answer. Bertie huffed.

'They danced too slowly.'

'You mean they danced away from you?' Melling replied. Pierre and Patty laughed.

'They'll be back,' Bertie stubbornly lamented, dropping beside Melling.

'Maybe when the check comes,' Patty said, tones teasing rather than sarcastic.

'Oh, I'm banking on it,' Bertie wittily rejoined with a shameless grin. 'The bishop should embrace the fact that he moves diagonally.'

'I'm stealing that quote,' Melling said with a laugh, always keen to arm himself with a rejoinder.

'As if you haven't been taking notes since we met, dear chap. I swear, had we been at Huxley together you would be a wiser man, now.'

'I would certainly be more outgoing,' Melling said, turning to Patty. 'Perhaps less a man of words.'

'Here, here!' Bertie shouted, raising his glass. 'Leave the words for fat, old Huxley academics. Let *us* drink, dance and spend our fathers' money!'

V

Doctor's Orders

London, May 1969

'Olivia Rosewood, eh? She was certainly cryptic back in the day.'
'Women always seem cryptic to you, Harry. You understand men better,' Detective Melling replied. He was in the cigar-den of his oldest acquaintance's Kensington home. They were couched in brown-leather armchairs below *Saturn's Bespoke Tailors*. Dr Harry Saturn, Melling's friend since their lives began, was a retired surgeon who took to running his late father's tailoring business. He had short grey hair and a skinny physique, almost grasped by his narrow fitting clothing. As customary, Harry was in braces, resting a pensive hand under his pointed chin, widening his grey eyes as he listened. The doctor had joined Melling at Huxley but had chosen a different career path. Their lives had always lain side by side however, and each man viewed the other as their superior; they were stuck within a cycle of personal inquisition, each man reliant on the other for particular wisdoms. Today, it was Harry's turn to bend an ear.
'That's not quite just, Robert. Remember Cindy Fairbourne? She always took to me.'
'Intelligent men never make claims based on exceptions,' Melling laughed, relighting his *Romeo y Julieta*. Harry chuckled in response, cutting the end of a Dominican.
'Why is it then, old boy, that our society seems to suggest the opposite to that axiom?'
'That's because,' Melling said, inhaling slowly. 'Humanity is determined to live in dichotomy: acting in opposition to what wisemen preach, then referencing the same wisemen for their actions.'
'A phrase for everything, Robert. That's what my father used to tell me. That boy has a phrase for everything.'
Melling chuckled, then turned serious.

'That's probably the part of my job I loathe.'

'What's that?'

'The incapability of saying the correct thing to someone's family. Death has this amazing ability to render the most appropriate consolation useless.'

'I suppose that's true. But then again, you were able to console Olivia. Do you really intend to go to Huxley tomorrow?'

'If Olivia asks for my opinion on the matter, how can I refuse?'

Harry nodded in response, lowering his thick brows.

'Shall you be needing my assistance, just call. I am with you in everything, until death and after, as you know.'

Melling smiled through yellow smoke.

'Harry, I expected you would say that, but am grateful all the same. You know what this makes me think of?'

'What, Robert?'

'You remember Dockery?'

That made Harry Saturn's eyebrows burrow sharply. Nostalgia and pain seemed, for a moment, to take twin residence inside his eyes.

'I will *never* forget Dockery. A horrific ending for such a young beau... I didn't sleep for weeks.'

'You know, at the time I never understood why he did it. He was never a malcontent – if you catch my reasoning?'

'He was far brighter than any other of his classmates,' Harry said with a grimace. 'He seemed so happy with himself and the world. So ambitious. I would never have known that Dockery suffered.'

It had been a gorgeous spring day, but Harry had housed a look of such peculiarity that Melling, intuitively, had expected bad news. He could never have expected to hear that Dockery, a boy who both students knew well and who lived in the dormitory just opposite, had hanged himself at just twenty-one years of age. Both were heartbroken. Their fellow student's suicide betokened so much more than just misery's final straw. It spoke to the fragility in each man's condition. Something despondent and isolated lay buried in everyone. They had also discovered how suddenly your perception of things could change, and how little one truly knew anybody else. Most of Dockery's closest friends, Melling included, had felt the unbearable stain of guilt, as though they should have been able to notice things that another had mastered how to disguise. To this day, Harry Saturn could not decipher just where he and the others had gone wrong, but Robert Melling thought slightly differently about things. After years facing self-demise, whenever Dockery passed into his mind, he became more and more convinced that the young man's end had been something other than melancholy entirely, something Melling would probably never be able to pierce. It was an ineffable assertion. He wouldn't insult his death by pretending to know about Dockery's emotional state at the time, nevertheless, the death lay like a half-smudged tombstone inside Melling's mind, dated but not fully satisfying its proclaimed causes. In fact, he would long have let the dead stay dead if it were not for one crucial detail. None of the students had been given any glimpse into the note Dockery left behind, but a certain Isabella Tamwhaite, a close friend of the family's, had disclosed how 'unreadable' it had been for the boy's mother. Suicide notes were usually far too easy to interpret, painfully so, almost making them more burdensome for they revealed just how tortured the poor soul had been. Any suicide which raised more questions than it answered, was one Melling found hard to let go of.

'Old Huxley,' his friend continued. 'I still cannot believe it. I truly thought we'd left that place behind. Oh, how I loathed it.'

'You didn't like the professors, that's all. There is a large difference.'

'Actually Robert, I detested the professors just as much as I despised the medieval prison which leading academics seek to call an institution.' Melling laughed.

'You know that I share... *many* of your sentiments, but does Jane realise just how cantankerous you're becoming?'

'Cantankerous? That isn't the matter at hand. The problem is with British academia.'

'Enlighten me.'

'Well,' the doctor said, leaning forward in his chair. 'Huxley, like Cambridge or Oxford, is destined to teach the same rigid courses for centuries. The problem, as I was saying, with British academia, is the assumption that we have it all figured out. That there's nothing left to know.' His irritated scowl sharpened the wrinkles that centred above his eyes, swirling alongside the smoke that rose in front of him.

'The consequence of a lack of new knowledge is decades of stagnation,' Melling murmured, sucking in the severe vanilla of his Cuban tobacco.

'Who said that?'

'Some European physicist, I think, said something similar.'

'Well, that explains it. No *British* academic would ever have the humility or intelligence to render themselves unknowing.'

'You should write some axioms of your own, you know?'

'Oh, who would listen? Certainly not those bastards at Huxley. Egoist, self-serving...'

The sentence's conclusion was smothered in murmured curses. Melling just laughed.

'I'll be sure to let them know what a success you are, stationed in your father's basement.'

'Oh, bugger off,' Harry said, though acknowledging the truth with a chuckle.

'I used to want to stay in academia, remember?'

'Better that you didn't. Lorelei was right about it – then again, your wife always knew better for you. Anyway, you had a great mentor there: that Farway chap. I never did.'

'For me, Huxley's main flaw is its rigorous overworking of students. Do you remember how obscene the workload was? I don't think it's healthy.'

'Public love it.'

'That they do,' Melling said with a nod. 'They love hearing how stressful and laborious a place it is, as if that's all a university is meant to be.'

'I wanted to quit so many times.'

'You weren't the only one.'

'What really makes me cringe,' Harry added, 'is that Huxley has become some cultural credential all on its own. This person said this, and well, they went to Huxley so it must be true – how many bloody times must I hear that? A lady at the station tried to force that assertion on her friend the other day; I told her she was ignorant.'

Melling burst out laughing, choking on smoke.

'Did you at least explain why?' he asked with a wheezy throat. Harry just shrugged.

'I explained to her that if she was willing to unquestioningly believe in the public's apotheosis of Huxley, Oxbridge and other such draconian places, all filled with privileged and whingeing, young white lads who desperately desire to be men, well, she had better not be on a train to work, because that ignorance can't be paid for.'

'Jesus…' Melling blurted, laughing and coughing once more. 'Since when did you become so ruthless? You're really starting to sound like your uncle, you know?'

Harry shrugged.

'You know I'm right. Everyone thinks Huxley just makes people geniuses, or that being a Huxley student automatically makes you a world leader.'

'I'll say one thing about Huxley, though. You can't deny how breathtakingly beautiful it was.'

'I will agree that our Fleuraline was gorgeous,' Harry said. Their college had been unique amongst the medieval backdrop of Huxley, styled more as a Tuscan villa entrenched within impressive British gardens. 'But you mean to say that *you* could overlook the underlying presence of spectres roaming those cobbled streets?'

'What?'

'Surely a man as sensitive as yourself couldn't avoid wincing at the atmosphere of death which clung to that place?'

'I daresay Harry, I had no idea you went in for such melodrama. I mean, spectres, really?'

'Don't start. You and I both know how many strange things that place has seen.'

'Centuries prior to our studies, my friend. We've progressed since the Middle Ages.'

'It isn't just that. Stop pretending that land wasn't cursed, whether by the past or by the present occupants. I know you felt it too. Huxley was just relics haunting future relics.'

'And Huxley's ghosts always meet,' Melling said quietly.

'What was that?'

'Nothing. Is that what we've become then? Relics?'

'Soon enough we all become relics, Robert.'

'How depressing,' Melling murmured, recalling a particular night during his second year at Huxley. He'd been walking home at midnight, crossing Apollonia's Bridge, when he'd heard a dismal scream. The sound almost seemed to have been aroused from inside himself, and for a moment he'd wondered if he had even heard anything. Then, in a panic, he'd surveyed the darkness below him in vain. Harry was right. There *had* been something distressingly and ineffably timeless about the place. But spectres?

'Robert?' Harry Saturn asked, warily scrutinising his daydreaming companion. His voice murdered the look of loss in his friend's eyes.

'Sorry, what did you say?'

'If you'd fancy some Scotch before you go.'

Melling shook his head, allowing his cigar to die out.

'No, I probably shouldn't. I have some affairs to settle in Covent Garden.'

'Robert.'

'Yes?'

'Just remember that you aren't a student anymore.'

'I saw myself in the mirror this morning, my friend. I don't think that delusion will come any time soon.'

Harry chuckled, but it lacked humour.

'I'm serious. Don't let the professors, or the setting for that matter, dictate who you are.'

Melling was surprised by the remark, but equally touched by his friend's concern. At heart, Harry was a worrier.

'Thank you for the advice,' Melling said with a warm smile.

'Listen to me,' Harry replied, grasping Melling's shoulder and lowering his brows. His grey eyes demanded attention. 'You are not part of Huxley, Robert. Not anymore. Do not let anyone make you feel like you are. You owe it nothing.'

Melling nodded, appreciating his friend's worry, even if it was unwarranted. He gave him a hug, and Harry smiled. 'Doctor's orders.'

VI

To the City Full of Dreams

'Stand away from the doors!' shouted a rail officer who jumped down onto platform seven of Kings Cross. Detective Robert Melling was sitting in a first-class coach, waiting for Huxley, and pondering on his past. A family of three then boarded the train. The parents could not have carried larger smiles.

'Just think, Huxley College,' the father said, voice full of idolatry. He was middle-aged, slightly plump with greying hair, putting a loving hand on his wife, a blond of healthier physique and lighter locks.

'If I get in, Dad,' the daughter, clearly a teenager, replied. She had hair like her mother's and looked her spitting image.

'But just imagine it,' the father continued. 'You'll be made. Who knows what sort of people you'll meet!'

'They can't take my examinations for me,' the girl sarcastically said, earning a pejorative look from her mother.

'Now dear. Just think of who we know who went to Huxley: the Fergusons, the Josephs, the Thorps! Some impressive people, indeed!'

'Jonty Adams,' the father added. 'He tells me he had the best years of his life there.'

'No wonder he's so dull now,' the daughter rejoined, and Melling chuckled from afar as he watched the exchange. He was reminded of Harry's remarks the day before about the assumptions people made about Huxley College. It was all too clear that parents, with all the best intentions, helped to propagate a narrative that perhaps needed revising.

'That's awfully cruel,' the mother dismissed in a raised voice, as the family began to walk further away from the detective's seat. 'After the internship he found you, you really ought to be more grateful.'

'He absolutely insists you apply to Dunfield College, you know?' the father said excitedly. 'You must remember,' he continued as his voice began to dilute with distance, 'that the university's colleges are all unique. Jonty says you'll love Dunfield! I always told him you could be a Dunfield girl!'

With that, the family found a new carriage and left Melling in a renewed quiet, hearing only the eager humming of the mighty mechanisms beneath him. He lit a cigar, and exhaled ponderously in his seat, relishing in the cedary vanilla of the habano. The train groaned as it finally escaped the enclosure of the station and ventured into the damp London air. Melling's thoughts began to chug along with the transport. It was the only direct train from London, and there had been a sentimental dismissal of ever updating the mechanics; this train was outdated to say the least. One was already stepping backwards in time before they arrived at the timeless landscape of Huxley.

Not a single soul at Huxley knew he would be coming. Now that he was headed there, he realised how little he had considered just what he was actually going to do. He had been too absorbed by the pain behind Olivia's voice to think his actions through. Where had Lucy Rosewood been living? What had she been studying? Where should he begin his investigation? How covert was he to be? For a meticulous man, he had treated the entire affair rather irrationally. Where would he even stay? He shook his head, exhaling slowly. The one thing he knew for certain was that, for Olivia's sake, he wouldn't allow a single person or occasion to get in the way of the truth. He wasn't sure how long it would take, but he would uncover whatever it was that had so disturbed Olivia – even if that ended up being foul play! At the notion of foul play, he recalled Gladys' parting frown.

'You broke your promise,' she had muttered, busying herself to avoid his gaze.

'I had to!' he had professed, but to no understanding. Gladys had simply relied on the promise of prayer to look after him. Melling did not feel comforted by the notion, but instead, combed his mind for professors who still inquired after him when the situation demanded it. There was Dr Alfred Farway, who had seen Melling as his undergraduate protégé, and still wrote to him on occasion. Farway had been the man to almost convince Melling to remain in academia, and he was certainly indebted to him. Perhaps he should use him as a foothold into his sweep of the university? Then again, he wasn't entirely sure; the man was devoted to the place and would surely despise an investigation. It was probably better to steer clear of such fanatics. Melling was also unsure how old the man must be now – if he should burden him! In any case, there were many boutique lodges in the area and, after all, Melling's determination would surely prevail. He closed his eyes, reiterating that thought.

The train roared northwards towards Huxley, passing through the wet, British countryside, and the water vapour whistled through the open window. Whilst he contemplated, a far-off voice, cast far below Apollonia's Bridge, called out to him.

VII

Streetcars and Desires

Paris, October 1938

'*Un autre café, mon coeur?*' Robert Melling was asked by his waitress, Lucille, who he had come to know personally after making her café part of his morning routine.

'*Non merci, ma chérie,*' he replied to the tall, thirty year old hostess with farmer-blonde hair. She was the mother of a clumsy young lad of eleven, whose father had died of pleurisy years prior. Melling was fascinated by her industriousness and constant smile among long days and difficult clients. He had endeavoured to always have his coffees with her and had even begun teaching the boy English on Sundays after their weekly picnic. He also knew it gave Lucille time to prepare for Monday morning. These past two days she had listened to him wax lyrical about a beautiful opera singer. Lucille had found his long looks charming at first. Now she found him comedic and, though she wouldn't admit it, irritating.

'*Encore cette femme?*'

Yes, he thought. *Still the same woman.* He nodded; she tutted, picking up his empty mug, and moving on to another table.

I should have talked to her…

But then again, what if that had spoiled her? What if knowing who she was would ruin her sublime effect? What if meeting her would prove to Melling that not even this unnamed 'she' could cure his longing for that which only art could express?

The curse of an over-read mind, his friend Harry would say. Then again, maybe he wasn't over-read at all, simply stupid. After all, he was spending family money to 'find himself' abroad. People said it was a frivolous luxury only for the rich, but Melling knew the richer truth to his bourgeois gallivanting. The languorous lifestyle of finding oneself was a naïve luxury, only for the naïve. What did that even mean: to find oneself? He was sprouting half poetry, half philosophy to Parisiennes so that he could bed them. He was the most pathetic version of an upper-class hero one could imagine.

You have too much time on your hands, rang his father's voice. *Maybe if you worked more, you could think less.* That thought irritated him because deep-down he knew it was true. His father had worked his entire life to provide him with the best education, and here he was using that education to consider and contemplate, socialise and seduce. He wanted to emulate the poets too much. He often forgot how many poets had gone hungry. All his life he dreamed of acting the hero, longing for some epic romance. Not just in love but in everything. He wanted to do something great. To *be* great.

He looked at his unworked hands and felt a pang of irritation. With that, all too suddenly, his enthrallment of the performance two nights before melted down into a new form of internal intensity: determination. Then and there, he refused to end up like Patty's friend Pierre. Not for who he was, but for what he had said: *She and I can always look back to it wherever we end up.*

He looked back at Lucille, considering how little time she had for herself, nor to think about who she was and spin narratives about life. Every day she rose at four to deal with the baker, cleaning her café from six to be open at seven. She shut the doors at four, then went to get her son. She cleaned, cooked, taught, washed, and kissed goodnight. She had no time for *perhaps*. She *always* smiled. Melling was embarrassed to be so free in the face of her routine. Then again, she seemed even more at ease within herself than he was. He was nothing next to her because he had earned nothing save what had been handed to him. Grand philosophies didn't pay her bills.

Melling shook his head with resolve. He left money for his coffee, took his coat and headed for the door. He was going to demand a romance of his life and make it something worthy of an orchestra or the stage. Not just in love, but in *everything*. He was going to do something with an education most people could only pray for. He was going to live *actively*. He was going to affirm who he was. What was it Nietzsche had said?

Such beings are not reckoned with; they come as fate will come.

He rushed from the café, sprinting into the late-afternoon wind of a Parisian October. He didn't even register his surroundings as he raced off.

'*Attention!*' a familiar voice called from behind, but he registered it too late. Before he could pivot, he crashed into a delicate frame, both of them tumbling onto the pavement. A ruffling woosh joined the thud both bodies made on impact, and Melling sat-up inside a flurry of sheet music his victim had clearly dropped.

'*Je suis vraiment désolé…*' Melling began. 'I am such a bloody fool!' He started to hastily pick up the papers and turned to the person who he had backtackled. 'Are you –'

He couldn't finish his sentence. He was too astonished. Two cinnamon irises widened at him in confusion.

'*Quoi?*'

'I… I…'

The woman sighed with a laugh.

'*Mon dieu! Ce n'est vraiment pas mon jour!*'

Still stunned, Melling took in her raven hair, cascading beneath a red chapeau. He could not believe what he was seeing. Straightening her blue coat, she sighed again at him, her face revealing a sentiment of disapproval.

'I just… I'm so sorry,' he said weakly in English.

'It is okay,' she responded melodiously in his native tongue. 'You look like you have talked with a ghost. I was told the English are awkward, *mais…*' Her look turned sympathetic. 'Did you fall badly?'

'No!' he exclaimed, picking up the rest of the sheets and standing in front of her. 'I just… my God, I can't believe it.'

'*Quoi?*'

He couldn't believe that a foreigner could enliven his own language so eloquently. He also couldn't believe that a ruby-red cap coalescing with cinnamon eyes could ever conjure such beauteous comparisons. His father would slap him if he ever said such a pretentious sentence out loud. He *could* believe however, how Paris must have felt when meeting Helen. Here he was regretting his decision not to meet the singer who had plagued him and here she was: that very medium of artistic madness, standing on the everyday Parisian pavement, looking at him with a bemused expression and seeing him in the most pathetic light. What the devil had just happened? It wasn't even coincidental. It was weird. Some people claim that when you think too much about things you attract them, but Melling considered such people idiots. Yet here they were. He was going to visit her after the opera, but she had found him outside of her artistic field. He couldn't have planned it. He was on the back foot.

'I think you have hit your head, *Monsieur.*'

'No! I just…'

Pierre's voice rang in his head again.

She and I can always look back to it wherever we end up.

The singer who had played Béatrice frowned.

'*Êtes-vous sûr de ne pas être blessé à la tête?*'

'No! My head is fine. I am so sorry. You must think I'm such a strange man. I just, I was shocked. You don't understand, you see…' He ran a nervous hand through his hair, feeling paralysed to admit the truth yet blurting it out all the same. 'I was just thinking about you and then I bump into *you* and that's… that's… that's just the most bizarre thing.'

She looked taken aback, but then the furthest tip of her red-wine lips curled to the right. He had never felt so unpoetic in his life.

'*Vous pensiez à moi?*' Again, the tone of her voice was void of all negativity, and she seemed to find the statement somewhat amusing. Possibly even flattering. 'Maybe it isn't such a bad day.'

He had to smile at that.

'Well, I'd get your coccyx checked first,' he said with a nervous chuckle, still not quite forgiving himself for his confession. Her cinnamon eyes widened with intrigue.

'*Pardon?*'

'Sorry?'

'Get your coccyx checked,' she repeated in a low voice, imitating his English accent and finishing with a giggle. 'What is a… coccyx? *Est-ce que je le dis correctement?*'

He didn't respond. He was both too caught inside and too disorientated by her playful attitude. Melling had just knocked her to the ground, confessed that he, a complete stranger, was thinking about her; she didn't seem to care at all, now teasing the way he spoke. '*Mon dieu,*' she continued through his silence. 'Am I being rude? The Americans are not like the British, so I cannot know.'

'Americans,' he muttered stupidly, her autumnal twins narrowing in response to his expression. Then she laughed again. When she had finished, she noted that he was still silent. Rather than shy away from his awkward confusion, she humoured him.

'Well, let's see. My neighbours are American, and I grew up watching American movies. All I know of English are these things.'

'Your English is excellent,' he blurted out stiffly, and she smiled, pretending to fan herself and raising her voice into a histrionic swoon. '*Mais merci beaucoup, chéri*. You are too kind!' She pinched his cheek to stress the theatre, and the playful dramatics finally reminded Melling that fate had brought him his Béatrice, and he was about to make fate regret handing him the opportunity.

Get control of yourself, man, he thought as she grabbed the sheet music in his hand. His hands stiffened in defence, and the burnt sienna of her gaze glinted expectantly.

'Sorry!' he said, tension forcing the words to land stiffly. He let out a nervous chuckle, releasing the pages. 'I just realise that this must make me the strangest person you'll meet this week.'

She shrugged, beginning to reorganise the papers.

'It is only Tuesday.'

'I think I'll still take the crown,' he said, earning an examination of his looks. She tutted.

'*Non,* it would not suit your head.'

'Well, thanks,' he said, looking down, and she smiled before turning back to her papers. He rushed to break the silence. 'Listen, you have to allow me the chance to explain all this weirdness.'

'But you are always talking,' she replied with a sarcastic smile, looking up and earning another nervous laugh from him.

'I promise I'm not usually this bumbling, half-silent Englishman that I now appear to be.'

'When you say, the chance to explain. You mean to meet you again?'

'Well, yes. You see I —'

'So, you say nothing now, asking me to meet you again so you can explain yourself? I am not sure I can talk for two.'

As she spoke, he analysed how pathetically his *carpe diem* determination had fled. Had he not just reorientated himself in that café? Had he not demanded a new version of himself? He was supposed to claim his present! He was meant to sweep people off their feet! But these thoughts made him realise that he still had expectations of what romance was meant to be. All he knew was how the damsel responded when the hero acted. Fate was cruel to shock his system so soon, but it was also gracious enough to show him how much of an overeducated idiot he truly was. This hero had stuttered, and this damsel was not like the books. She was being her authentic self and truthfully, she did not seem like she needed a hero at all. He could never have imagined that this laid-back, humorous lady in a red cap would be behind the previous opium of opera.

This rare aesthetic heiress had in this strange moment finally made him see. She was not the bridge between art and reality in the way that he had deliriously and selfishly romanticised. She was simply who she was: an opera singer as well as someone kind enough to entertain an awkward stranger. The categorisations of the intellectual were a farce, indeed all categorisations were, trapping every person who spoke their language. Her cinnamon stare had now turned to her watch, and he could see that she was about to bid *au revoir*. That would be it. A familiar sensation returned sooner than it had originally fled: determination. What was it Nietzsche had said?

They come as fate will come.

'Listen, I tackled you, then trapped you in a conversation with yourself.' She raised a brow.

'Trapped me?'

'It all started two nights ago. You see, I was at the opera, and I was completely overwhelmed by your performance. This is going to sound ridiculous, and I completely expect you to walk away, but I will never forgive myself if I make the same mistake I did then.'

She began to smile at his excitement. 'I was going to demand to see you backstage and tell you that never before had a person managed to weave the threads of art and reality so masterfully as yourself.'

She laughed at the extremity, but he kept going. Besides, she still seemed unable to produce a sound that would offend the ego. 'And you're right! I *am* too British in my stiffness! But it's more than just a cultural image. You see, I always choose art over reality, too afraid of what a real-life hero would do, scared to think of how dull life could be if left to the genuine man and woman. But I can't do it any longer. You must let me know you.'

She blushed at his outburst, looking down at her music. After some worrying seconds, her eyes met his again.

'You are a performer, aren't you?'

'No, I -'

'*Pas comme moi.*'

Not like me.

She took a step toward him and peered into his eyes as if she had already diagnosed him entirely. 'You live your life by performing. That is how you make yourself an artist.'

'But I am done!' he said in hyperbolic assertion. 'I can't do it anymore. I can't look at someone like you and imagine what would be said.' As he spoke, he realised how intense and pathetic he must sound, but he kept going. 'So no, I am not asking for the chance to explain, I am demanding it. I am not letting you out of my sight. I thought I was going to have to go to watch you perform every night, but…' He was desperately seeking a conclusion to this outburst, but the words he found himself choosing seemed to have been decided by some foreign source. 'I guess, what I want to say is: can we please share a bottle of red and talk about how you came to be?' He sounded deflated, and the words surprised him more than her. She blushed further.

'It is only eleven,' she said, but the chuckle which followed hinted he could raise his hopes.

'Well,' he said with an almost exhausted laugh, 'I imagine it will be a long story.'

She fidgeted with her music, seemingly toying with the idea.

'It *is* a long story,' she admitted, then she laughed. 'Okay, *on y vas.*'

He grinned like a lunatic. '*Mais, à une seule condition.*'

'Name the condition?'

'You say again how much you liked my performance.'

VIII

Poverty and Beauty

Huxley, Huxshire, May 1969

Standing outside the dull brown of Huxley Station, Melling gazed across the verdurousness of Huxley, wondering how Harry could have misremembered its beauty. He was on familiar cobblestones, though if memory served, the town as well as the actual institution lay to the east, perpendicular to the northern meadows he now surveyed.

He walked slowly along the barren station, wandering towards the drivers who were awaiting passengers. There weren't many, and Melling well knew that Huxley would always be one of those places where cars were sparse. The cars themselves seemed to belong to at least two decades prior, and the detective was reminded of how slow time was here. From the Medieval to the Renaissance, Victorian to Post-War, Huxley's clock staggered along, layering itself via physical remnants.

The only inkling of modernity came from a pair of youngsters: two lads, and like many of the smokers who loitered outside of Melling's London home, their hair was far too long, and their trousers far too tight. At least, that's what Gladys ranted in complaint when she rapped on the window for the umpteenth time. Melling for one enjoyed the daring colour schemes of nowadays youth. Every generation was determined to bother the previous in their own ways. Seeing these two unkempt lads however, only helped to unsettle Melling. In his traditional overworn suit, careless of colour, he felt invisible in his *alma mater*. He wasn't sure what to expect upon arrival, but he was already facing the fact that things moved on, even if the cars didn't.

A man of roughly fifty or sixty, dressed in a long overcoat, was interrupting people as they passed. The detective noticed a look of hopeful clarity in his shrunken gaze.

'Detective Melling?'

Melling nodded, and the man beamed through the cold; he extended a hand. 'I am so glad to meet you! I am Dr Louis Starling, a friend of Harry's.'

'Harry told you I was coming?'

'Naturally. He doesn't have many friends here, but I definitely owe him more than one favour. He asked if I might look after you, and be your chaperone, so to speak. He mentioned you knew Dr Alfred Farway, but wanted you to be with someone *he* knew, so, here I am.'

Melling's grin broke across his cooling cheeks. So, Harry had been his true, as well as his slightly controlling, self, utilising this kind man to make things easier, and to make sure Melling had a friend.

'I cannot thank you enough, Dr Starling, truly. I had no idea Harry had done so. He is awfully secretive sometimes.'

'Indeed,' the stranger said with a smile. 'But this way please.' He took the detective to a dated black Ford, the doctor clearly also having refused to meet modernity; he carried his case into the back. Melling found the passenger side, rolling down the window to not burden the man with smoke.

'Don't suppose you could spare me one?' Starling asked as he sat down.

'Certainly.'

'Thank you. You a cigar man?'

'Most definitely. One thing I missed during the war was not having a Trinidad. I'll settle for a cigarette any day, but they just don't feel the same, you know?'

Melling laughed as the car lurched away from the station.

'So, did you tell anyone I was coming?'

'The Chief Inspector of Huxshire. His department takes care of serious crimes in Huxley seeing as we are part of the larger county.'

Melling nodded, recalling the geography.

'That may create an unnecessary fuss seeing as there hasn't been any indication of an actual crime.'

Starling smiled knowingly.

'I wouldn't worry. Harry instructed me that you would probably want matters under the radar, and well, Inspector Todd is an old friend.'

'Excellent,' Melling replied.

The car soon found the outlining forests of Huxley town and Melling watched as the purple horizon illuminated the ageless woodland and shrubbery; they crunched defenceless twigs as they passed. Eventually Starling meandered left as the woods receded, finding the valley's clearing. When they swerved out of the shadowy green, Huxley was revealed as its gothic towers came into view. It was as though the Ford was a time machine, driving into the Middle Ages. Not a single rock nor roof belonged to the 20th Century. Huxley was, put simply, a dense cluster of old-way architecture, cohabited by old-way people. Small, ancient dwellings competed with modern shop-windows, though these latter designs were painfully discordant to the timeless foundations they were attached to; the vendors tried their best to blend into the world they had chosen, meaning that one would only remember the consumerism of the age when they met a shop head-on. Looking onward at Huxley as a whole, however, was akin to reading the memoirs of some Angevin herald. Huxley was a historian's Galapagos. Gazing into the stony roads, Melling couldn't avoid the overhanging castle which stood threateningly above, menacingly proud in the distance.

'Huxley Hill,' he said in a low mutter.

'Incredible how the sun colours it at this time of day, isn't it?'

'I forgot how positively ominous it was.'

'Ominous? I thought Harry was the fearful one.'

Melling chose to smoke instead of reply, and Starling drove them through the ever-narrowing streets of the town. No matter where one was, the gothic towers of the old castle stood thunderously upright against the darkening pink of the sun's rays. He remembered the walks he had taken there, as well as the voices of the tour guides. The authorities always hammered on about the legendary sundial that had been installed for God knows what reason other than to keep time. The locals treated it as some enigmatic, brilliant feat of man. It was pretty, Melling agreed, but it was ultimately just a copper sundial in a castle courtyard.

'With a sundial of one and a quarter metres in length,' he murmured with a half-smile, remembering the enthusiastic description of the guides.

'I'm sorry?'

'Nothing. I just... you know when the tour guides drone on about the sundial?'

Starling chuckled, then he put on a nasal voice.

'The castle was built in 1427 at the commission of Baron Huxley. Since then, it has seen forty-five alterations and additions. Just three have occurred after the seventeenth century, one being the side tower added by Queen Victoria's niece.'

'Very good, very good. Then you have the sundial and... I forget the last one.'

'It's the gift shop,' Starling replied, and they both had to laugh. Then Starling summoned some camp-fire theatrics: 'and do you know why the sundial's gnomon is one and a quarter metres in length?'

'Nobody knows,' Melling said, joining in on the gag.

'Indeed,' Starling replied in a mock-haunting voice. 'Part of the castle's many mysteries.'

'I promise Harry's the one who goes in for ghost stories, not me,' Melling tried to assert, but in reality, he well-knew how easily he could be swayed by the whiff of the supernatural. There was more than one occasion in his career where the irrational had coalesced with unforgettable goosebumps and shivers. One night in particular, in Trennunburg, Germany, was still awaiting a credible explanation.

You're not in Trennunburg now, he corrected, looking up once more at the domineering structure which seemed to exist beyond the horizon.

'It'll be dark soon,' he said. 'Is there much point asking around for Lucy Rosewood's details?'

'We're meeting with Inspector Todd tonight. I believe he has all the details you need.'

'Perfect,' Melling replied as the town widened into a drop. Ahead of them, the castle roared from above the religious side of the old dwellings, protecting the stony avenues beneath. Huxley was divided into two, either side of the river. To pass from one part of town into the next, the car had to cross the fifty-five-foot ravine that buried the watercourse below. Generations of Huxley lords had pushed plebeians and merchants away from the grandeur of Huxley Hill until a newer town had risen. The degradation of Huxley bourgeois blood had slowly exfoliated Huxley Hill into a forgotten relic, locals leaving the dwellings closest to its summit. Fast forward to this century and, well, Huxley Hill was a monument, with all variety of people living in the lower parts of the old town, including a few of the university's colleges. It seemed

Starling's home was there too, and murky memories began to barge their way through for Melling as the Ford's front tyres kissed the cobblestones of the only way into that part of Huxley.

'Apollonia's Bridge,' Melling whispered, peering across its equivocative edge. The drop was always deeper than one recollected. Starling didn't affirm. The bridge was barely alive, with two or three groups walking across.

'You need to slow right down here. It's the law as we don't have many cars in town. Too many pedestrians at risk if we go quickly. No one ever really drives.'

'I remember,' Melling said, slightly out-of-it. They crawled over the medieval structure. A young couple were dancing halfway along, and Starling waited patiently for them to move. Melling looked to his left, noting a young woman with auburn hair and bruised feet, shivering in evident cold. Her face was shadowed, but she eyed the detective curiously. For a moment, he forgot where he was, struck by her sinister paling eyes and how they contrasted with her dirtied, elfin features. The left corner of her lips turned upwards halfway between a snarl and a smile. She didn't seem real to the detective, more a caricature.

Starling's Ford crawled away from Apollonia's Bridge. They found the barren streets of the old town. The medieval met the mysterious on this side of the ravine, the stones closer to eradication and to the first footsteps of Huxley's settlers. The authorities had managed to limit the potential for renovation, locals settling for maintenance or partial conversion. They crept upwards along the winding stone road for two-or-so minutes until they slowed into a domestic close where one medieval construct seemed to have been converted into at least ten dwellings.

'Here we are,' Starling said with a smile, stopping in the middle of the terraced structure. The building was as stone made as the rest of the town, but this particular abode was dressed in unkempt vines. The house was number 18. Melling took his case and followed the doctor up the broken footsteps. 'Now, my wife is out, but you'll no doubt see her in two days if you're still with us.'

'Well, that'll be delightful, if I am.'

Starling smiled, opening the door to reveal a simple home, decorated in dark-silver wallpaper. Walking inside, the detective was met by oddly pompous golden couches that jarred with Huxley's ambience. Starling noted his surprise.

'My wife works in interior décor. She's creative at home.'

'Lovely.'

'You'll be on the landing, Detective.'

With that, he showed him up the rickety stairs towards a room clearly untouched by Mrs Starling's creativity. It housed a dull bedstead uncomplemented by greying walls which were evidently birthed as white.

This certainly matches Huxley's atmosphere, he thought.

'We don't have many lodgers,' Starling said in apology.

'Not at all, it's perfect. Dr Starling, I really don't feel able to explain just how thankful I feel for your hospitality.'

Starling smiled.

'The least we can do for you, Detective. Downright tragic what happened to that poor girl.'

'You knew her?'

'No, but my wife asked around. Supposedly she was the top of her year at Dunfield.'

'So, Dunfield was her college,' Melling muttered, recalling the idolatrous father on the train who had urged his daughter to apply there. 'I remember it. It was fairly academic when I was at Huxley.'

'Where were you, Detective?'

'Fleuraline.'

Starling nodded with a competitive smile.

'Your college has fallen down the ranks a touch since you left, I'm afraid. My own Sackville is now topping the Huxley table.'

'I had a few friends at Sackville, actually.'

'Oh, fabulous. Anyone I might know?'

'Potentially,' Melling said with only half interest; his appetite was not for small talk. 'Dr Starling, I don't mean to be rude, but is there anything else you might know about this girl?'

The man offered a rueful smile.

'Not at all, Mr Melling. I am here to help, of course, but I'm afraid the answer is no. If you were asking about that boy at Marlowe, however, then I might be able to say more, but for the moment I –'

'Wait, what boy?' Melling interrupted.

'Well, a second-year there just passed away, and under peculiar circumstances I must say.'

'When?' Melling asked with some aggression. 'What circumstances?'

Starling stepped back.

'Why Mr Melling, two weeks ago I believe. But is it so important?'

'Two students die within three weeks of each other, and you don't find that strange?'

'I can assure you we all found it strange, but young folk nowadays seem acutely susceptible and vulnerable to their… inner struggles, let's say.'

Melling froze.

'Inner struggles. You mean to say that this was a suicide, too?'

'Well, no, not quite.'

Melling began to grow irritated.

'Not quite a suicide?' His voice was raised in incredulity. 'Dr Starling please be clear!'

The doctor took another step back, wrinkles widening in a mixture of pity and worry.

'I apologise, Detective. I didn't realise this would be so crucial. Come down for a glass and I'll explain everything to you as I understand it.'

The detective regretted his over-excited outburst and apologised.

'No. *I'm* sorry, Dr Starling. This incident has me quite agitated, and well, to add another death into the equation could change things a lot.'

'No apologies, please Mr Melling.' He extended an arm towards the stairs. 'Please.'

They made their way back down to the golden divans, and Melling took a disconcerted seat. 'What's your poison?'

Scotch, Debussy and a Cuban cigar.

'I'll take a Scotch if you have some?'

Starling nodded and returned from the kitchen with two shallow glasses. Melling traded his glass for a cigar, and both gentlemen took a moment to light and swallow the virgin touches of each vice. Starling seemed immensely pleased to be smoking Cuban tobacco rather than the previous Gitanes.

'This boy, then,' Melling began. 'Who was he?'

Starling put his glass down and exhaled slowly, guiding fumes upwards.

'Well, his name was Samuel. I knew his father once upon a time – a good man, and his son was supposedly the same: kind, meticulous and ambitious.'

Melling half-smiled.

'Ambitious?'

'Yes. Though I am told that his ends took to the melancholic.'

'But he *didn't* take his own life?'

'No. It was an accident.'

'What was?'

'Well, picture this for a moment,' Starling said, slowly re-setting the scene and taking another sip of whisky. There was something about the old ways, about a hedonistic parley, about a drink and a smoke, which the newer generation were both turning their nose up at, and yet also losing the advantages of: a man at ease was a man who could both divulge and take-in. 'Samuel was a history student,' Starling continued, 'who achieved sound grades. He was an active member of the politics society. Wanted to go to the house apparently.'

Melling listened intently as Starling spoke. 'One night, a girl at Trinity, she crosses Apollonia's Bridge and finds him standing on the ledge, peering into the water below.' Starling looked up sorrowfully and took a long drag.

'I'm listening.'

'Well,' the doctor unwillingly resumed. 'He wasn't himself apparently. Singing about being a baker's daughter or something.'

'Baker's daughter?' Melling echoed in understanding, though it clearly made Starling uncomfortable.

'Right.' He downed his glass and began to tap his foot nervously. 'The girl swears it on her life. Is that normal in your experience, Detective?'

'Well, not exactly. Suicide doesn't signal madness, but I guess: tell that to Ophelia.'

'Ophelia?'

'Oh, you know, Shakespeare's Hamlet? Ophelia turns mad after the death of her father and starts to sing about an owl and a baker's daughter. I'm guessing our friend was pondering the consequences.'

'The consequences?'

'She drowned,' Melling stated flatly, thinking of the harsh Huxley watercourse which wrestled along under Apollonia's bridge. Dr Starling squirmed in his seat, nodding his head.

'Oh yes, that's right… so, you're saying that…'

'Drowning was certainly floating around inside his mind. What else did this girl say?'

'She said he was drunk and kept singing. She managed to talk him down, but, well, as he stepped down, he slipped.' Starling sounded pained by the irony.

'God,' Melling said in disgust, the usual deep vanilla of his cigar tasted of dated methanol. 'But, again, even if he was thinking about it, that doesn't mean he would go through with it, *per se.*' He paused in disconcerted thought for a few seconds, then sighed. 'This will remain an accident, I suppose.'

'It really disturbed Sheryl.'

'Sheryl is your wife?'

Starling nodded, and Melling began to picture the young lad falling as he had stepped down. There was *certainly* an irony to such an action, a step towards life becoming a leap into death. It was almost disproportionately ironic to the point of sheer hilarity. It was sometimes so that such shocking twists of life were so discordant to how life's narrative was meant to pass that, as one reacted to them: humour, pain, shock and disgust seemed to coalesce into an ineffable sensation. Melling had once been reminded by a professor of ancient theatre that it was no crime to laugh at death in a performance, for laughter was often grief's way of communicating surprise.

'It is a disturbing account, if true. I want to speak to the girl though, and hear it from her.'

'I'm sure Inspector Todd will sort that for you.'

Melling nodded, then sat ponderously, rolling his cigar in his palm. Starling was taciturn, silenced by his own story, and Melling's own concerns slowly wisped into an unreadable fog like the smoke that glided over his knuckles and ears. In his mind, the fumes of deliberation swirled into the shape of an auburn figure, gazing from the bridge; Melling let them rest there. Somewhere, deep inside his subconscious, a known voice called out to him.

IX

To Sleep, Perchance to Dream

'The inspector is meeting us at the *Abenborg*,' Dr Starling explained as they found a familiar side-alley.

'Was a frequented haunt of mine,' Melling said, recognising the dilapidated stones which were eroded by the feet of eager students – or so he first assumed. He himself had taken this very alley towards the overhanging sign of the *Abenborg* many nights as a student. When he had been a first year it was a place for him and Harry to talk to girls. Now, when Starling pointed to the wooden sign, Melling noted how much the letters had rotted away under the harsh rain of Huxley autumns.

Upon entering, he poignantly realised that students no longer visited the *Abenborg*. Familiarity assaulted him, with the smell of spilled lager and cigarettes conjoining with the worn leather of the couch seats of his, once favourite, evening pub. Every drinker was as outdated as he was. He recalled the two students by the station whose hair and clothes would make Gladys shout. He was the old Huxley: so were the others who sat on the aged barstools. Then again, there would always be another who pointed into the past and deemed it older. As outdated as he felt, every generation would share his feeling at some point. So, it went. For a brief second Melling recalled his old friend Patty, a music journalist who had shared some special moments with him in Paris. Her only consolation in an earlier death was that she wouldn't become a lost old woman, invisible to the young, forgotten by the city itself. Soon enough they would all be relics, haunting future relics. And somehow, Huxley's ghosts would always meet.

Across the semi-crowded middle-darkness a man waved to Starling, and both doctor and detective ventured through the chiaroscuro to join him at his table. Waves of cheap cigar smoke trailed behind each man as they carved through the wake of the pub's fog. Everyone was smoking. Clearly, little had changed in terms of the establishment's tobacco tastes. They found their seats opposite a gentleman in a buttoned-down brown chemise. Inspector Todd had a military cut, and his blondish hair seemed to be fashioned from one thousand dots of a greying, yellowy-white. His jaw was unflatteringly rounded, yet his hazel eyes emanated intelligence in a conventional way, though, not necessarily in a common-sensical way. He took Starling's hand with a smile.

'Louis! It's fantastic to see you.'

'How are you, Caspar?'

'Well, old boy, quite well.' He turned his eyes to Robert Melling with anticipation. 'And this must be the awaited detective? How do you do?'

'It's a pleasure,' Melling said, offering his hand. 'Thank you for meeting with me so soon after my arrival.'

'Not at all, not at all. It served me to come down from Huxshire this evening, so you see, it all worked out quite conveniently.'

The inspector pulled out a box of cigarettes and offered a smoke to both men who declined in favour of Melling's *Romeo y Julieta's*. All three took a few moments to light their cravings.

'So, not that I particularly want to pass over pleasantries,' Melling began. 'But would you mind if we got straight down to the matter at hand?'

'Not at all, Mr Melling.'

'Thank you,' the detective responded, shuffling his cigar case back into his pocket. 'So, what can you tell me about Lucy Rosewood?'

'Top student, kind girl, ambitious.'

'Ambitious,' Melling said in drawn-out repetition.

'The perfect student?' Starling added leadingly, not really as a question.

'That's right. A shame how it all unfolded. A student gave an emotional speech at a recent Dunfield service in her honour. Incredibly moving.'

'How so?' Melling asked.

'Oh,' Mr Todd stumbled, clearly not understanding the interest in the question. 'She cited some Egyptian scripture to see her off, so to speak.'

'Seems particular,' Melling observed with a raised brow.

'Well, they were both protégés of a certain Professor Robora. He's a professor of Ancient History. Lucy Rosewood, as a philosophy student, topped the modules which he offered. Well, honestly, the words felt very fitting. Beautiful way to send off her classmate. You could tell she was finding a way to pay homage to a lost friend through something they'd shared. But the most moving aspect was the chanting.' He paused to take a brief inhalation.

'Chanting?' Melling asked.

'Yes, some students had clearly organised a beautiful closure in her honour. Incredibly touching.'

'Well, what did they chant?'

'I was never much for Latin, but I believe it was ad lucem – no, in luxem. Yes, in lucem, or something to that effect.'

'Into the light,' Melling said in translation, and Starling nodded in acknowledgement. Clearly only Inspector Todd was ignorant of the meaning.

'I've never heard that said in Latin before,' Starling noted.

'Neither have I,' the detective said in agreement. 'I would like to speak to that classmate of hers. The one who gave a speech?'

The inspector coughed before answering.

'She was quite overwhelmed, so she's gone back home to be with her family.'

'Understandable,' Melling said through thin lips. 'I would like to speak to Lucy's professor.'

'Professor Robora?' the inspector asked with an apologetic chuckle. 'I'm afraid you can't.'

'Robora, I've never heard of him. He must be new?' Starling suggested.

'He is indeed, joined two years ago. He was highly recommended by a cohort of well-established professors.'

'Hold on just a moment. Why can't I see him?' Melling asked.

'Well, the professor is currently at a religious retreat in Oxford. Won't come back until Wednesday.'

'So, you can see him over morrow,' Starling proposed to Melling, and the inspector nodded. Melling sighed, biting on the end of his cigar in thought.

'He's a real pillar of the community here at Huxley,' the inspector said with a strong smile. Melling exhaled from his rapidly diminishing cigar. 'I'm sure he is. What did he tell you about Lucy? I'm assuming he was interviewed?'

'Well, there weren't really interviews as such, being that this was a suicide.'

'Right,' Melling said in flat acknowledgement. 'So, what did he say?'

'Well, he was in tears, obviously. Really affected by her passing, said he was happy that she was at least at peace.'

Melling listened intently. He was greatly disturbed by this funeral service – whether it was beautiful or not. He knew he was coming across blunt, but he was here for Olivia, not to make friends.

'Don't we all,' Starling said, glancing at the splintering end of his cigar. Without taking his eyes off the inspector, Melling took his silver case from his pocket and left his cutter on the table for his host to use at leisure.

'Well, I never knew the poor girl,' Melling admitted. 'Only her mother. Currently,' he looked around him and lowered his voice, 'I don't even know *if* she took her own life. I never learned of the details.'

Starling grew visibly tense, but the inspector, accustomed to the nature of Melling's world, answered calmly.

'Lucy's neighbour at Dunfield, a smart boy called George Goodwin, when she hadn't answered the door for two days, he went to the porters asking where she was. They immediately broke into her dorm.'

'What did they find?'

'This part is truly dreadful,' the inspector said for Starling's sake, but the doctor nodded his head, thumbing his cigar nervously. 'The girl was there alright, had been for some time.'

Melling was accustomed to the horrors which someone could do to themselves, but he wasn't expecting to hear the following words. 'If her floor hadn't been made of carpet, George Goodwin would have been met by blood flowing out from under her door.'

'She slit her wrists?' Melling asked.

'Not initially,' the inspector replied with a slight shudder. 'The girl had carved two lines from her toes to her waist with a kitchen knife.'

Starling stifled a whimper, looking down at the floor to quell his disgust.

'Now, why would someone do that?' he croned in horror. Both he and the inspector then looked to Melling for expertise.

'I haven't heard of a person doing that before… specifically that, I mean. It is a touch inventive, I would say, for a cause such as melancholy. I'm not sure what to make of the line of incision.'

'So, you don't know?' Starling asked, almost condemningly.

'Well, it depends on her motive. Carving seems more of a ritual.'

'Ritual? She was a twenty year old, Kentish young lady. Where on earth would such outrageous sentiments even arise?' Inspector Todd asked with incredulity.

'I'm just giving you my thoughts,' Melling rejoined bluntly, not exactly sure why he didn't want to conjure hypotheses in front of the inspector. 'At the very least,' he said flatly, fighting against his rising wall of pity, 'it's odd. Is there anything else?'

'Yes,' Inspector Todd said before a big sigh. 'She left a note.'

'Can I see it?'

'Certainly not. It has been sent home to her family.'

'Well, what did it say?'

'Exactly what you'd expect, though quite intelligently worded.'

'How so?'

'She asked her mother not to feel sorry for what happened.'

'That's a ludicrous request,' Starling scoffed.

'Indeed,' the inspector said.

'So, in what way was it *intelligently* constructed?'

'Well, I'm no academic. However, she'd attempted to centre her message around the truth; how it was unpleasant but needed to be said. Stuff to that effect.'

'Asking her family to accept reality, I suppose,' Starling suggested.

'Yes, I guess so. Though, it did end rather confusingly, not sure what to make of it. Maybe her mother would understand.'

'Well, don't spare the details now inspector,' Melling said, sitting up straighter.

'Right. Well, if memory serves me, she said that by dying she could save everyone fourteen years.'

'That's it?' Melling asked in irritation. 'That's all you remember?'

'That's all there was detective, believe me.'

'Fourteen years of what?' Starling sighed.

'Is that all, inspector?' Melling repeated.

'Yes, that's all I know.'

'What happened to her room?'

'All cleaned out. Everything that was hers has been boxed-up and sent to the family.'

'Dr Starling said that there was a boy?'

'Not that I know of –'

'Not with Lucy Rosewood. There was a boy who fell from Apollonia's Bridge. What do you make of it?'

'Well, I thought you were here for Miss Rosewood?'

'I am, but then I learn that a boy falls to his death whilst debating Ophelia's suicide not three weeks before. Clearly, he was on the cusp of jumping before somebody intervened.' He then forced himself to remain conversational rather than overly concerned. 'What do you know about it, just out of interest?'

'Well, I don't know about the Shakespeare, but he slipped as he came down. We fished the body from the river the following morning when the girl came forward. Got the corpse out before the first team rowers would find it.'

'She waited until the morning?' Melling asked, puffing slowly. Inspector Todd shrugged.

'Too overwhelmed, I guess.'

'Why do I get the feeling that people are doing far too much guessing,' Melling said quietly, 'and not enough investigating?'

'Now, Mr Melling, that's quite out of turn. Two students have tragically died, much to the sorrow of their university and townsfolk. We *are* grieving and taking these matters as they are. We are not, you won't mind my saying so, throwing random speculations into the air, and reading into things too deeply. Don't you think the families and friends of those involved have suffered enough? We do not need you coming here and mixing up the dirty water as soon as it has settled.'

Melling shook his head, choosing to ignore the ignorance. Starling soothed the outburst on his behalf.

'Caspar, the detective is merely frustrated. You will recall that he was acquainted with the girl's mother, which makes him personally involved. He isn't slighting the department or yourself, he simply wants answers.'

'Well, the answers are there in the note detective,' Inspector Todd huffed. Melling sighed, taking his silver case of cigars from the table. He noted he had sighed a lot since arriving.

'I think we'll be heading now, Mr Todd. I trust you can procure a meeting for me with the girl that tried to stop the jumper?'

'He *fell*.'

'Right,' Melling said in cold affirmation. 'I'll be here all day tomorrow. Get me a meeting with her, please.'

With that, he walked away from the stifling table and pushed through the old door to the outside haven of the cold, night air. He shook his head, rubbing his left temple. He felt sick. He heard the door open behind him.

'Well, Caspar *will* give you that meeting, but I must say, you ought to be more careful next time.'

Melling whirled around in irritation.

'Don't tell me you agree with him?'

'Detective, unlike most of the men here, I look at the details, and see what they suggest. If you are as disturbed by the incidents as I think you are, then by God, I can't ignore the peculiarity of it all, either.'

'Then what are you saying?'

'I'm saying that maybe,' Starling said, evidently distressed to be uttering the words, 'you need to be as below the radar as you originally intended to be.' It was clear that it had taken a lot of the man's energy to admit such a thing.

'I didn't think our inspector would be the one who I couldn't have an open dialogue with,' Melling said with a shake of the head. 'But opinion ceded'.

'The people here: they like things open and closed. They want to see it all as a misshapen tragedy, because well, they can't start making it bigger than that or the students, *and* the university's reputation, will run riot.'

'Dr Starling,' Melling began.

'Louis, please.'

'Well Louis, it seems to me that the inspector is afraid of more than just causing an upset amongst the students.'

'Yes, he is irritable, but he has had a tough go of things at home recently. He's a good man, believe me. I just think that resistance won't help anyone; I know how difficult it will be for Caspar to confront a blot on Huxley's honour, so perhaps it *is* better for you to stay slightly out of the way and present him with conclusions rather than yet unanswered problems? But come. It's late. Let's head back for a good night's rest. Tomorrow might lend more answers.'

'Okay,' Melling said in submission, not finding the will to finish his cigar, let alone investigate things further. He cut the end and returned the stub back to the case.

They walked through the blended moonlight in pensive silence, passing along the empty stone streets without a word. But when they found the doctor's road, Starling paused.

'Mr Melling.'

'Robert,' Melling corrected, also tired of the formalities.

'Thank you, Robert,' Starling said. 'What did you make of the girl's note? I mean to say: what do you think she meant by saying she had saved her mother fourteen years?'

'Not much, I'm afraid.'

'Well, you see when I was a student here, I twilighted philosophy.' Louis Starling seemed paler now in the moonlight, and Melling realised that something about the note had struck a chord.

'Go on.'

'Well, it was just that aspect of how her letter was centred around truth. It keeps mulling over in my mind.'

'She was too intelligent for it not to be relevant to what she did,' Melling concluded with a shudder. The doctor thinned his lips.

'I think that the fourteen years has to do with the philosophy which she studied.'

'Go on.'

'For some reason I remember the number fourteen. I just, for now, can't quite articulate the memory, but I know that something about it is familiar. Back in the *Abenborg* you were saying that her...' he swallowed for a moment. 'You said that her death might be ritualistic, and I just, well, fourteen years really stood out to me.'

Melling nodded.

'Philosophies find their way into people's *raison d'être* all the time. Sometimes, more disturbingly, they also worm their way into someone's reason *not* to be. I think for a philosophy student it wouldn't be a stretch to see a perverse intellectualising behind it all. Same could be said for their chanting, I suppose.'

'They're an overintellectual sort,' Starling said. '*In lucem*. I confess I am really touched by the way they framed her as finally at peace. Into the light.'

'It's peculiar,' Melling muttered to himself.

With that, they returned home, Melling bringing a glass of Scotch to his bedside. He knew, as was custom these past few months, he would wake up needing it. As his head hit the pillow, the inspector's words became a resounding mantra in the detective's mind.

In lucem.

There was something awfully specific about Lucy Rosewood's funeral service which unsettled Melling. Something about a fellow student using Egyptian scripture *to see her off*, as the inspector had put it, deeply disturbed him. What then of the chanting? Was he thinking too much about something rather harmless?

In lucem.

He repeated the words until he fell asleep.

X

Somnambule

Paris, October 1938

'*Le Somnambule?*' Robert Melling noted sceptically, looking at the inky green letters hanging over the black-painted bricks of the unknown restaurant. Having agreed to a bottle of red, the good-humoured and beyond beautiful opera singer had vowed to take him to a place he would never forget.

'*Oui, Le Somnambule,*' she echoed. 'The sleepwalker.'

Melling had to shake his head.

'Strange name for a restaurant.'

'I know many people who do this,' she defended, and he laughed.

'I was going to say that it perfectly describes a British politician.'

She looked up at him, eyes a curious cinnamon.

'*You* remind me of a politician.'

'A politician!' Melling repeated loudly. 'That's not a compliment.'

'*Oui,*' said the smiling belle. '*Trop Anglais.*'

'*Tu sais que je parle français,*' Melling asserted, beginning to grow annoyed at the notion of being *too English,* but she just smiled disarmingly, squeezing his shoulder.

'And if you spoke Swahili, should I say you are *Africains?*'

'That's not the same thing.'

'*N'est-ce pas?* Language cannot make a person change. *De toute façon,* do you *not* want to be English?'

'Well of course I do,' he said with a shrug of obviousness.

'I think you do, and you also do not.'

'I thought it was you who was meant to be telling their story.'

'Well,' she said, grinning. 'Wine will make you talk.' With that, she asked a passing garçon for a table, and the next thing Melling knew, they were seated on the ruby cushions of an outside divan, a fire-pit placed cosily to their right. The décor was Turkish in design, and they were practically the only people present: two strangers ensconced on an outdoor sofa, surrounded by Ottoman greens, stone greys, and wine-splashed burgundy.

'*J'adore cet endroit*,' she murmured, burying her back into the cushion behind her.

'I'm glad you showed me this place.'

'Aha! I believed you as a man who likes these sorts of places.'

The waiter, a young and patently French lad, probably no older than nineteen, was quick to demand their order.

'*Juste une bouteille de vin*,' his companion said, and the host left them with a menu. Melling's mahogany-eyed madame was full of smirking expectation.

'Is this a test?'

'*Peut-être.*'

Maybe.

'Do I not, at least, get the name of my examiner?'

'*Je m'appelle Lorelei*,' she replied with a chuckle. 'I thought I said already.'

'To be honest, I was still calling you Béatrice in my head. After your performance.'

'I thought you were going to find out: the real me?'

The way she mimicked his earlier confession irritated him. He nodded in response, eyeing the wine list but not actually reading it. '*Et toi? Comment t'appelles-tu?*'

'Robert Melling.'

'Robert,' she repeated with a slight accent.

'Are you from Paris?'

'Burgundy.'

'That explains the wine snobbery,' he said with a chuckle. 'Burgundy it is, then!'

'That's cheating!'

'You should have kept your cards closer to your chest.'

'You play?' she asked, suddenly sitting up straighter. It was clear she *did* play.

'Depends which game?' he replied cautiously.

'I play all games,' she said, reaching in her bag and, to Melling's surprise, procuring a deck of cards.

'You carry cards around?'

She shrugged.

'There is much waiting at work. We always have to come in, but we are not always rehearsing. So, we all just drink and play.'

'You drink a lot?'

She shrugged again.

'I'm from Burgundy,' she offered, and Melling smiled.

'England has rules, well, unwritten rules about drinking and working.'

'You English have many, many rules,' Lorelei replied, shuffling the cards on the stone table. The speed of her quick movements suggested her fingers had evidently done this many times. She was about to bridge the cards when a thought struck her. 'Where do you work?'

'I, uh, currently don't work,' Melling said slowly, almost unwillingly, and she grinned interestedly.

'And you can offer me wine?'

'I didn't say it would be good wine,' he rejoined with a wink, and she had to laugh. As if on cue, the waiter returned, and Lorelei watched him carefully as he ordered. He had only now begun to pay attention to the words. He had learned about wine when dining with the aristocracy at Huxley College, but this menu was full of subtleties he did not understand – there went his chance to impress. The waiter coughed in expectation, then offered the answer to his confusion:

'*Uniquement Bourgogne et Champagne.*'

Lorelei sniggered, and Melling shook his head. She had taken him to a place where Burgundy was the only red on the menu.

'Burgundy it is then,' he muttered, repeating his earlier joke, and they both had to laugh.

'*Désolée!*' his companion said with a honeyed laugh. 'But a handsome stranger tells me he's been thinking about me, then offering me a drink; an average wine would ruin the poetry of that.'

He hated to be reminded of his all too forward awkwardness, but also had to consider her remark a compliment. The waiter coughed again impatiently, and Melling panicked, searching for a name he recognised. He hurriedly ordered a bottle from the *Côte-de-Nuits*. The man sneered before hurriedly taking the wine list back. Lorelei just looked at Melling with doe-eyed curiosity.

'*Vosne-Romanée?*'

'No good?'

She just smiled with new comprehension.

'I am now beginning to understand you better.'

'How do you mean?' Melling asked, feeling somewhat nervous about the order. Lorelei placed the deck face-down on the table, then took his hand, searching his gaze for a second, before placing it onto the deck.

'Is there where you say abracadabra?' he said in a low murmur. He felt slightly delirious.

'We each take a card. Who is lower must answer a question.'

'I can't decide whether I'm lucky or unlucky today.'

'Just stop thinking things and take a card,' she ordered. He did as she said, placing an eight of spades onto the table. As she took her card, the waiter returned, opening the bottle and asking who would like to try. Lorelei pointed to Melling before placing a six of diamonds face-up. Melling swirled the ruby liquid around in his glass, noting the impressively nuanced shade of brownish purple that dominated the centre, with edges that were almost lilac. The aroma was an intoxicating mixture of clove, strawberry and spice, and his initial sip from the cold glass was divine: a seductive teasing of earthy berries, cedar, with hints of vanilla. Clearly the name had stood out to him for a reason. Lorelei watched him carefully as he put the glass down next to the cards, realising he could ask her a question.

'Okay,' he began as the waiter poured them both a full glass. 'What don't I know about this wine?'

The man left, and Lorelei searched into the burgundy, humming quietly as she watched its legs climb down the inside.

'*Bon, c'est un excellent pinot noir,*' she ceded, gently lowering her elfin nose and inhaling. Melling wondered if they would smell the same things.

'But I have to say,' she added with a giggle. '*Everyone* says *que c'est délicieux.*'

'How do you mean?'

She tapped the bottle before responding.

'This is *Domaine de Montille*, very talented wine makers, *mais tous les vins,*' she paused, switching to English. 'All of the wines from this area are famous, not just in France.' When she finished, she looked at him to see if he understood what she was implying, but he had already sussed her point.

'I just ordered a bloody expensive wine, didn't I?'

She laughed outright.

'*Oui.*'

'Thanks for stopping me.'

'This is my fault?' she blurted, still laughing.

'Well… yes.'

'You have this I'm in control determination, so I thought you were trying to impress!'

'I *was* trying to impress you,' he said in raised voice, then he laughed dryly and looked down.

'At least it is not a grand cru!' she said, stroking his arm sympathetically, eyes widening in a doe-like manner.

'At least,' he repeated sarcastically. She took his hands and apologised.

'I feel bad,' she continued. 'You can ask me some questions; we don't draw cards.'

'Yeah, that'll pay the bill,' he laughed, but truthfully, he was glad for the opportunity.

'When did you realise you had a voice that could demand its own genre?' The question was all too honest and had left his lips before he could think twice. Lorelei just smiled.

'When I was very, very small, my father gave me piano lessons. He made me start singing when I could name any key he played.'

'So, you have a gift.'

'Maybe,' she said, shoulders shrugging again.

'That wasn't a question,' Melling affirmed. 'I'm not quite sure you're aware of the effect you had on me.'

'You said I made both art and reality,' she elucidated, clearly not forgetting his earlier compliment.

'You *connected* them,' he corrected, taking a sip of his wine. 'All my life, art has fulfilled a lacuna within me that reality just can't seem to solve. Maybe I've read too many tragedies or romances or whatever, but, after all I've seen in the lines of verse or the pages of epic, life always falls short of art.'

'That was a lot of words,' Lorelei said, unimpressed, smelling her wine.

'You studied at an expensive *université?*'

He nodded. '*Évidemment.*'

'But you,' Melling continued despite her comments. 'You made art come to life.'

Lorelei blushed.

'*Merci.*'

'*Ceci n'est pas un compliment,*' he corrected, desperately hoping to convey his seriousness.

'You think too much,' she replied evenly. '*Mais, merci.* I have only been working for one year at this new company. So far it is going well.'

'One year and already the main part,' Melling added, reaching in his coat pocket for a cigarette. She gave him a pejoratively downturned brow when he began to light it.

'*Fumer c'est mauvais pour la gorge.*'

'I'm not a singer.'

'I think smoking will damage you.'

'Ah, *oui?*' Melling said in nonchalance, taking a drag.

'Ah, *oui?* You don't ask me where I heard this? Now I understand why you do not work: it is because you do not truly care about who you are.'

'That's quite the claim,' Melling said evenly, somewhat annoyed. She ran the risk of rudeness. 'You hardly know me.'

'Mhmm.' She leaned back further into her cushion. 'So, tell me why you do not work, then?'

Melling shrugged again.

'That's not easy to answer.'

'*Tu es perdu.* You are lost. I was lost also, but I had not read enough books to know it. You can intellectualise… I think this is the word. We are all pushing a rock, but you can think about the rock, the hill, your reasons for… for pushing. Is there even a hill or rock? These questions you think and,' she stopped to laugh. 'You have time to think. Somebody made you feel too smart, and so you are not happy.'

'That's hardly a fair comment,' Melling interrupted, but Lorelei continued.

'*Réfléchis moins.* You are a con artist. Me, I am honest. You need to think less. It does not matter what you have read. Books cannot tell you who you are or who are people. You think about *les personnages*…?'

'Characters?'

'Yes, characters. But you do not know who *you* are.'

'That's not exactly –'

'*Non*. I see in your eyes that you feel. You feel a lot?'

Melling had to nod in reply. 'You are not happy,' she continued, and he had to nod again. Lorelei took his hand and squeezed it. 'You are not happy because you are not living; you are always thinking. *La vie*,' she began, tapping his head with her index finger, 'does not need to be big words.' Then she gestured toward the table. 'It can be wine and music, *mais*, not always. Life can be simple. Innocent. Not everything must be exceptional.'

He hadn't anticipated such an authentic attack, somehow overloaded with empathy. He smiled and she returned it. He was also irritated that she felt the need to explain him to himself, and still, she had managed to do so in a manner no one had yet done.

'You actually made me realise that before telling me it.'

'*Quoi?*'

'I was determined to go backstage after your performance.'

'*Vraiment?*'

'Have you ever read Dorian Gray?'

'Oscar Wilde?' she asked, and he nodded.

'I felt like Dorian when he sees Sibyl acting, falling in love with a woman of the stage.'

Lorelei blushed. 'Then, well, I realised he only loved her because of her profession, not for who she was.'

Lorelei shook her head.

'Too much thinking!'

'But what if –'

'*Non*,' she interrupted. 'We are talking now, not thinking.' She took his hand and made him take another card. He obliged, even though she had asked him a handful of questions already. Hers was a six of spades and his the mere four of clubs.

'*Ma question*. Where did you study?'

'Huxley College. *Vous le connaissez?*'

'I told you already! You are a politician!'

'I studied with a few,' he chuckled. 'Yes.'

'But you are not *really* like them.'

'My dad hoped I would be.'

She *tsked* loudly in response.

'I can see that many people have been putting different ideas into your head, but who do *you* want to be?'

'We didn't take cards,' he said, and she sighed, choosing an ace and turning triumphant.

'*Encore la même question…*'

He shrugged but her brows became downturned once again. 'Stop that!' she called out, imitating his sagging shoulders.

'I'm just not sure,' he defended, but she gave him a knowing look. 'You're going to laugh.'

'*Je déteste cette phrase.* The person laughing will not be the one who pays the taxes.'

She had a point there.

'Well,' he said, speaking softly. 'I was thinking of joining the London Police. Scotland Yard, that is.'

'*Mais vous êtes trop timide!* How can you be a policeman if you are so shy?' She jabbed his shoulder as she teased, and he had to smile.

'Well, I didn't mean a policeman!'

'What then?'

'A detective,' he said. She sat back with folded arms, smiling at him.

'*Pourquoi?*'

'Well, I don't really know, to be honest.'

'*Bon,*' she concluded, grabbing her glass. 'Then it is perfect for you! No thinking!'

He laughed outright, clinking his glass against hers and taking a satisfied sip. She looked at him suspiciously for a moment. '*Mais…* you *have* been thinking a lot about this.'

'Well, it might not be the right move for me.'

'*Qui a dit ça?*'

Who said that?

'Well,' he said, 'no one really but —'

'Your father?'

'I haven't actually told him.'

'Then who?'

His eyes fell to the deck. She sighed when she noticed and waited for him to take a card: it was a nine. Hers was a Queen.

'I'm starting to feel like there may be some sleight of hand going on here.'

Lorelei laughed, then the interrogation continued.

'Why not be a detective?'

'Well, I have literally had the best education one can get,' Melling said slowly, feeling as though the statement spoke for itself, but Lorelei gave him a blank expression in return. It was frustrating that she didn't immediately appreciate what countless back home would. 'And so,' he clarified, 'I have many options.'

'Many options,' she repeated with a laugh. 'What does this mean?'

'Well, you know, a Huxley degree could open many doors.'

'You would be too bored,' she said. '*De plus*, there are too many lawyers and accountants.'

'Well, there was also the option of academia.'

'*Académie?* You want to stay at university?'

'Is that so bad?'

Lorelei yawned. 'Oh, come on. There's an honour to it.'

'You wish for honour?' she asked, but her eyes quickly widened in understanding. 'Oh, you want to be like the heroes in your books.'

'Something like that.'

'There is no heroism *dans l'académie.*' She pronounced heroism without the 'h'.

'But there is! At least I could try and arrive to some sort of meaning to things.'

'*À quelle fin?*'

'I'm sorry?'

'Every philosopher wants to find an answer!' she said, as though she herself were a philosopher. Like every teacher, she was also determined to make Melling realise his pitfalls. 'If there was an answer, then things would be easy! *Non*, I can see that it isn't enough for you. *Je sais…* you want to be more. I think you are not being honest with yourself. I like you as a Mr Detective. Who is telling you to stay *dans l'académie?*'

Melling's thumb drummed against the table in discomfort. '*Qui?*'

'Well, there's someone who's been really good to me at Huxley, a professor of mine, Dr Farway – Alfred Farway. He's helped me get to where I am now, and well, you can already see I'm not the best at making life decisions and –'

'Life decisions,' she repeated, grimacing as though the phrase was sour in her mouth. 'The job you pick is not the end of your life! You are young! You need to do what you want to do! You cannot always keep reading books! Life is happening *now!*'

'But what if it's the wrong decision?' he defended, but she scowled. For an awful second, Melling thought she would leave, but, instead, she grabbed him; before he could ask what she was doing, she kissed him into silence. He was stupefied. She tasted like Burgundy; the kiss was over before he could savour it. Pulling away, she grinned at his expression. 'What was that for?' he whispered in pleasure.

'Life is happening now,' she said. He slowly accepted that yes, she had indeed kissed him.

'I… I'm not sure I understood the lesson,' he replied, cheekily. 'Maybe I need to be shown again?'

She pushed his smiling cheek to the side and grabbed her glass.

'Just try and think less,' she said, now looking him in the eyes. 'I think you will be a good detective.'

'You hardly know me,' Melling murmured. He knew many of his friends wouldn't have the patience for such a conversation. Her stubbornness was annoyingly unrelenting – if she was not piercing at an inner truth, he would have complained. Then again, probably not.

'I think this professor has made you too many expectations.'

'Dr Farway just says I have potential, and that means a lot coming from him. He thinks I could really be at the brink of new understanding if I stay at Huxley. It could be a great opportunity.'

She shook her head.

'You think you *need* to do this.'

'Sorry?'

'You feel oblig… *obligé…*?'

'Obligated? Maybe.'

'*Ton père?*'

'I certainly owe it to him to make something of myself.'

'You think being a professor will make him happy?'

'I'm not sure what will make him happy,' Melling said in defeat, gazing down into his wine. 'You know, in a moment of certainty this morning, I promised myself I would apply to Scotland Yard, and I –'

He was interrupted by a chuckling groan.

'Robert,' she began, stealing his attention. 'He will be happy if you are happy. *C'est très simple.*'

'If only it *were* that simple.'

'But if it was not, it should not matter. If you really want to be like the hero in your books, you should take a risk. *En plus*, I have read about this Huxley place before,' she added, looking up at the sign of the restaurant with a defiant smirk. 'They are all *somnambules!*'

He had to laugh. Whether she was right about them being sleepwalkers or not, he was rapidly realising that this was a woman who wanted a risk-taker so long as she agreed with what risks were worth taking. She had a one-sidedness, and yet she was brimming with empathy. Her assertions were fiery, yes, but her intention seemed pure. Then again, his best friend Harry Saturn claimed that Melling was guilty of blending beauty and truth. Had someone less alluring slashed him with so many stubborn questions, Melling would probably not be sipping his wine with such a goofy smile. What *was* certain however, was that her cinnamon stare eclipsed any feelings of her not appreciating his point of view.

XI

No Imp, Simply Perverse

Huxley, May 1969

Feeling himself sweat in the cold, night air, Robert Melling stood before the black pathway of Apollonia's Bridge, admiring the open nothingness on either side as it slipped over the shallow ledges. Halfway across, a silhouette caught his eye. Barely visible, standing out as darkness against darkness: she beckoned him with outstretched arms. He took a tentative step towards the lyricism of her voice. Closer he went, step-by-step towards desire. She walked away, asking him to follow. Follow he did, towards the middle of the bridge. Stopping, she motioned to the ledge with pointed fingers. He assented, dragging his wet feet onto the stone as he clambered onto the side.

He peered into the darkness below. The voice promised pleasure soon. She was beside him on the ledge now and glaring into his eyes. He recognised them; they reminded him of a Christmas cinnamon. Her shadowy locks were blown sideways by the breeze that coughed upwards from below the chasm he overlooked. She kept glaring and Melling swallowed. The sleepwalker's apparition urged him to stare deep into the abyss of the beloved baker's daughter.

Maybe that's who she is, he thought in dizzying confusion. She asked him to follow her. He certainly would.

Then, with reaching hands, she stepped forward into the nothingness, and he watched her cascade into the nightmares below, hurtling towards his desires.

'Everything goes with you,' she cried as she fell, and he peered after the disappearing voice. He wanted to join her. Aching with desire, he let his left foot dangle over the ledge, flirting with his craving.

'Detective!' a voice shouted from behind him. His foot found the ledge again. *Her* voice told him not to listen, agitated from below. 'Detective, get down, please!' the contender begged from behind.

'I know that voice,' Melling said to himself. The voice from the abyss started to fade, and his mind slowly roused.

'Robert get down from there,' Starling implored again. Feeling her control slip, the woman screamed from below. Melling saw her wading toward him in the darkness.

Finally, he thought, stepping forward and hearing the scream of Starling graze against the sonorous roar of *his* woman. Her hands found his, coldly intertwining with his sweating fingers and pulling him forward. With a last smile, he let her pull him down. But as his heels lifted from the ledge, a human arm snaked about his waist, suspending him from the call of death and wrenching him back to safety. The woman's hands broke free as she collapsed into nothingness. Melling fell backwards, tumbling onto the shelter of the bridge, with Starling's haggard breathing close to his ears.

'Have you lost yourself, Detective?' he shouted, putting a thick coat around Melling's body. Melling didn't realise how cold he was until Louis Starling drifted into perfect focus before him. Then he began to quake brutally, teeth chattering. He was struck dumb by wakefulness; everything had been clear... he had been in Starling's guestroom and then... then what? How on earth had he arrived here?

'What... what... happened?' he stuttered, words stumbling out of his shivering mouth.

'You were going to jump! Are you mad? Here I thought that the *boy* was insane! You're meant to be the one saving us from this absurdity!'

Melling was mentally wrestling with that painful droplet of memory which refused to solidify. Such was the way with dreams. You were alive to everything, fully aware of the subconscious. Then you were confused, desperately chasing images that only revealed themselves to closed eyes. To waken was to lose.

'Get me inside,' the detective croaked, eyeing his bluing feet. His toes were dirtied well into the nails, but currently, he couldn't feel them. Starling just dragged his fingers through his hair in exasperation.

'What happened, Robert?'

'Truth be told, I've not been sleeping so well recently.'

'Wait,' Starling said with a cold laugh of incredulity. 'You're saying you thought you were dreaming?'

'You don't honestly think I'm out here for my health, do you?'

That made hist host sigh, biting his lip in disbelief.

'Come on,' he said in slow relenting, finally coming to terms with the situation. 'Let's get you home.'

He helped him up, and in slow torment, the detective hobbled back to number 18. As they walked, he began to consider the state that he was in, and for the first time since his nightmares started, he began to feel afraid.

'Louis?'

'Robert.'

'That's never happened to me before.'

The doctor turned with a sympathetic sigh as Melling continued. 'I cannot thank you enough. I'm now just realising what would have happened if you hadn't been there. How did you even know?'

'I heard the door close. I almost blamed the wind and went back to bed. When I stepped outside, I saw you at the bottom of the hill in your nightgown.'

Melling shuddered.

'If you hadn't heard, then…' he swallowed. 'If it wasn't for you Louis, I would be at the bottom of the abyss like that boy.'

The doctor looked at him matter-of-factly as they made their way up the hill.

'Robert, I'm… I'm at a loss for words. I'm just so glad I *did* wake-up. Truth be told, when I saw you talking to yourself on that ledge, I had never been so afraid. It scared me because for the first time since these deaths, someone has arrived with some aggressive common sense, asking the questions that *need* to be asked. Then, you walk yourself onto the ledge in a crazed state. I thought you were suicidal!'

'That's not it at all,' Melling said with a sigh. 'I still have my wits, just not when I sleep.'

They walked the final stretch of the darkness to number 18, and once arrived, Louis lit the fire, procuring some blankets. He walked into the kitchen and poured them both a Scotch, taking the liberty of offering Melling his own cigars. Fumbling the Cuban, and placing it in his trembling mouth, he let Starling light it for him, heaving a sigh of pleasure as the warming fumes burned like a gratifying furnace inside his lungs.

'I'm concerned, Robert,' Starling eventually began. 'About everything. My wife and I both are.'

'You should be,' the detective asserted, 'but not because of what happened to me out there.'

'What *did* happen out there? Because, from where I was standing, it looked like a madman's suicide.'

'Well, in a way, I guess that could be what it was, but I just don't know.'

'How do you mean?'

'Did Harry tell you about my wife?' Melling asked, taking a sip from an unsteady glass and revelling in the inducing burn. Louis looked down in apology.

'He did. I'm sorry for what happened. Though, I don't know the particulars.'

'I fell in love at first sight, Louis. She had my soul and more.'

'What happened?' Starling whispered.

'She was an Opera singer in Paris. I was staying in *L'Hôtel des Rêves*, the so-called hotel of dreams, but she was by far the dreamiest apparition I could ever have imagined. I proposed months after I met her; that's how certain I was. War still managed to make us wait – though that's another story. Anyway, we were happily married for a long time after it all stopped. Our life was *our* life until... one day, last year, she received a letter concerning some accolade in Vienna. It was one of the highest awards in her art.' The glass became smaller in his hands, and he had to force his tears to remain unwept. 'I lost her.'

'I'm so sorry,' Louis said bluntly.

'Since then, about a week after her death, I came home to Kensington. The first night I awoke and felt like I was dying. I couldn't explain it, but I thought that my heart was physically failing in my chest.'

'I've never heard of such a thing,' Starling remarked in consternation, chewing broodily on his cigar.

'I hadn't either, but the sensations were disturbingly real for someone living.'

'What did you do?'

'Well, the feelings would subside eventually, and I would take to my piano and cigars.'

'True medicine,' Starling said, chuckling humourlessly.

'The feeling occurs after nightmares I can't remember having. In fact, the nightmares are more constant than the physiological angsts. I thought it would all leave with time, but it hasn't.'

'So, standing on the ledge?'

'That has never happened. As far as I am aware, the dreams have never made me a sleepwalker.'

'Okay.'

'My doctor thinks the tragedy of losing her has pushed me towards a stress and melancholy so intense, it's become nocturnal.'

Louis seemed relieved once the context was explained, but relief was a borrowed feeling, competing with an evident horror. 'So, what were you dreaming, in God's name, that brought you outside?'

'That's the other side of the coin, I'm afraid.'

'You mean, you don't know?'

'I haven't been myself doctor, and well, my own doctor isn't able to offer me anything other than palliatives.'

'I may have something there,' Louis reluctantly responded. 'It's unorthodox. But it could help you.'

'What is it?'

'Well, it's far beyond my understanding, that's for sure. Someone runs an outside practice, if you can call it that, on the other side of the bridge. And well, he isn't exactly a friend but, I have heard that he deals in such… matters.'

Melling nodded his gratitude but neglected the suggestion.

'If it's all the same to you, Louis, I think I'll take my chances without a witch doctor.'

Starling smiled without mirth.

'I don't blame you. But, if it's all the same to *you*, Robert, I'll be tying a bell to your hands.'

Melling laughed until he realised that Starling was being serious.

'Very well,' he said in acceptance. 'I suppose it's a simple solution.'

XII

Shed From the Bosom of the Morn

'More eggs, sleepwalker?' Starling asked from behind a large mug of coffee. It was breakfast, only a few hours since both gentlemen had relinquished the Scotch in favour of sleep. Melling raised his bell-tied hand, which he had kept on out of humour, his usual defence against the serious, and twitched his wrist with a rueful smile. Its copper jingled quietly.

'I'm full, thank you.'

Melling was pleased that Starling had decided to make light of last night's incident. The detective himself, was carefully attempting to deny his brush with death, and it vexed him greatly to try and recall the dream which had led him to the bridge in the first place. From outside, any idea of sunshine was weakened by the omnipresence of clouds, stretching to the very edge of the horizon. It was a dark morning indeed, somnolent as the bags beneath his eyes.

'What's the plan, then?' Starling asked, browsing through the paper.

'While you're off at the surgery, I'll be visiting Dunfield to find out more about Lucy and well... maybe speak to her friends from the service.' He sighed. 'I may do some other, quiet things.'

Starling grimaced at the suggestion.

'I'll sleep safer when the dots are matched – though I don't think there is any foul play. However, there *are* certainly questions which need addressing.'

The detective nodded, though after what the inspector had relayed at the *Abenborg* last night, he now did not doubt, even in the slightest, that there was something undeniably rotten in Huxley. Indeed, he had used Starling's phone to call Olivia Rosewood; the notion of fourteen years was as equally confusing for her as it was for the detective.

He stood up to clear his plate, but as he did so there was an aggressive knock on the front door. Melling and Starling looked at one another. The doctor rose to answer, and the detective began putting their plates in the sink.

'Caspar?' Starling voiced in surprise. Melling left the kitchen to see why Inspector Todd had come.

Standing in the half-light of the overcast day, the inspector seemed irritated. He was dressed in a functional grey suit, and his polished brown shoes glinted in the detective's eyes.

'I wasn't expecting to see you so soon in the day, inspector,' Melling remarked.

'Morning Mr Melling. I'm here to assist you today.'

'Chaperone?'

'Things will be a lot easier for you with me by your side.'

Melling nodded but knew when someone was here to oversee and control, rather than aid.

'Did you contact Trinity about that girl who was there the night the boy fell?' The inspector nodded in response. 'Great!'

'We have permission to talk to her after lunch.'

'Well, what do you suggest we do beforehand?'

'You wanted to see Dunfield College, because of Lucy Rosewood?' Melling nodded. 'The master there would like to speak with you.'

'When?'

'At half-past the hour.'

'Well,' Melling chirped, grabbing his coat. 'There's no point in dallying then.'

He nodded at Starling, then joined the inspector in the overcast outdoors. He slipped on his heavy coat, immediately reliving last night's near hypothermia; he had forgotten how cold it could get here, even at this time of year. Starling's little copper bell rang quietly as Melling slipped it from his wrist.

'What's with that, detective?' the inspector asked.

'A sleepwalker's warning,' he replied, turning away.

'I wanted to apologise, Mr Melling.'

'Please, Inspector Todd, I am the one who needs to apologise,' Melling said somewhat democratically. 'I didn't intend to disregard your hard work. I was tired from the journey, and still emotional about Lucy Rosewood.'

'I appreciate that,' his *chaperone* accepted.

They walked downwards into the town, Melling noticing that it was busier than the day before. Students and locals alike could be seen wandering about the cobbled streets, their feet tapping lightly on the stones as they went. The peopled presence made the town far more pleasant to behold, the attendance of individuals collectively living their lives indemnified the cold, lifeless aura of the architecture around them. The modern clothing of those younger walkers however, jarred with that architecture for that very reason. 'You see, detective,' the inspector went on, 'we have had various complaints from parents after the incidents, begging for answers which we have not been able to provide. People won't allow us to stay in our lanes.'

'Stay in your lanes?'

'We aren't psychologists. We're policemen, and as a consequence, we can only deal in evidence. The fact is, two tragedies happened, and though I can understand the impetus behind grief-fuelled speculation, when people start hoping to find speculative truths in these incidents, they end up drawing connections when there simply aren't any to draw.'

'Just to clarify,' Melling interrupted, noting how much his deceased wife would have detested this man's circumlocutions. 'You're saying this boy, Samuel, from Marlowe, is not connected to Lucy Rosewood?' He tried to sound impartial.

'And I am sure that once you examine the facts you will feel the same way. Were both students… disturbed? Of that we can all be quite sure, and it fills me with great sorrow knowing that if they had only been helped earlier, things could have been drastically different. My heart goes out to the parents, it really does.' The inspector finished by looking expectantly at Melling. The detective nodded in solemn acknowledgement.

'I understand your grief, inspector,' he said, and they began to walk up an incline towards the merchant district of the old town. Here, numerous market stalls were placed in squashed unison, creating a labyrinthine pathway of outstretched hands and cacophonous discount-calling. Melling smiled at the vendors, eyeing the various trinkets, fruit and pottery.

'Things haven't changed much since you were here, have they?'

'Not much at all,' Melling admitted. 'Students just wear different clothes. We're almost at Dunfield, right?'

'Good memory.'

They walked until the mercantile road ceased, exposing a Gothically erected wall of stone upon stone. The building had once been an old church, but the academics had demolished it, keeping the grandeur of its defensive entrance. A student in a black gown walked through the open, wooden gate.

'The oldest gate in Huxley,' the inspector said didactically, motioning Melling through.

The detective stepped inside, instantly struck by the silence of the verdurous courtyard he had walked into; he had completely forgotten how beautiful individual colleges were at Huxley. The walls of Dunfield stretched further than he could now see, encapsulating freshly cut lawns and illustrious bushes of floral splendour. With its manicured grass of oriental jade, patches of Robin Hood woodland that somehow coexisted with majestic gardens, and structures straight from the pages of history, Dunfield was breathtakingly beautiful. Huxley's colleges were microcosms of loveliness, quiet treasures reserved for the academic few who were fortunate enough to study here. The building behind the first lawn was as medieval as the town itself, built from dark brown brick with pointed arches above each window. Melling remembered walking someone home from dinner when he was a student, leaving her right by that very same shade of brown. The inspector saw his nostalgic expression and smiled.

'Come on,' he said. 'The master wants to give you a tour.'

'Does he?' Melling said in a sleepy murmur, watching the students who walked hurriedly across the pathways in smiling groups. The gentlemen walked on through the stone archway of the redbrick manor, and Melling ran his palm across one of the four Corinthian pillars holding the bricks in suspension. They ventured into a pink and purple garden where students were reading on benches; some even braved the cold grass. They were all uniformed. Melling felt at home. The sun had poked its head through the clouds for just a moment, and the green blades became available for the shivering bees who braved the morning chill. Melling inhaled the perfumed garden, smiling away his unease.

'I must have come here one thousand times,' the inspector said with a grin. 'But every time I do, the novelty of beauty strikes me just as severely.'

'It's stunning,' Melling affirmed with a smile. He even had to shield his eyes from the sun as he looked ahead at the grey, stone walls protecting the garden's rear. Then, appearing from an arch in the wall, a man in a heavy cloak made his way past the students.

'I told the master why you were here.'

'Let me guess,' Melling answered, unable to resist an aggressive irony in his response. 'He came to put my heart at ease, and place the watered lilacs at the front of my mind, so to speak?'

'He hopes you can see his college for what it truly is.'

'Well, he picked a good hour for it,' the detective responded in reference to the sun. 'But just remember that Miss Rosewood saw these same lilacs every day. That didn't stop her from carving herself with a kitchen knife.'

The master's cloak was black velvet, and, in the slight breeze of Dunfield's microenvironment, it danced behind him in silent waves. The man was beaming, nodding at each student as if they were old friends. He must have been older than sixty, and his locks were a dark grey. He was incredibly handsome for an older gentleman, and, as Melling was about to realise, despite his experience, he had a slight youthful twinkle in his agate eyes.

'Caspar Todd!' the master called out with a smiling sigh, widening those agate irises. 'Thank you for bringing our esteemed guest,' he sang, turning to Melling and cupping his warm hands around the detective's. His voice was musical and pleasing to hear. The man had one of those gravitational presences; Melling felt himself positively attracted to him – as though he needed to impress him. The detective only remembered his purpose when the lilacs of the shrubbery came into view behind them.

'Master Gabriel Dunfield,' the inspector introduced. 'Meet Detective Robert Melling.'

'How do you do?' Melling offered. The master beamed a honeyed smile.

'Mr Melling, it is a great pleasure indeed to meet so esteemed an alumnus. Tell me, have you been back to Fleuraline since arriving? I know Dr

Alfred Farway holds you in the highest regard. He would really love to see you. He thinks he is in his last few Huxley years. Perhaps even of mortality. It would be gorgeous for someone like you to meet him full circle.'

Melling smiled politely.

'The professor is kind to remember me, though, I have not really had the chance to indulge myself in the nostalgia just yet. We still write on occasion.'

'Yes, you have had a lot on your mind, I can see that clearly. But hopefully, we at Dunfield can perhaps ameliorate your dilemma, and lighten that burden you've decided to build upon those curious shoulders. Dr Farway has insisted that I attend to you personally, seeing as you are his *protégé.*' The man's eyes seemed to sour as he pronounced the last word, but only for a moment. Melling smiled again in response and thanked the master for his kindness. 'I was here when you first became a student of his, you know? I had just finished my doctorate. He always spoke of your intellect.'

Again, Melling thanked him for his compliments. 'Please, let us walk and enjoy this sunlight. Such a rarity for us at Huxley, as I'm sure you're aware. Inspector, if you wouldn't mind seeing Dr Hazel, she's waiting for you in Old Court.'

Inspector Todd nodded at both Melling and the master, then wandered back to the entrance. Meanwhile, the master had turned to his students in the garden. 'I feel so incredibly blessed to be the master here at Dunfield. It was my ancestor who founded this college, and I feel closely connected to him, though he is far beyond.'

'*In lucem,*' Melling murmured.

'I'm sorry?'

'Apologies,' Melling said. 'The inspector told me what some of your students chanted at Lucy's service. It was on my mind. A certain Mr. Robora was her professor, I believe?'

'Ahh, yes,' the master said with a frown. 'We are indeed very grateful that Robora chose our college. He has been so enlightening to so many students.'

'Like, Lucy Rosewood?' Melling suggested, and the master smiled ruefully.

'Yes, like Miss Rosewood. Clever girl. Very clever indeed. Ambitious young woman. I remember when I first met her, I felt she was destined for great things in academia, but alas, neither Robora nor myself were aware of her condition.'

They had walked beyond the wall into a new courtyard filled with well-watered evergreens. Here, the pathways were crushed into sandy pebbles which crunched underneath their feet. The smell of pine was almost overwhelming. 'You see, Lucy was acutely sensitive to sadness, but I can assure you that this is rare amongst our students.'

'So, she told you she was unhappy, then?' Melling asked as they meandered through the wooded garden.

'Not to myself. However, she confessed to Robora in times of confidence.'

'You said you weren't aware of her condition?'

'We were unaware of the true extent of her confusions.'

'Confusions, Master Dunfield?'

'You would call her thoughts stable?'

'Well, she certainly knew what she was doing when she carved through her –'

'Detective please,' the master hastily interrupted. 'I cannot have my students hearing such horrors. It *is* exam time soon, you know?'

Melling looked at the ground, severely disturbed by this man's priorities, but he needed his questions answered.

'I apologise Master Dunfield, I really do. I don't mean to be out of turn, but, you see, Miss Rosewood's mother is a friend of mine, and I promised her that I would reach the truth of the matter.'

'The truth…' the master murmured musically.

'Yes.'

'The truth, Mr Melling, is patently clear in the letter she left behind. I am told that Caspar, our inspector, divulged its contents to you?' He stopped by a stone fountain, void of water, but he peered deeply into it as though there *was* perhaps a bird splashing about which Melling couldn't see.

'He did,' the detective slowly acknowledged, 'though I must profess it all seemed rather vague to me, and to her mother, I might add. It posed more questions than it answered.'

'But isn't that the way with truth, detective? Those who speak it often pose the unquestionable, but people question all the same. Miss Rosewood begged her mother to see the truth – it's all there, written in ink.'

'Pardon me, Master Dunfield, but her plea of fourteen years was hardly *enlightening*,' Melling defended. He thought he heard the man chuckling, but then again, it could have been the slight wind which had now begun to whip around his shoulders. 'Let us be honest, Master Dunfield. Lucy has left us with uncertainty, and I am determined to uncover the causes.'

'Mr Melling,' the master reiterated as his lips twitched into a sardonic grin. He clearly enjoyed reading more deeply into matters than others could. 'The truth was there, whether one chooses to see it or not.'

Melling was waiting for the man to divulge what he clearly thought he knew that the detective didn't.

'I think more can be revealed by the body. I think her corpse says more?'

'And just what do you think it says?' the master challenged, turning his scrupulous gaze onto the detective. The previous melodiousness of his voice had been diluted.

'Well, clearly Lucy killed herself a certain way for a certain reason.' He briefly looked around him, then lowered his voice. 'The carving was certainly a vile method, and she would have suffered a great deal in the process. She wouldn't have done it if there was not a specific motive for doing so, I'm sure of it.'

'You seem plunged in ambiguity for someone who professes themselves so certain,' the master declared, somewhat irritably.

'Well, that's what happens when all are determined to avoid the pursuit of truth.'

'There he goes again with the truth,' the master announced in the third person. There was no mistake this time: he *was* chuckling, and Melling's patience was dwindling. He forgot how supercilious these academics could be. 'Come with me, Mr Melling,' he said, motioning onwards with his arm, past the trees to the ending walls of the college.

They walked away from the secretive pines, exposing the thundering grey halls of Dunfield's dormitories to the left, and an idyllic structure of paling Italian baroque. 'Have you been to the

Dunfield Library, Mr Melling?' the master asked, pointing to the building on the right. It was certainly beautiful, and quite imposing. The shallow shrubbery clung to its foundations and whirled around the stained glass windows, painted on which, Melling could make out the story of the nativity. On the left side of the library there seemed to be a spire tower attached, which housed a large blue clock with golden hands that glinted in the choking sunlight. 'You must join me in the tower,' the master insisted.

'I'm not sure. I didn't come here for entertainment.'

'Nonsense,' the master rejoined, renewing his cajoling timbre. 'I insist.'

The next thing Melling knew, he was walking through the trimmed grass of the final lawn, joining the man towards the library. As they walked, Melling noted the peculiar smile that twitched the corner of the man's lips. It was not happiness; the detective knew that outright. It was, however, disturbingly pleasurable, as though he was holding something back which gratified him. They passed more students who smiled at the master, and upon arriving at the greying stones of the library, Melling took a moment to watch the particular indentations of age which affected each piece individually.

The inside was better suited to a prince than a student, and Melling surveyed the countless editions of greens, yellows, reds, browns, even purples. The walls were a luscious red which accentuated the oiled char of each bookcase. The room was pleasurable to behold in a way which only a library could be. Melling had always adored reading, and he felt that every man who lusted after knowledge found it impossible not to feel this ethereal affinity to a storehouse of comprehension. What made such spaces so gratifying was the fact that they stood as a token for potential learning. One was destined to purchase one hundred books for every ten they actually read. However, readers still found themselves at the counter with their arms full, attracted by the improving promises of each title or the cultural glamour associated with the author. Whatever the reason, libraries were a sanctified impending of information, an assurance of understanding which housed infinite pages of future delight. Despite this atmosphere however, the room was unbearably warm.

'Literature, wasn't it?' the master murmured in his ear. His voice touched the detective's skin the way music scratched out from vinyl. It felt antecedently natural, yet secretly artificial.

'Pardon me?' Melling whispered.

'Your study was literature, was it not? Before you turned your mind towards punishing bad behaviour.'

He made Scotland Yard sound like a nursery.

'I wanted to be a detective,' Melling corrected, swallowing pathetically, realising how dry his throat was.

'And pray tell,' the master continued, smile turning sour, 'do you not miss your Huxley career, *detective?*' He scowled to utter the last word, and the uncomfortable blend of self-assurance and bitterness realigned Melling with his purpose, nudging him out of his lull. He remembered when he had been so torn about which path to take, academia or crime. He knew that both this man, alongside his mentor, Dr Farway, felt he had chosen the wrong career.

'I made the right decision,' Melling asserted, more confidently now. He hadn't realised that returning to Huxley would find him feeling like an unsure student all over again. It was just the effect those in charge of the institution had. They always made one question themselves. Flashbacks of Dr Farway's influence over him resurfaced as a young woman with bobbing curls of rusted copper came over to greet them. She was in a gown and, despite the heat, was wearing a thick scarf.

'Master Dunfield,' she greeted. The master beamed at her and grasped the detective strongly by the shoulder.

'Detective Melling, allow me to introduce Miss Lea Algrin, the brightest female physicist we have the pleasure of housing here at Dunfield.'

The girl curtseyed and her cheeks turned crimson.

'It's a pleasure, Detective Melling. How are you finding Huxley today?' Miss Lea's voice encapsulated all the innocence of youth with its melodious tones, but for some reason, Melling got the inkling that her greeting was planned.

'How do you do Miss Algrin? The master is proving to make it quite a special visit, indeed.' He eyed her scarf once more. 'Though, I must say, this library, though grand, lacks ventilation. I would personally feel close to death in that scarf of yours,' he added with a well-meaning chuckle, but her cheekbones burned into a deeper ruby.

'I… I… I'm not sure what you mean, detective?' she asked, looking down and running her hand nervously over the material. The master coughed in intervention.

'Our detective didn't mean anything by it, Lea, no, nothing at all. One is more susceptible to heat at our age, is all.' He soothed her embarrassment with a dismissive laugh, and Melling, though he felt apologetic for upsetting the girl, found the situation acutely strange in a manner he couldn't quite articulate. His father often said that academics were so awkward you'd think it was you who said the wrong thing. Besides, these thoughts were quickly forgotten when Miss Lea Algrin excused herself, and the master guided him to the wooden door at the side of the room.

'Are you ready?'

Melling nodded, following the man towards the door, which opened with an obtrusive creak. The outside air, thrown down from the top of the spire, played with Melling's wispy hair. The light from above also cascaded down the stone steps, revealing the dull greys of a medieval spiral. 'This way,' the master beckoned, starting his ascent with an eager smile. Melling followed, spiralling upwards and leaving behind only the muted thuds of his shoes against the stone slabs. Within a minute, the light from above was more revealing, until their winding ascent opened into an exposed stone cube, all the sides of which were unguarded and bare, save the front, where the lapiz blue of the giant clock eclipsed the sunlight. The rays kissed around its edges like a golden disc with a centre of black onyx. Above him was a golden bell with its mechanisms hidden from view.

'I hope it's not half past the hour,' Melling said, and the master chuckled with disarming mirth.

'Remarkable isn't it, detective? I like to come up here and survey.'

Melling stood behind him, and it *was* true: the college was truly stunning from this height. 'I took you here because I want you to see Dunfield for what it is. You see, the professors, students, mothers and fathers were all devastated by dear Lucy's passing. My wife and I have cried many nights since. But,' the master paused, 'those of us who are lucky enough to be a part of the Huxley *community* are still able to see things for what they are. You, detective, so long parted from our way of life, I fear, have begun to villainise the place in defence of the person.'

'I'm not quite sure how to respond to that, Master Dunfield,' Melling admitted with a sigh.

'A detective who focuses on suicide. Is it not so? I wonder if you yourself can spot the juxtaposition. Do tell, how a man asked to investigate a suicide can be labelled a detective? What is there to detect? Surely the culprit is the deceased? A sort of self-homicide, if you will?'

'Well, whilst one cannot deny the logic to your semantics, I must say that no suicide is ever so open and shut. There is always a cause, or string of causes, which, when one identifies, can be used to prevent similar tragedies in the future.'

'So, you *are* here looking for somebody to blame,' Dunfield spat, almost disgustedly.

'Master Dunfield, I –'

'Huxley is blameless, Detective. Blameless! What happened to Lucy Rosewood was indeed a tragedy, but it is rendered even more so when the cause, as you have termed it, is thrown onto those who did everything in their power to nurture her and help her to flourish.'

The master seemed truly astonished and offended; he was pained. 'Huxley was her home,' he added, voice wavering, 'and you come here, searching for villains in the land of the innocent. We set people free here, we do not constrain them.' He turned accusatory, eyes full of challenge. 'Or is that how you felt here? Constrained? Where would you be now if not for us? What would you be without Dr Farway? Without Huxley? Lucy's case, though tragic, is simple to explain –'

'But that cannot be the truth!' Melling shouted, and the master's lips twitched in their sardonic way yet again, though only for the briefest of moments. Melling wondered if he had even seen them move. He met the detective with his harrowing stare.

'And just what do you know about the truth, Detective?'

'That it is always there when one looks hard enough,' Melling defended, holding the man's immeasurably deep, agate gaze.

'What of Lucy's truth?'

'That remains to be seen,' Melling said but the latter just sighed in disappointment.

'Look at you. Still looking for someone to blame. Did she not already cite her truth in that note?'

Now it was Melling's turn to shake his head.

'That note was saturated with ambiguity, and sadly,' he said with a frustrated raise in voice: 'no one wants to tell me the meaning!'

The master paused, taking a slow step away from the detective and gradually exhaling into the, now dying, sunlight.

'As much as Dr Farway tried, you were not much of a philosopher were you, *boy?*'

'I'm sorry?' Melling asked, trying hard to reign in his anger at the condescension.

'Seven years of silent inquiry allow a man to find truth,' the master recited and Melling noticed that his eyes seemed to look for a world that neither man could truly see. 'But it takes fourteen to discover how to pass that truth on for others.' He turned back to Melling. 'These measurements were translated from Plato's texts by Renaissance writers, some of them even translated here at Huxley – texts Miss Lucy Rosewood was all too familiar with as a philosopher.'

'Wait,' Melling recalibrated, feeling the pinprick of nausea threaten to invade him. 'You're saying that when she claims to save her mother fourteen years, she's referring to some sort of *truth?*' He felt dizzy speaking the words into existence, and his voice fell into an almost resigned whisper. 'Just what truth do you think that is?'

'Well, I would suppose, though it's just a guess, the ultimate truth?'

'That which only death can answer,' Melling murmured to himself in realisation, suddenly growing too agitated to control an outburst. 'She thought she was showing the way to life's understanding! My God! How awful! But that's… that's… insanity!'

The master did not affirm but stood watching the detective with his constant scrutiny. Melling felt his stomach scrape away until only a poignant emptiness remained; he turned around to think, exposing himself to the view he had neglected: the omnipresence of Huxley Castle. Atop Huxley Hill, it taunted him. Stepping forward for a better view of all the castle's towers, he paused tentatively at the edge of the landing. At the sight of the empty lawn below, the vaguest sense of familiarity exposed itself to him, and for the most modicum of moments, he felt almost asleep. Reality, in that meagre minute, didn't quite feel real enough to be considered consciousness. The detective was completely, mentally destabilised.

'Detective?' the master said, evidently curious. His voice was like the cautious cooing of a huntsman before the fox, and the man's fluctuating pitch brought Melling back into the present. He walked away from the edge, releasing a long exhale.

He relived the past few minutes of exchange. As much as the master had superciliously withheld his wisdom, the man had finally brought some clarity. Lucy did seem deceived by some cruel interpretation of her... perhaps it could be said: her *own* interpretation of philosophy. It broke the detective's heart to acknowledge this. His irritations with the master were annihilated by the realisation of just how tragic Lucy's end had been.

'I'm sorry, Master Dunfield. It's just a lot to process, if true.'

The man's agate eyes turned outwardly sympathetic.

'When Professor Robora spotted the comparisons to Plato, I too was shocked – *horrified!* It is indeed a dreadful loss. But you see,' he furthered, grasping Melling by the shoulder. 'When the truth of the dead is left behind, it does not serve the living to point new fingers.'

Melling sighed in defeat and lowered his head.

'I guess you're probably right about that.' He was too demolished by the facts to ask further questions. The possibility of a young girl killing herself in search of some ultimate truth was just one more thing to keep him up at night. He suddenly wanted to be alone. 'Thank you for the information, as well as the tour. I'm afraid that I have not been sleeping well as of late and so –'

'Not at all, not at all,' the master said with his honeyed chimes, taking Melling yet again by the shoulder.

'If she chose to see death that way, then,' Melling began with a long exhale, trying to find some semblance of a silver lining.

'See it as a sunrise, Mr Melling, not a sunset,' the master offered.

It was true that suicide could always be interpreted as someone's sunrise. After all, it was mostly just a sunset for those left behind. The person leaving the world was often freed from their worldly sufferings. Melling looked down in defeat once again. Nevertheless, the notion of a sunrise seemed ill-suited. Lucy had been deluded, God knows why, by something almost too queer for a young girl to have imagined on her own. It sickened Melling that she could have done what she did not due to troubles, but due to philosophical answers. She hadn't been releasing herself from suffering but, if the letter was true, then she had been chasing philosophical answers life couldn't offer.

Together, they walked away from the clock, down the stairs and out of the library into the darkened morning. The sun, like Melling's spark, had been smothered under nauseating clouds; from down below, the clock felt less imposing, the decaying daylight turning its golden hands into a dull bronze. The master walked the detective back to the courtyard where they had begun, and Melling found himself apologising for his targeted questions. Said apology was then crushed beneath the rhetoric of politeness, and the request of calling-in should the detective need anything.

As soon as the master departed, Melling felt assaulted by his internal vexations. His head ached with questions he didn't have the heart to answer. He turned slowly on his heel, walking through the arching passage of staring students and out into the original emerald of the opening courtyard. But approaching the gate, it was not Inspector Todd's parental scowl which greeted him. Instead, he was softened by the comforting grin of his new companion: Dr Louis Starling.

'What are you doing here?' Melling asked, half-awake. His voice was barely audible to himself.

'Well, I couldn't stand another minute waiting at the practice, so I left early to join you as I promised Harry I would.'

Melling smiled his gratitude, but it was a weak endeavour. 'Everything alright?'

'Where's the inspector?'

'He asked if I could stay with you while he attends to some matters. He wants us to meet him at Trinity earlier than anticipated, so we can speak to that young lady.'

'When?'

'In an hour.'

'Good, then we can have a coffee, because I feel like I want to sleep the day away.'

'I know a place.'

He took the detective out of the microcosm of beauty and back into the cobbled world of Huxley town. Leaving the enclosure, Melling felt an instant freedom, releasing a tension in his shoulders he hadn't even noticed. He was able to collect his thoughts for the first time since standing atop the library's tower. It was ineffable to say the least, but the atmosphere of Dunfield, beautiful as it was, seemed to hold an aura of sedating confusion. He had been drugged by eloquence and that schoolboy feeling of not knowing how to express oneself properly under the scrutiny of one's superiors. The vendor-filled streets, on the contrary, cared not for the detective's thoughts; the paths were *awake*, demanding wakefulness from their occupants.

He relayed all that had passed to Starling, who clung to every detail with hungry and worrisome eyes. By the time he had finished, they had lowered into the town centre, Starling taking them to a sequestered café. It was opposite a longstanding chapel, newly renovated. They sat down for coffee, and Melling immediately silenced himself with a much-desired smoke. Starling too, now privy to Lucy's philosophical quest for deathly truth, quickly shared Melling's sombre complexion.

'Fourteen years,' he said in soft disgust. Then he grew more animated: 'that's the most tragic thing I've ever heard. I knew I recalled it! I suppose we're lucky this Robora fellow pointed it out.'

'How on earth will I be able to tell her mother?'

Melling couldn't comprehend how something like this could happen. Sure, young adults turned to suicide all the time, but when did they take their own lives in search of a higher truth? Suicide was an escape from life, it wasn't meant to be an answer to it. His heart kept breaking every time he acknowledged Lucy Rosewood's actions. An all too familiar feeling ruminated inside of him too: he felt glad for not having a child who bore his name. With the things he had been forced to see in the century he was born in, well, he was often relieved not to be a father.

'Tell me something, Louis,' he began. 'How does the world allow something so unbelievably dreadful to happen? Sometimes, I really find myself falling completely out of love with life. As a parent, you do everything right: you love your son or daughter, you raise them to learn what's right and what's, well, undeniably wrong. With hope, prayers, and rigorous childhoods, sometimes they manage to further their pursuit of knowledge at a coveted institution like Huxley. Maybe it's Cambridge, Oxford or wherever.'

'Just when you think you've managed to do it all correctly, you mean?' Starling suggested in quiet dejection. 'As though they can only succeed from there?' The doctor had clearly picked up the exact frustration the detective was trying to convey.

'And after all of that, they convince themselves to take their own life,' Melling spat, coldly. 'How is that a solution?'

Starling had to shudder under the detective's painful truth, thinning his lips nervously. 'I've seen many deaths in my harrowing career. Many,' Melling continued. 'I've spent countless nights trying to process the secondary grief of when a child dies. That's all I am to the situation: a secondary, and still, it kills you.'

For a moment his mind was cast back to Horsham station in Sussex, where the exfoliated remains of Jacob Wenley lay scattered across the tracks. He was a student too, and it was only recently that he had been forced to behold the spectacle of his suicide, limbs ripped apart by an uncaring train. He tried to banish the image from his mind. 'But *this*,' he uttered, chewing his dying Gitanes cigarette. 'This is a whole new method of horror because it isn't melancholy, nor fear, nor a thousand other reasons. It was the pursuit of some perverse version of distorted truth.' His lips quivered as he thought of Olivia Rosewood's daughter, the daughter of someone he used to study with every day, carving a kitchen knife up her legs. It was all too much, and he couldn't keep control any longer. He struck a bewildered fist onto the table, startling the doctor. 'Bloody ridiculous!'

Tears began to pass slowly down Melling's cheeks, and he wiped them away. An individual droplet managed to evade his snubbing hands; full of determination, it reached his chin, dangling there as though it was afraid to fall onto the cobblestones. It took the length of a cigarette for Melling to find his voice.

'I still need to know why she cut her legs. Was she torturing herself at the very end or was it ritualistic? And what of the boy on the bridge? Are we just going to chalk that up to coincidence? Every aspect of my instinct is demanding that I see a correlation. But, then again, what if it really was an accident?'

'I know you don't believe that!' Starling corrected, leaning forward. 'I know I abhor the fact that you feel you need to be covert in my hometown, but I can now no longer pretend to doubt your fears. There is something sinister about Lucy's death... so sinister that it makes the boy's accident appear even more disturbing. Why doubt yourself?'

'It was just... that master, he made me feel so illogical. I felt too, well, almost embarrassed, to bring up the boy on the bridge.' He shook his head at his own weakness. 'He was so sure that she was an anomaly, and well, suicides generally are.'

'Your job asks you to make equations out of people, right?' Starling asked, and Melling was once again cast back to Sussex, where Constable Whaites had posed the same question.

'That's all that we are to each other, at least, that's what I otiosely try and affirm, because rationality is the only weapon against misery. It's dangerous to become subjective in my line of work. Stick with details and probabilities and you can delude yourself into thinking that you are somehow separate from the destructions that people are willing to do to themselves.'

Starling scoffed, seemingly caught in thought.

'I'd say it's clear you are far too involved in the deaths of others, Robert. You obviously care more than you're advised to in your profession. But at what cost to yourself?'

Melling didn't want to gratify the rhetoric behind that question, so Starling asked another. 'Why did you become a detective of suicide?'

'I'm not even sure why I became a detective at all,' Melling said weakly, eternally unsure of himself. 'I was drawn to the idea of playing an active role in the world. I'd read enough books to start a library, brainwashed by authors, poets and playwrights into thinking that everyone could make something of themselves. I guess that the jobs all my friends were after didn't seem heroic enough. Then the war happened.'

'That really just speaks for itself, doesn't it?' Starling said before laughing dryly.

'How could I not re-evaluate everything after that horrendous cock-up of a half-decade?'

'I wish I discussed it more with Sheryl,' Starling replied. 'But how can you explain it to those who weren't there?'

Melling nodded pensively.

'History books are going to do their best, but it just won't land like the shrapnel did.'

'Well bloody put,' Starling murmured. His eyes were not facing his interlocutor but facing Dunkirk's horizon, German planes circling above. He really thought he'd die that day.

'I get that our wives had to recalibrate too, and I know that life wasn't exactly a picnic or anything, back home. The blackouts, sirens and…'

'…the blitz…' Staling said, almost as a hush. He could hear the whirring of the engines above.

'But *being* there,' Melling emphasised, shuddering under his own smoke as distant, deeply repressed memories fought their way to the surface.

'You don't need to go further,' Starling whispered, recognising a look on the detective's face that was mirrored on his own.

'Anyway,' Melling digressed, avoiding the putrid imagery of mud, blood and misery that had now been reawakened. 'The war made me realise how little it all mattered.' He motioned to the threatening glare of the castle whose spires still managed to dominate the horizon behind them. 'None of these conventions and ideals truly matter, not in a general sense, anyway. I suppose I realised that one could have the best degree, the connections, the car, the house, the religion… whatever it is that people covet… it could be anything. Whatever your idealised securities, whatever stories you spin to make you think your life is on track, you can still be shot dead in a war you didn't even start, you know?' Melling even found himself laughing ruefully at the irony. 'When I realised that these things are all just attempts to grapple with the existential dilemmas of being a human being, that they could crumble at any point, I started to think more about a career where I could enact some good. Even being married is a crutch that the so-called divine can rip away at a moment's notice.'

His wife's smile danced in his remembrances for a few moments until Starling interrupted his daydream.

'Olivia Rosewood will never know how much this means to you,' he said with a sorrowful smile. 'But I will. I just want to thank you for being the one person here who's actively looking into the misery that others avoid. Don't stop asking those questions now, not when this place *needs* you. If Huxley has a problem with identifying such misery, then you need to correct it.' He had extended a hand of support, and

Melling shook it with his cold palm. He managed to nod a half-awake smile to his new friend.

'It means a lot to me that someone is here to support me, Louis. I can't explain just how grateful I am. Thank you.'

Before they could trade any more assurances, Melling used his newfound support to mentally give himself a kick in the rear, shivering an uneasy pinch out of his spine. He checked his watch and fell back into his determined seriousness. 'Can we get to Trinity within ten minutes?'

'Absolutely,' Starling alleged, seemingly glad to get moving and ponder less on life's cruelties. They left the café feeling, somehow, both cathartically rejuvenated and simultaneously more miserable than when they had arrived.

XIII

Filled With Crazy Lumber

As they walked through the colder streets of the early afternoon, Melling felt the castle watching from behind him. The clouds grew more numerous; Huxley seemed determined to amass all the countryside's vapour without shedding a single drop of rain. Trinity was positioned on a busy street, and Melling found it incredible how these colleges could contain entirely different worlds that were isolated from outsiders' eyes. Their walls blended perfectly with the panorama of their surroundings: Huxley was a medieval labyrinth of seemingly endless narrow roads and side-streets, stone upon stone, but pass through the correct door, and you stepped into a different universe. Outside Trinity's domineering black gate, an elderly porter with a green bowler hat stood guard.

'Afternoon gentleman,' he croned in a hoarse voice. Melling wondered if he might be slightly too old for his career.

'Afternoon,' Starling returned with a smile.

'What brings you to Trinity?'

'We have an appointment with Inspector Todd,' was the reply, and the man sneered at it.

'Ahh, so you're the ones stirring up a fuss for Miss Collier.'

'Well, that depends on who she might be,' Melling said in quick rejoinder, using an obviously false smile as an invitation for confrontation.

'Careful, Mr Melling,' the man jeered, 'do watch your *step*.' He laughed to himself, leaving both the detective and Starling in confusion. Still chuckling, the porter pulled the gate open with some effort, revealing a wide expanse of lawn which stretched for a space at least three times the courtyard at Dunfield College. The grass here was less maintained; in the middle, a huge stone fountain was enclosed inside a cage of statues, making the grounds appear more capacious by contrast. Both men stepped across the invisible threshold with a humbled outlook.

'How on earth are they hiding this behind here?' Melling exclaimed with a laugh. 'How could I ever forget this?'

'My wife says Huxley permits one to step into new worlds,' Starling said.

'The inspector is waiting for you in Ferrum Court,' the porter rasped from behind them, and Starling shuddered as the man hobbled away. Both men found themselves conceiving a dislike for the porter, though neither one could quite articulate as to why. Melling passed it off as some idiosyncratic personal distaste, reaching for the cigarette case in his pocket; it clinked as it scraped against his cigar case. He pondered on his purpose here in Huxley and decided to drop his silver case of Gitanes on the gravel before the lawn – leaving himself one to smoke of course. Starling noted the action with a raised brow.

'What are you doing?'

'Allow me a little mystery, would you?' the detective answered with a wink.

'Will do,' Starling replied, somewhat bemused. But with a shrug, he turned his gaze back to the expansive landscape before them, turning rueful. 'As much as the colleges are breath-taking, I do have to admit that I am no fan of this place. I mean Ferrum Court in particular'.

'What about it?' Melling asked, lighting his Gitanes as they began to walk.

'Weren't you ever told of Dr Thomas Ferrum as a student?' Starling asked, but Melling shrugged. 'Well,' Starling continued, placing his hands awkwardly in his pockets. 'Every student hears the tales of a darker Huxley.'

'The spectres that second-years conjure in order to keep first-years on their toes?'

'The very same,' Starling allowed with a chuckle. 'But he, Thomas Ferrum that is, *did* exist. He lived in the buildings behind these lawns.'

'Let me guess,' Melling said in chuckling suggestion. 'He got up to no good?'

'More than just no good. Evil is the appropriate description. He was a student of the late German physiologist, Eduard Hitzig, and used to dissect animals from the woodlands nearby. He did it for research – discovered a lot about spinal nerves and their connection with the brain.'

'As appalling as vivisection was, a great deal of humanity's beloved scientists weren't strangers to it. Though I detest to say it, we benefited a lot from the results.'

'Unquestionably so, Robert. But that was not the evil I was referring to. You see, Ferrum became transfixed by the soul. He was desperate to see how science might confirm the divine, tracing biological impulses as evidence of something spiritual. Nevertheless, being the religious man that he was, he didn't believe animals had souls, meaning that they were rendered useless subjects for his experiments.'

'What then?' Melling asked, somewhat aware of where this tale was going.

'He used human beings,' Starling said with matter-of-fact distaste. 'He felt that if he could electrocute certain areas in the brain, he might be able to trace the soul's boundaries via the body's reactions. But the person needed to be alive.'

'Who on earth would volunteer for that?' Melling asked ironically, chuckling to avoid the seriousness of the story.

'Well, that's just it, Robert,' Starling said, pausing for a solemn swallow. 'No one did. About a year after he had supposedly ceased his experimentation, people began to disappear.'

'You're sure this is a *true* story?'

Starling nodded.

'He was careful in his crimes, choosing poor, unwanted prostitutes whom no one would go looking for. Strapped thirty or so into his chair and electrically lobotomised them.'

He paused as Melling choked on smoke. 'None of them survived.'

'That's horrendous,' the detective said in a low mutter, fighting back a shudder. Then he tried to make light of it: 'no wonder they're using that story to scare first-years.'

'I believe the university lobbied a name-change, but it was reversed by the Chancellor. Something about maintaining our history with dignity.'

Now Melling really had to laugh.

Having crossed to the other side of the lawn, they followed the stone walls of the moss-grown building to Ferrum Court. Melling shook the story out of his shoulders and attempted to ignore the claustrophobia of the narrow passages which wound towards the back of the college. It didn't help that the students seemed to have abandoned the place. They rounded another corner, Melling baffled by how long the college stretched on for; this patch was home to a quad of daffodils. The brickwork was a lighter shade of brown here, and Melling could see a door marked as the master's office. They walked on past walls of overhanging vines until they reached a proud building of reinforced lime mortar, evidently the medieval foundation of the college. Some students were passing listlessly in front of the dirtied doorway, smoking cigarettes. Starling chuckled as Melling passed them, flinging his own to the ground. Then they ventured into the building of Dr Thomas Ferrum, the criminal vivisector.

XIV

Blinded With an Eye

The inspector guarded an empty, dull classroom from the outside. Upon seeing the doctor and detective, he frowned.

'You're late. The girl does have better things to be doing, you know?'

'What's her name?' Melling asked, ignoring the irritation. 'An apology is always better with a name.'

The Chief Inspector of Huxshire sighed, rubbing one hand over the other's knuckles.

'Judy Collier. She's doing a doctorate here, specialises in Renaissance Europe, or something to that effect.'

'Thank you, Caspar,' Starling said on Melling's behalf. The inspector opened the door, but before they stepped through, Melling slapped the outside of his coat.

'Oh dear,' he said. 'I think I dropped my cigarettes.'

'Really?' Starling asked, immediately catching on to the ruse, but evidently uncomfortable under the acting.

'Inspector Todd, I do hate to inconvenience you, but you see, it was my father's case. I really don't want to waste any more of Miss Collier's time. As you pointed out, I've wasted enough already. Would you mind retrieving it for me? We took a smoke by the entrance, just after we stepped in. I'm so sorry to be such a bother but it has sentimental value – I hate to think of it lying there for anyone to find. You'll know the entrance better than Starling,' he added, hinting that Louis could stay behind, thus planting the idea of him behaving as a minder; not that a Scotland Yard detective should need one. The inspector huffed, giving Starling a look that ordered him to watch the detective like a hawk. Starling smiled reassuringly, and to Melling's delight, the man obliged him with a stiff expression.

'Not at all, Mr Melling, I understand. As a detective, you have full right to talk to her without me being present.' Then the man's eyes narrowed. 'I'll find it quickly.'

As he left the building, Melling winked at Starling. Then, he pushed the door open into the poorly lit room.

Miss Collier was slouching in a chair in the middle of the room. With blonde hair reaching folded arms, she glared two frosted-blue eyes at both gentleman as they walked in. She was dressed for the outdoors even though the room itself was far warmer than the outside. The blinds had been lowered halfway, so the already meek sunlight did little to brighten the stuffy room.

'You're late,' she said with some irritation, adjusting her grey scarf.

'And do forgive us for it, Miss Collier,' the detective replied politely. 'But good things come to those who wait,' he added with a chuckle. Judy Collier did not laugh; she scowled at the cliché.

'You speak like you're from another century,' she returned in a voice which, though it chimed with youth, ended sharply, inflections aiming at cutting down accusers. 'Anyway, I already said everything that happened that night.'

'Well, Miss Collier, though I trust the inspector at his every word,' the detective began. 'I wanted to understand the story for myself. If you don't mind, that is?'

She shrugged in acquiescence.

'Excellent! Let's start with what you already told the inspector, then? You were the last person to see our Marlowe undergraduate alive, isn't that right? His name was Samuel, I believe?'

Judy Collier let out a loud sigh.

'That's right,' she eventually said.

'Sorry, Samuel who?' Melling asked sweetly, jarring against her lacking enthusiasm.

'Caspar didn't tell you?'

'*Caspar?* Oh, I see. You and the inspector are on a first name basis, then?' She shifted in her seat.

'I guess.'

'Look, Miss Collier,' he said with a notion of stern impatience. 'The less forthcoming you are, the longer you will be here, do you understand?' She shook her head insouciantly and pouted, glaring back at him. Then she stole a glance at the door.

'Am I under suspicion?'

'No. This is just routine. But the more evasive you become, the more secretive you seem.'

She faked a yawn.

'Fine,' she said with deep disinterest. 'His name was Samuel Cadence.'

'Did the inspector tell you that, or did you know him before you saw him on the bridge?'

'I knew him,' she said cautiously. 'But not well. I mean, we'd met a few times at a –'

She paused for a moment.

'Yes?'

'A reading group.'

'Do go on…'

'At Marlowe College,' she said, drawing the words out slowly. She had all the caution of a deer on a dark road.

'How many times had you met?'

'I have no idea. Maybe once or twice?'

'What were you reading?'

'I'm sorry?'

'This reading group… tell us about it?' Melling asked in perfumed tones, taking a seat in front of her, and turning slightly towards the window.

'Why?'

'Miss Collier…'

'Edgar Allen Poe,' she eventually said.

'So, it wasn't Hamlet, perchance?' Melling asked.

'No. It's been Poe this whole term.'

'You've no doubt read it, though?'

She nodded.

'Of course. I study Renaissance literature, so…'

Now Melling nodded.

'Did you know Samuel was referencing Ophelia on the bridge?'

'What do you mean?'

'Your report said that he was claiming to be a baker's daughter.'

'He was drunk!'

'How drunk?' Melling asked.

'I don't know. I didn't *ask* him.'

'So, what *did* you talk about?' Melling inquired, keeping a calm poise. Starling remained impassive behind him.

'We didn't talk! He was singing when I saw him.' She began to sound hysterical. 'I told him to get down. I begged, I –'

'It's quite alright,' Melling said. 'I know you were deeply disturbed by it; I can see that.' He could see she needed reassurance. 'Just so you're aware, no one is blaming you for anything.' He waited for her breathing to slow before he continued. 'So why didn't he listen?'

'I don't know, I don't know,' she repeated, her bravado slipping slightly. 'I told him he would regret it –'

'So, you knew he wanted to jump?'

'Like I said,' she replied, gazing emptily at Starling instead of Melling. 'I've read Hamlet, so I made the connection.'

'What were you doing before all of this?'

'What do you mean?'

'Well, I'd like to know why on earth you were there, at that time of night, in the first place?'

She swallowed nervously.

'I…'

'Yes?'

'I have trouble sleeping,' she concluded, the corner of her lip twitching into a smile. 'I hear I'm not the only one.'

Melling's blood ran cold.

'What are you talking about?'

She couldn't possibly have known about his sleepwalking escapade. Then again: the victory in her lips was palpable. 'Answer the question,' Melling said flatly, but Judy just shrugged, murdering her smile.

'A lot of my friends go for walks when they can't sleep. Either that or a cigarette can help.'

Melling felt the sickly rise of unease travel up his forearms. Then again, her smile was gone, and she couldn't possibly… unless the inspector had given her the ammunition. After all, Melling had mentioned sleepwalking to him that morning, hadn't he? But why would the inspector be giving her conversational leverage? Besides, it had been the most passing of mentions this morning, not even an admittance. But the look in her blue eyes demanded unease all the same. He coughed, ashamed that he'd allowed her bravado to build itself up again. Intuition told him that she was underselling her relationship with Samuel. He decided to change his angle.

'So, did you know that Samuel was failing his studies?'

She seemed about to object, then she took a slow breath.

'What's that to me?'

'Well, he must have had his reasons for wanting to end things,' Melling alleged in a calculated manner. Then he added: 'cowardly reasons though they may be.'

He turned to Starling. 'Don't you think, Louis? I mean, realising that he wasn't quite academic enough for Huxley? Could make any student turn to drink. The problem is, when one sobers up, they're still a failure regardless of how much —'

'He wasn't a failure!' she interjected. 'Or a drunk.' Her lips were trembling.

'I thought you barely knew him?' Melling asked and her cheeks turned crimson.

'I don't... didn't... I...'

'Right,' Melling interrupted. 'You're going to start telling me the extent of what you know, or I am going to assume you had more to do with it than you're letting on. Now, let me tell you, not only will I assume the worst but,' he placed two authoritative palms on the table, 'Inspector... *Caspar*... Todd, won't be able to help you.'

'Okay,' she said quickly, her façade diluting. 'I knew him.'

'How well?' Melling asked, and now her whole body began to tremble along with her bottom lip. A slow tear ventured down her left cheek. It rested on her chin for a devastatingly long minute, then she wiped it away.

'We were in love.'

Starling inhaled in surprise.

'I'm sorry,' Melling said, almost as a whisper. 'So, you went down to the bridge to stop him, didn't you?' His mind was all sympathy now. She stared emptily into his eyes, having regained composure; still her left shoulder twitched. 'It's alright. You can tell me. You were trying to help him, weren't you?'

She nodded slowly, and Melling found himself pitying this poor girl more and more by the second. He was about to ask a subsequent question when the door opened behind them, and the inspector's voice intruded.

'Your case took a while to locate, Melling but I…' His eyes passed over Judy Collier's expression. 'Detective!' He ran over and wagged a finger in the detective's face. 'How dare you! I allowed you to see her in order to understand her side of the story, not to bully her whilst my back was turned. How dare you expose this impressionable girl to your blaming —'

'Caspar!' Starling interrupted with a yell, silencing the room.

'It appears Miss Collier had omitted some crucial details,' Melling said. 'Though I had not hoped to upset her, she told us something important.'

A peculiar expression of disbelief made its way into Inspector Todd's eyes, and for a moment, it looked as though he was glaring at the poor girl, who, in turn, looked down bashfully.

'Well,' he said, almost to the floor, eyes becoming less alive. 'What did she say, exactly?'

Melling's brows creased in confusion, not quite understanding the inspector's irritated reaction.

'That she and Samuel were in love, and that she went down to save him. It isn't damning whatsoever, but I would like to know why she lied in the first place?'

The inspector looked down and mumbled to himself. 'Sorry Inspector? I didn't catch that,' Melling asked. The man looked at him, and his dejected state quickly became professional once more.

'Well,' he said slowly. 'You must forgive me for my outburst, Detective. Do understand that I am only looking after our students. I don't want them to think that they are being subjected to unmerited accusations.'

'It is quite alright, Inspector. Though, again, I was *not* blaming Miss Collier.'

Judy Collier still avoided the inspector's eyes as Melling turned to her. 'And I'm sorry to have upset you my dear, but you see, I had a suspicion you were lying about Samuel. I did not mean to discredit his memory, but I had not, and *still* do not, mind you, have the slightest idea of why he was down there. But you do, don't you?'

She didn't respond. 'I think you'll find that we'll all benefit from the truth.'

At the notion of the truth, she looked up at him with a new gaze. Again, for the slightest of moments, Melling would have testified that the hint of a sardonic smile played with the corner of her ruby lips.

'The truth?' she asked, and Melling was uncannily reminded of Master Dunfield. 'Are you sure?'

The inspector tried to interrupt but Melling silenced him with a hand. He encouraged Judy with his eyes.

'The truth is the only thing I am here for, Miss Collier.'

She rested her chin on interlocked hands and sighed. She looked at the inspector, who said nothing, but Melling wondered what his eyes were telling her. She sighed again, then turned her frosty gaze back to Melling. She seemed truly pained to be speaking, but at the same time, there was something about her look that he didn't trust. Judy Collier, as distraught as she seemed, also appeared inauthentic. The detective was well-versed in performance, and her eyes certainly revealed the tinge of performativity. Yet those tears had been real.

'He was, I guess you could say, melancholic. Didn't have parents or many friends, but he had me,' she explained, voice trailing off.

'So, he wanted to escape this world?' Inspector Todd suggested flatly, not really asking. She nodded.

'He told me he was going to end it that night, and I thought that I had talked him out of it earlier that day. We were meant to meet late. I was going to check up on him after I finished an essay.'

'But he didn't show up, did he?' Melling asked, sympathy rising in his chest. She shook her head.

'No.' Her voice chimed hollow, and the inspector placed a consoling hand on her shoulder.

'We're sorry for the loss,' he said softly from behind her.

'He was pure,' she pronounced, matter-of-factly. 'Heart as a feather.'

'Pure?' Melling repeated, stalled by her choice of words. She began to cry, and the inspector shot the detective a meaningful glance.

'Mr Melling, I think it's best to stop this. I'll make sure she's looked after. After she's had some food and rest, I'll make sure to get a full report. You have my word.'

The detective looked at Starling, who nodded.

'Okay,' Melling assented to the inspector, who handed him back his silver case.

'Thank you, Caspar,' Starling said. Before they left the room, Melling stopped by the door.

'Miss Collier,' he initiated tentatively, and she looked up through wet, blue eyes. 'I'm so sorry for your loss.'

She snivelled.

'I'm sorry too.'

With that, Starling and Melling left Ferrum Court, both feeling confused and morose. Despite the perturbing nature of everything, it was Judy's final comment that had unsettled the detective the most.

He was pure… Heart as a feather.

Why were people stating such obscure sentiments around death? There was Lucy's classmate who, as the inspector had said just the other night, had given *an emotional speech at a recent Dunfield service in her honour… She cited some Egyptian scripture to see her off.*

Melling had found that an all too particular notion at the time. Inescapably random. As was Judy Collier's recent word choice: *pure… Heart as a feather*, which became even more so when placed side by side with the fact that students had been chanting *in lucem* for Lucy.

Were students imparting their philosophies, esoteric as they might be, onto the dead to console themselves? Had the likes of what professors such as the infamous Robora been teaching, been taken by students as a means of grappling with mortality? He should be careful not to conflate what he had heard about Lucy's mourning service with what he had just been told by Judy. All the same, was this bizarre concept of feather-like purity supposed to console her in such times of trial in the same way that others had relied on such strange thinking? Then again, should such specificity really be so alarming? It bothered Melling that they would say such things about death. But these were no ordinary people: so well-read that they could decorate death in ways foreign to most. Was that all it was? Melling could not fully flesh out why it bothered him beyond its mere particularity. It *was* definitely an exclusive consolation. Clearly Huxley students were overly armed when it came to exploring demise. This was certainly an issue if these students took to melancholy, as had patently been the case for Lucy. Lucy had philosophised her own death, looking for an ultimate truth. Was that just eloquence at its very disturbed limit? Not just consolation for a corpse, but self-consolation before becoming a corpse?

If two students had died, regardless of their proximity in time, was it so terrible for other students to find their own ways of explaining these circumstances? Huxley was a stressful place; angst and sadness were rife amongst an overworked student body. Perhaps all Huxley needed was a means of identifying and helping the sufferers? To be overread always meant that death could become aggrandised – surely Melling had been doing the same sort of melancholic philosophising his whole life? Times were changing, and these were no ordinary students. It would have been rare not to use the metaphors of heaven and hell in his day. But these days? He once more reminded himself that Lucy was not Samuel, and Judy was not Lucy's friend at the funeral service. The cases were separate.

Still, the conversation between Starling, Melling and the inspector at the *Abenborg* pub came back to him once again.

But the most moving aspect was the chanting… I was never much for Latin, but I believe it was ad lucem – no, in luxem. Yes, in lucem, or something to that effect.

'Into the light,' Melling translated out loud once again, earning a look from Starling. Melling quickly shook his head in dismissal of himself, turning his eyes back to the building they had just left, staring after answers he couldn't find.

Staring into those outdated stones was like staring into the Mediterranean: one could feel all of its recorded history in some perpetual moment. Here, in the sunless gloom of Ferrum Court, he saw that a translucent spectre was staring right back at him. It was the ghost of the building's old scientist, Dr Thomas Ferrum, still giddy with electricity. He watched the detective with a snickering expression, wondering if he would ever figure out the true story behind those two words that so bothered him, or indeed, what they asked of the person speaking them.

In lucem.

The detective shuddered under the glare of Huxley's history.

XV

From Error to Error

Melling woke to the rattle of metal. He coughed loudly, somehow startled by an indescribable surge of fear. He wiped his lazy eyes and gazed listlessly in front of him. In the darkness of the early morning, he felt for the bell on his left wrist, but his fingers could not find it. Slowly, his eyes adjusted to the black and white of nocturnal sight, passing from the end of his bed to the open door. He almost screamed when he finally noticed the darkened figure standing in the doorway.

It was a woman, though he could not decipher her appearance beyond her blackened silhouette. His lips numbed in panic, and though he wanted to cry out, his jaws failed him. Only a pathetic squeal broke from his throat as he sat there in upright dread. The person walked confidently into the room. She was noiseless. As her pale appearance passed into the delicate moonbeams of the dying night, he thought that he recognised her. Now standing at the foot of his bed, her expression was, once again, obscured by darkness.

The detective still hadn't moved, but felt his stomach fill with terror when she placed two grey hands on his covers, digging her corpse-like fingers into the duvet. To his incredulity, the haunting apparition crawled slowly towards him, crittering sluggishly and deliberately, almost denying herself her victim. She was seduced by her own attack, deterring each movement in relish. Melling's ears were ringing now, drowning the sound of footsteps from outside his room. Immobile, he closed his eyes in pathetic submission as she finally reached a raking finger forwards, itching for contact. Though he wasn't facing his fate, he could literally feel the lifelessness emanating from her limb. It was then that a shout from Louis Starling cracked into the room.

'Robert?'

The detective didn't move. But, when the ringing in his ears had ceased and he hadn't felt the cruel touch of death's maiden, he slowly opened his eyes. Nothing. 'Robert? Are you alright?' the doctor asked, coming concernedly to his bedside. Melling blinked in confusion, moving for the first time since seeing the hallucinated spectre. His back cracked at the sudden release; it felt as though he had been sitting upright at a desk for hours. Could it have been a hallucination? Had he not been awake? He shook his head in slow disbelief, raising more questions of concern from Louis. The spectre's shape began to dilute in his mind. 'What time is it?' he asked, voice almost an imperceptible croak.

'It's four in the morning, Robert,' was the response. 'I thought I heard the bell, and I came to check.' He looked at Melling's bare wrist, then in surprise, he looked around him until his fretful eyes found the copper trinket cast aside onto the floor. Picking it up with a look of unease and distrust, he rung it gently with a slow hand. Melling cringed beneath the tolling rattle. 'Why did you do this?'

'I didn't,' Melling protested with a shaky swallow. 'I swear. The sound of it falling woke me. It was off already, I promise.' His guilty pleading made Starling sigh. He offered a solemn look as he placed the bell on the desk to Melling's left.

'That isn't good, Robert. It really isn't. If you did that whilst asleep, then… I don't really know what to say.' He shook his head. 'And why were you so afraid when I came in? I swear, it was like you were under attack.'

The detective didn't answer, wetting his dry lips in discomfort. 'Robert?'

'I thought I saw something,' Melling said, getting out of the bed on uneasy legs. He walked to the half-curtained window in curiosity, gazing out into the empty moonlight.

'Saw what exactly?'

The detective turned around, crouching uncomfortably low to look under the bed. Nothing. 'Saw what, Robert?' Starling asked, growing more anxious. Melling stood up and sighed.

'I'm not sure, Louis. I'm really not sure. I thought I recognised them but now…'

'So, it was a person? You saw someone in here?'

'Well,' the detective replied guiltily. 'I could hardly see anything in the dark, but… yes. I thought it was coming to take me somewhere, I could feel that, but I don't know where. The more I think, the less I remember. It was all clear and now, slowly, it disperses into nothing.'

The doctor sighed, shaking his head whilst his guest spoke. 'I know that it's out of the question, but –'

'You felt that did you? Felt what exactly?'

'Louis, I know this is all sounding ridiculous! I usually don't go in for spectres either, but –'

'So, it was a spectre, now?' Starling sarcastically rejoined. 'Here I was being disturbed by Ferrum Court, and here you are…' He shook his head again. 'I'm sorry, Robert. I don't mean to make you feel isolated in your experience, but these dreams of yours are really starting to bloody well wear me down. In the daytime you're a man of impeccable reason and morality, but at night, you become susceptible to these wild ideals, and well, frankly, the contrast scares me. Harry promised that you would rid Huxley of darkness, if indeed there was any, but you seem to invite it whenever your eyes close!'

Melling looked down. He was ashamed of Starling's admittance.

'I'm sorry, Louis, I really am. I wish I knew what these dreams all meant, or why they're plaguing me in this way.'

The latter sighed.

'Don't apologise, but Christ, I can't believe I am still even pushing this myself.' He ran an anxious hand through his withered hair. 'If you *are* going to stay here, I want you to see that practice I recommended – that contact of mine who deals in things like this. Unorthodox though it might be, he's the only man who might be able to explain these… premonitions.'

Before the detective could respond, Louis Starling left the room and Melling heard his footsteps patter down the stairs. He decided not to stress how he couldn't possibly have been dreaming, for it was the bell itself that woke him. Then again, he had walked to the bridge whilst asleep, so perhaps the figure was a figment of his perturbed thoughts? It had to be. These hauntings felt all the more disturbing because he didn't understand them at all. If he was the director of this dark performance, how come he was always left on a cliff-hanger? How come the certainty vanished with every second he was awake? Then again, he had felt awake when he saw it.

He was probably losing his mind. If he hadn't been sleeping, that meant he was probably becoming a lunatic. That was a thought he quickly crushed.

Let's not go down that road just yet.

He noted that it was now a quarter past four. Refusing to subject himself to another terror, he crept down the creaking stairs of Starling's home, taking a bottle of Scotch from the kitchen to the golden couches of the living room. Turning on the lamp to his left, he lit a cigar and sighed away his vexations, watching as they wafted out of his mouth. One wasn't meant to inhale cigars, but years of dependency had required a stronger sensation.

The afternoon had culminated into a taxing evening. The inspector had failed to call with any details regarding Miss Collier's account of events, and he and Starling had sat at home conjuring a thousand theories, all of which left more questions unanswered than they responded to. In fact, the men's 'logic' grew less logical the more they contemplated how all this sadness was connected. Eventually taking to bed, the detective had realised that therein lay the problem: these deaths could *not* be linked. They simply refused to be. He had come to Huxley to uncover the reasons for Lucy Rosewood's death, subsequently jumping at the notion of another suicide. Perhaps *he* was the problem? After all, Master Dunfield had illuminated the details of Lucy's letter, disturbing as they were. Her death *had* been explained, at least to an extent.

All the same, his instincts ordered him to ignore the rational and cling to the irrational. The less likely the deaths of Samuel and Lucy seemed to be correlated, the more he found peculiar reasons to assert that they were. Then there was Miss Judy Collier and the way her harsh, blue eyes had tried to avoid the truth. If she knew why Samuel had wanted to jump, why hadn't she said anything? Why hadn't she tried to explain his deathly purpose? Out of love? The notion seemed ridiculous. Surely, she would seek to alleviate the confusions around his name? The most frustrating thing though: why in God's name did Melling feel as though every person in Huxley knew something he didn't? That paranoid sentiment ate away like an ulcer in his mind every time he walked over the town's persistent cobblestones.

*

The morning's crows cackled above the chimney of number 18; a sidelong glance at the mirror atop the cupboard to Melling's left made the detective regret his early morning pondering. The lines around his eyelids had crinkled two-fold since his first meeting with Starling. His host's coffee hadn't done much to rejuvenate him.

'Listen, Robert,' Starling said, making another pot. 'You know you are welcome here, whatever you decide to do. But I implore you to consider what I said last night.'

Melling nodded with a smile, about to respond when the phone rang. The detective anticipated the inspector's report, but Starling's greeting of 'hello darling' revealed his wife on the other end of the line. Melling sighed, returning to the paper, though not two minutes into Starling's husbandry remarks, he began to sound confused.

'No? What do you mean? No, we haven't been there at all.'

Melling dropped the paper, guided by an instinctive awareness that Huxley was again about to trample all over his reason like a spooked horse. 'And you're sure it happened this morning?' he asked, growing animated. 'Last night? So, you're sure that they're in hospital?'

Now Melling's curiosity spiked uncontrollably. 'Okay, darling. I love you. Yes… yes… I must go.'

The doctor slammed down the receiver, mouth searching for words. He turned slowly to Melling's eager gaze, internally weighing the news. 'A student fell from his dormitory window last night at Fleuraline.' His voice was of a tone an author cannot find the words to describe. If there were a phrase to perfectly encapsulate how one sounds when they finally begin to accept that something truly dark has found its way into a place they love, well, such was the tone of Starling's voice. Hitherto, as much as things had disconcerted the doctor, he was still hoping that coincidence would eventually find its way into the equation. But coincidence seemed to have taken a holiday. 'He didn't die,' he continued. 'He's been rushed to hospital in Huxshire. Sheryl wanted to know if we were there too.'

Melling said nothing for a moment, thinking that his heart had forgotten to cooperate. He didn't have time to articulate his thoughts however, for Starling was already rushing to the closet, reappearing by hurling Melling's coat at him, then speeding for the door.

'After you doctor,' Melling murmured.

XVI

Se Offendendo

'Alexander Dawn. Rushed in via ambulance at roughly half-past seven in the evening after falling from his bedroom window,' Melling said to Starling, reading the report. A nurse was ushering them through the white corridors of Huxshire Hospital. She was clearly a graduate, with a dark ponytail and local accent.

'That's correct, Detective…?'

'Melling.'

'Well, Detective Melling, he was brought in just as it says. Suffered two fractured shins, his left knee, as well as six ribs. He was lucky he didn't puncture a lung.'

The doctor seethed between his teeth at the details.

'Must have a headache the size of Mars,' Melling murmured.

'I'm just surprised his spine wasn't an issue; his vertebrae certainly didn't face good odds,' Starling explained in disbelief. 'Never mind a concussion of dangerous proportions, I'll wager he's lucky to walk. Did you see the boy? Is he able to talk?'

'The young man is definitely lucky to be alive. He is just about stable. He hasn't spoken yet; he drifts in and out of consciousness. He acknowledged his parents this morning – if you can call it acknowledging. Someone else just stopped by to see him. I believe it was the inspector.'

Melling and Starling traded a look, the latter taking the report.

'It says that the drop was roughly eighteen feet. There's just no way his spine didn't break,' he said in disbelief. 'Unless he landed on a softer surface and was on his front. Then again, he'd most likely have a broken neck. The doctors must be citing miracles.' Then he turned to Melling with a careful tone.

'If he didn't fall, he wasn't expecting to survive this. Nine times out of ten, a fall from this height onto a hard surface, at the very least begets a broken spine or a fractured skull, neither of which you are getting up from.'

Melling exhaled at the news.

'He wanted to end it.'

'Only nineteen,' Starling added as they stepped into a waiting room.

It was entirely empty, save from a hurriedly dressed couple who the detective figured must be married. The only other person in the room was none other than Inspector Caspar Todd, who, like Melling, did not appear to have slept. At the sight of Starling and the detective, he got up from his chair in anger.

'Just what do you two think you're doing here?' He cast an ireful glance at the nurse who took a worried step back, and Dr Starling placed a concerned hand on the man's shoulder.

'Calm down, Caspar. We heard the news from Sheryl and well –'

The man irritatedly pushed Starling's hand away.

'You have no business being here.'

'We *don't?*' Melling began, voice dripping irritation. 'Don't be daft. This sort of circumstance is exactly why I'm here.'

'You're here because we allow you to be,' the inspector spat. 'This boy fell. He did not –'

'Just like Samuel?' he was interrupted. 'Are you going to tell me that Lucy Rosewood died by accident too?'

'There you go again, Melling,' Inspector Todd replied, as the nurse hurried away. 'Looking for answers to questions which aren't being asked.'

'Only because fools like you aren't asking!' Melling shouted in frustration. 'For God's sake! How many students have to die before you decide to look at the problem?'

'Just what problem would that be? You're a *suicide* specialist, and you certainly hold no sway over matters here. I thought you already knew why Lucy Rosewood died. That's what you were here for, wasn't it?' He stared threateningly into Melling's eyes. 'Didn't Master Dunfield explain her suicide note? Run along and tell her mother what you learned, and for the last and final time, stop poking your incessant nose into matters where it doesn't belong.'

Melling felt like striking the inspector across his scowling face, then hurling all sorts of profanities at him, but managed to rein in his temper when he heard a lady start crying behind him. She was immediately consoled by her husband. 'That's Mr and Mrs Dawn,' the inspector related, now in lower tones. 'They're not sure their son will wake up.'

'Wake up?' Starling whispered, and Melling felt a pang of nausea begin to ruminate inside his stomach.

'He slipped into a coma this morning after internal bleeding,' was the reply, the inspector turning to Melling. 'So, he isn't going to answer any of *your* groundless interrogations.'

Melling swallowed nervously, feeling nothing but devastation for the parents of the young man. If the situation had been different, he would have found a way to talk with them. He knew all too well, even on a personal level, how it was to be young and hopeful, to lose a loved one to suicide, and then have to deal with detective jargon from a man you didn't know. After shouting with the inspector, and with the boy now in a coma, he decided it might be best just to leave, at least for now. He was too empathetic a person to push a situation like this further in front of the grievers. Exhaling from a tight jaw, he looked at Starling and motioned to the door. They left the waiting room without saying a word.

As they made their way back it was Starling who broke the silence.

'Those poor parents. I can't believe they have to go through something like this.'

Melling sighed before answering.

'I only made it worse. I should have realised who they were and –'

'Stop! You were arguing on their child's behalf, and just because he's in a coma, that doesn't mean that our reasons for coming here should change. We should give them some time to process the incident and for Caspar to calm down. I've never seen him so angry.'

Melling nodded, not entirely listening as he eyed the nurse. She was taking a folder from a noticeably tall gentleman in a long black overcoat which draped over his gloved hands. 'Michael?' Starling asked. The masculine figure turned with a kind smile, exposing a middle-aged countenance with thinning grey hair and compassionate maroon eyes. 'Louis, what a pleasure. But... what are you doing here? Is everything okay? Where's Sheryl?'

'Sheryl's fine, Michael. She's away right now. We're here to check on a boy who fell from his dorm last night.'

'My God,' the tall man said in a low whisper. 'That's dreadful.' Then he turned to the detective and extended a hand. 'Apologies, I'm Michael Crown.'

Melling smiled.

'Detective Robert Melling.'

'Detective?'

'That's right. I am looking into a recent student tragedy. Shouldn't say much else I'm afraid.'

The man's face grew solemn.

'It's not Lucy Rosewood by chance?'

'How did you —'

'Michael's the main funeral director in Huxley, but he's also a coroner,' Starling explained.

'What a dreadful, dreadful incident that was. Heart goes out to that Mrs Olivia, the mother I mean. Poor lady. We spoke on the phone. I had to discuss moving the body. That's always the worst part.'

'Grief has this amazing ability to render any consolation useless,' Melling said.

'It does indeed,' the tall man approved, turning a curious glance back to the detective. It wasn't often somebody fully understood the difficulties of a death-dealing profession. It took someone with actual experience in such morose matters to properly understand the painful realities of a career where one was always standing outside death's door. Melling had recognised the recognition in Michael Crown's eyes.

'So, what brings *you* here Michael. I trust everything is alright?' Starling asked.

'Oh yes, all fine for me. Just handing Miss Laetitia some documents about an inquest from last month. But listen, gentlemen, I'm afraid I'm on the clock today.'

'Not at all,' Starling said with a tired smile. 'Good to see you.'

'You too Louis, and you as well, Detective Melling.' He smiled and went to the exit. Still, before he was out of the door, he turned on his heel, retracing his steps. 'Say, Detective. About that Miss Lucy Rosewood. Did you have any explanation for the shape on her legs?'

Melling swallowed, intuition ordering his heart to sink.

'Shape?'

'Well yes. You know, the peculiar symbol she drew around each knee?'

The detective's fingers numbed at the new information, and in the corner of his eye he noticed Starling stare confoundedly at Michael. 'Say, Inspector Todd forgot to mention it, eh?' the man continued. 'Was the strangest thing. None of us at the morgue had seen it before. Do ask him about it, we're all curious.'

After his matter-of-fact request, he turned to leave, but Melling finally found his words.

'Wait!'

The coroner turned. 'Just what did it look like?'

'Well let's see. It looked like a sort of bowl, sliced around each knee.' He turned to look around him, then decided to lower his voice in front of the nurse. 'Then, two lines were drawn from the middle upwards. The right was shorter than the other. Honestly, it was a while before we even realised she had drawn it on both knees.' He lowered his voice yet again: 'the blood obscured the symbolism.'

'We didn't know that,' Starling murmured.

'No? Well, do have a think.' He turned to Melling. 'With your expertise, I figured you may have a better clue. In fact, why don't I show you? Just to be sure.'

He took a pen and paper from the nurse's desk, then, sure enough, he traced an upward facing semicircle with two straight lines drawn out of the centre, one just slightly longer than the other. It almost looked like an upside-down toadstool.

'Seen it before?' the man asked, but Melling declined. 'Well, do let me know if you do.'

Melling was too absorbed to notice him leave. In fact, he had already disappeared as soon as the pen had left the paper. He combed his brain for any sort of symbolic similarities but fell short of even a grip of understanding. He stared into the page for what seemed minutes. Finally, he wrenched his eyes away, almost grunting under the effort. His heavy judgements fell onto Starling.

'Your friend, Caspar...'

'I know what you're going to say, but listen, he's a good man.'

'Then why would he lie? He said that she had drawn lines from her feet to her knees.'

Here he was feeling guilty for putting the man on the spot in front of Alexander Dawn's grieving parents, and now… 'He couldn't have just made some sort of mistake, Michael just told us that he knew,' he reasserted.

'I don't know,' Starling said in uncomfortable admittance. His pitch had risen sharply. 'It doesn't make sense, but there *has* to be a reason.'

As Starling reasoned an excuse, Melling recalled their conversation in the *Abenborg*.

The girl had carved two lines from her toes to her waist with a kitchen knife.

'Carved! He specifically used the word carved – even his mind was offering language more relevant to the truth. He lied to our faces, and I'd like to know why.'

With that, he tore the symbol from the notepad and sprinted down the corridor back to the waiting room.

When they made it back, the inspector was the only person there. The parents were evidently inside the boy's room. He looked up at the gentlemen before him, and his eyes liquefied into anger. However, when he registered the avenging black of Melling's harrowing stare, he swallowed. Sometimes someone intrinsically knows when they are about to be discovered. It is as though guilt is aware of its own clock.

'I thought I told you to leave,' he said, weakly. All the certainty had been wrung from his voice.

'We were about to, but then your friend Michael Crown drew a nice little picture for us.' Melling held up the drawing and the inspector's face pallored into an anxious white.

'Where did you get that?'

'Like I said, it's from a man who said he saw these carvings on Lucy's knees. He also assured us *you* knew about them.'

The inspector began to fidget, saying nothing, and Melling thought he was going to split the man like an axe does a log. 'Answer!'

'Listen, you have to understand,' he began to plead. 'I was doing it for the benefit of everyone. I told you she carved lines to her feet because well, it simplified the matter. Carving is carving! I thought you would start asking questions that we wouldn't be able to answer, and I thought it would help us put everything to bed…' he trailed off, falling dejectedly onto a chair. Then, to both Starling and Melling's surprise, he began to cry, head in hands.

'So, you interfered with the investigation, just because *you* decided it was for the best?' Melling understood why. 'You thought that my input was dirtying the calm waters of Huxley's reputation? Am I right?' His voice turned seethingly low; he was too appalled to even recognise a human before him. He could see that the man had placed an ideal above the truth. Huxley was too precious for him to objectively investigate. 'You thought my input was dirtying your calm waters? Your calm waters?'

The inspector sniffled but didn't respond. Melling exploded. 'You've clearly been drowning in those damned waters! Not to mention that your students are willing to drown *themselves!* And yet, you think, by omitting symbolism from Lucy's death that you were doing it for the benefit of others? I can't even see how someone in your position could manage to conceive of such a pathetic, immature… how you could even…' Wrath and disgust displaced language, and he too was forced into silence.

'You have to understand…' the man finally began to defend. 'We can't have people thinking that Huxley has a problem! I thought you would leave it at Lucy Rosewood, but then you started to prod Judy Collier and –'

'So, you admit it!' Melling interrupted in disgust. 'You admit that it goes beyond Lucy! You don't want me to see just how bad the situation is! And you overlooked some things with Miss Collier, did you not? By the way, you still haven't shown us the report you claimed you would write up. Were you even going to ask her more questions, or were you hoping I would forget? As if I could forget that students were taking their own lives here! You're an inspector for God's sake! An inspector!' Melling's hands were combing through his thinning, oily hair. His voice had cracked. 'You're the one who's meant to right Huxley's wrongs, and yet, you fell in love with an ideal that was too fragile to uphold. You had to rely on deception just to keep it from bursting!'

'But Huxley –' the inspector started, getting to his feet; Melling threw him straight back into his chair.

'Enough!'

He itched for his revolver. He lowered himself to the man's level, staring straight through his watery eyes. His voice was a predatory growl. 'If you defend Huxley one more time, I'm going to dangle you from Apollonia's Bridge, and see how you like the taste of the cold abyss below it. Your intuition knows what mine does: Huxley has been infected by something sinister. But you're too cowardly to confront it!' He was trembling from his anger, so he took a step back to poise himself. 'As an inspector, I expected better from you, I really did. But I finally see how far you've fallen from the code of your career. From now on, you tell me everything I ask, or I am going to charge you with unlawful interference. Any more omittance, childish indifference or denial, and I will find a way to put you in one of the rooms that our friend, Alexander Dawn, is now lying comatose within. Now,' he continued, still trying to calm himself. 'I *will* allow you to handle your affairs with these parents, simply out of decorum. But you will also send over Judy's report by the afternoon, with a phone call to go with it as a reminder. If Starling hasn't been called by five in the early evening with the news, at the very latest, I'm writing you up to Scotland Yard.'

'Mr Melling, I,' the inspector stammered. 'I just want my community to stay the way it is.'

'Huxley cannot rest on its laurels. But none of that is even the point... avoiding the truth is the worst thing a man can do, especially when Britain's brightest are carving symbols into their knees before slitting their wrists.' With that, he left the waiting room before what he was saying would make him fight the inspector in a berserk fury.

Melling was too bewildered, enraged and disgusted to think straight. One thing he knew for certain: the inspector had desecrated his duty and the obligations of both men's profession. From now on, Melling's tentative and diplomatic behaviour was over; he saw his wife scolding him with her gorgeous laugh, calling him *trop Anglais*. Well, that would now need to stop. Intuition had told him that things were severe at Huxley, but he hadn't been able to confirm just how severe until this discovery. If local law enforcement were too busy looking the other way, then there had to be something especially wrong in his old student home. Indeed, Melling felt a sorrow gnawing into his gut the more he considered the inspector's actions. It had offended him, deeply so, that a man in the same profession could place an ideal above the self-murder of children.

'Robert, I, I had no idea,' Starling said once they were back at the reception. 'My God. I had no idea that he would do something so foolish. To lie to us... to avoid facts... I never suspected it.'

'Nothing you can do for him now,' Melling muttered matter-of-factly, thanking the nurse as he stepped out into the late-morning chill. The sun was hidden behind the omnipresence of the Huxley clouds, and Melling exhaled his vexation. 'And no one can blame you for not suspecting your friend to lie. I don't hold it against you for seeing the good.' He looked at Michael Crown's sketch once more. 'Anyway, there's something I'd like to do whilst our no-good inspector is occupied.'

'What's that?'

'Well, we can't question the comatose lad, but we *can* search his room, and maybe ask around for some witnesses.'

But as they walked to the car, Starling paused, earning an expectant look from the detective.

'Robert I... I think I will tell Sheryl to stay away for a while. I can't really put into words why I think it's for the best. But I... just until things get sorted I...'

'I understand,' Melling said, face turning more empathetic. 'I understand completely.'

XVII

Dead-end.

'So, here's what we know,' Melling ruminated as they left the car parked in the new town. 'New' was a contemporaneous term of course. Melling had always thought that 'later' was a more suitable adjective for the setting, equally medieval as the old town. 'If Master Dunfield is correct, Lucy's letter tells us that she killed herself to reach some form of ultimate truth. So, this drawing needs to be connected to truth in some way.' He began thinking about the boy in the coma. 'Bugger.'
'What?' Starling asked.
'We should have checked if the boy had this symbol! We would have immediately confirmed whether it was correlated.' He kicked a loose stone in irritation, annoyed at his short-sightedness. These past few days made him wonder at what point he had started to lose all those detective skills that had served him in his career. In Huxley he felt he was behaving more as a spectator than a detective. 'Right. If we use Fleuraline College's phone, we can get the inspector to find out. Now that we know he withheld information, we should also make sure he keeps us informed. We should also know what the jumper's body, I mean Samuel from the bridge, looked like.'

They hurried up the winding stone streets, climbing the ascending cobblestones to Melling's former college. The detective hadn't yet weighed the nostalgic importance of returning to his past; student suicide had created a mental queue which was too long to permit a reminiscence of golden university days. Now, walking up a familiar incline, the days of old at long last managed to worm their way forward.

When he had been a student, his days had passed in a manner well-known to most adults, whose university period seemed like a bubble of everlasting timetables, friendships and fallacious pressures, absent from the reality of the world outside. Melling had loved his Huxley experience despite the intense academic stress. The constant quest for new knowledge, the awareness of prestige, and the beauty of buildings so old they seemed to breathe history itself. But now, the mixture of adolescent demise and dangerous nightmares had polluted the beauty of his former life, besmirching the idealised portrait of those days that seemed untouchable inside his memory. In some cruel perversion of Proustian sentiment: the remembrance of Melling's past was now subject to the terrorising reconsideration of present realities. Had his past housed more than he had been privy too? The place he used to love now disturbed him. Students he used to be happy for, he now pitied. The men he used to look up to he now deemed short-sighted. Some contagion dwelt in his former home. For how long?

As the antecedent instincts from preceding footsteps led him up the hillside of the new town, the notions of death against dandelion days at his former college probed yet another sour tasting memory: the loss of his friend and fellow Fleuraline, Dockery. Dockery had been one of Huxley's brightest, and Huxley, in many ways, had failed him. Of course, it was the fact that Dockery's suicide note had failed to answer any of his mother's questions which had forced Melling to remain distrustful of classifying the lad's demise as mere melancholy; however, the parallels this drew with Lucy Rosewood were not immediately obvious to the detective at this present moment. Melling was certainly haunted by the sickening symmetry both deaths spelled out for the stars which governed Huxley, but with so much of the present on his mind, he failed to consider just what the similar peculiarity of Lucy and Dockery's letters might suggest, and possibly even share. Perhaps the decades were too distant, too distinct for the detective to fully consider a correlation beyond the hauntingly dubious deaths of two young academics – both of whom the university had failed to protect.

The sun felt as though it may be setting the higher they walked, and as the clouds began to swallow its struggling rays, Melling forgot that the afternoon chimes of the colleges' clocks were yet to strike. His past further revealed itself to him as the streets grew less defined, and the shops, sparser. Fleuraline was an atypical college. His former professor, Dr Alfred Farway, had enjoyed labelling it as eccentric – particular for its aversion to Huxley's cobblestones and inserted gardens. The other colleges had forced nature out of the ground, but

Fleuraline had always been engendered *from* nature. Closer to the countryside greens of the old Midland meadows, the college had forced pathways onto verdurous land, and dug foundations into grassy mounds. The basalt and granite buildings were always painted white as the founders had wanted to avoid polluting the colours of the fertile land, which, they had dignified as a shrine to British floral history. The result was that Fleuraline appeared more like an aristocratic country estate than a college.

The grassy road began to widen as the cobbles diminished. Once they rounded a final corner, Melling found himself face to face with his cherished past. The shallow white walls of the enclosure did little to hide the white buildings of his former dormitory and study rooms. As he and the doctor stood in front of the thin bars of the revealing black gate, he gazed on the faded purple of the bee orchids which lined the gravel path behind it, complimented by the rows of buttery parnassus. The delightful duo created a smudging line of glorious beige. It finally felt like Spring.

'I forgot how beautiful it was,' Melling said in slow stutter, earning an agreement from his companion. He imagined he could hear dew falling from petals, brushing the murmuring wings of insects.

'I never really come up here much; I should make the time for more visits. Then again, the Fleuraline master doesn't allow many guests to survey the grounds.'

'Makes the parents think it's more exclusive, and ultimately, all the more willing to pay their way in.'

Starling had to laugh, earning a smile from a gentleman in a light brown bowler cap, waiting behind the gate. Starling waved.

'You ready?'

Melling nodded, and they walked on.

'Good morning gentlemen and welcome to Fleuraline College. How may I help you?'

'I'm Detective Robert Melling, and I'm here on Inspector Todd's behalf,' Melling announced, handing over his identification through a gap in the gate. The man had been smiling kindly but raised a brow when he read the detective's credentials.

'Well, Detective, is everything alright?'

'We hope so. You see, we're here about Alexander Dawn.'

'Ahh, poor fellow,' the porter said in dismay. 'We're all praying for that one.'

'We've just come from the hospital,' Starling said. 'Sadly, he's slipped into a coma.'

'My God,' the man said, blurting the words out. 'That's terrible. Do they think he's going to make it?'

'We're unsure. We didn't want to disturb the parents at the time.'

'Understandable.'

'Though my professional guess, as a doctor, is that he's incredibly fortunate to still be with us.'

'I'll say. Boy fell from twenty feet.'

'Twenty? The report said it was eighteen?' Melling said, finally rejoining the conversation.

The man shook his head knowingly.

'No, sir. Alexander lived in the Veratrum; on the third floor to be exact. That drop is no less than twenty feet. Put a definite shock into the couple that were sitting on the lawn for a romantic evening.' The man even chuckled. 'Anyway, I'll take you to my colleagues who will surely be able to help.'

They followed the man down the beige tunnel, walled in by the overpowering evergreens which lined up on either side of the path. It was like a meander through a Tuscan wood.

'So, what did they find in Alexander's room?' Melling asked, but the man shook his head.

'They ain't been in his room yet, as far as I'm aware. The ambulance was rung in the late hours, and he was brought away. We been so busy this morning, and police haven't come yet, so it is too early still for anyone to have checked the room.'

'Can *we*?'

'Well sure. I'll have my colleagues send you there.'

They wandered through the rowed garden pathway towards the giant white building of what was aptly named the Magnolia. At the central hub of the college, Melling was plunged back into his past, peripatetically walking as a curious undergraduate. He had always found that the Magnolia appeared more as an Italian manor, something stolen from the pages of some early Victorian novel. When the sun had shone in those everlasting summers he had joked and walked along the pathways with his peers. Time had seemed timeless. As the years had passed, the detective had begun to see the university in a new light, still with respect, but with more objectivity; now, he felt all too uneasy at the sight of the beauty around him. It jarred with his mental landscape, heavy with the horrors of human action.

Noting the sun collapse under an expanding cloud, he suddenly appreciated what the poet John Keats had been attempting to encapsulate when writing *Ode to a Nightingale*. Natural beauty always managed to float above the melancholies of human existence. The poet had summed up that truth with perfect poignance: *But here there is no light*. Melling had studied this poem in this very location. Back then, he had been too untouched by life to appreciate how painful those words truly were. How being a person in the world was marked by efforts and grunts; even creators toiled on end to find beauty. But the natural world never seemed to try. It achieved without struggle. There was an intrinsic effortlessness – a childish carelessness. A bird cannot write music, but it can sing in tune on pure instinct. It does not know its own death. It does not sing to lament. Such purity is hard to mimic, glimpsed perhaps in the soft kindness of a grandmother's smile... the promise of a lamp glow in a far-off window...

'But here there is no light,' Melling murmured.

'Robert?'

He turned to the doctor who was motioning to join the porter indoors. They followed inside, and the scent of oleander danced along the detective's nose hairs. A balding gentleman of roughly fifty smiled his greetings. The detective explained his purpose, and whilst the man led Starling to a phone, the porter from the gate vowed to take them to the Veratrum and Alexander's room.

Melling took in the spiralling emeralds of the capacious Versailles lawns that spread between the marble-white country house buildings. It was almost absurd how such a Spring-touched setting could still permit such a wintry wind. He was led through the rosebush pathways which guarded the Veratrum. The bleeding blush of the petals spilled onto the gravel, and the detective became heady under the heavy tug of their scent. Here, the dangling branches of the proud trees invaded the space above their heads. The overgrown beech became an arching canopy. Then, at the end of the pathway, the trees dispersed to reveal the proud, snowy basalt of the Veratrum's cuboid floors.

'Welcome home, Detective,' the porter said with a chuckle. Nostalgia wriggling inside Melling's stomach like a lost worm, they walked inside.

The drowsy daylight was immediately replaced by the effulgence of newly installed indoor electricals. The walls were no different to the simplicity of any other student accommodation, and the floors could do with cleaning. The Huxley spell was shattered. They continued upstairs to the third floor, and the porter led the way to number 32. Knocking on the door as though he were respecting would-be privacy, he turned a rusted key into a narrow lock and Melling's spine shivered under the sound. The man pushed the door open. The first thing the detective noticed was a cleanliness. The room was again the product of standardisation, with a shallow bedframe supporting a yellow mattress with bleach-pale sheets. A bookshelf stood half-full; a desk was neatly organised. 'Window's still open,' the porter said sorrowfully.

'Any chance you can lead my companion here?' Melling asked, unsure if he wanted an extra pair of eyes which didn't belong to Starling.

'Sure,' the man relented, evidently hoping he could have lingered.

Melling's search was otiose. He ransacked the drawers of the closet: nothing. Under the bed: clear. The boy hadn't even left a note. He looked at the window, noting the size of the frame. He himself could squeeze through, supported by the wide ledge underneath. He peered outside, noting a student jogging under the tree branches. Casting his eyes downwards to the lawn, twenty feet below him, he swallowed. It was certainly a deadly height. A slight ring began to twitch his eardrums and he closed his eyes, imagining the rush of wind which would have dragged against the boy's cheeks as he plummeted to near-death. The detective began to rock back and forth on his heels as he imagined being in the boy's place. The whistling was welcoming; the journey would have been rapid – no doubt surprisingly so. Melling knew how one's expectations of falling were woefully inaccurate. One sometimes daydreamed the feeling of declining into oblivion, slipping away from a great height… the ground was almost forgotten. It was as though life would end mid-air. At that thought, Melling stepped away.

He waited on the bed in annoyance, biting his fingernails. Not five minutes later, the porter returned with Starling. The former needed to return to the gate, and was evidently irritated. He asked if they might lock the door and return the key. Melling on the other hand, was glad he and Starling would have some discretion.

'Any news?'

'Caspar is saying the doctors aren't allowing him to check Alexander's body.'

'Poppycock,' Melling said with restrained anger. 'Let me guess, he's saying the jumper's body, Samuel, showed no signs?'

Starling nodded, and the detective raised his voice. 'For goodness sake! And how do we know that's the truth?' He saw a peculiar look in his companion's eyes. 'What is it, Louis?'

'I just lied to him.'

'How do you mean?'

'He asked where we were, and I said we were calling from home. I never expected that he would put me in a position where I felt like I couldn't tell him the truth.'

Melling smiled without mirth.

'Doesn't matter much. The room yielded entirely nothing.'

'You're serious?' Starling asked in half-defeat, putting his hands on his hips with a long exhale.

'Not even a note. I hate to admit it, but maybe our cowardly inspector is correct. This may just be a fall. It's foolish to rely on intuition alone Louis, and I find myself clinging to it, nonetheless. I guess we have to hope the boy wakes up, because if he doesn't, we've only got Judy Collier to help prove my wild theories. Damnit. We *need* evidence.' He got up from the bed and stretched, really starting to feel this morning's fatigue. 'Let's go.'

And yet, just as the doctor stepped outside, something on the bookshelf caught the detective's eye. 'Wait!'

Unsure, but desperate to drag out his hope, he walked trepidly to the bookcase, eyes scrupulously anchored to one particular title. He took the book, moving with slow deliberation, silently praying for a miraculous connection. He thumbed the velvet spine, staring at the author's name as though it held the answer to all his questions. If there was a clue to Huxley's riddles, this might be it; it was the only thing he could tangibly connect to anything else, and yet, it was a mere book. He ignored an inner voice which said that retirement was on the horizon.

'What is it, Robert?'

Melling raised the book as though it spoke for itself. Starling just shrugged.

'The Pit and the Pendulum,' Melling said, stressing each word. 'By Edgar Allen Poe.'

'What about it?'

'Judy said that she and Samuel were at a Marlowe reading group, remember? They were reading…'

'Edgar Allen Poe!' Starling interrupted excitedly. 'Maybe Alexander was part of the group too? But,' he paused, turning sheepish. 'How does that help us?'

'Well, in the beginning I didn't think twice about students reading together. But if Alexander was in the same reading group as Samuel; well, if both lads try and jump to their deaths, we ought to ask Judy who else is in this group. They may know something she doesn't.' He sat down on the bed, opening the book.

'Is it issued from Marlowe library?'

Melling analysed the beginning, then sighed with a shake of the head.

'Doesn't say. We'll just have to talk to Judy or find the group at Marlowe.'

As he flicked through the pages, his finger rubbed against a different material. 'Hold on,' he said, finding an envelope and pulling it free. His entire body tightened under what he saw. 'It can't be,' he managed to say, words falling from his mouth in clumsy whisper. Goosebumps trickled down his arms.

'What is it?' Starling asked, making his way over in concern. He too was immediately horrified. For there, in the top right-hand corner of the envelope, was the same mark Michael Crown had drawn for Melling in the hospital. It was the symbol Lucy had carved into her knees. 'Is that…?' was all Starling managed to utter. They looked at one another as if they had just discovered the holy grail.

'Well, we won't know anything if we just stay here dumbfounded,' Melling eventually muttered in mock-courage, opening the letter. His confidence was immediately replaced by shock. He stared at the writing, unable to process what he was seeing. He grew sicker with every sentence; he felt a belt around his chest. 'Lord in heaven,' he said, voice a dying croak.

XVIII

Schöne Leich

Vienna, 1968

'*C'est comme dans les romans*,' Lorelei whispered into Melling's ear before the concierge led her on a tour. It was a wide suite, full of red and gold. The windows were the height of two floors despite the lack of stairs, filling the area with light; it burned into poppy cushions and crimson curtains. The hotel was the oldest and finest Vienna had to offer. Situated just across the street from the *Staatsoper*, the pride and joy of Austrian opera, Melling and his wife were staying here for that exact reason. She was to accept an award for a musical career of excellence, retiring from the art form a few years earlier, thus concluding a professional tenure that had lasted over twenty years. Now the world of opera was tipping its hat to one of Europe's greats, and Melling could not be prouder. He wanted everything to be perfect. That was the least she deserved.

He noted the size of the fireplace and sauntered over, immediately struck by the smell of chestnuts. It made one fancy a smoke, so Melling struck a match, throwing its dying end into the fireplace after eagerly lighting a Gitanes. He stepped out onto the balcony, immediately spotting the *Staatsoper* not one hundred metres away. His eyes then spotted a couple crossing the street mid-flow, weaving between cars, and narrowly avoiding the honking jaws of a snarling tram; it barrelled noisily onwards along its designated lane. For a second, the detective thought it would have hit them, grunting in fear as the pair scraped past. With his cigarette tight between his teeth, he shook his head. People really ought to be more careful. Crossing the street was a stupid way to die.

He heard the door to the suite close, and the graceful footsteps of his happy wife coming to join him. He turned just in time to see her walk through the balcony door, grinning.

'*Quelle vue*,' she said, raven curls beginning to lift under the slight breeze. She seemed mesmerised by the sight of the *Staatsoper*. Tomorrow night's acceptance speech was dazzling inside her eyes. Sauntering over to him, she wrapped confident arms around his waist, cinnamon irises glowing. '*Mon amour*, you are stressed.'

'I'm not that stressed I –'

'*Je sais*,' she interrupted. 'I know you are tense because you are quite an overcontrolling man. You want my weekend to be perfect.'

He was about to tell her how much her happiness meant to him, but she briefly kissed his lips shut. 'You do not understand that I am always going to have the perfect weekend if I am spending it with you.' Her voice was so linear in its authenticity, so perfectly matching the emotion behind her eyes, that the detective shed a tear. That made her laugh, kissing it away. 'Remember when I thought you wanted to be a policeman?' she giggled. 'I knew straight away that you were too sentimental!' She was amazing at being able to be blur the boundary between intimate passion and humour.

'But a detective….'

'*Justement*,' she confirmed. 'I saw that you were a brilliant man. I could see how beautiful your mind was.'

'You were so sure I should be a detective. I really had no idea why you were so assertive.'

She turned to the ledge behind them and placed two tanned hands onto the white stone. He joined her, picking up the cigarette he had left; it had been fighting for life in the breeze like a trapped insect. Looking over, he saw a silver champagne holder filled with melting ice, but empty of champagne itself. 'As much as I was smitten back then, I didn't even appreciate how well you saw beyond the messy manifolds of my mind. I thought you were just exaggerating, but I quickly realised that you had figured out my sense of self better than I could. I just want to say that I love you for that.'

She turned to him with a loving gaze, placing a warm, olive palm onto his cheek.

'You are always a man of lovely words. Your eyes had this look in them, even though you didn't want to sound like it was a good idea. You said 'Scotland Yard', and your eyes told me how much it spoke to you. I hated hearing you talk about all the reasons you should not do it.'

Time and time again, Lorelei revealed herself as someone who just wanted people to do what made them happy. Often, it seemed as though she couldn't even recognise societal conventions. Whatever objections, normalities or 'one cannots' somebody suggested, she laughed in the face of. That made for arguments when dining in London, but he always took her side. She broke away to stare down the face of their hotel, peering into the hats and hair of the walkers below.

'What is your secret?'

'What secret, darling?'

'You are never afraid of heights.'

'You cannot get over a fear of heights, Lorelei.'

'Many people say you can.'

Melling sighed before responding, taking a long drag.

'I personally don't think one ever gets over any fear.'

'*Jamais?*'

'Never.'

'I am afraid, I think, because I worry if I have the urge to jump. Do you understand?'

'The imp of the perverse,' Melling murmured.

'*Quoi?*'

'Edgar Allen Poe said that there is no human feeling so demonic and anxious as when we are on the ledge. Look long enough and your body feels like you might just jump.'

'*Je pense qu'il a raison,*' Lorelei agreed, stepping back, and earning a laugh from Melling. He wrapped her in an intense hug, immobilising her under his loving embrace, nose pressed against her hair. 'And what do you smell?'

'Still the chestnuts of the fireplace,' he said. 'But come on, I promised you sight-seeing.'

As they turned for the room, something caught her eye.

'Oh look! A streetcar!' she said, pointing. Sure enough, there went the tram again, honking wildly as it lurched past eager tourists.

'We'll start with that then.'

They turned indoors, but a rasping crack made them jump. It took a few moments for Melling to detect that this was merely the sound of falling ice in the champagne bucket. They laughed when they realised how pathetic a thing it was which had so startled them. But that was the way with the speed at which ice melts. It was one of those lazy, quotidian things. Hard and certain, it melted innocuously and forgotten until it reminded you it could not stay solid forever.

XIX

Bolts of Bones

Huxley, May 1969

'Robert!' Starling trepidly asked. The detective had been too stunned to react. The words were written and signed by Judy, that much was abundantly clear... but why she would want Alexander to... The detective's heart didn't know whether to race or rupture. 'Robert?'

Weakly, with pale hands, Melling passed the letter to his companion and waited patiently for the sound of horror. He didn't need to wait long.

'My God,' the man cried, slumping onto the bed. 'My God! It can't be true!'

Melling's thoughts were hardly coherent. All he knew was that things were far worse in Huxley than he could possibly have imagined. 'What you will discover!' Starling repeated, reading aloud from the letter. '*Discover?* My God she was as delusional as Lucy!'

The mention of Lucy Rosewood kick-started the detective into the present. He turned to Starling and took the letter from his lifeless hands. Returning his eyes to Judy's perturbing prose, he read and re-read the letter, intending to fully understand what he was seeing.

Alexander,

Tomorrow you take the final step, and for that, we salute you. Think not on what you will leave behind but consider what you will discover. Yours is the path towards eternal understanding, to the answer which for all the living remains unanswerable. For you, life's torture ends.
They are deafened by ears and blinded by sight, but you will be liberated!

Illumination takes courage, but remember, there is nothing more necessary than the truth.

Courtier Collier

'My God,' Melling said again, further anxious to note the ominous, ever-elusive symbol in the bottom right corner, almost a co-signature.

'That Judy's eyes were saying more than her mouth would allow was obvious, but I just can't believe she was hiding all of this! Lucy's symbol is there, which means it's connected. Judy must have led Samuel to his death!'

Now that the full understanding of Huxley's darkness draped upon him, he had to lean on the desk. His watering eyes stared blankly at Starling who seemed unwilling to acknowledge what he had just heard. 'It's the… it's the students…' Melling managed to say, voice a futile croak, his sorrow then morphing into anger. 'The students are the problem themselves. Could their professors ever have dreamt such a thing? Cheating their way to life's ultimate truth.' He slammed his fist on the desk and heard it crack, letting out a piercing cry of anguish. There was a guillotine of silence in the room, slicing through both men.

When Melling found his voice, it was full of gravel. 'For some Goddamned reason, students are convincing other students that some philosophical answer awaits the dead and that living without that answer is clearly not acceptable!'

'I just don't believe it,' Starling whispered. Melling had guessed that there was something dark which needed addressing in Huxley. Perhaps he may even have conjured half such a hypothesis. Yet, there was no way he could truly have arrived at such horror on his own. It was too absurd to have been thought up. It was too disgusting.

'We need the professors' help. They know their students better than we do, but first, we need Judy. She implies a collective. But how many? How many students share this ludicrous notion?'

'Those poor parents,' the doctor managed to say, sitting on the victim's bed, slowly awakening to Huxley's dark truth. 'Students convincing other students to kill themselves… was there ever something so… so…'

'The very language makes me shudder. It's littered with academic weight.' He walked over and joined the doctor. 'Look. We have eternal understanding, liberation and illumination. Then deafened by ears and blinded by sight.'

'A trapped soul?'

'Indeed. No wonder it took that Professor Robora to read through the lines of Lucy's letter. It's all so academically perverse only a professor would understand.'

But not even the professors could have interpreted such a murderous philosophy. They would need to be told soon. He wondered how Master Dunfield would react to learning that something so disgusting had been happening under his nose.

'Evidence at last,' Starling said. 'Though I wish to God it did not exist.'

'This letter is more than enough,' Melling asserted. 'We need to find out who else was part of this group. They were clearly using reading as a cover. Huxley has all forms of student-led academic leisure which the university encourages. It's an easy cover for them to…' The reality of the situation struck him anew, and he paused. 'I still can't bring myself to believe it. I could never have, in my wildest hypotheticals, even dreamed of it.'

The reading group was the truth that had hitherto eluded him. Judy could say it with a straight face because it was the perfect cover, because a reading group it was not. They were not here to poeticise nor analyse. It was a group of sinister instruction. They goaded you into breaking your spine, hiding their letters in the spines of novels. Was that how they had turned Lucy? If he had just…

He gasped in realisation as Olivia Rosewood's phone call returned to him. In his mind's eye he was standing in his Kensington kitchen, receiver to his ear. Her voice squirmed out from his heavy memories. *Please don't think less of me for saying it. But she wasn't herself. I cannot explain it, but something about my poor girl's last moments doesn't make sense to me. She was reading things too serious… too morbid.*

'I've really been asleep,' Melling said to himself, feeling all too guilty. Starling gave him a look, but the detective didn't want to meet his eye. The devil of it had been in what she had been reading! If he had just connected those dots sooner… then maybe Alexander Dawn wouldn't now lay comatose. Maybe. But then again, who could have imagined one could fall into a group so philosophical it led to… 'We don't have time to waste!' he blurted. 'Who is to say when the next victim is due? We need to get to Trinity and find Judy.'

XX

Bewilderments of the Eyes

Moments before midday, they were once again back at the old gate of Dunfield College. The original porter was absent, but the gate was open this time, revealing the wide-reaching lawn, now littered with students. Both men stepped inside, finding the porters' office. A balding gentleman with kind eyes was laughing with a younger adolescent who Melling would have deemed a student if they weren't wearing the same attire.

'Excuse me.'

'Morning, sir,' the older man said. 'How can we help?'

Due to the overcast nature of the greying sky, Melling had forgotten it was still morning. He handed over his identification to a pair of raising brows.

'I'm Detective Robert Melling, and I'm here on Inspector Todd's behalf.'

'Is everything alright?'

'I'm not sure,' Melling said, trying not to give too much away. 'Can you tell us where Miss Judy Collier is, please?'

The man's lips thinned in thought.

'Well yes, I suppose we can. Johnson, would you find her timetable?'

The adolescent replied in the affirmative, pouring through a thick, white binder. After a few moments, he was mumbling her name, tracing an unwrinkled finger over her details.

'Let's see here. Judy Collier. Says here that she should be in. No classes today and our library is only open for borrowing. This time of day, she'll probably be in her room. Yes, definitely in her room.' He seemed almost proud of his deductions. 'Studies a lot that one.'

'Can you take us?' Melling asked, noting that these two were far more welcoming than the Hydean character who had sneered at them on their last visit.

'Johnson will take you,' the balding man said with a smile. The adolescent returned to his binder.

'Let's see. Back of Ferrum Court.' At the mention of Ferrum Court, Melling cast Starling an ominous look as the man fished a skeleton key from a drawer.

'Oh, can I quickly use your phone?' Starling asked. 'Go on,' he waved to Melling. 'Let me call the inspector and see what I can glean. I'll come after you as quickly as I can; just find that girl.'

The signalling chimes of the afternoon resounded over the lawn as the younger porter, named Johnson, led Melling past the curious students in dark blue gowns. As they walked, Melling relived Starling's gothic horror story regarding the murderous scientist: the savage Thomas Ferrum. His lips twitched for a cigarette, but he denied the craving.

'Is it true what they say about Ferrum Court? Did Ferrum really kill those women?'

The porter sniggered.

'Why, it's as real as the truth. Yes. Butchered those ladies as though it was his profession.'

'But I thought he electrocuted them?'

'Aye, that he did,' the man replied as they wandered through the darker, narrower alleyways which led to the building of their conversation. 'But he butchered them too. Spread their remains so they would fit in shallow graves.'

'How vile.'

'Yes. Vile. Students hear him laugh.'

'Oh, that they claim to do so I have no doubt,' Melling said, chuckling to avoid his growing unease.

'Well, you can always count on a few who hears him.'

'Do you know anything about Miss Judy Collier?' Melling asked as they made their way past familiar daffodils.

'Nothing more than that she's a shut-in. We have too many students for us porters to know personally. We aren't concierges, you know?'

Melling nodded in agreement as the familiar medieval brown of lime mortar announced the presence of Ferrum Court. The porter led him through the standardised entrance, growing more silent the further they progressed into the subdued corridors. Soon they had arrived, and the man knocked politely as though he was in fact a concierge. They waited in the quiet dimness. They waited longer. The man knocked again. 'Miss Collier?'

Still silence. 'Well, Detective,' he concluded. 'I'm not sure where she is.'

'Open the door,' Melling ordered, and the man drew back. 'Sir, I don't mean to disrespect the –'

'Listen to me,' Melling said, voice stern, thinking about the boy who was now in a coma and the student who might be next. 'Open that door, or I'll have Inspector Todd place you under arrest for a failure to cooperate.' His palms were wet with anticipation. The porter gulped, clearly afraid of the consequences of authority.

'Okay,' he said with a nod, hands trembling slightly. The sound of the key rattling against the lock broke the silence of the darkened corridor. After some agonising moments, the porter managed to steady his hand. However, the door only opened partially. 'That's strange,' the porter muttered, but Melling didn't waver. He pushed the fool aside and, taking a second to brace himself, shouldered the door with all his might. It gave way with a groaning creak, swinging open with some speed and the detective followed it through, his loss of balance causing him to fall. Expecting a carpeted platform, Melling was stunned by the stiff clutter which he landed on. He felt as though he had landed on some sort of wooden contraption. It crushed beneath his weight.

'Detective!' the porter yelled, helping him to his feet. 'Are you alright?' Melling massaged his shoulder for a moment, tensing his jaw when his body whispered its irritations.

'Quite alright. Though, I wasn't expecting whatever that was.' He looked around him in astonishment. The room was vaguely lit by three dying candles which dripped blood-red wax onto the carpeted floor. Their lux was dim, so Melling could not ascertain just what he had fallen onto.

'I will have to inform the others about this.'

'You do that,' Melling murmured. 'And while you're at it, send my colleague my way. Just before you go though, would you mind finding the light in here?'

'Yes, sir.'

Melling heard a hand fumble against the wall for a switch, but to no avail. 'Ahh, here it is.' He heard a click and waited. Nothing. 'I guess that would explain the candles,' the porter said.

'Maybe,' Melling answered, unconvinced. The detective knew these candles betokened something sinister. 'Leave me a torch if you have one. And remember to send my friend Starling here as soon as possible.'

The porter handed him a pocket-size torch and fled from the room. His disappearing steps could be heard for a minute until they died with his presence.

The detective turned on the torch and slowly moved it around to establish his whereabouts. The room seemed just the same as any other at Trinity, though Miss Collier had clearly exercised her own preferences. In the corner lay a mattress without a bed frame. Shining his torch onto the candles, he saw that they were dangerously close to burning the carpet. He stooped down, mindful of his sore back, still shocked by impact, and blew them out one by one. The sound of the last exhalation was followed by the noise of the door swinging shut behind him.

He turned rapidly, pointing the torch in defence, now submerged in near total darkness. There was only the sound of his breathing. Judy's window had to be closed, and there wasn't a draft, so how then had the door shut? Melling scrutinised it in the meagre torchlight. It seemed untouched. He shook his head, ignoring the sensation that began to dance along his spine. He walked to the door, feeling the handle in his sweating hand. He reopened it slowly and found little resistance. Peering outside into the corridor, he wasn't sure whether to be reassured by the silence the gloom offered or to turn timid. He tried the light again but with no prospect. Sighing, he took a fragment of wood which had broken his fall and wedged it into the space between the door and its hinge. He had never liked to be startled, and felt a small pinch of satisfaction for his childish contest.

The corridor's half-light did little to support his vision but at least now the veil of black was slightly lifted. He began inspecting the girl's desk under torch-light, finding nothing but the clutter of crumpled paper and half-used pencils. Deciding now to inspect what had broken his fall on the floor, he didn't see the door swing shut, but heard the lock rattle against the latch. Jumping in surprise, he wheeled around, pointing his torch as though it was a weapon. He remained silent as a corpse for what seemed an eternity, searching for a sound in the black; his temples glistened with consternation as he waited for the intruder's footsteps to reveal themselves. Silence. He had that near-mystical human suspicion of not being alone.

'Hello?' he inquired into the darkness. 'Who's there?'

He was left unanswered until… Yes! The sound of frantic footfalls faintly emerged from down the corridor. Were they fleeing? No. They were getting closer. The crescendo grew until the steps ceased outside the door. The detective's heart pounded.

'Melling?' Starling called from outside, pushing the door open. His lamp was bright, and the young porter was back with a larger torch. The detective coughed, shoulders drooping in relief.

'Sorry we took a while; the hospital didn't know where the inspector was. I left a message with his department, asking for a call when he was available.'

'Thank you,' Melling said, taking his first step forward since the door had closed. Now that they could see better, he examined its hinges, moving it slowly backwards and forwards. Starling gave him a look of confusion.

'You alright?'

'I'm not sure,' Melling said, more to himself. The porter walked into the corner of the room.

'Ahh, she's placed something over the window, but I can't for the life of me get it off.' Melling heard him struggling.

'What would it even be?'

'Not sure, Detective,' the man replied. 'Sometimes students nail in their own make-shift curtains. We remove them of course, but we can't be everywhere, at all times.'

'Okay, I appreciate that,' Melling responded. Truthfully, he couldn't think straight with this fool acting so sarcastically. 'Can you by any chance give Marlowe College a message that I want to speak with them?'

'Sure,' the man relented, leaving them the torch.

'Everyone's curious,' Starling observed and Melling chuckled. He was glad to be alone with the doctor.

Now that they had sufficient light, they began inspecting their whereabouts more accurately, starting with the debris which had broken the detective's landing. Starling picked up a finer piece of shaped lumber, turning it over, then yelping and throwing it to the floor.

'Damned things!'

'What is it?' Melling shouted, his heartbeat rising.

'Apologies, Robert. I was caught by surprise is all. I never did like puppets. Even as a boy.'

'Puppets?'

'Well, whatever it was, its smiling face was *not* appreciated.'

'Wait a minute,' Melling paused, shining his two torches over the floor. He rifled through the mess and discovered three puppets about the size of his forearm. He studied their faces. One was painted over, one housed a three-digit number, and the one Starling had thrown down did indeed remind one of a haunted circus figure. Melling shuddered.

'The number one hundred and twenty-five is carved into this one. Why?'

'I haven't the slightest idea, Robert.' Starling replied, shaking his head. Melling took the figures to Judy's desk, ruminating on what it all meant.

'I have never been so uncertain in my entire career.'

'Well, that does not console me in the slightest,' Starling offered, dryly.

'Though we can't assume this is relevant to her... I don't even know what to call it... I can try and analyse based on ritual. We would just have to view it through her philosophical lens. Unfortunately, philosophers didn't care about puppets. Actually... wait! What's the rest of the stuff laying around?'

Shrugging, Starling examined the floor.

'I'm not sure. It seems to be more wooden paraphernalia and, wait, some sort of white sheet. Looks to be torn from a pillowcase.'

'I landed on the whole thing when I broke through the door,' Melling said, joining him in assessing the assemblage.

'What are you thinking?'

Melling looked back at the covered window, then at the white sheet. His eyes found the extinguished candles.

'Of course! These candles were burning when I came in!'

Starling looked about him, growing more excited as he whirled his lamp in the middle-darkness.

'So?'

'It's slightly medieval for a renaissance scholar but look: the candles would have cast a light onto the puppets, forming shadows on the pillowcase.'

'But why?'

'I was being facetious when I said that philosophers didn't care for puppets, but have you heard of Plato's cave allegory?'

'Naturally. You mean that... surely not?' Starling's voice was wavering.

'A soul enslaved,' the detective murmured.

Dr Alfred Farway, his Fleuraline professor who had considered him a protégé, had been the very man to introduce the detective to Plato's work. The ancient philosopher had been obsessed with the true essence of things – that higher semblance of nature which humans couldn't perceive because they were too transfixed by their watered-down surroundings. The life one saw was mere shadows compared to the bright light of higher truth. To explain this concept, Plato had compared reality to cinematic shadows on the wall of a cave, dark projections of a truer and brighter reality. 'It is a philosopher's duty,' Melling said, droning his professor's words, 'to show people the light from outside which is casting these very shadows.'

'Some might call it the divine truth we're all looking for, hidden behind a puppet-show,' Starling added.

'A puppet-show where the spectator is a prisoner,' Melling clarified, eyes falling back onto the eerie face of the puppet before him. 'Judy clearly saw death as an escape out of darkness and into truth.'

Neither man said anything for a few moments, both weighing up what they had concretised. There was not a single doubt in Melling's mind that Judy Collier, who had sought to *liberate* Alexander from what she had deemed life's tortures, was paying homage to some dark perversion of Platonist thought. The Metropolitan Police Service should count themselves lucky that Melling was so well-read.

'Pass me the letter, Louis.'

The doctor pulled the letter from his pocket and laid it on the desk; Melling scoured the prose, matching his thoughts with Judy's devilish dictums. 'She calls it illumination, as though Alexander is going towards Plato's enlightenment.' His eyes eroded the message again until he had to shout her clauses in renewed disbelief: 'blinded by sight! My God it makes perfect sense. If Plato thought that we were being tricked by what only appears to be real, then clearly Judy finds herself some prophet who is set to liberate her fellow scholars.' The more he understood Judy's role, the more Melling began to grow faint. 'I don't want to believe it, and if we were anywhere else, I would laugh the notion out of the room but…'

'Huxley is a place of philosophical minds,' Starling concluded for him.

'Exactly. The concept is almost too ridiculous to be logical, but if you apply it to the right contexts then…'

'Huxley students are almost the only people smart enough to be so stupid.'

'Exactly! We have a girl convincing a boy to commit suicide to reach some Platonist truth, and then we have Lucy Rosewood, the reason I came here in the first place: she was a philosopher who used Plato's notion of truth as the foundation of her suicide letter. Clearly, she was deluded by the same philosophy. The connection is there, and Judy is clearly responsible for Alexander. Did she influence Lucy too?' The last sentence he asked in almost a whisper.

'Do you think Judy invented all of this?'

'It would have taken such a Huxley academic to dream it up, but that one would chose to indoctrinate another…'

That Judy could be responsible for the death of Olivia's daughter made him so angry it was hard to continue talking. Already having seen Lucy's symbol in Judy's letter to Alexander had been difficult to handle. How on earth was he to explain this to Livia? Currently there were still too many unanswered questions but finally, as absurd as it all seemed, the detective was now sure he was following the right thread. Lucy Rosewood referenced Plato when she claimed to have saved her mother fourteen years; Judy Collier took this thinking further, rhetorising life as entrapment, and death as liberation. Both girls were united by this Platonist notion of ultimate truth, and death as an escape towards it.

Clarity turned him further sombre. 'Louis… I just don't want to believe this. I cannot. I refuse. How could a student hold so much power over another?' Melancholy crunched into the detective. It was all too much. 'They're still children for God's sake!' He thundered an exasperated fist onto the desk, rattling it so that a few pencils fell to the floor. Starling placed a saddened hand on Melling's shoulder, but the contact sent a static shock through them both. The light above them flickered, as if in response to the passage of stunning electrons. After a resuscitating gasp, the bulb finally sparked into life, illuminating the room entirely. Melling cast his companion an anxious glance. 'I don't suppose we asked the porter to sort the fuse?'

Starling shook his head, switching off his torch. Melling did the same, trying to ignore his renewed sense of unease. He discreetly looked at the door, remembering how it had continued to close.

Let's not engage in such stupidity.

Scolding his timidity, he chose to ignore the coincidence of a static shock and a bulb breathing to life. Both men now turned to take in the room more clearly. With light came understanding.

Undeniably, the scattered remains of Judy's contraption didn't require further inspection. It was obvious that she had been fashioning her own perverse puppet show. For darkness, a black sheet had been nailed into the window edging. Looking down at the contraption once more, Melling had missed a detail. 'Pillow feather?'

He motioned his eyes to the giant white feather which lay between the broken wooden pieces. Starling saw it and shrugged, turning back to the puppets on the desk. Melling took the feather and placed it inside his jacket pocket. It was then that he considered the burning candles with new importance. 'Louis, we need to go. Now!'

'What why?'

'Now!' Melling insisted excitedly, taking him by the arm. 'The candles were on; she wasn't expecting to be gone long.'

Realisation dawned in Starling's eyes as he was pushed out of the room. He handed Melling the puppet, evidently hoping to distance himself from its eeriness. The detective killed the room's light and closed the door behind them. He yanked the key with some excitement.

It would not be an asymmetric interview like last time. Entrapped by her return to Plato's puppet show alongside her handwritten letter to Alexander, there was no way she would offer anything less than a full confession. The detective was sure of it. As they raced down the creaking stairs, disappearing from Judy's hallway, unbeknownst to them, the light inside her room began to buzz with pleasure as the ghost of Thomas Ferrum flicked his torturous switch. He was enjoying this electric game of cat and mouse.

They brushed past two confused students as they cleared through the ground floor, pushing through Ferrum Court's darkened entrance into the smothered daylight of the early afternoon. Melling hadn't realised just how claustrophobic he had felt and welcomingly drank in Huxley's oxygen. He eyed the students who were milling around the entrance. 'We need to be hidden, but I don't know where we can go,' Melling said, chewing his finger nervously as he scanned the area for a place to steal away and still have a clear view of the entrance. His hungry gaze rested on a bench, conveniently placed behind a bush. 'There!'

But as they crossed the lawn the detective's heart stiffened. The familiar, frosted-blue eyes of Judy Collier gazed expectantly at both of them. She stood just a few metres away. For an eternal moment, neither the gentlemen nor the girl moved. She seemed frozen in time, eyes almost pouring through them. Then their arctic blue passed over the puppet which Starling had thrust into Melling's hand. Instantly, the twin-wrinkles of fear and frustration crouched around her gaze, swirling with the crimson in her cheeks. Melling followed her stare and immediately foresaw how she would respond. In that micro-second, he realised that his spontaneity had led to blunder. 'Bugger,' he muttered. Judy spun on her heel, pushing through the students beside her as she took off in a full sprint.

XXI

Into the Glories of th' Almighty Sun

The wind whipped through Melling's hair as he ran after Judy, struggling to match her youthful pace and energetic strides. He dodged the abrupt corners of the stone buildings, narrowly missing a professor as he exited an unseen passage. Judy never stopped. Instead, the fugitive cast erratic looks behind as she tore across the college. At the sight of the open gate, she did not slow; she ripped across the dazzlingly wide lawn, weaving through the curious eyes of fretting students who, in turn, stared at the panting detective and his slower companion, both screaming for the girl to stop. The gate was unencumbered and she, gazelle-like, jumped pliantly through and onto the streets of Huxley. The retired lion, Melling, almost tripped as he stumbled through the wide gap, shoes clacking against the cobblestones as he staggered on.

They shot through the busy meanderings, dodging the locals who watched the chase in startled wonder.

'Stop!' Melling called as they descended the medieval roads, but Judy paced onwards, evidently aiming to lose the detective in the town's centre. They ran on, the gradient lowering so that Melling continuously fought for balance. Inhaling raggedly, he started to recognise where she was heading; Apollonia's Bridge was now in view, singing a luring welcome along the siren-hiss of the Huxley wind.

Down they went past cursing vendors, Starling jogging in exhaustion further and further behind. Twice Melling thought she had disappeared, and twice he had seen the dark blue tint of her flowing gown ducking away between the growing crowds. He had pushed past adults and screamed at unobservant children as they barred his pursuit, and after crashing into a waiter who stood outside a café, he had neglected to apologise; he shoved the man away, desperate to remain in range of the fleeing girl.

The bridge that had so tormented his sleeping psyche was now close at hand, and the thought of running up the steep hillside of the new town on the other side was already conquering his slipping resolve. Luckily, Judy was barred by a crowd of spectators cheering at a shirtless street acrobat who pranced and twirled in the lagging light. The performer almost appeared as a pagan hierophant, beckoning for the sun to find its way out of the clouds. It could not. Judy was unable to push through the throng, and Melling began to minimise the gap of pursuit. As she cast an agitated look backwards, the detective was now close enough to read the undeniable fear in her blue eyes. Caught in the intensity, the seconds drew longer breaths. He stopped before her, panting.

'Judy Collier,' he shouted. 'You're under arrest for the attempted murder of –'

She never allowed him to finish. Instead, shouldering an onlooker in the back, she slithered through the crowd. The detective was not so subtle. 'Everyone move!' he yelled, pushing past the stubborn bodies until he too was inside the acrobat's ring. He saw her gown slip through the other side, and he screamed for some space, barging through two men who were too slow in responding. He followed Judy's trailing blue as she ran onto the bridge.

The crossing was dense. He had to weave through the locals yet again, bellowing for space. His heart was groaning for oxygen, and his subconscious begging for something he couldn't articulate. He grunted as he pushed past more bodies. Fortunately, Judy was also barred, and Melling heaved in relief when he saw her stop before a particular pod who blocked her way. It was a busload of tourists who were listening to the informing shouts of a guide. Judy looked about her in exasperation and this time her resolve seemed to slip. She stepped backwards from the crowd. Had she too, had enough? Had she realised that the detective would refuse to give up? Perhaps she knew she couldn't outrun her culpability.

Melling closed in, gasping for air. 'It's over,' he said, pulling his identification from his coat for emphasis and earning some curious eyes. 'It's over, Judy.'

Her eyes dripped defiance. 'You might outrun me here, but the police will have you in for questioning before the day's end.'

That spurred an angry recalcitrance, and she began to shout.

'You won't stop anything!' Her eyes were glinting something sinister. Something unsuited to an adolescent. Melling stepped even closer, onlookers slowing as they passed. 'There will always be another.'

'Another what?' Melling shouted in fear, taking another step closer. 'Another what, Judy?' he repeated, coming closer still. *Her* fear had fully left her frosty eyes, outdone by a sneering that ate away her youth until only a malicious snarl remained. 'Judy, let me help you,' he tried again, but she only laughed.

'They already have.'

Before he could ask her who 'they' were, she pushed a bystander aside, and sprinted to the bridge's edge, climbing onto the shallow ledge.

'Wait!' he screamed, conjuring a sound of such hopelessness he thought he was in a play; the audience around him were instantly silenced. The bridge's entertainments died as all heads turned.

Stuttering with a thundering heart, he sprinted towards her, but it was too late. Judy Collier walked off the bridge as though the ledge continued. She disappeared so fast that a blink would have eclipsed her. Melling roared inarticulate sounds in protest, arms pounding onto the stones where she had stood. The sun finally parted the clouds and spotlighted her blue gown as it trailed into the dark waters below. The bridge was full of screams.

*

The bridge was cleared by police; the only people who were not Huxley officers were the exhausted Starling, the melancholic Melling, and a homeless young woman of dirtied auburn; she watched from afar as the detective lay crumpled against a police car, mind unfolding in wearied madness.

Nothing Starling said prompted an answer. Melling's only recognisable company was the memory of her last step, which reoccurred over and over inside his head until it became a one-footed walk into death.

'It wasn't your fault,' Starling eventually said, thinking that the detective was perhaps feeling guilty. But Robert Melling still refused to stare anywhere but straight ahead, reconfiguring her endless footstep, rewatching her die. Starling looked wretchedly upon his companion and sat beside him on the stony bridge, back resting against the car behind them. He couldn't bare the silence for long, nor the dejected look in Melling's hollow eyes. 'It wasn't your fault,' he repeated.

'Even though it wasn't my fault,' the detective eventually… trepidly… replied. His eyes remained fixed on the ledge. 'I can't help thinking how I could have saved her.'

'But you –'

'And every time I think that I'm reminded of that look in her eyes. Don't you understand, Louis? She thought she was *saving* herself. Somehow death is the escape. Death was her answer. She thought it would save her, but not from me, from life itself. Tell me how, in God's name, we have people barely older than children, smiling to their deaths? Because she wasn't frowning! No, she welcomed it. Lucy, Samuel, Alexander, now Judy. Four people, just students, who *wanted* to die! Not because they were suffering, but simply because death promises answers. Some philosophy that is!' He spat that last phrase out, gurgling on his own pent-up saliva. He was crying but he didn't bother to wipe away the tears. 'If somebody doesn't explain all of this to me soon, I think I'm going to slip away.'

Starling did not know how on earth to begin responding, but followed Melling's gaze to the spot where Judy last stood. 'And I should probably see her as evil for what she convinced Alexander Dawn to do, but all I feel is loss. He's in a bloody coma because of her and still…'

'Right now, Robert,' Starling carefully began. 'You have the burden of all their deaths on your shoulders because you're the only one asking why students are brainwashing others into taking their lives. Hell, we're the only ones who know.'

'It's wrong,' Melling said. He didn't recognise the sound of his own voice. 'And as angry as I am at whoever it was who started this. Well, all I want to do is make them realise how worth living life is... anyway...'

The sun had been struggling the entire day but now, for just a moment, it managed to pierce through the grey and pour benevolently onto the space between Melling and the ledge. Clambering to his feet, he watched as the drifting clouds pushed the sunlight along the ground. It lingered on the bridge's edge, illuminating exactly where Judy had stood like a spotlight from above. He recalled how, moments earlier, her blue gown had glinted away into the nothingness below the bridge. He now watched the focusing beam, caught by its coincidental pause. Childishly, he pretended that the light might lead somewhere.

'Dr Starling?' a gravelly voice inquired from behind, and Melling turned.

'That's me,' Starling said, getting to his feet. A podgy man in his thirties with a bushy moustache extended a hand. Melling was reminded of a younger Constable Whaites – his retinue in Horsham after the law graduate, Jacob Wenley, had been ripped apart by a train. That particular day would always haunt him, just as this one would: that much he knew.

'Pleasure to meet you, Doctor,' this new gentleman said to Starling with a kind smile. 'We received your calls to the department about the inspector. He regrets to inform you that he's had a family emergency and seeing as he hadn't left us the report you were asking about, I'd say it's stuck in his house until he comes back.'

'Did he say what happened?' Melling asked, earning a disapproving look.

'His wife, I think.'

'My God, that's awful,' Starling said with all the unhoneyed tones of honesty. 'I hope Claire's alright.'

'I think she's fine for now but, well, she's been unwell for quite some time. He won't be more than a day away if all goes well.'

'Thank you,' Starling said. Then the gentleman looked at Melling, and to the latter's surprise, he seemed happy to see him.

'You're Detective Robert Melling?'

'That's me,' Melling muttered, taking out his London identification. The man shook his hand before eyeing it carefully.

'I'm Sergeant Lynne. You've been convening with Inspector Todd before now, yes?'

Melling nodded.

'Well, I'm sorry that this is the first time we've met. You see, we'd expected Lucy Rosewood's death to be a simple explanation, and well, we already considered Samuel Cadence's demise to be an open-and-shut affair. We had not expected,' he paused, looking around him almost guiltily. 'We hadn't expected you to find some new information that we'd missed.'

'Inspector Todd *told* you?' Melling asked in surprise, and the man looked taken aback.

'Well of course, Detective. But then,' the man looked about him again before answering. 'He came clean about withholding information regarding Miss Rosewood's tragic end.'

'He admitted that?' Starling asked, his inflected pitch indicating how happy he was that his friend had not entirely lost his way.

'Sadly, he did. We were going to give him a week's leave for negligence, but then, our captain took pity on him. You see,' the man said, casting earnest eyes to Melling. 'That man is just a lover of Huxley, is all. He's built it into some kind of bubble. Hates the idea that every now and then that bubble must burst.'

Melling nodded, unsure of how to respond. This frankness was too disconcerting considering he had spent the last few days being treated like the enemy. 'Unfortunately, as I said, his wife has taken a bad turn. So, in light of everything, the captain wants me to firstly, Detective Melling, personally thank you for all the work you've done these past few days.'

Melling was stunned. 'And secondly, well, get to the bottom of the mess you've unearthed,' he added with a chuckle. 'So, would you mind telling us everything you know?'

Melling swallowed again, stupefied at how events could suddenly have turned for the better.

'You're willing to listen?' he asked, earning a disapproving look.

'Yes, please,' the man asserted, eyes glinting with a touch of humour. 'I wouldn't be very good at my job, otherwise.'

Melling and Starling traded looks of relief.

'Well, what I have to say goes further than simply the symbols on Lucy's knees, Sergeant.'

'I'm all ears.'

And so, Robert Melling explained his whole story: beginning with his arrival in Huxley, imparting what he knew about Lucy Rosewood's death and how her letter had focused on dying for the sake of the truth. The man was unsurprised, but upon the news of Judy Collier's note in Alexander's room, signed with Lucy Rosewood's symbol, he began to pale.

'So, you're telling me that Miss Collier convinced Alexander to commit suicide, or to try to?'

'There could be more like her,' Melling asserted quickly. 'At least, she said that someone had helped her! Judy wasn't the first, at least I don't think she was. We broke into her room and found her Platonist puppet show.'

The Sergeant's lips thinned.

'Puppets?'

'Yes. Plato thought that reality was basically a shadow of truth, a sort of a puppet show. One of her puppets has the number one hundred and twenty-five carved into, though I'm at a loss for the reason behind that.'

'And you chased Judy here, yes?'

'Well, you see, she saw us and ran. I didn't want to let her escape, and well…'

The man nodded, deliberately avoiding the edge of the bridge with his eyes.

'So, about this reading group – at Marlowe, was it?'

'That's our lead right now. Probably their disguise. We think that if we can find all the members then we can get to the bottom of how this all started and who is left to save.'

'Okay, Detective Melling. Is there anything else that might be of help? Bear in mind that my team is already sweeping Miss Collier's room as we speak.'

'Well, no, that's it.' He handed over the letter written to Alexander, fumbling around in his inside pocket. His fingers brushed against something soft, and he suddenly remembered the feather.

'Oh, wait. This too!'

The man eyed the long feather suspiciously.

'Where'd you find that?'

'Judy's room.'

'Because she had invented a makeshift puppet theatre from wood and her pillowcase,' Starling added. 'Though the feather seems larger than the ones I find in my pillows.'

The Sergeant eyed it with a peculiar stare.

'It may be part of some ritual?' Melling suggested but Sergeant Lynne simply nodded. Clearly, he was bothered by everything he was yet to understand. Melling realised that he was forcing the man to face a darker truth than he had first considered.

'We'll do our best to figure that out.' A forced smile returned. 'Well gentlemen, once again, Huxshire wants to thank you for all that you've been doing. I know good work when I see it.'

Melling frowned.

'Is this a 'we'll take it from here' speech, Sergeant?'

The man smiled, half-closing his russet eyes.

'Not at all. I'm just letting you know that we *will* be following this up. I'll be heading over to Marlowe myself with some officers to get to the bottom of everything. If she did mention this reading group, her letter being found in that book like you mentioned, well, we will unearth it all soon enough.'

'But can we –'

'Detective,' the sergeant interrupted. 'Don't take this the wrong way. But in light of us having been slow on the trigger, so to speak, the captain is asking that *we* follow through from here.'

'Here I was thinking that I was being valued.'

'Don't take it personally, Detective,' he said. 'I'm sure the politics are the same at Scotland Yard. Picture yourself in our shoes. Especially with one of your own having withheld information!'

Melling shook his head, hating the bureaucracy of his world sometimes. Then again, he appreciated that there was an urgent need for Huxshire to take control. It was also a relief to see them acting. He started to feel as though maybe he could have been more open with them from the beginning. Perhaps if he had gone into the department first thing, then matters may have been different?

'Just make sure you call with the news,' he sighed in defeat, feeling somewhat relieved that his burdens were no longer going to be entirely his own.

'Will do,' the man said. 'We process early in the morning, so expect a call at breakfast. We'll dissolve this misled group of students, sure enough.' He shook his head again. 'My God, can you believe it?' Yet he seemed confident that all would be taken care of and shook both men's hands before leaving.

These past few days Melling had felt he was trespassing, tiptoeing around the sensitivities of those in charge. Now he was being thanked and promised action. He should be elated. Instead, he was uneasy.

'Stop thinking too much about it, Robert,' Starling said, clearly reading the worrisome lines that stretched across the former's forehead. 'Here we were feeling isolated, and now you're getting the help you need.'

'I wouldn't call it a *deus ex machina* just yet,' Melling muttered, rubbing his temple, and earning a half-chuckle from the doctor.

'You've been all alone with this. I think you've earned a break.'

'It's all so sudden.'

'Come on, Detective,' the latter said, motioning to the end of the bridge. 'One last stop.'

XXII

No Streetcar, Just Desire

'Maybe this can wait,' Melling said to Starling, earning an encouraging hand that squeezed his shoulder.

'You heard the sergeant. They'll call in the morning, so that implies another night where you might try to take the bell from your wrist.'

'I told you,' Melling sighed. 'I didn't *try* and do that.'

'Which is exactly why we're here, Robert.'

They were standing outside the jet-black door of 3, Abbot Close: the home of Starling's old acquaintance who supposedly dealt in matters such as Melling's. Starling had deliberately avoided the notion of experimental science, but Melling could tell that he didn't agree with the gentleman's practice.

'We haven't even called-in,' Melling protested, unwilling to have this pseudo scientist scour his brain.

'He isn't exactly… busy,' Starling said, rapping on the door.

'You mean he lacks a reputation. *Great.*'

After a few moments, the door swung open, revealing a handsome man of some height. His hair was excellently dark, but trimmed, complimenting the fitted white chemise that clung to his shoulders. Harry Saturn would have liked his style. At the sight of the doctor, he beamed, which widened his dark blue irises.

'Louis!' he exclaimed in a weighty German accent. 'What are you doing here? It has been so long. Do come in!'

'Afternoon Calmet,' Louis Starling replied, remaining where he was. 'Allow me to introduce Detective Robert Melling.'

The German smiled, extending a strong hand to the detective.

'Calmet Traum. How do you do?'

'It's a pleasure,' Melling said. This was certainly not the man he had been expecting.

'And to what do I owe that pleasure?'

'Well,' Starling began.

'Ah,' the tall man interrupted. 'You're here because of this,' he cooed, pointing to the dark rims which had dug trenches beneath the detective's eyes.

'That and some other things,' Melling said, but the man silenced him, growing animated.

'Patrizia!' he shouted behind him into the house, then he turned to Starling.

'Louis, you wait inside. Patrizia will set aside some tea for you by the fire. You,' he boomed, turning to the detective with a deep voice, full of quirk and authority. 'My practice uses the other door. If you wouldn't mind taking the next street over and walking back? It's also number 3.' With that, he pulled Starling inside, and slammed the door shut.

'Well then,' Melling muttered, turning back along the stone street. He almost missed the back entrance for it was buried at the end of a short set of steps which disappeared from view. Clearly these were old servant's quarters. He walked down and knocked on the door. Before the third rattle of his knuckles, the smiling scientist was beckoning him in.

'Welcome, Mr Melling,' he said, almost as a host, pulling him inside with warm hands. The first thing which the detective noticed was the overwhelming scent of incense which hung on his shoulders and wiggled under his nose as soon as he stepped into the cavern light of the room. 'Right this way,' the man sung, and as the door closed, Melling almost struggled to find his figure in the gloom. He followed over cushioned carpet which soothed the toes through his shoes. He felt like he was walking through some sort of hedonism den, with red candlelight guiding him onwards, and Moroccan rugs closing him in from both sides. The aroma of sandalwood and vanilla spiked his nose hairs, and his eyes began to water as they walked.

The tall figure of this enigmatic man named Calmet pushed open a heavy oak door, revealing a dark leather sofa that slept opposite a red-cushioned chair. Melling could hardly place the colours of the room as it was so cluttered with instruments and worldly paraphernalia. He noted three broken globes, at least a dozen lamp steads without bulbs, various contraptions that bewildered him and ones that enticed. There were maps of countless countries strewn across the floor, and

Melling was afraid to step forward and murder a continent with his feet. The ceiling supported just three oil lamps, which somehow added the scents of rosemary and ginger, complimenting the visible incense that clung to the damask walls. Behind the sofa was a long wooden tables piled high with half-open volumes, and Melling could already see that many of these books were painted with the negligence of spilled candle wax.

'What is all this?'

'Oh, that is all part of my practice,' the man hummed with a low-timbred chuckle. 'Please, lie down,' he suggested, guiding Melling to the black sofa, and adjusting a silken pillow at one end. Melling hesitated. 'Please, Detective, or you'll never know about that woman who haunts you.'

Melling's heart jumped.

'What? How did –'

'Mr Melling,' the man interrupted with a musical voice. The sounds became sonorous and lulled his ears; he began to forget his question. It had initially burned inside him, desperately seeking an answer, but almost immediately, it had died in the bud; Melling even found himself questioning his angsts. The detective could hardly recall why he had even come, what even worried him; what could, after all, be so pressing? 'That's right,' Calmet said in soft, lulling echo. 'Just relax, Mr Melling.'

The detective found himself lying back, feeling the silken pillow ease against his neck. It was perfumed, its scent a mixture of red wine and oceanic sand. The sensation of waves crashing onto a darkened shore made him feel dizzy. 'That's good,' Calmet whispered. 'Very good.'

Gradually, Melling didn't realise who was speaking, nor did he know why he was even trying to figure out where he was. Above his sleeping eyes, the German doctor began gently swinging a pocket-watch to and fro. 'Auf Wiedersehen…' the man murmured.

*

Melling awoke to the crushing scent of chestnuts; their woodland musk swept through his throat as though he was smoking them.
'Cigarette,' he whispered.
'Not here,' instructed a man from above him. 'Listen.'
Then an ataraxious accent joined the smell of chestnuts.
'That's suicide too, you know?' she lulled from over his shoulder. He stared into the fireplace before him. He struck a tall match, recognising that he was in a hotel; he knew the room's lush, wide red interior without looking behind him. Indeed, his body wouldn't allow him to turn and face the woman, but in his mind's eye he could see her silhouette, cast against the dated backdrop of the cognisant decor. He lit his dry cigarette, wetting its tip on his unplaceable lips and drowsily inhaling its lethe-ward expulsion. He staggered slightly.
'Careful,' the woman said, almost singing the word.
'Careful,' whispered the man above. Melling coughed into the fireplace, adding cancerous smoke into the burning chestnuts.
'Air,' the seductress said, offering the detective an escape. Melling staggered onto the balcony, pushing the white-framed door as he lunged outside into the uncaring dark. He ventured slightly onwards, finding the stone edge with his hands. It iced against his fingers, and he fumbled, dropping his cigarette. The mouthless embers sailed downwards into nonexistence. His mind told him that this was a street, identifiable with the sounds of cars and peopled chaos. He, however, was isolated from them in terms of vision, seeing only the final sparks of his Gitanes disappear into an obscurity. 'That's where you're going anyway,' stated the woman.
'Falling,' Melling mumbled in anaesthetised intoxication.
'Falling,' she beckoned.
'I ca… can't,' he stammered, hearing people scream below him in the street, gradually losing feeling in his limbs at the speed at which ice melts. The horn of a distant tram grew closer, teasing him.
'Melt,' instructed the woman.
'No,' Melling said, voice barely even a croak. His face numbed against a single tear. It ventured towards his chin, pausing mournfully where it found the oxygen, hanging there in eternal trepidation.
'Melt,' repeated the other voice, almost questioningly.

'Orders,' Melling slurred. He licked his lips; they tasted like chaos and chestnuts. The voice grew in comprehension.

'Solve the equation, Detective,' she mouthed from behind him.

'Everything goes with him,' yelled Constable Whaites from below.

'Yes, everything goes with you,' the woman lullabied in repetition.

'So, do you,' Melling mumbled in an intended determination, feeling nothing but the smell of chestnuts. As he faded into obscurity, his eyes bronzed into embers. The tear droplet fell whilst a lady screamed. On the street below he heard someone say goodbye.

'Auf Wiedersehen,' murmured the male echo, and its familiarity jolted him awake.

His heart raced into a frenzy, and he sat up with a start, gasping for oxygen. A warm, steadying hand pressed his shoulder.

'Breathe,' Calmet instructed. '*Breathe.*'

Melling did as instructed, slowing his heart, and leaning back in exhaustion, reminding himself that he was back in Calmet's practice.

'What... what happened?' he asked, voice coming out as a meagre rasp. Calmet smiled.

'What do *you* think happened?'

Melling rubbed his temple with a sweating palm, slowly sitting up.

'I feel like I died, and yet... it felt familiar... almost like it had happened before.' He felt guilty for saying so, believing himself to be a madman but Calmet's smile remained.

'You were dreaming, Detective,' he explained, offering an expectant look.

'But how? I was just lying down and then...'

'Chestnuts?'

'Yes,' Melling affirmed, head beginning to throb. 'I could smell them. I was in... I was in...' He focused, struggling to rein in his escaping memory as it fled.

'You remember?' Calmet asked, and Melling closed his eyes to think.

'There was a voice, no, two. There was your voice and...'

'Yes...'

'... and...'

Slowly, as he focused, the dream came back to him, like the way food reminds us of its flavours: the familiarity is always there: dormant until prompted. The more the details came back to him, the more his head began to ache; the more the information stirred from inside him, the more he realised that this was the dream that had been plaguing him since his wife had died. 'My God.' He sat there, rooted to his seat, mind breaking into one thousand unanswerable questions, all of which led him back to her. 'Lorelei,' he whispered. Sitting there on Calmet's couch, in desolation, he realised that the voice of his dream belonged to Lorelei, his wife. Not only, but he could finally for the first time in months, actually see the dreams he had been dreaming. He could finally see *her*. Lorelei was tethered to every single one of his sleepless or tortured nights. Calmet looked happy to notice the look of hopelessness and discovery which shared a space in Melling's insomniac eyes.

'Grief is universal,' the German said, earning a distrustful and puzzling look from Melling. 'Which is why I can tell you that your plight, though mystifying, is actually common.'

'Wait a minute. Just so I understand your directness. You mean to tell me that I've been thinking about my wife in my dreams this entire time because of grief? My grief has not been foreign to me, so how come I can't remember *her* until now?'

'Ah, well,' the man continued with a steady smile, pulling a golden pocket watch from his waistcoat, and swinging it backwards and forwards. 'You haven't had me.'

'You hypnotised me?' Melling asked in incredulity.

'Well, no,' Calmet offered in defence. 'At least, that isn't quite the term I'd prefer. All I did was help you navigate between your subconscious and your conscious.'

Melling stared at him without response.

'What?' he finally managed.

'Well,' the man said, getting to his feet. 'Your dreams are a part of your subconscious, you see.' He walked over to the table of opened books and took a thin vial of purple liquid back to the detective. 'You must realise, Mr Melling, that it's hard for a person to control the inner workings of the mind. Your subconscious does most of that for you.'

'That much I do know, or at least, I've read about the theories,' Melling muttered, growing impatient. The doctor pulled the cork from the vial and handed the lilac solution to the detective.

'Drink,' he instructed. Melling hesitated, but the man's eyes were steadfast. Sighing, he swallowed the drug, surprised by how sweet it tasted.

'What *is* that?'

'Well, like I was saying, it can be hard for the conscious mind to get the subconscious to reveal itself. This solution helps to cement the link we made already.'

Melling wasn't sure if that was true, but he already found his headache subsiding. 'It works fast,' the grinning German observed. 'So, why don't you start by telling me where you were?'

Melling closed his eyes to think, but this time the memories swam into consciousness easily.

'It was a hotel in Austria,' he recounted, feeling sadness creep into his heart. 'My God, that was our final time together.' As he surveyed the dream, he realised that it was not the same as it had always been. The memories of his past nightmares now shone before him with the upmost clarity, Calmet's medicine clearly working. He could see Lorelei in all her various shades of beckoning, night after night in London. Just now, when under Calmet's hypnotic trance, Lorelei had not been alone. 'I could hear *you*... and a constable I met recently. Why?'

The man shrugged in response.

'Well, I was helping your mind stay focused. After all, this is the first time I've been in your head, Detective. As for the constable, I can only assume that what he represents has been on your mind recently.'

'But what about my wife, because...' It was then that Melling's mind passed over the past few nights. 'No,' he whispered, realising whose voice had cajoled him to the bridge, and whose figure it was which had climbed onto his bed. 'I've seen her!' Melling blurted out. 'My God, I saw Lorelei jump and I –'

'You only *thought* you did,' the scientist said with a frown.

'*No*,' Melling corrected. 'She tried to pull me over the edge of Apollonia's Bridge! Why would she want me to die?'

The man shook his head with a knowing gaze.

'Mr Melling. All that we have done today, is link your conscious to *your* subconscious. The figures you're seeing are only what *your* subconscious is creating.'

'Yes, I *understand*,' Melling said in irritation. 'But why would *my* mind make her do that to me? It doesn't make sense. I have no interest in jumping off bridges, thank you.'

Calmet chuckled.

'When a man is thirsty, he dreams of water.'

'Haven't we all had that before?' Melling replied sarcastically.

'So, what that tells us is that our desires can manifest themselves in the subconscious.'

'Well, why would I want her to want *me* to die?' Melling asked, thinking that he had caught onto the meaning. 'That makes even less sense.'

Again, Calmet just shook his head.

'The question you should be asking, Detective, is why you might want to join her?'

'I'm sorry?'

'Your dreams are often playing on those desires that you've buried deep down, allowing you a cathartic space to fulfil those desires.'

'Catharsis? You mean dreams are like performances for the stuff we haven't acknowledged?'

'Exactly! Sometimes that's enough and our cravings are purged. Other times…'

'It isn't enough,' Melling murmured, and the man nodded.

'That is the most dangerous sort of desire, Mr Melling. Our subconscious has a funny way of getting its way.'

Melling felt exhausted as he listened, the anxiety of sleep now teasing into his neck and shoulders. But as he took in the diagnosis, he relented to what his true desire was.

'I want to be with her,' he said flatly. 'I mean, of course I do. She was the love of my life, so why wouldn't I want to join her? She was ripped away from me, and I never thought my soul would recover. But that doesn't… that doesn't mean I would do anything! That's ludicrous, irrational!'

'Mr Melling, would you have gone out onto Apollonia's Bridge if you were truly in control? Louis has told me that you almost died that night. Do you find *that* rational?'

The detective shook his head, voice flat with helplessness.

'So, what does this mean? How do I stop this?'

'You make peace with your buried emotions,' Calmet said quietly.

'I suppose I never did,' Melling slowly acknowledged, taking off his heavy coat and procuring a cigarette from his silver case. 'Do you mind?'

'Not at all.'

'You see, she was an opera singer. I used to love her music,' Melling continued, lighting his Gitanes and sighing at the sensations it conjured. 'I fell in love with who she was in reality just as much as who she was on the stage. She was my Sibyl Vane.'

'What happened?'

Melling lay back and stared at the ceiling.

'We were engaged just months after we met. That's how in love we were. After the war, we moved in together in London. We were happily married for a time. Happiness seems to fall short, really. She's been my rock all these years but last year...' he had to pause, sucking hard on his cigarette. 'She was honoured with an award for her profession; there was a ceremony in Vienna.' His lips began to tremble as he spoke, and his dreams subsided, making way for the nightmare of his memory.

*

Vienna, 1968

The sound of the tram's desperate breaks groaning under the weight of deadly momentum seemed to last longer than a lifespan. Ironic how they would signal the ending of one. It was peculiar how so miniscule a moment could transform into one's longest recollectable memory; these seconds were somehow withheld, too afraid of what the implications might be if they were allowed to pass.

Lorelei had spotted an old friend, all too excited to celebrate with one she used to sing with. She had leapt forward, sprinting across the road to greet her. But she never looked. She and her husband had been on that very tram the day before; Lorelei had learned to speak English from American movies and novels, so she called them streetcars.

Melling had looked up too late, or rather, just in time to see the tram driver slam the breaks in horror. He had been stunned, eyes widened, mouth agape. Sound escaped him. The man eternally armed with a quotation was struck dumb. He would never again fully reunite with his old affinity for language; his linguistic flexibility often relied on a levity for life, something a tram would steal by doing nothing other than following its route. War had chipped away at his ability to engage with comedy, often even cheerfulness, but a streetcar would entirely snuff-out Melling's very foundation for happiness.

The seconds could not hold back forever. Time, proverbially, waited for no man – a perennially propagated cliché that had survived history because of its certainty. The problem was that no matter how much one knew that tragedy could one day strike, they somehow, subconsciously thought they would see it coming. But tragedy is never on the horizon. It always arrives from under the eyeline. Tragedy sneaks up on you. Despite its inevitability, tragedy always arrives unexpectedly; one is destined never to fully process it as a result. The guillotine falls but has always been falling. Thus, Melling learned the cruel spontaneity of the reaper's scythe. It swung down with the passing seconds. They ticked forwards. They rolled onwards like the tram, unable to restrain themselves, allowing the thud of Lorelei's frame and the final, creaking jolt of the stopping streetcar. As time collided with Melling, the tram collided with his wife.

A lady screamed. Soon many others joined her. Melling watched it all unfold like a detached spectator, unable to reconcile his urge to sprint towards his lifeless wife with his deadened feeling of heavy revulsion. Indeed, the urge to vomit surprised him; he had not realised that tragedy would so demand a yearning for some sort of expulsion. Around the body, individuals spoke frantically and loudly. Others were more callous to the heartbreak, too eager to pass on into the very place where Lorelei was set to receive her honours.

Next he knew, Melling was by her side, hands cupping blood as though he could pour it back into her broken skull.

'Lorelei, Lorelei, Lorelei,' he whimpered.

She hung in his arms, herself for a final second.

Then the back of her head opened fully.

Melling couldn't feel anything.

Her brain fluid was under his fingernails.

It took four men to haul him away from her body.

XXIII

What Shall My West Hurt Me?

Huxley, May 1969

It had taken Robert Melling ten minutes to finally stop crying. Calmet had helped him to sit up and calm himself. Then, under the pretext of giving him a moment to himself, he had stolen away.

Melling felt better for sobbing. He had tried desperately to restrict his grief when Lorelei had passed. He wasn't sure why he had done so, considering there was no one left in his life he needed to be strong for. Everyone save Gladys and Harry had left him. Nonetheless, after the overwhelming realisation of who had been plaguing his dreams, he felt as though his dam of woe had finally collapsed, making way for the floods of relief. He recalled Calmet's explanation of repressed desire, and corrected himself. Lorelei was not plaguing him. Of course she wasn't! He was fashioning her from his own grief. Months of denial had embedded her into his subconscious.

Sitting on the hypnotist's sofa, he realised a great irony to his situation. Here he was dejected by the prospect of students ending their lives, when he himself, deep inside the mysteries of his mind, desired the same fate. He shuddered under his lack of control. He had conjured his murderer out of the memories of the woman he loved. He had stepped onto the bridge's ledge to stand beside his dead wife, guided by some internal wish for reconciliation.

'But would I even join her?' he muttered to himself. Of course not. Lorelei was gone, and if he passed, he would be gone too. Life begins and ends with its occupant. There was no second destination. If Melling's unconscious was allowed to expose itself untamed, the detective might look for a lover who no longer existed. He might find her at the bottom of Apollonia's abyss.

Make peace with your buried emotions, Calmet had prescribed. He would try. He had to try. Thanks to this German psychologist who, truthfully, behaved more like some modern wizard, his mind had been revealed. No matter how much he believed that he was in control of himself, there was a sinister side to him which would assume responsibility when he could no longer keep his eyes open. He didn't want to die. The very thought of a nothingness frightened him. It appalled him.

'Apologies,' came Calmet's musical timbre from the room's entrance, interrupting the detective's thoughts. 'I was trying to find my card.'

'Your card?'

'Why yes, just in case you would be requiring my services back in London.'

'So, that's it then?' Melling asked, now irritated. 'I don't even know how to handle what you've shown me. How do I stop my… *subconscious*… from overwhelming me?'

'You have to accept your desire,' Calmet repeated.

'But I *have* accepted my desire!' Melling said.

'Well then I suppose you won't be needing my card, after all then, eh?' Calmet maintained with a rueful smile.

'So, that's it?'

'Well, if you say that you've made peace with your desire, then yes, that's all.'

The man walked over to his desk and ran a long index finger over some of his books. His voice turned serious. 'Mr Melling, if you do not accept your desire, you are going to push it further down into the realms of your subconscious until it strikes out ten-fold.'

'But I'm not sure what else to do,' Melling complained, getting up and coming over to Calmet's side, who was busy pouring over some sort of French scholarship. 'Tell me how I can fix this.'

Calmet looked up at him with regretful eyes.

'Resist it and your soul grows sick with longing,' he murmured with a saddened smile.

'You're saying I have to yield to my desire for it to no longer be desired?' Calmet nodded. 'But that's ludicrous!' the detective blurted with a raised voice. 'If I die to stop myself from wanting to die, then I'm already dead. You're nonsensical, Mr Traum.'

Calmet shook his head with a tut.

'I'm not suggesting that you do any such thing, Mr Melling. I am simply telling you, that if you don't make peace with your desire to experience the cold touch of death himself... or perhaps herself in this instance... you will forever be taunted by her.'

'But I already told you,' Melling repeated in exasperation, 'that I *have* come to terms with it!'

'And I told you, Mr Melling, that if you don't yield to your desire, and I mean *truly,* consciously yield to it, it will remain buried.'

'So, help me,' Melling cried in appeal. 'Because I'm at a loss to –' he paused, eyes landing on the far side of the hypnotist's table, to where some unrecognisable writing was beautifully painted with careful strokes. He could make out a bird which reminded him of some sort of Egyptian hieroglyph, but the other seemed more recently familiar.

Despite his frenzy, something more powerful, more alluring, beckoned him. There are, at times, those rare moments when one seems to connect with some sort of inner hunch which one can hardly put into words. Sometimes you're thinking about someone, and they walk past you. Other times, you think a number and lo and behold, it races past you on the back of a bus. There is something potent to that mysticism which many Westerners are willing to both simultaneously quietly acknowledge and loudly brush aside as mere coincidence. The feeling Melling was experiencing was of a similar calibre. This was one of those instances where the slightest inkling of suspicion was enough to suggest a tsunami of implication, where one just *knew* they needed to ask a specific question, choose one of many doors, pick a certain number. There was a palpable uncanny to this sensation; it squirmed within and begged you to unearth its mystery.

Melling forgot himself for a moment, guided by this uneasy thread, walking past Calmet to the opened book. He traced his hands over the symbols, familiarity pounding its way into his thoughts. He focused on the vertical semicircle that had so attracted him. It was tauntingly familiar though not identical to the symbol that had so frustrated the detective since he first saw it. Something instinctively told him that his frustrations were about to end. His gut informed him that Calmet Traum would decipher what others could not.

'What is this?' he asked, throat incredibly dry. Calmet came over with an air of nonchalance.

'Those? They're just hieroglyphs. I used to trade archaeological artefacts, so I needed a dictionary and I, well, still read through sometimes. Exquisite language when you get to understand it. They function alphabetically, logographically and syllabically. Truly incredible how they utilised it. Did you know that there was an incorrect dictionary circulating for quite some time which people used for the decryption of ancient sites? Egyptians weren't the only ones to use them either but –'

'How many do you know?' Melling interrupted, mind beginning to buzz with the hum of discovery.

'In Ancient Egyptian? Well,' the man paused with a smile. 'Most of the –'

Melling cut him off by rumbling around the table.

'Do you have a pen? And paper? I mean paper I can write on?'

Reading his distressed excitement, Calmet was quick to act.

'Well, yes, *natürlich.*'

He hurried out of the room, but within moments, returned with some yellow paper and a steel pen. Melling quickly began drawing the symbol that Michael Crown, the coroner, had seen on Lucy's knees. Here, what was carved in blood was relayed in rich, black ink. He stepped away, eagerly eyeing the hypnotist as the man looked at the drawing.

'Do you know it?' he asked, pulse kicking inside his dry throat as he waited agonisingly for the verdict. 'Well?'

Calmet hummed to himself and tried shifting the symbol on its side.

'Are you sure it's not upside down?' was the eventual response.

'Upside down? No, why?'

'Well, this particular symbol is recognisable, but only when inverted.' He turned the page around, muttering the word 'amenta' to himself.

Now the semicircle faced downwards with the lines declining down the page.

'Yes,' he concluded slowly. 'It *is* the amenta.'

'What's the amenta?' Melling asked, curiosity practically bursting.

'Well, as I said, the one you've drawn was upside down. But this way, it represents the underworld. I used to see it at sites on the Nile's West Bank.'

'West Bank?'

'Yes, where the sun sets. Are you sure your version isn't the wrong way round?'

'The way I've drawn it is the right way, though that is frustrating to admit seeing as you've explained it as something else. You're sure it doesn't mean anything the other way?'

'Well, if it was drawn that way on purpose, it may be positive, but, no, I don't think it can be. You see,' he said, pointing at the semi-circle, 'the amenta symbolises the underworld by mimicking the falling horizon of a sunset. A sun cannot set upside down, not even in Egyptian mythology, and to me it would be too strange to attempt to pair death with the sunrise anyway.'

Melling's pulse felt like it was propagating stones.

'What did you say?' he whispered. His thoughts were forcing him to recall a specific sentence uttered by someone whose identity was still shadowy in his memory. Traum gave him a strange look.

'Well, instead of the sun setting, if you reverse the symbol of passing into the underworld, it almost becomes heavenly. Though that is me finding a meaning. Perhaps if you wanted to see death as a sunrise it could work. But then again, there are other symbols for both the sunrise and death.'

Detective Robert Melling didn't listen to that last part. Instead, the man's notion of the setting sunrise leapt about inside his skull like a cornered animal. His palms trembled as he fought for his recollections. Then, suddenly, he felt the iteration that had been calling from beyond his consciousness gasp for air. He was cast back to three days ago, speaking with Master Dunfield atop the library. The master's advice played against the ears of his memory. He had dismissed the tragedy of Lucy Rosewood's death in favour of something more poetic.

See it as a sunrise, Mr Melling, not a sunset, he had said.

Huxley was her home, and you come here, searching for villains in the land of the innocent. We set people free here, we do not constrain them.

'We set people free,' Melling whispered aloud, each ghastly syllable falling heavily from his lips; he no longer noticed the room around him. He reached out for the table in front to steady himself, mind now racing onto Judy's letter to Alexander.

They are deafened by ears and blinded by sight, but you will be liberated.

Liberated.

We set people free here.

Here was the missing piece to Huxley's puzzle.

We salute you, Judy had written. *We*. This 'we' had plagued him since he'd first read her letter. Who were *they?* He had thought it was some perverse, melancholic student group masked as a reading society. He had believed that students were influencing others to see death as some ultimate truth. 'My God,' he whispered, looking straight at Calmet but not perceiving him; Master Gabriel Dunfield's sardonic smile eclipsed the figure before him.

And just what do you know about the truth, Detective?

He had known. The master had known all along.

I would suppose, though it's just a guess, the ultimate truth?

No. Melling had not mistaken the master's smile that day. He *had* known – had even revelled in Melling's bewilderment. He was only feigning a guess, all too glad to parade Plato before someone he knew to be in total ignorance. Dunfield had been completely aware that death could signify ultimate truth.

Frenzied mind becoming further frantic, Melling retraced his investigation, recalling the living Judy and her tears.

'I think you'll find that we'll all benefit from the truth,' Melling had told her. Yes. She had smiled too, exactly like the master.

The truth? Are you sure?

There was no denying it. She had resembled him uncannily. She had lied her way through their meeting, and it all made complete sense. In Judy he saw the master's duplicitous, rhetorical stare, and knowing what he knew about Judy, he was crushed by the realisation of just who Master Dunfield was and what he was capable of.

Yours is the path towards eternal understanding.

Illumination takes courage, but remember, there is nothing more necessary than the truth.

How could the master have turned a bright young girl into a cold, philosophising murderess? Judy had told Melling she loved Samuel, but there was now no doubt in the detective's mind that she was responsible for his death too. Answering questions raised new questions, and he began to itch for the inspector's report on the matter.

'The report,' he murmured, finally finding himself back in the hypnotist's presence.

'Everything alright, Mr Melling?' Calmet whispered, eyes laced with worry, but the detective just pushed him slightly with his hand. Walking to the couch and pressing his distressed palms onto his head, he rocked to and fro. 'Get Starling down here, now.'

'Can I – ?'

'Now!' he shouted, not even looking up as the overexcited doctor disappeared to fetch the other doctor.

Not a minute later, Starling burst through the door, eyes flaring in distress.

'Robert,' he shouted, rushing forward. 'What is it?'

'We have been deceived! How could we not have seen it?'

'Seen what?' his friend asked, Calmet waiting quietly by the door. His excitement, however, was audible.

'Get me a phone,' Melling said, getting to his feet.

'Seen what?' Starling shouted, but Melling was already imploring.

Calmet guided both men down the left of the corridor to an unkempt office of stacked paper. A phone protruded from the sea of black and white. Melling rifled through the phone book until he found the number for the Huxshire Police. He needed to get through to the sergeant or his team. All the book had was a reception number, and after five painful rings an indolent voice answered.

'Huxshire Police, how may I help you?'

'Hello!' Melling began in a raised voice. 'This is Detective Robert Melling. I need you to get word out to Sergeant Lynne and let him know that he's looking in the wrong place.'

'I'm sorry, sir. I'm not sure what you mean?'

'The sergeant and his team are meant to be at Marlowe College in Huxley. But he doesn't realise that his objective is in the wrong place. Can you find him, please?'

'Okay, sir. One moment. Let me get back to you.'

'What's happened, Robert?' Louis Starling implored. Melling kept the receiver to his ear as he spoke.

'It's not the students, Louis. Well, at least, their doctrine comes from another source. Mr Traum explained to me the meaning of Lucy Rosewood's symbol.'

'Which is?' Louis asked, growing further animated.

'It was a hieroglyph! But it was upside down. When it was the right way round, it was the Egyptian way of writing the underworld. But something he said.' He turned to Calmet. 'When you said that it symbolised the sun setting, not the sun rising, and that it would indeed be perverse to see death as a sunrise.'

'What are you talking about?' Starling interrupted.

'If the symbol was upside down, it was meaningless.'

'I'm not sure what you mean.'

'Her death was a message, just like her note. Calmet said something that made me realise the truth!'

'You mean all this stuff about the sun? You still haven't explained!'

'Well,' Calmet said. 'If you wanted to show the sun rising instead of the sun setting, you wouldn't use that shape. You see, it represents the underworld exactly because that semicircle is meant to show the sun crossing the horizon. The lines are the last struggling rays.'

'So, if you did want it to be the other way round,' Melling said, 'it would be a rather positive way to look at death, which got me thinking. Do you remember the conversation I had with the master at Dunfield? After imparting what Professor Robora had made of Lucy's note, he said something peculiar to me.'

'That it takes fourteen years to teach the truth?'

'Yes, but there was something else too. When I realised that Lucy wanted to arrive at some ultimate truth, a notion which the master had rather enjoyed explaining I might add, he'd told me to see her death as a sunrise not a sunset.'

Starling tied the pieces together but didn't want to agree.

'That's just coincidental.'

'Is it?'

'He is just putting a positive view on things!'

'Exactly! Think! Whoever is influencing these students to desire death is convincing them that their pursuit will reap the reward of life's understanding.'

Calmet Traum exhaled painfully at this information and rested a wearied head against the door frame of the office. 'And so,' Melling continued. 'They aren't seeing death as the end but as a discovery. Don't you see? The master couldn't help himself. He also told me that his job was to set people free! *Liberation!*' he insisted in an exasperated tone. 'Just like Judy wrote in her letter. Why do you think he kept harking on about truth? I just chalked it all up to him being a supercilious academic but now I see.'

'Illumination takes courage,' Starling said, repeating the other aspect of Judy's letter. He looked heartbroken, and Melling knew why. 'The specifics match-up: sunrise. They think they are being enlightened.'

With Starling's observation, Melling now finally grasped how the information had been there from the beginning.

'*In lucem,*' he said. 'Into the light. The chanting at Lucy's funeral service: into the light,' he repeated. 'Sunrise sheds light. Remember what Inspector Todd told us? Perhaps even he knows.'

Starling paled.

'No… it can't be. No! I would have known! That sort of evil you can feel from a man.'

'*Can* you?'

'Caspar… Caspar… No. He wouldn't.'

But before Melling could answer, the voice returned to his ear, and he held up a hand for silence.

'Yes, I'm still here,' he said into the phone. He devoured the reply, but within moments his eyes dilated in fear. 'No, I understand. I think I have the wrong information   no, don't worry about telling him. No, not at all… yes, that was the incident on the bridge… and now? No, honestly… don't call… my mistake really… thank you.' He slowly lowered the phone, feeling his hopes die.

'What is it?'

'Sergeant Lynne carried out his last duty today after Judy jumped. The lady said she had not been told of any of Huxshire's officers going to Marlowe College, and she wanted to tell me that the sergeant was now on leave.'

'On leave?'

'He had only been by the bridge because it was an emergency. We shouldn't expect him back until next week, apparently. In short: he lied to us. Just like the inspector.'

'My God,' Starling said in shock, taking a step back. 'He'd said that Caspar was on leave too.'

'It was a set-up. No doubt his wife is fine. We've been played.' Melling's voice was dripping with anger now. 'They would have, no doubt, given us false information tomorrow morning too.' He turned to the hypnotist who seemed to be clutching at reason.

'Is it true?' Calmet asked, finally speaking now that Melling offered him his eyes. 'Are Huxley's professors killing students?'

Every ounce of Melling's body was disgusted by the fact that his response was in the affirmative.

'There is no doubt in my mind that there is a lot more happening than even we currently understand.'

Then the faintest tickle of a budding opportunity warmed his thoughts. 'But at this moment, nobody knows that we know.' His lips actually began to twitch into an angry smile. Disgust became fuel for determination. 'For the first time since I've arrived,' he said, his mind already strategizing in a way that was second nature. '*We* have the advantage.' He looked at Starling with a grin. 'Huxley thinks we are still in ignorance, meaning that they are on the back-foot.'

Starling met him with a stare that dared to think bravely.

'So, what do we do?'

'We need to call London.'

XXIV

Dead Ringer

Robert Melling blurted awake, bathed in the sweat of his night terrors. He looked around the darkness of Starling's guest room, noting the slivering silvers of moonlight as they sprang through his half-closed curtains. The moisture of his midnight anguish made him shiver. He ran an anxious hand over his left wrist, feeling the cool copper of Starling's trusty bell.

A gust of wind licked against his damp torso, and he shivered anew. Why was there such a draught? His window was closed but his feet felt like they were standing on frozen stone under his blanket. His teeth began to clatter, the trembling bottom jaw gnashing against its brother above. Melling quivered, feeling less and less at ease. He lay his head back against his pillow in frustration, though it only made him dizzy. He knew where he was, but he felt like he was standing on a ledge, despite laying down.

The air began to part his wispy hair, and he sat-up in annoyance, now face to face with a figure who sent his pulse fleeing from his shivering body. His wife was in front of him, her eyes mere inches from his. Her hands, like iron stakes, pinned his covers to the bed. He recognised her enchantingly black locks as they drifted over her cheek bones. Her eyes were the same as the night she'd passed, their golden shine of chocolate topaz seeming to contain a hidden furnace. Her ever-visible empathy, however, was stolen. Death had suited her in disgust. Her lips were metal dead, the space between her browning teeth an empty black.

'Lorelei,' he whispered, barely audible between the repeating bites of his chattering teeth. 'Lorelei, I love you,' he said, holding her stare. Calmet Traum's warnings flooded his mind and he tried to stabilise his shuddering jaws, aware of how he needed to clamp down on this subconscious situation. 'I love you, but I can't *join* you.'

The woman's shineless, burgundy lips stretched into a malicious smile, marring the purest face he had ever known with a hag's scorning grin. *No!* She was *not* Lorelei. She was some demonised perversion that his subconscious had conjured to take him by his weak-willed hands to the grave. 'I want to live,' he cried in defiance, but his wife didn't respond. Instead, her bottom lip dropped, exposing the slightest shine of dull brown. It took a second for him to realise that this was his copper bell, lying on her hideously grey tongue. Safety and reason were no longer tied to his wrist. Staring at the fearfully enigmatic spectre, fully undone by his unconscious, he couldn't help but whimper. 'Please, please; I miss you so much but… I don't want to die.'

The figure closed her mouth, lifting an icicled index finger which she reached towards him. 'Don't!' he begged, voice faltering. Her finger found its destination, imparting its glacial shock onto his burning forehead. His breath failed with the connection, and the last thing he heard was the screaming warning of a streetcar's impending horn.

*

Melling gasped for oxygen, writhing in the sweat-laden sheets of his bed. He immediately jumped up to search for the haunting spectre of his wife.

Nothing.

The window was closed, and the moonbeams that had forced their way through the curtains illuminated an empty chamber. She was gone. In angst, he ran his hand over the bell of his wrist, overcome with relief when he felt the slight friction of the cold contours.

What did it all mean? He had already considered himself awake, so had it been a hallucination engendered by his subconscious? Or had he dreamt that he was not asleep? Poignantly returning to his damp sheets, he stayed upright in contemplation.

Make peace with your buried emotions, Calmet had instructed. Was he any closer? He had tried to deny any semblance of reconciliation. He felt that tomorrow night she would haunt him still.

He tiptoed out of bed, careful not to disturb Starling's much needed rest, and helped himself to a glass of Scotch and a seat. He reached for his silver cigar case and pulled a *Romeo y Julieta* free. After lighting it, he exhaled his sadness, seeing visions of Lorelei in between every wisp of smoke. He hated himself in that moment for two reasons. Firstly, he loathed that his mind was perverting the coveted image he had of her. Now, when he closed his eyes, he saw her snarling grin biting over his copper trinket. He used to only see her playful indifference to anything supposedly serious. What's more however, he hated the fact that he had been outmanoeuvred by the controlling murderers of Huxley College, and he loathed to think how many more there were in this depraved cult of irrational inducement. He had no refuge. Night-time he was haunted by his former love, daytime by scholars from his past.

He had however, mentally already begun his counterattack. He had phoned his superior, Chief Artegal, who had promised to provide the men and arresting power, granting them the full authority of the Crown in their overrunning of the Huxshire Police. Yet his boss would only offer new recruits, and he hardly wanted anyone to have a weapon. Artegal wanted to keep Melling as the only experienced and reputable man in Huxley. Unfortunately, that would make things harder for the detective. It would suit his objective if things were kept quiet, but he was feeling the pressure of sole responsibility. Artegal wished to keep things clean not in terms of attack, but in terms of the aftermath.

'Don't blow half the damn university up,' he had coughed into the receiver. Melling wasn't sure the man properly appreciated the gravity of the situation. He was always under the pressure of someone else's reputation, leading to a smothering of carnage; it was like throwing a grenade into a cave. In Britain there was always a reputation to consider, and Melling understood that this was part of Huxley's problem. Reputations should not just be inherited, then propagated through ideals alone. They had to be continuously re-evaluated, re-earned. Above all, reputation couldn't become an obstacle for justice.

Melling had asked if his friend Harry Saturn could come as a civilian. He would need someone with experience whom he trusted. He also knew Huxley well and had a stellar war record: both would be helpful. Artegal had acquiesced. Calmet Traum had originally been overwhelmed by what he heard but, showing himself a true gallant amongst a sea of culprits, pledged himself to the cause. Harry was no less sickened to the heart but vowed to help gather a troop of Melling's colleagues from Scotland Yard and take the earliest train to Huxley in the morning. They would probably arrive by midday if Melling was lucky.

Melling's idea was to take the university *and* the police station simultaneously. Nevertheless, it would be difficult to orchestrate such a manoeuvre under the circumstances. The simple avenue of academic attack would be arresting Master Dunfield, though one had to make sure he was arrested in-time with the Huxshire takeover. A simple idea, harder to execute. Melling instinctively saw Dunfield in some sort of arch position, so he planned to use him the way armies used to take capital cities, hoping that the rest of the country would then capitulate. But take him too early and the police might catch wind; inversely, take Huxshire first and Dunfield and his colleagues might escape. Take someone high enough up the leader board and names could be revealed later, so he couldn't afford to lose the man. Then they had to consider the arrival of support: too many bodies leaving the train station might notify the wrong person before things could be implemented. One just didn't know who might be on the side of Huxley's debauched society of murderers. Who might be watching them for just such a move?

Melling had intentionally left things alone to make it seem like he had taken Sergeant Lynne at his word, but it was likely he was still under scrutiny.

Yet, as far as Melling had come to understand who his enemy was, the motives behind these truth-pursuing academics were still unsolved. The true identity of Huxley's evils demanded many theories, and Melling itched for the full story. To him, some form of pseudo-philosophical cult seemed likely, and he was impatient to bring them to justice – perhaps too impatient. Sitting in Starling's living room, for a moment Melling was reminded of a case which he had taken in Germany in the fifties. Children had gone missing, and the clues left behind had also taken to the perverse. He shuddered at the uncomfortable memory. British reputation had also played a key part in shaping misery back then, and it had seemed impossible for the detective to make heads or tails of anything. However, with Huxley, minor details had begun to reach the outskirts of sense.

The ritualistic nature of Lucy's death supported the notion of some suggestion of cult or religious suicide, and the fact that Judy had used the same symbol signalled a defining emblem. Ideologies required symbols to latch onto. This was a social rule that was often overlooked. Even evil could become seductive when symbols were at play. He had gone to war in opposition to those who had truly understand that notion. Ideology was powerful. It was, conversely, also the reason that suppressive regimes censored the intellectuals first. Subversion originated in intelligence. He understood clearly that the academically minded students of Huxley were especially malleable to such indoctrination. They were at the foothold of new thinking, and indeed, were encouraged to see themselves as the pioneers of thought. This supercharged the bias of authority, allowing those young student-philosophers who sought to understand truth to meet death with a smile. Were all those under influence as altered and obsessed as Judy Collier? That seemed unlikely. Perhaps there were those who took longer to take. A cold flush of horror stole through him.

What if they resisted? He grew more impatient at the notion, wrestling with himself to remain seated, fixating on Judy's tears. Why had she cried? This too, unnerved him. In all his years as a detective, he had never failed to distinguish between crocodile tears and genuine weeping. No. Those tears were real.

The sound of a door closing somewhere along Starling's road caught his attention. He glanced at his watch. Almost one in the morning. Strange to be up this hour. He remembered that he had in fact been the one to prove this statement, bewitched by his dreams into walking onto Apollonia's Bridge. This sprouted a vague remembrance of his interview with Judy Collier.

'I'd like to know why on earth you were there, at that time of night, in the first place?' he had asked. It was ironic for him to direct such a line of questioning when he too had ventured there in the witching hours. But she had played with that irony, hadn't she?

'I have trouble sleeping,' had been her excuse, as would his have been in light of his night-time wanderings. He choked on his smoke. He would have had to say the same!

'The same,' he muttered in astonishment. His mouth dropped open, and he hardly managed to catch his falling cigar.

I hear I'm not the only one.

Yes! She had thrown the accusation back onto him. Her smile had carried a hint of triumph. Certainly, how could she possibly have known unless she had seen him? The notion was ridiculous then... but now? Why would she have come out that night at all? She could not possibly have been on the bridge, for they would have seen her. She had no cause to be out, surely? Was she visiting the place of her deceased lover, perhaps? He shook his head at his own conjecture. It seemed unlikely. But where would she be going to? Understanding slowly dripped into his churning thoughts. It accumulated first as a puddle, then gradually flooded into full comprehension.

He shot up from his seat and raced to Starling's door, rousing his host from a peaceful sleep.

'What is it?' he asked in alarm, no doubt expecting the detective to be engaged in some nightmarish danger. 'Are you alright. Are you *really* awake?'

'Yes, yes, I'm fine. But we must get dressed now. Right now!'

'What for?' his friend asked, rubbing sleep-deprived eyes. Melling tore open his curtains to illuminate the room in moonlight.

'Quickly!'

He raced to his room and threw on the clothes which had been laid out for tomorrow. Once dressed, he returned to hasten the doctor to the door.

'Let's go!'

'To where?' Starling said with a sleep-hungry whine, growing more tense.

'I know where it's all happening,' Melling said triumphantly, and he grinned.

'*What?*'

'I know where the bastards are!'

XXV

So Dark are Earthly Things

They were outside in the frightening cold of Huxley's old town, staring at the deadened streets. A shallow level of thick fog had accumulated, lapping at the gentlemen's ankles.

'Where are we going?' Starling asked.

'One hundred and twenty-five,' Melling whispered as they stood on the reddish cobblestones. 'Do you remember where we saw that number?'

'Of course, it was carved onto one of Judy's puppets.'

'Exactly. Since then, I have been conjuring infinity and more scenarios as to its relevance and well, nothing was satisfactory. But then I asked myself why Judy Collier had said that she wasn't the only one who had trouble sleeping. Do you remember?'

'I do,' Starling muttered. 'It had felt like she was trying to win the argument.'

'Precisely, Louis. I realise *now* that she was.'

'But how could she have seen you?'

'She *must* have seen me. But why and where? Not on the bridge.'

'Because then we would have seen her in the town's opening,' Starling quickly reasoned.

'I inferred the same. But we walked through the town back this way.' He traced the downward path to illustrate his narrative, then he pointed his finger to the immense castle that roared in the moonlight above them. Her spires pierced the darkness beyond, scraping the surface of some northward hell. 'To get to Trinity, one needs to start from the ascent to our left. Which means, she may have passed us if she had come down the path from above.'

'But that leads from the castle?'

'Indeed, it does,' Melling affirmed with a grin. 'Which brings us to our number.'

'How?'

'One of the castle's many mysteries,' he said, looking to Huxley Hill.

'The sundial!' Starling said in budding realisation.

'Precisely. A sundial whose gnomon is exactly one and a quarter metres in length.'

Starling smiled in bewilderment, muttering a half-earnest notion of disbelief.

'I don't believe it.'

'One point two-five metres; enter our lucky numbers.'

'Seems slightly conjectured,' Starling mused, always a sobering voice.

'That it does… but hear me further. If Judy had seen us, she would almost certainly have needed to be returning from the castle to cross our path without us being able to see her. If so, she was coming from that direction at an hour when she really ought not to hold any sort of business at the castle. Knowing now what we do about our ritualistic enemies, the sundial's gnomon seems the likely origin of Judy's numerical fixation. There might be some history which we never knew.'

Starling began to pale.

'I always entertained the mystery as just that: entertainment, in truth thinking it was just a trivial matter, but maybe…'

'It *is* particular enough to Huxley's history to actually hold a mysterious truth.'

'So, do you think we can maybe get a glimpse of who these people are?' Starling asked, gesturing towards the castle.

'Well, it would be ridiculous to assume we'll be lucky enough to catch them in the act of anything particular. But at the moment, I can't sleep, and I am itching to investigate any sort of clues to confirm my theory. It's a reach – that's for sure, and yet, if they do their deeds in the dark, then maybe there are some clues to be found during twilight hours. After all, to catch a thief, you need to wake with the thieves.'

Melling looked up at the mass of darkness, where the moonlight had managed to outline the figure of the imperious Huxley Castle. Its arrogant glare challenged the detective.

'As if I'll be able to sleep after this. I say we investigate.'

*

In some darkened parody of Fleuraline's meadows which lay to the opposing side of Huxley, where the cobble-stone streets began to fade away in the face of luscious and vivacious grasses, Huxley Hill, inversely, grew less alive with every increase of incline. The detective noted how the streets began to be replaced by unpaved mud, with the roots of neglected trees sprouting forth unseeingly, as if to grab at the fleeting ankles of passers-by. The town's mist had likewise abandoned them, and both gentlemen felt increasingly alone as they walked up the uncaring terrain, rising towards the threatening abode of former Huxley barons. Looking behind through the ever-autumnal branches of leafless trees, so bare and broken that they were hardly living, the dying glints of Huxley's lampposts seemed to twinkle their condolences from afar in honour of the detritus that lay around.

'I forgot about this,' Starling suddenly said, and Melling returned his gaze upwards, finding the moss-devoured tombstones of the old settlers who had been buried in the outer grounds of the castle. 'You know that they ran out of space here, supposedly?' Melling said as they walked past the black railings which separated them from the hundreds of gravestones, all cracked, dirtied, and forgotten.

'It's true. One of the plague years struck Huxley particularly badly.'

'Did they really dump bodies in the river?'

'You would have thought that they might have known better, being enlightened. They say that the real reason was due to a shortage of men, as well as horses, who were willing to bring the bodies up to the main burial ground.'

Melling shuddered. Society used to be so different. Borderline alien. He wondered how future generations would look back on his lifetime.

They left the buried behind; their only company the gangling arms of leafless trees scraping along the black earth. They walked on to where the terrain became muddier until they rounded a corner, putting them face to face with the threatening glory of Huxley Castle. In the magnificent lux of the full moon, Melling was momentarily astonished by the ruby shine of the proud and expansive stained glass windows. They were embedded inside the tall walls of Norman stone which pierced the cloudless sky, with one hundred slivers of light escaping through the numerous turrets. The grassless land melted into the lower foundations of reinforced rock, and Melling was dwarfed under the medieval glare before him. 'So, what now?'

'I must confess that I hadn't really thought beyond this moment. It is unlikely someone is here tonight, but we do need to be careful. We need some sort of vantage where we can see everything. Besides, we still need to get inside.'

Starling nodded.

'The original Baron Huxley didn't allow for many hidden passages. He was a paranoid man apparently, so wanted his guests and guards readily visible. If there is anyone here already, then it may be too risky to...'

A sense of rebellion suddenly reached his eyes, and he adopted a mad sort of grin. 'There could be a way, though you have to be prepared for a slight climb and, well, best not to discuss it now.'

Melling was not assured by this sense of potentiality, but something in Starling's gaze made him too excited to question things. If Starling had an idea, he would follow it.

Hugging the darkness, Starling guided them in a stealthy manner, keeping to the shadows to remain in obscurity. They wandered around the outer walls of the castle which had met their share of corrosion. Melling noted that the Norman stone which had built these foundations was crumbling with time, fading with the hands that ran their tourist fingers across the material. Soon, they were at the castle's rear. 'We're at the motte-and-bailey,' Starling elucidated, guiding Melling into a grassier terrain than the front. 'Do you remember it?'

Melling stole a glance behind him, then nodded at Starling in the affirmative.

The motte was the feudal mound which hoisted the stone structure of defence above it, otherwise called the keep. Most keeps had been built on artificial earth in the Middle Ages, but Baron Huxley had relied on a natural mound that had originated long before any settlers had set foot in Huxley's verdurous land. The keep was a classically Romanesque design, with the same tint of brown as its stone. It peered over the structure to its left, the bailey, which was the fortified rear of the castle. Despite the peaceful existence of the original settlers, the Baron had seen himself as a sort of William the Conqueror, owing to his French ancestry. This was why the structure was Norman in design. Melling watched the moon glare through the turrets and plain windows, finding it difficult to picture just how he was supposed to climb the battlement. 'This way,' Starling urged, walking towards the right side of the tall mound, where a stone wall seemed to step down its side like a jagged staircase. The detective watched, in surprise, as Starling began scaling the grass of the mound until he was able to climb, with some difficulty, onto the side of the wall.

'Where did you get this wild idea?' Melling whispered loudly, offering a shoulder of support.

'I'll explain when we're in,' the latter said, clambering to his feet, then helping Melling find his way in turn.

With some grunting efforts, he hoisted himself up the wall, just like his companion had done; they began their trepid walk. It was slippery and, once or twice, Melling had to interrupt cowardly thoughts as the gradient steepened. Starling had never seemed so alive, poised like a predator; now however, as they reached the outer walls of the keep, he had his heart in his throat. He stared down the twenty-metre drop which separated them from safety: a small vantage which connected two towers. They would need to jump down onto it. 'I remember reading about a riot when the second Baron Huxley was in power. The townsfolk wanted to protest the fact that a university was to be built within the town. The locals had snuck in from the rear in just the same manner as we are doing now,' Starling whispered.

'Protesting education in our way,' Melling said. 'So, now what?'

Starling nodded to the vantage. 'Seriously?'

'With the high-stakes, I figured: in for a penny, you know?' Then his voice drooped like a flower. 'I never realised it was so high.'

'We can always turn back, Louis,' the detective offered, but his host shook his head with resolution. 'Well then,' Melling muttered, looking down. In the twilight, he couldn't see the ground, but one would certainly *feel* it. His lingering eyes saw less than his imagination. He heard the rush of midnight wind that would guide him to his destination. He leaned forward. His fingertips tingled.

'Robert?'

'Right, sorry,' Melling said, shuddering. He brought his eyes back to the vantage.

'How should we do it?' Starling asked, but Melling knew that talking would only lead to talking oneself out of the deed. So, before he could think too long about it, he leapt onto the vantage, landing with a heavy boot and curse. It was not elegant, but he was safe. It took a few cajoles and curses until Starling was beside him; they laughed at themselves for a moment until Starling led the way into the tower and down a staircase. All that Melling could hear was the sound of his breathing and the muted thuds of his footsteps, until they escaped into a poorly illuminated walkway. Starling was more confident of his whereabouts now, guiding Melling past statues and portraits until they found an open landing which surveyed the main courtyard. The beams of the ceiling around him seemed to be made of ivory; they had been ribbed in the Norman style, making chevrons of zigzagging mouldings.

They looked across at the moonlit courtyard, eyeing the copper sundial, a brilliant bronze under the moon's rays. This was what they had come for. There was no one.

'What now?' Starling asked in cautious whisper. Melling glanced back at the doctor, exhaling nervously.

'I needed to confirm my own theory, but now that I'm here, I'm not sure how to do that.'

'Well, I can't see anyone, so it's probably safe to explore.'

'Maybe this was a stupid idea.'

'No,' Starling interrupted. 'I know exactly why you wanted to come. With all the mystery, you've craved some sort of answer, and the idea of this place and this dial seems to provide one.'

'I'm not sure why I anticipated something other than this empty courtyard. I mean, what was I really expecting? Dunfield and an animal head?'

Starling shook his head with a half-smile.

'That would probably raise more questions than answers.'

Then, Starling walked across the landing to survey the halls from above, all of which led to the sundial. 'But it doesn't even look like there's so much as a night manager around.' He turned to Melling. 'Shall we walk?'

The detective nodded.

They made their way down winding stone steps towards the lower level until the light of the moon led them to the courtyard. Melling looked at the dial in all its midnight glory. The copper was well maintained, lacking even the tiniest blue imperfection. Clearly the locals took pride in their history, and Melling now wondered if there might be another reason for this maintenance. 'No animal head,' Starling murmured, but as he did so, both gentlemen were startled by an altogether different noise. It was faint and seemed to come from the floor of the courtyard itself. In fact, it was more of a low vibration. Both men froze. 'What was that?' Starling whispered as the noise passed again. Melling shook his head. It was now landing like a distant hum. His pulse quickened as this hum grew, seeming to emanate from the walls of the courtyard. It was as though the centuries-old stones were groaning. The noise amplified once more, and Starling offered a panicked stare. Melling motioned to exit.

They scarpered up to the landing from which they had first surveyed the courtyard. Mindful of being noticed, Melling rested his head against the cool stone of a thick pillar, concealing himself behind the medieval material without barring his vision. Starling following the detective's suit by hiding himself behind another pillar.

'Something's happening!' he said in aggressive whisper. Something *was* happening. The hum had become even louder and affirmed Melling's stance on what the noise was: it was humming itself, and it had reached a frightful crescendo.

It was chanting.

It was people.

People, coming from somewhere, were calling in unison, now in such a harmonised horror that the darkened courtyard seemed wide awake. Neither Melling nor Starling could initially identify just who this twilight chorus were. But then…

'God in heaven.'

Figures were striding through the courtyard in a march towards the sundial, all robed in red like monks in velvet ruby. There must have been at least ten of them, all moving in single file, chanting together, voices carrying into Huxley's moonlit sky. Their music was well-rehearsed, pitches prowling along with purpose so that the very air seemed to oscillate. The ground grovelled and the walls whispered in response. Melling's eardrums pinched like the sound of a clinked wineglass.

As the first figure reached the sundial the course diverted slightly, and sure enough, they snaked around the copper mechanism, maximising its circumference by circling around its outline. The meaning behind the singing was inaudible despite its volume, becoming even less pierceable when all the figures assembled: the group became eerily quiet, now murmuring their incantations into a mystifying whisper that dispersed like vapour.

'What are they saying?' Starling asked, carefully quiet, but Melling watched on in silence, his heartbeat audible inside his skull.

After two more minutes of chanting, they all stopped, as if on cue. There was a loud silence for a few moments until the figure furthest from the detective rolled down his hood, revealing the dark grey hair of Master Dunfield. Seeing the man, Melling's first reaction was to choke back a startled cry.

I was right.

He could hardly think. He hadn't even noticed Starling's catlike crawling, but the doctor was suddenly beside him, placing a warm hand on his frightened shoulder.

'You were right. You were bloody right about all of it.'

'We were right to call London. Clearly this is a bigger group than we understood. Who knows how many they are?'

'Someone's coming.'

In walked a figure with the same robe of darkened red, but behind him trailed three wide-eyed students in college gowns. A blonde boy and girl were whispering excitedly to a brunette, and the robed figure stopped before the dial and bowed. Melling couldn't believe how chance was finally on his side. He was finally meeting the truth.

There was silence from all for a while. Then Master Dunfield finally spoke, his lyrical voice resonating around the stone walls of the Norman court. Melling was again disturbed by how handsome the man was despite his age.

'Courtier Robora. Welcome back to Huxley.'

The person rose and dropped his hood, revealing a gentleman with thinning brown hair. He could not have been more than thirty, and his aquiline face held all the semblance of aristocracy.

'So here is the famous Robora,' Melling muttered. Here was the man he had been told to be in awe of from the start. He now understood why he was able to translate Lucy's suicide note. He had given her the

Platonist ideals in the first place. He may as well have co-signed the letter to her mother.

'Courtier Dunfield,' the professor replied to the master, his voice not quite as able to pass throughout the castle's court. 'I have carried out my ordered duties. Now that I have returned, I am at last able to present to you,' he then motioned around the court. 'To you all: our new *umbrae*.'

'Shadows,' Starling whispered in translation of the Latin.

'Well let us indeed,' the master sang, opening his arms in welcome, 'remove the obstacles to the light of truth, once and for all.' There was a cheer from the robed figures, who descended upon the students in applause and congratulations. Melling wasn't sure whether to feel alarmed or to laugh at the hyperbole of the process. The students appeared overwhelmed. They smiled and giggled for all the world as if they were the sole honour of some fête or degree.

'Do they actually know what they're joining?' Starling asked, but Melling shrugged. Some of the figures had broken off and returned with similar robes of red, which the juvenile trio traded-in for their black gowns.

'With this shift of attire,' the master shouted, 'we witness the brave choice you have all made. Putting on these robes, you abandon the constrictions of your studies and open yourselves up to the pursuit of life's true ambition: the truth!'

There was a murmur of excitement from the hooded members.

'They seem too naïve to know the significance,' Melling whispered to Starling. 'I have read a great deal on such matters, and well, the indoctrination can be slow. Often, it is the promise of disclosing the unknown which seduces the victims.'

'They don't look like victims to me,' Starling said, shaking his head, and Melling just sighed in quiet acquiescence. The students were overjoyed by these robes and what they represented. Seeing such confident, jovial faces, one could easily forget the disappearing body of Judy Collier, walking to her death.

Professor Robora made the three students kneel before the dial, and the robed spectres sat cross-legged in their original positions. Dunfield walked slowly to Robora's side, and paused in front of the first, the blonde boy, who stared at the man's feet in trepidation.

'*Tenebris!*' Dunfield shouted.

'*In lucem!*' the boy roared in reply. He was still staring at the floor, and Melling felt the singular hairs on his arms tingle in disgust as Master Dunfield tapped the boy's head. The student, who had clearly been informed of the ritual, looked up, and slowly rose to his feet. He took the master's wrinkled hand and kissed it. Melling squirmed.

'Courtier Michaels. Welcome to your journey into the light!' When the man spoke, it was as though the moon had spotlighted him, the music of his voice rising with the vapour of his breath. There was a round of applause and cheering from the gathering, save from Robora, who stood controllingly beside the two girls who were still silently kneeling. 'Welcome to liberation!' Dunfield yelled again, earning applause. 'You may join your fellow courtiers.'

The boy rushed off to join the circle, and the exact process was then repeated for each of the girls, both of them passionately yelling their rehearsed phrase, then kissing their innocent lips on the guilty fingers of Master Gabriel Dunfield.

When the initiates had withdrawn to the circle, all hoods faced Dunfield. He was once more spotlighted by the moon. His voice penetrated the entire courtyard, singing along the creaking Huxley wind.

'*Credo ut intelligam.* We believe so that we may know. For centuries, Huxley has housed some of the world's brightest minds and deepest thinkers. Huxley's finest have changed and re-changed the world every decade, but,' he paused, shaking his head. 'But many amongst us are still living life through a narrow tunnel. Reason and rationality allow a man to navigate the world, but this is no mechanism for the soul!' The leader was impassioned, and one could feel the transfixation of the entire robed mass. Something palpably spiritual was happening. 'Mathematics cannot be one's rudder into truth, nor science a sail for the spirit. As a keeper of the truth, as a courtier, it is my duty to make the most important distinction for my *umbrae*: the material as opposed to the metaphysical – that which only philosophers have had the courage to illustrate. As Huxley students, you are all too aware of the material. Academia is the arch analyser of the physical world, for knowledge behaves as a lifeboat on the ocean. Knowledge is buoyancy. Knowledge allows a man to be superior, to overtake, to manage, to discover. But knowledge is not necessarily truth. For what truth are we even speaking of? *Umbrae*,' the man implored, walking up to the young initiates. 'I beg of you to recognise that though your minds are some of the sharpest in your generation, you are only racing ahead on the plane of the material. What can your books, your studies and your conclusions offer you in the afterlife? How can your knowledge of *earthly* things translate into a knowledge of that which exists beyond the tellurian or the terrestrial? False knowledge is not truth, it is misleading misdirection. You may conquer the world's challenges, but your soul may wither and starve in the process. Do not neglect the metaphysical in favour of the material! Knowledge is not necessarily truth, for one must know beyond the plane of reality to truly pierce the divine! Your eyes and your ears are liars! They remind you of existence: they keep you ensconced inside a narrow tunnel of what you can perceive. But…'

At this point he let silence speak for an aggravating minute. 'You are the most fortunate scholars in your generation, for you have already realised that there is more to knowing than what you are currently able to know. Many priests have spent their days saying that a rich man could never pass through the needle eye of heaven. Since that is a well-grasped idea, let us adapt the parable. A man who spends all his time reading romances will soon find it hard to find love in real life; his notions of what romance should be are based on false images. This is our rich man: weighed down by the heaviness of his fabricated ideals. He cannot afford true romance with the lies he has bought. The lies he learns. The lies he propagates as his own experience. This too is humanity, for all of us are trapped by our ideas and so-called knowledge, thinking that what we have experienced is the true essence of things, when what we experience is but a smudge on the glass of truth. We are all the rich man, weighed down by the material, sinking in the sand of false knowledge, destined to stare up at the divine and sigh. However!'

Another aggravating minute passed as the man walked slowly around the dial. 'There are some of us who have managed to shake loose from materiality's shackles. Some have looked above the clustered chaos of society and what people are destined to call real life – that which is unreal. Real is referential, and our points of view feel so natural that to lose them would be alien. You three,' he thundered, pointing at each of the students. They were the only people besides Dunfield and Robora whose hoods were down. 'You have stood on the highest branches of academic success and used such training to open your minds and understand that, yes, there is a greater, finer, more divine truth to things. You have begun to think beyond the material. Beyond convention, beyond shapes and nouns. You have begun to consider outside of what has been offered as explanations... what your studies can offer you. You have started to deconstruct yourselves. Who else but such bright minds as yourselves could do so? Your intellect doubts beyond what has always been dreamed up as fact. Your enlightenment predecessors were some of the last humans to both doubt and dream in unison, questioning all and proving everything. You take up their baton tonight, in the season of rebirth!' At this final line there was a huge cheer, followed by rapturous applause.

'We are in the season,' Robora repeated in a reedy voice, taking over from the leader. 'Where the smartest are smart enough to identify all they do not know. The time has come for true discovery! There is a symmetry to such a time, for as we accept and guide these new courtiers on the pathway towards liberation, we do so in proximity to the final breaths of others. We say farewell to some of Huxley's bravest, looking up with a grin and tear, knowing that they are now at rest with the truth, or soon will be.'

'*In lucem,*' Dunfield intoned, followed by shouts of repetition from the others.

'*Credo ut intelligam,*' Robora responded, echoing Dunfield's earlier phrasing. 'The hardest element of finding the truth is the sacrifice required in discovery: we believe in order that we may know. The divine is at the end of our existence; we cannot meet the divine unless our existence ends.'

'*In lucem!*' Dunfield shouted. Now the chanting began anew, this time with hands interlocked.

Robert Melling did not fully grasp all that Dunfield's monologue had meant, but that mattered little. He understood perfectly what he was witnessing. Huxley housed an organisation of intellectual indoctrination, where students were being seduced down the path of truth to some supposed light. They would die for some crude blend of philosophy and the divine and...

Melling's heart began to itch. It... it...

It paced painfully. The detective started to panic.

Why was his heart beating so fast?

His vision smudged.

He worked his jaws.

They numbed.

His lips didn't feel real.

In lucem.

Dunfield and his chanting hoard grew louder until the detective's eardrums wept a high squeal. It felt like an iron bar was inside his brain. His fingers raked the stone wall.

What's happening to me?

In lucem.

His mushy mind squirmed for sense as his heart continued to throttle in alarm.

A belt was around his chest.

He wanted to scream.

'Robert,' Starling whispered, tugging his sleeve. At the contact, the detective sputtered into normality, grumbling, then sliding down the wall. He lolled his head back with a heavy exhale. His heart slowed. Panic packed away its things and... slowly... left him.

Dr Starling was watching him in horror, face to face with him now, eyes widened in shock as Melling's own were deflated. He was corpse-like to the doctor, who scanned his friend in deep worry.

'Robert, what's wrong?'

Seeing such anxious eyes, Melling immediately plunged into the stone water of the present. He waved the man's worry away, and clambered to his feet.

'Nothing,' he said, voice a gravelly croak. The courtyard tilted; Melling managed to stay upright.

What had happened?

'Robert...' Starling whispered insistently, but the detective offered his best attempt at an easy smile, nodding his head back to the courtyard. Starling was *not* convinced, but the spectacle of the chanting robes was enough to distract him, or at least to keep him quiet.

Melling left them chanting as he vivisected his spirit, seeing the group, but not noticing them. His mind's eye was inward, analysing this new feeling of panic. It had been a sudden attack, like when he would wake up in bed, seized by a heavy dread. His heart had only ever betrayed him at night, when his psyche was the most slippery. He had never felt such an overpowering before he had closed his eyes.

It's spreading.

He had to accept it. His condition was worsening, no doubt triggered by Dunfield's lunacy.

Is that where I am heading? Lunacy.

Sooner or later, as he had tried to tell Constable Whaites back at Horsham station, the man who internalises his vexations was destined to scream at the moon.

He certainly wanted to scream now, after witnessing this chanting hoard initiate three new students. That this could have grown from the foundations of academia made logical sense, but it was still sickening. If he and Starling hadn't witnessed these students pledge their own death, then their days would have been numbered. Melling, if he acted correctly, could enforce order onto this madness. He could save these youngsters before the bridge's ledge was a cemented thought in their minds.

The detective had lost his focus; he seemed to have blinked, and the scene had changed. All the so-named courtiers were now standing before a small set of weighing scales.

'What's on the balance?' he asked, straining to see.

'Nothing.'

Then, every member of the group procured a white feather, roughly twenty centimetres in length, from inside their robes. The detective wanted to punch himself! How could he have forgotten about Judy's feather? He recalled handing the feather to the sergeant, reanalysing how the man had viewed it.

Where'd you find that?

He had eyed it so mysteriously. Was he too, one of those hooded deceivers? He had to be. After all, he had lied about going to Marlowe. Was he amongst them now? Melling would give anything to run in, gun raised, lowering every single one of their hoods. A stronger part of him wanted to toss a grenade right into the midnight mass.

The members, one by one, placed their individual feathers on the left scale of the balance, until only that of Dunfield's was absent. The scale had dipped ever so slightly under the gentle pressure of soft white.

'New courtiers! By joining us in this ritual, you are drawing attention to another reason that you have been chosen. You see, we do not only seek those who seek to understand. We seek those who *deserve* to undertake that journey towards understanding. Those, who know what is right, and are willing to hang the colour of their souls in the balance.'

'I am pure,' the boy said twice, who was followed by each of the girls in procession. Dunfield placed his own feather on the other side of the balance, then shouted his omen:

'*Tenebris...*'

'*...in lucem!*' the red figures responded. The stone court was draped in silence, with only the cooling wind of the early morning.

Tenebris in lucem.

Melling knew what it meant.

From darkness into light.

XXVI

Magic That Hath Ravished Me

'See, it says it right here,' Starling said, pointing to the dusted page of an old index on Huxley. He read the information aloud to Robert Melling and Calmet Traum; they were standing in the German doctor's library. 'The copper sundial was installed in 1867 at the request of the university, donated by an academic institution from within the university itself.'

'You're sure that the dial was one and a quarter metres in length?' Calmet asked, earning a nod from both gentlemen. 'And about the feathers in balance too?'

'Saw it with my own eyes, Calmet,' Starling maintained. 'Why, what do you know?'

The German tapped his foot nervously, then found a dark-burgundy armchair to light a cigarette. He sank into his seat and exhaled his nerves.

'Have either of you gentlemen heard of Richard Lepsius?'

Neither the detective nor Starling were able to answer in the affirmative. 'Well then,' Calmet muttered, oozing deeper into his armchair. 'He was a 19th century academic, and a prominent Egyptologist.'

'Did he have anything to do with the symbol you translated for us?' Melling asked, but Calmet shook his head. He was deeply disturbed by something.

'*Nein*. But he was the first to introduce the world to the Book of the Dead.'

'The Book of the Dead?'

'Since the writings on tomb walls in the Old Kingdom, the Egyptians believed that when a person died, their soul would navigate the underworld, governed by the god Osiris. He, alongside forty-two judges, would determine if the person was worthy of paradise.'

'This book, explains that?' Melling asked. Again, Calmet shook his head.

'Not really. You see, before one could even reach their ultimate judgement, they had to pass through various evils that could end up leaving them tortured forever. So, spells and manuals were created that could be buried with the dead, and help the soul reach the hall of truth.'

'The hall of truth?' Starling repeated, sitting on a sand-brown sofa.

'Yes, where Anubis would provide a balance that could weigh the deceased's heart against the feather of truth, which belonged to the goddess of justice: Maat.'

'My God,' Melling said excitedly, interrupting Calmet. 'Louis, try and remember what the inspector had described about Lucy's funeral service. Someone had cited, what was it, some Egyptian scripture to see her off,' he quoted. 'This must be it!'

'Well,' Calmet continued with growing concern. 'If the heart was lighter than Maat's feather, then the person had lived an honest life and could pass over to paradise. But, if they had not, well, then they were devoured.'

His words were left unanswered for a few moments as both Starling and Melling attempted to piece together what they had heard. It was then that more details returned to the detective.

'Remember what Judy said about Samuel! She had called him pure, remember? She had pronounced it in such a horrifyingly matter-of-fact way.'

'You're right,' Starling whispered.

'Heart as a feather, I believe, were her exact words!'

'But none of this makes any sort of sense,' Starling said. 'This Egyptian death book says how to survive the underworld, but aren't these students dying to reach some sort of philosophical truth?'

'Dunfield's speech was pretty clear about that,' Melling said in agreement. 'Knowing beyond earthly things requires one to say goodbye to earthly things.'

'Well, maybe these scales are more symbolic of the journey they're taking?' Calmet offered.

'Symbols and ritual *are* a necessity for such groups to function,' Melling said. Then after some moments, he began to see that he was perhaps taking the wrong line of thought. 'I think we're treating this too much as a Huxley problem.'

'Meaning?'

'Right now, we're caught in the Huxley daydream, assuming that because this is an elite institution, things need to reach some sort of higher-level explanation. However, let's just appreciate that wherever it is found, a suicide cult will always be an absurd idea. Not even Huxley should be allowed to explain away the ridiculous.'

'Right you are,' Calmet muttered.

'What I am saying,' Melling said to Starling, 'is that none of this can possibly make sense in *any* setting. I have read into such indoctrinating circles before, and the simple fact is that they are never without mismatched historical embellishment. A glance towards the past always helps to cement a notion of mysticism or ancient credibility, when in reality, we would never expect a future generation to use our modern day in such a way, centuries down the line, right? As if the letters L or N, for example, could have the same gravity centuries later in the same manner through which a hieroglyph betokens the divine, or the unknowable? Our daily symbols could become mysterious to future historians.'

'What you're suggesting is that this book Calmet is referencing is more of an embellishment?'

'Even Huxley is young compared to Egypt,' Melling replied. 'They didn't mention Egypt at all last night, but the ritual was there. Clearly, it's the ceremonious weighing of the scales which not only helps cement the ideas of their philosophy, but sanctifies it. The language they use: pulling from Plato, the Enlightenment, Egypt. It's all coded to shroud their doctrine in transcendent proof. They draw across time and the globe to highlight an overarching thesis: the overarching truth that awaits us all.'

'I follow you,' Starling said. 'What was his name, again?' he added with a turn to Calmet. 'The man who wrote the book?'

'Richard Lepsius,' Calmet said. 'But I should say he translated and compiled rather than he wrote it, but in any case, it was chapter one hundred and twenty-five in Lepsius' publication which outlined this process of the heart and feather.'

'The sundial's length,' Starling blurted.

Calmet Traum nodded solemnly.

'I don't believe it,' Melling muttered. 'And it really bothers me that they would use such ancient thinking to provide a moralistic element to their philosophy.' He thought back to the speech Dunfield had given at the castle not seven hours ago. 'That eligibility. We seek those who deserve to undertake that journey. That's what Dunfield said. His exact words were: those willing to hang the colour of their souls in the balance.'

'I am pure,' Starling added. 'The students all repeated that.'

Calmet's brows lowered in greater concern, especially when Melling reminded both of them that Judy had described Samuel in the same way.

Heart as a feather.

'If I am not mistaken,' the German doctor said flatly. 'Saying that you are pure is part of the spells through which souls were meant to navigate the Egyptian underworld. Perhaps your master feels that his students must show themselves to be pure before they can reach paradise, in this case: truth?' Calmet was growing further distressed by his own suggestions. There was something which weighed on him in particular – Melling could tell.

'*Credo ut intelligam,*' the detective replied flatly, following Dunfield's Latin. 'They kept saying one needed to start with belief before they could reach true knowledge. Eligibility seems to run parallel with that. The moral aspect was strangely Christian too. They mentioned the soul and the divine, but that may just illustrate their ideas.'

Calmet did not respond; he was muttering to himself, eyes filled with something the detective could not decipher.

'I am not sure I can ignore it any longer,' he whispered.

'Ignore what?' Melling asked.

'I wished it was not so… but must I be forced to think of it… must it be… Hermeticism?'

'Hermeticism?' Melling asked, clinging onto the last word.

'It began in Alexandria in the first few common centuries, when the Greek god Hermes was joined with the Egyptian Thoth, of wisdom. Together they made this being they called Hermes Trismegistus.' He was no longer sitting. He marched around the room anxiously. There was an evident heaviness in his eyes.

'There are too many deities entering this conversation,' Melling said, struggling to contain Calmet's vast knowledge. 'This Trismegistus? Was he a god?'

Calmet was in a deep conversation with himself.

'Calmet?' Starling prompted, getting his attention.

'Well,' Calmet finally said, looking at the floor. 'He *was* worshipped like a deity, but he was described more as a magical author of the sacred text called the Hermetica, which outlined his opinions on the divine, alchemy and astronomy.'

'I've never heard of this,' Melling said.

'Hermeticism argued for an absolute power, or what was called: the one.' His voice was hollow as he explained.

'The one,' Starling repeated.

'We often call it the monad.'

'You mean like Neoplatonism?' Melling asked. He knew that a later form of Platonism had been obsessed with this idea of the monad. It was a singular, divine totality, separate, pure and beautiful. Calmet looked up at Melling, eyes filled with a sort of wonderment, but glazed with an immense melancholy. He spoke mechanically now, mentally elsewhere.

'Whether in the stars, or in mathematics, it represented a sort of supreme whole which one could strive towards. Its parallels with a Christian God are all too easy to identify.'

Melling knew this well. People today often overlooked the Greek influence on European Christianity. Plato's obsession with the singular, ethereal models of higher understanding, those pure, abstract ideals of reality, that which he called the forms, had pervaded western consciousness in so many ways. 'Neoplatonists were obsessed with a complete, divine source: the monad. Much like Plato, they focused on sacred perfection, but in an absolute sense, not just in terms of goodness, kindness, beauty. They thought, especially the famous Iamblichus, that magical rituals could help you to get closer to this place of perfection.' With that, he looked at the floor once more and began biting his finger again, cigarette dying in his other hand. This agitation was now really bothering Melling.

'So, what does this mean for the ritual we saw?' Starling asked.

'The ritual you saw was not theurgical in nature,' Calmet began, noting the indifferent eyes which both gentlemen showed at yet another esoteric term. 'Theurgical. What I am saying is that this ritual you saw doesn't specifically relate to this idea of the monad. That is to say, this sense of divine oneness.'

When he saw Starling and the detective nod in understanding, he continued. 'Your professors were referencing the Book of the Dead, but the Egyptian influence in Hermeticism was only borrowed. Egyptian ideas on gods and rituals were simply incorporated into Neoplatonism's way of thinking.'

'Now I am lost again,' Melling interrupted with a hopeless sigh.

'Plato is considered one of the world's greatest philosophers, yes?'

Melling nodded in agreement. 'But there were many who developed and changed his ideas in notably influential ways. Many Neoplatonists, for example as I said already, felt that certain rituals and that magic, could help you reach this ultimate power which they deemed: the one. The Egyptian practices were incorporated to help with such an outlook. You might see Hermeticism as a more mystical, ritualistic, corrupted Neoplatonism.'

'In layman's terms?' Melling asked, needing a more concrete simplicity to latch onto.

'What I am saying is that Huxley's cult seems to be highly Hermetic in nature. As you have established, they are clearly in search of some ultimate truth, like Platonists, but the rituals which they use to support their cause cannot actually be found in Plato's thinking. But their Egyptian occultism *is* highly Hermetic. Hermeticism promises ancient wisdom, similar to how these professors are promising ultimate truth. Their rejection of false knowledge in favour of a divine truth is like a Hermetic approach to the universe.'

Calmet was now back in his armchair, lighting another cigarette. He was staring at the floor. He was clearly agitated by something within himself, and Melling had a theory as to why the man had suggested this Hermeticism in the first place. Why had his mind gone there? Why had his remembrance of such ideology also arrived with a look of guilty terror? Melling wasn't sure what to ask. He was certainly already piecing matters together in a way that appreciated the fact that Calmet was evidently a well-intending man, and yet...

'You're awfully familiar with something so specific, you know?' the detective began.

Calmet nodded slowly, swallowing purposefully. 'Is there,' the detective said, sitting down on a nearby chair to appear less threatening. 'Something else you want to tell us?'

Starling looked frightened when Calmet finally raised his head. His words were solemn.

'Want and need are not the same,' he confessed with shaky breath. 'You see, detective, it is not just I who am full of revelations today. You have revealed something to me too. I wish you had not come. I had pushed these thoughts away these past days, imagining it was not related but I confess, now I must accept it is.'

Melling could see the man was more sorrowful than secretive, and so he offered him his most empathetic look.

'I wish I had not come either. Then I would not have to face the reality of things.'

Calmet exhaled heavily before responding.

'I have not seen Dr Starling for quite some time, and though he will never admit why he avoids me, it is not lost on me. I am *not* a stupid man.'

'Calmet…' Starling said, beginning his defence, but the German raised a hand for silence.

'It is not an accusation, old friend. Our minds share similar circles, and yet along the way things change. Science is our god, but we have different methods of prayer. You were always respectful to my, as they termed it, wild ideals, but once I left the university you were right to stay away.' There was some painful silence before Calmet turned to Melling.

'You see, Detective. I was disgraced.' He uttered the last word in disgust. 'As if it was what I had tried to do.'

He took five long drags before continuing. 'I took a position at the university to bring what I had been learning in Switzerland to British academia. Ours is a growing field, but with many doubters. It has taken time for Freud to be less of a cultural debate and more of a scientific prophet. I had a mentee in my early years at Huxley. She was one of the sharpest minds I have ever had the pleasure to engage with. She was always asking new questions, proposing new experiments, new interviewing techniques… new ideals.'

Melling was already seeing where this sombre story would conclude. He guessed with the conclusion of the girl's life. 'I will spare her name,' Calmet said, 'though you can find it in the papers at the time. I cannot bring myself to make her real once more.'

Starling gulped, and distant dots in his eyes were finally coming together.

'I remember,' he whispered.

'Just tell me what happened,' Melling said.

'She began to say that we were always at a limit. That it was of no importance to interview, to study, to... to test for answers. Our condition as humans made us ignorant. She began reading ancient wisdoms, including the Hermetica. I was concerned, but for a time it helped her research. She seemed *so* hungry for answers! I knew... knew something was not right but I kept my silence. In the end she took her own life for the sake of our research. She left me detailed plans of how I was to test her brain... I was...' he shook his head in disgust, smoking to stop himself talking. Both Melling and Starling were stupefied, waiting for further information. Eventually Calmet continued. 'I was horrified. I couldn't believe I had allowed myself to put my research first, and *her* second. I had failed her.'

'When was this?' Melling whispered.

'Some fifteen years ago. I was finished, of course.'

'The university held you in disgrace?'

Calmet let out a dry laugh.

'*Nein*. They wanted to *help* me. They didn't want me to punish myself, so they said. They tried to keep my name out of it. It was *I* who was finished. I moved to this side of the town and decided my days were over. But I didn't want to leave Huxley. To abandon her felt wrong. I know she was no more, but I couldn't leave. It was a long time before I set up my practice and by then the professionals were sickened by my name. I was not controversial. I was a killer. So, you see, Detective Melling, why I know so much about something so particular, and why I believe I may have discovered the ideology behind your group. It is because I have known them longer than you. I didn't *know* until you told me, but that girl was part of it. Since yesterday I had avoided my past, hoping that she was not linked. But she is. I must face that now. And, well, I have spent years reading and re-reading all that she was obsessed with, trying to find meaning. Ask me anything, for I have studied everything about it.'

'I'm really sorry this happened, Calmet,' was all Melling could say. Matters were made more real by this confession. It was patently all linked. Huxley was polluting its brightest via Hermeticism. Though Melling didn't fully understand the finer details of just what that meant, even if Calmet did, the importance of what it meant for the lives of those indoctrinated was dangerously obvious.

He was overwhelmed, especially by Calmet's confession. He would be haunted by this girl forever. 'I suppose it's a stroke of luck that it was your practice I found, Mr Traum,' Melling began quietly. 'And I'm sorry you were taken down the nightmares of memory. Starling and I can take our leave. Rest assured I will make whoever did this pay tenfold.'

Calmet's eyes dripped defiance; they also dripped tears. His voice was sterner now.

'The worst thing you could do is leave me out of it! Please, Detective, please! I have to be a part of this for *her* sake!' He was standing now. Pleading. 'And you *need* me because I have tortured myself with Hermeticism more than anyone on this earth, believe me. I had never seen this symbol until now: this inverted amenta, but you have to let me discover with you. Do you understand? I *need* to know.'

Melling stood up and placed a hand on Calmet's tense shoulder. Culpable as he was, Melling didn't blame him for his past. If anything, he rather respected the man for holding himself accountable and still trying to continue his profession. Melling squeezed the man's shoulder with a rueful smile. He decided it was probably best to keep him focused on solving the present rather than punishing himself.

'Let's start at the beginning, then. Because this philosophy is incredibly complicated. Help us.'

Calmet had more tears falling from his eyes and sniffed before smiling. '*Natürlich!* Please sit.'

*

Calmet's mood was now neither the disgraced yet enthusiastic witch doctor, nor was he the sorrowful confessor. When people disclose their greatest weights, they fall into an open calm. Calmet had nothing to prove and nothing to repent. Of course, he had a vendetta to settle with Huxley – as much if not more so than Melling. But now he was humbly sitting with newly dried eyes, quietly explaining all that he knew. He was in a state of relief. There were no pretensions in the room, just truths, questions, and answers.

Melling was still greatly confused by what Hermeticism was, and was probing the man for clarity.

'What I am saying,' Calmet attempted to explain, 'is that Hermeticism is very similar to Neoplatonism in the sense that it cannot escape Christianity's grasp. There is a sense of an inner self which is constrained by the physical world, and that certain magical rituals can lead one towards a divine singular: a wholeness, that which is called the monad. The rituals these professors enacted at the castle are highly Hermetic in nature. They stress an otherworldliness, and they relate to Egyptian scripture. The Book of the Dead has never been part of Hermeticism, but Egyptian wisdom has. Hermeticism promises ancient wisdom, rejecting the world in favour of a secret truth. Why these professors have used the Book of the Dead as a source for their rituals I am not sure, but Egyptian wisdom in general is a Hermetic approach.'

'Phew,' Melling huffed. 'So, again in layman's terms, there is some sort of unreachable spiritual whole, or truth, like a sort of god, which they might be hoping to reach?'

'Right,' Calmet said. 'The mystical secret to life is the promise through which they enact their rituals in the first place. You said that they chanted: *credo ut intelligam* – I believe so that I may understand. So, the belief in what they will find after death comes first. The rituals support this. They help them believe.'

'And the feather ritual?'

'If they are prioritising those whose souls are deemed pure, then there must be some form of selection involved.'

'Those bastards,' Melling muttered.

'Isn't it so incredible how something so pagan is also so Christian?' Starling mused.

'Well, welcome to the realms of Hermetic academia,' Calmet said. 'It is well known that Plato travelled to the eastern magis and sorcerers to learn of their trade, which has led many to view human magic as the real root to wisdom. Now, because Plato believed in a human soul and a divine being, a Hermetic stress on ritual magic has been able to transform Platonists and Neoplatonists' ways of thinking into a sort of religion, reliant on magical ritual to protect and free the soul. Avoiding the evident non-Christian rituals, a concern with the soul appealed to the renaissance Italians, who chose to see the Hermetica as a pagan prophesy of the one, true God. Marsilio Ficino was therefore asked to translate the work, which he did, and this allowed its rituals to permeate into Renaissance society. However much modern science likes to condemn Hermeticism as irrational, it was fundamental in the progression of mathematics, astronomy, and the rest of science.'

Melling was amazed by Calmet's mind. He himself knew that the occult could not so easily be divorced from Renaissance science, but Calmet spoke with such a fluency on things. He began to realise how much of a secret weapon the man was for the investigation.

'I think I understand,' he said, running an anxious hand through his oily hair. He remembered that he had not bathed since yesterday and made a mental reminder to wash as soon as the day's arrests had been carried out. 'Do you really think Dunfield, and his group are Hermetics, then, if that's the right word?' Melling asked.

'I know it completely,' Calmet responded. 'I have chased them for fifteen years, but I did not know it. Their adoption of the Book of the Dead does need further explaining, since that is not a part of the Egyptian world that ever found its foot in Hermeticism. More importantly, however, their desire for death needs further explanation. Hermetics tend to search for the hidden secrets of the universe, so I would contend that this cult, whoever they are, find death to be the ultimate theurgical ritual. They may not call themselves Hermetics, this I will not deny. But they have certainly learned from them. I know that these beliefs are responsible.'

Melling's skin, once more, began to itch. His head whirred with fatigue, repulsion and the absorption of complex, novel understanding. More importantly, his mind burned with a singular question: had Huxley always housed such evil? If the sundial's nascence could attest to the birth of this organisation of murderers, well then, Melling had been as much a student under its presence as Judy Collier, Lucy Rosewood, Samuel Cadence and Alexander Dawn.

XXVII

Old Cats

In distrust, Robert Melling was paying special attention to the gentleman in a long overcoat who was standing outside Huxley's train station. The sunlight was, as per the custom of the town, crouching in secrecy behind the greying afternoon clouds.

'What's he doing?' Melling asked himself, leaning against a black Ford. There were numerous of the old-fashioned taxis, with drivers awaiting future fares from the impending London train, and Melling had attempted to scout for anyone who might become an enemy to his cause. He was finishing one of his beloved Gitanes, whilst Starling waited in Calmet's blue car behind him. Maybe he was over paranoid.

If he was lucky, there would be the promised officers chaperoned by his oldest acquaintance, Dr Harry Saturn, who he had last left smoking in the cigar-den of his Kensington tailoring service. Recalling their conversation, he realised how many of Huxley's ticking seconds had wearied him with their passage. Time had seemed to warp with an unbearable longevity, and his sleepless nights and distressing conjectures had only served to make the days grow longer. Learning of the murderous Hermeticism which had invaded the walls of his former *alma mater*, well, that was just the nail in the coffin of his psychological burial. It had been mere days since he had seen his friend. It had also been decades. They were years apart in what they had seen.

He followed the man's movements towards the station. He disappeared inside, and moments later, the train which Melling was expecting pulled in with a whistling shout. Minutes after, the familiar figure of Dr Harry Saturn was strolling into the half-light of Huxley's afternoon, and Melling saw nostalgia wash over his intelligent grey eyes. Soon, their knowing gaze passed over Melling and he smiled ruefully, making his way to the car. He was closely followed by two men in dull-brown trench coats. These new recruits were dressed as American gangsters, minus the hats.

As was arranged, no greetings were made, and all three men were inside the Ford before a word was uttered. Melling threw down his cigarette stub, then dropped into the driver's seat. Only once the door was firmly shut did he speak.

'I am so glad you're here,' he said with an exhausted smile.

'Me too my friend,' Harry replied. 'Your week has proven rather fantastical, though I am sure Marcellus and Sebastian can help with that.'

Melling nodded his greetings to the gentlemen in his rear view, then turned his attention forwards to the station opening.

'How many?'

'Excluding us, we have eight more coming.'

'I was wanting so much more than just new recruits.'

'Indeed, old boy. But your chief, Artegal I believe his name was, has left us wanting.'

Melling clenched the steering wheel tightly.

'So, what do we have?'

'The ten officers have only a few pistols between them, I'm afraid. Something about going about matters quietly. He told me to remind you of this. Anyway, I took the liberty of asking Gladys to show me your Smith & Wesson. Who knew you would have needed it up here?'

'Ahh, Gladys,' Melling murmured warmly. How right her reservations had been about Olivia Rosewood's phone call. 'Let me guess. You brought your own revolver for yourself?'

Harry Saturn nodded with a guilty smile. 'Good,' Melling affirmed. 'I need you sharp, Harry. I wanted you to come because I need someone who has seen hell before – someone I trust. Chief Artegal has reputations to consider even when student suicide is the matter at hand.' He lowered his voice, eyeing the boys in the back. 'I haven't dealt with the lads he's sent with you, and I wasn't allowed anyone with authority, so I need someone who has pulled a trigger many times before. So long as we wave our pistols, and we orchestrate things perfectly. Then we should be fine. Huxshire is not exactly a Texan detention centre. A few guns will suffice,' he repeated. He didn't feel wholly assured by his mantra. He watched as two more men in long overcoats wandered to the blue car behind him.

'The others will take taxis,' Harry said. 'They'll rendezvous at Starling's.'

*

'I did warn you not to let Huxley consume you, old boy,' Harry said with a grimace, puffing on a long Dominican. They were standing in Starling's living room, waiting for the final two men to leave their taxi in the old town, and make their way to the rendezvous.

'You don't look so great yourself,' Melling said light-heartedly.

'I'm serious, Robert. When was the last time you slept?' Harry pressed. He looked immaculately dressed as always, his slim frame clothed in bespoke tailoring. His grey eyes held a lifetime of experience.

'Trust me, when these murderers are rooted out, I will be sleeping as soundly as a new-born.'

Louis Starling tutted from his golden sofa, turning to Harry.

'His nocturnal habits are part of the reason I told my wife to stay put on the Isle of Man,' he intervened with a half-earnest chuckle, and Harry raised a concerned brow.

'Your nightmares are getting worse, aren't they?'

'Only in the daytime.'

'That's not funny.'

'Indeed,' Starling added. 'I wouldn't call almost jumping from Apollonia's Bridge funny either.'

'What?' Harry's eyes became a heavy steel.

'Oh, don't look at me like that, Harry. Believe me, Calmet has sorted everything. I will explain all as soon as this is over.'

Harry seemed displeased with the notion and shot Calmet Traum a disapproving glance. It was then that number 18's front door received a knock from the final arrivals, who upon stepping in, were in similar attire to the rest.

'You lot are not exactly covert, are you?' Melling said sarcastically.

'It's better than uniforms, Detective Melling,' the man previously identified as Marcellus replied. His accent was thickly cockney. Despite this East End characteristic, his eyes were an Italian charcoal, and he had a similar European expression to Calmet. 'Chief Artegal suggested it.'

'Of course, he did,' Melling said flatly. Artegal was a great leader of Scotland Yard: meticulous, authoritative, and ballsy. Anything imaginative however, he left to his subordinates. Melling wondered when he would retire.

He gazed around the room at the eager faces around him, growing excited at the prospect of finally outrooting Huxley's evils.

'Right gents,' he addressed the room. 'We don't have much time as there's no telling when another student is due to engage in a stupid suicide. I know you've all been briefed on how horrifying Huxley has become, and the nature of the evil it is harbouring. Let me be clear: things are far more far gone than your wildest imagination could suggest. Huxley, if we are right, has been infested by such ghastly ideals for over a hundred years. Loving parents have hoped their children could find an entrance into one of the most sought-after and respected educations the world has to offer. Yet, some of these children, for in our eyes how can they be anything else, have been grossly misled and let down by their so-called educators. I think I can speak for all of us when I say that the men whom we're arresting are guilty of one of the cruellest evils imaginable. Gentlemen, this group, whatever they believe and whoever they deem themselves to be, are responsible for, as we know of, the suicides of Lucy Rosewood, Judy Collier and Samuel Cadence. All three were younger than twenty-three when they decided to leave this world, dying at the hands of a perverse philosophy. At this time, another student from my own past college, Alexander Dawn, lies in a coma for jumping from his bedroom window. What's more, we believe that one of the men responsible for this boy's condition, Inspector Caspar Todd, was the man permitted to console the boy's parents! Evil has, therefore, permeated Huxley's justice system, and it us up to us to balance the scales.'

The men around him nodded in eager excitement, murmuring their agreement. 'Calmet,' Melling continued, 'as a student of the ancients, believes the group's practices and rituals to be Hermetic. What that means is they might believe there is some sort of mystical answer which lies in death. We believe their intention is to seduce students into believing that life's ultimate truth lies beyond the final curtain of our existence. Their notions of the divine lie in embracing an early death. The fine print of their doctrine is not something we know for certain. What we do know is that there is perhaps one of the filthiest forms of foul play just outside this door. Students have come for scholarship, but jump off bridges, fall from dorms and even carve symbols into their bodies before slicing a final artery.' He paused to allow his words to seep in. 'When we have taken the criminals responsible, we will further learn of their ideologies. For now,' he paused, watching as each of the recruits hung hungrily onto his every word. 'For now, their decision to seek student suicide is ideology enough for me to itch for my revolver!'

The younger men began to murmur agreements, Harry grabbing some supportingly by the shoulders. Starling's eyes seemed electric, and Calmet nodded his head after every sentence. 'If there is a God,' Melling said, voice turning into a low growl. 'Rest assured that when these men eventually pass, they will find their truth in the fiery gates of hell!'

There were louder murmurs of aggression from the room now, with some shouts.

'We must be strategic if we are to be successful. We must enforce a top-down approach, taking Sergeant Lynne and Inspector Todd of the Huxshire department with our guns pointed. It is crucial that the good officers of the county know under whose authority we operate. They may not like answering to a gun, but remember that our revolvers are the cool steel of her Majesty's jurisdiction. We must make sure our authority is acknowledged. Even the innocent may not be inclined to put their own leaders behind bars. Know your credibility. Huxley answers to *us* now. Once the inspector and sergeant are arrested, we must guard those cells well, but more importantly, we must not allow anyone else to leave or perhaps get some sort of word out to others. There is no knowing who else shares in this group's wicked schemes. Harry will take seven of you with him, led by Starling, whose presence might ameliorate any distrust which you may encounter. Starling is, after all, a man some of them know.'

'Where will you be?' Starling asked.

'I will take our final three men to Dunfield, where two of us will take Master Dunfield himself in his study, whilst the others visit Robora. We have it on good authority that on this day and time, both gentlemen are likely to be in their offices.'

'It is also critical,' the London lad, Marcellus, said: 'that if any information can be gleaned from arrests, it must be called in as soon as possible. There is no telling which children may be poised for doom this very day.'

'Well said,' Melling agreed. 'Once Dunfield and Robora are under arrest, we will take them to Huxshire. There we can begin to ascertain who else is part of their abhorrent organisation. Calmet will remain here, and you have all been given the house number. Send all information through him if you can.'

The men all nodded their understanding. 'The sooner we have these men behind bars, the sooner we can prevent a mother from attending her child's funeral.'

'Let's get the bastards!' Marcellus shouted, and the group cheered, assembling themselves. Harry came over to the detective.

'They're young and they haven't been to war. Take Marcellus with you. He's seemingly the most adept.'

'Noted,' Melling said with a smile. Harry had been a sergeant in the Second World War, and indeed, had earned his stripes. There was no doubt that he would carry out the matters with the greatest proficiency. The younger lads were meant to be hardened and efficient in dark matters by nature of their profession; ironically, Harry, by virtue of being part of Melling's war generation, eclipsed them all. 'Take care of Louis.'

'Will do.' The man went to join his group but turned for an additional warning. 'Just make sure you don't fall for any lowered guards. No matter the age, these people are evil. Even old cats can leap when cornered.'

'I'm going to steal that one,' Melling replied with a chuckle.

'Detective Melling,' Marcellus said from behind him. 'I've been told to join you. Sebastian and Frederick will be coming to Dunfield College too.'

'Good. Tell them to be outside in two minutes.'

*

Melling had almost finished a second cigarette by the time they were outside the familiar gate of Dunfield College. It was already the late afternoon, and the wind had picked up, blowing the detective's smoke away from him. In his mind he chased the swirling grey, feeling his pulse quicken in trepidation. The yells of haggling vendors were carried across the wind from behind him. His mind was not being kind to him. He wondered how many at Dunfield were linked to Lucy Rosewood's death. He also wondered if there were any professors at Trinity who had been involved in this disgraceful business, and he kept revisiting having to chase Judy.

No one is going to die today, he reassured himself.

'You two,' he said, pointing to Sebastian and Frederick. 'You'll go with a porter to Robora's office. Say that you have some mail for him that needs to be hand delivered. He should be there now. He is for the taking.'

They nodded in angst and strode through the entrance, leaving Marcellus and himself alone for a few minutes.

'We're waiting for what exactly?' the younger recruit asked in his strong cockney accent.

'Too many of us at once needing a guide might send warning bells.'

Marcellus nodded in understanding.

'You feeling alright, Detective?'

'Me?' Melling asked in surprise. 'Sure.'

A few moments passed before he allowed more disclosure. 'Truthfully, not quite. I chased a student from Trinity just yesterday and had to watch her jump to her death.'

'Jesus,' Marcellus said, growing pale.

'No, I don't think he had much to do with it. But in answer to your question, this past week has truly overcome me. I'm anxious to leave, but more anxious for the discovery which our arrests will bring.'

'In a way, it's nice to hear you sound so human.'

'I'm sorry?'

'Well, it's just, we've all heard of your exploits. The Sienna case with those women – the twins, I mean. Then there's the boy who went missing in Germany.'

'Please don't revisit my past cases.'

'They're more talked about than you realise, Detective. I was just gonna say that with all the stories people tell, it's nice to see your human side.'
'You were imagining cold steel eyes behind a cold steel revolver?' Marcellus chuckled.
'Something like that.'
'Anyone who pretends that they aren't emotional is ill-suited to my field. As you must know, I prefer to handle suicide, and suicide demands a response from someone who can conjure the victim's perspective; a negative capability if you will.'
'A what?'
'Never mind,' Melling said, deciding to make a different point. 'You know, just recently, I had to inspect the shredded corpse of a lad just about your age. He had jumped in front of a train.'
Marcellus winced, but Melling continued. 'I am going to tell you his name: it was Jacob Wenley, and he was a student.' As he spoke, images of the dismembered boy at platform one, Horsham station returned to him. 'How much have you seen death?'
'A few times.'
Melling nodded. He could see some experience in those young eyes.
'Know their names?'
'About half of them, yeah,' Marcellus said, looking at the ground.
'In war, you kill without knowing who you kill. Their identities are subsumed under a general enemy. But in these wars of life, the ones for you and me, people of our profession. We must always preserve individuality: victim or aggressor. You want advice from someone with a timeline like mine? Well, never let humanity become abstracted. Never ever indulge in the idea of a cold pair of steel eyes behind a cold steel revolver. We are not in this line of work to bed women and shoot bad guys. We are not in a Western. There is no true heroism in our work. No sort of poetry. It *is* true that things can be eradicated down into the fundamental sides of a coin: dead or alive. But our reactions to the heads or tails of things are too murky for verse or screenplays to grapple with.'
Marcellus seemed to take it all in for a moment.
'My eyes aren't even grey.'
Melling chuckled.
Good lad.

With that, he glanced at his watch and threw his cigarette to the ground. 'Let's go.'

They hurried through the oldest gate in Huxley and, once again, Melling was struck by the beauty of the emerald shine of the manicured lawns, the rainbow of floral bushes and the polished brown of the medieval backdrop.

'Jesus,' Marcellus said, drawing the word out. 'Students really get to study here? It should be a museum.'

'Huxley is just relics haunting future relics,' Melling responded, stealing Harry's ominous epigram. There were two porters on duty in their light wooden lodge, and it was an elderly lady who showed them where Master Dunfield's office was.

'You can't miss it. It will be on the right side of the library behind the giant oak.'

Soon, Melling was staring up at the golden hands of the library's lapiz clock, which glinted atop the Baroque structure. The sun stole a glance through the overcast sky and peered through the stained glass windows, layering the shrubbery beneath with a watery glow. They hurried down the rightward path, past the evergreens until they found a gravel lane which diverted behind a towering oak.

'That'll be it,' Marcellus observed, voice wavering slightly.

'You ready?'

Marcellus nodded. 'Wait here,' Melling ordered. 'If he tries to escape or if I miss him, you keep watch.'

Melling hurried down the gravel path, footsteps crunching on the soft and sandy stones beneath him until he was outside a private lodge, seemingly stolen from the pages of a German folktale. With a strong wooden door, the timbered outside walls almost resembled a small cabin. It was isolated and tranquil. He read the golden letters which identified the murderer, and carefully opened the door, stepping into the all-wooden world of Master Dunfield's office. The deep oak floorboards were coloured by the red and yellow leather of the expensive folios that overflowed from his bookcases. A slight odour of damp air tugged the bottom of the detective's nose, and in reaction, his eyes found the half open window to his right which blew a slight breeze, carrying with it the sound of silence. Dunfield wasn't in. On the blushing red top of the master's mahogany desk, open, lay a giant book. Melling could imagine the weight in his hands, and pushing the door fully open, he walked towards it. The unlined pages seemed worn, with various unrecognisable names organised into messy margins. Some of those names had symbols next to them. Melling noted at least two that were in repetition.

—⊖— V̲

One was a small circle with a line through it, the other: a 'v' shape which was underlined.

'So, you figured us out in the end, did you?' a reedy voice said arrogantly into his ear. Melling was too startled to turn, and he let out a yelp of surprise. Before he could whirl around, a tight cord snaked around his throat. He was tugged backwards, his larynx crushed by wrenching hands. He pulled at the claws of his murderer but was unable to free himself. Struggling only made the cord stricter. His vocal cords burned in protest; his muffled screams grazed against a dented windpipe. He had recognised Professor Robora's voice as the same shrilling pitch that had helped to initiate the students at the castle. So, where this man had cajoled his students to their deaths, he would be killing Melling outright.

His bulging eyes became hotter, seemingly pushed from his skull.

He sputtered.

He was oxygen starved.

Robora yanked the cord ever narrower from above him in a murderous tug-of-war.

Melling became lifeless and limp.

He knew he was going to die.

He couldn't even feel his heart anymore.

His vision drifted.

The crying horn of a streetcar blared inside his ringing ears.

The lights came.

In lucem.

His lips tasted like chestnuts and chaos.

*

Louis Starling was nervous. At least, that's the word he'd chosen when Harry Saturn had asked how he was feeling. Shit-scared was closer to the truth, yet also no closer to summarising his angst. Starling had never been through such a tormenting few days; well, unless you counted the war. A Huxley local after a stellar student record at the university itself, the doctor had loved living inside such a picturesque, communal town – especially one which was home to some of Europe's brightest. He also loved his profession, lying comfortably in his bed at night under the appreciation of how his life was being lived.

These past few days had seemed to take the chime out of the grandfather clock on his mantelpiece. Huxley town no longer ticked by as expected, and with every horror that Robert Melling discovered, the more Starling began to feel haunted by a smothering guilt. The detective had been searching for those who the justice system would soon deem guilty, but a noose around the academic necks of Dunfield and the rest did not comfort Starling as much as it should. The more he considered the evil, for evil was the only word which could contain it, the more he felt that he too, should stand on the scaffold beside the primary culprits. How much did the law pay attention to the bystanders? To the secondary and tertiary passers-by with their heads in the sand?

Starling was a good man. He knew that. Good in a humble sense of the term; he was as good as any, average, flawed human being could be. He was good, he considered, because he pursued good. That was all any of us had. But how good could he really be when he had been blind to so much? Perhaps it would be better to say that he felt he was good simply because he did not consciously pursue the immoral. But goodness had obligations beyond avoiding evil, didn't it? Could he be blamed for what Huxley housed as much as those who had led students to their final breaths? The distance between the doer of the deed and the man ignorant to the deed was certainly far, but that did not leave the ignorant man free from responsibility.

'Penny for your thoughts?' Harry Saturn asked his long-time friend, causing Starling to jump. He cleared his throat, then turned to Harry's wise, grey gaze.

'Just how bloody foolish I have been to be another one of those who adored the place I lived in.'

'Nothing wrong with adoring a place,' Harry said, clapping him on the shoulder with a smile. 'But adoration cannot relate to perfection.'

They were standing in the new town, about three hundred yards from Apollonia's Bridge. They were waiting for the others to join them. As Starling knew the way best, he had left his car for one of the officers to use, with Calmet's blue Ford being driven by another. The other men would walk to the meeting point, though not at the same time. They had decided to split things up so as not to raise any brows, especially the image of fully manned cars; that would be hard not to stare at in a town where cars were rarely driven. They would pass Starling, and stop about two hundred yards further up the main hill of the new town on a previously identified side street. There, everyone would drive to the police station, hopefully now having avoided any obvious surveillance.

'I feel like I'm part of the problem,' Starling explained. 'Living ignorantly to an obvious evil.'

'Well,' Harry said. 'I can only answer that with my own opinion. Personally, I see an obvious evil as a purer form. I appreciate how you must be feeling, and I would agree that Huxley's reputation has certainly helped such horror to manifest. But fundamentally, this was not an obvious evil at all. Knowing and accepting evil is far worse than being oblivious to it. I would also argue that in your case, it is that you would never have been able to conjure such an evil in your own mind, being the man that you are, that helped you remain in the dark. As much as I detest the exceptionalism of the university, I know that they who live and work here are good people. In fact, in a place as this it can only be said that students are truly taught by those who want to help them reach new heights. At the end of the day, we can't start looking for wider explanations or blame due to a minority of wickedness. Don't take on a guilt that isn't yours. And as hard as it may be, don't now begin to condemn a place in the stead of a few godless people.'

Starling thanked him, though he was far from absolution. Biting hard on his molars, he watched his black car as it slowly crossed the bridge, stuck behind lazy tourists. Neither Starling nor Saturn spoke until the

Ford had disappeared into the predisclosed side street. The words they then chose were brief and quiet, almost in fear of discovery. Next came the other walkers, remaining apart from one another and ignoring both Starling and Saturn as they passed. Finally, after five or so minutes, Calmet's blue car began to cross. Starling watched it glide patiently behind the passing bodies. The doctor's eyes were hawkish, tearing apart every person who dared to dignify its presence. Anyone could be a threat to their operation, and Starling tried to control things with his stare. He knew he could do nothing but wait. Nevertheless, it comforted him to hold this semblance of authority, checking every soul who might contravene the detective's plan.

It was such a reptilian surveyance that made his eyes pause on the long coat of one middle-aged man. It was one of those strange situations where one focuses on something without really knowing their exact intrigue for doing so. There was something about this man's attire and the way he leaned to the side which beckoned recognition and further examination. Then there was the evident pace behind his speech. He was talking to a man who, due to the angle of exchange, Starling was unable to identify. The man's cigarette-smoking hand was wisping erratically as his mouth hurled words. Starling, somewhat subconsciously, somewhat over-alert, felt concerned by this pair, especially the familiarity the smoking man's overcoat jolted.

'A while since you've done something like this, eh old boy?' Harry said with a chuckle, tapping Starling on the shoulder.

'You could paint that on my face.'

'It is already a picture. What are you even looking at?' he asked as the Ford finally passed them.

'That man,' he pointed.

'The smoker?'

'Something about him I don't like.'

'Robert says paranoia is never a cause, always a symptom.'

'Meaning?'

'There's always a justified reason for it.'

'Doesn't he just bloody have a phrase for everything?' Starling murmured, still watching the erratic man.

'Well, sometimes he credits his success to his paranoia, so he may be confirming his own attitude.'

It was then that Starling understood the cause for his own suspicion, and it was this reference to Melling which led him to the root.

'I remember it now,' he sputtered. 'It was Robert who didn't like the look of him – he told me so when we came back home. He'd been standing idly by the station! What if he saw us there?' Starling recalled the man clearly now, without a cigarette at the time, but his overcoat gave him away.

'A Huxley local is spotted by the station, then, after a few hours, in the town. Is that so strange?'

'I suppose not,' Starling said in agreement, beginning to think that paranoia, despite Melling's quote, *could* merely be nerves. 'I think I need better self-control,' he said, earning another chuckle from Harry, who began to turn towards the hill.

'I think you'll feel much better when we've taken the station. Leave this jumpy fellow to his gossiping.'

But Starling did not turn with Harry, for it was precisely then that the smoker took a step to the left, revealing just who his interlocuter was. Starling gasped; it was a face so individual one could never mistake it. The man seemed to defy age yet embody experience all the same.

'Bloody hell!'.

Harry turned back.

'What is it?'

The chance of it was miraculous.

'That's Master Gabriel Dunfield.'

Something inside Harry Saturn's eyes detonated, and he didn't pause like his friend had done. He yanked Starling by the lapel, dragging him out of the murderer's eyeline.

'Did he see us?' he whispered sharply, despite being well out of earshot.

'I don't think so,' Starling said, stuttered words falling like pans down a staircase.

'Damn!' Harry cursed, punching the wall, then running a hand though his hair.

'What do we do?' Starling pined, borderline as a whimper.

Harry was all business.

'Snap out of it, man! We deviate from the plan is what we do!'

'But Robert –'

'We can't worry about him now,' Harry said bluntly. 'We have Dunfield right in front of us. Right now. We take him.'

'Take him, how?'

'Get up to the others, and drive down to him. Meet me there,' the latter replied, eyes inking into a revolver's heartless hue.

'What if they're waiting for Robert?'

'If they know our plans, then it's already too late to help him. It may already be too late for us and the Huxshire Police. We need to be fast. We take Dunfield, and then we take the station. We just have to trust that Robert can look after himself.'

'But –'

'Go!' Harry asserted, pushing Starling away from him. 'Get a car to me fast!'

With that, Harry moved away from the shelter of the side-street and turned his attention to the master. 'So, you're the bastard…' he murmured, loading his gun. Feelings long dormant began to stir. Old cats could still leap.

XXVIII

The Hell Where Youth and

Laughter Go

'Auf Wiedersehen,' Lorelei said from above. There was the sound of the streetcar screeching from behind him. He felt the rumble of the road under his back and knew that in seconds he would be dead. Lorelei was beckoning for him, her hands outstretched. She looked beautiful again.

'Falling,' he murmured.

He *wanted* to.

He was ready to yield.

He had waited long enough to rejoin her.

I am dying, Paris, dying, he hummed to his beloved. She wrapped him in a warm, ever-loving embrace.

Tu m'as manqué.

'Detective Melling!' someone yelled from aboard the streetcar, and the sound of gunshots jolted his mind into a dizzying frenzy. 'Detective!' the man yelled again as hands tugged at the corner of his shirt. 'Detective, wake up!'

Lorelei kissed him with hot air. 'Wake up!'

He did.

Lorelei's loving body vanished, the blaring horn of the streetcar disappeared, and the discomfort of the growling road was replaced by a hard wooden floor. The light of the master's lodge came into view, with the concerned face of Marcellus peering over him. His lungs burned in their plea for oxygen, and he rolled over in a fit of coughs. 'Are you alright?' Marcellus asked, placing a steadying hand over him. 'My God, you weren't breathing, Detective. I didn't think you would wake up… I think you were… dead.'

Melling wheezed as his larynx throbbed, and he passed worried hands over his throat. He slowly sat up, but horror replaced pain when his eyes passed over the bloodied figure who lay on the floor just two metres before him. Professor Robora was dead, caked in the deep red of his own blood. It had already puddled around him with a metre radius.

'Why did you do that?' Melling rasped, hardly able to produce a coherent sound.

'He was killing you,' Marcellus said flatly.

'How did you know?'

'I felt useless all the way up the road. I thought I better be outside the office, and well I wasn't even twenty metres out when I saw the door close after you had walked in.'

Melling exhaled in relief, soothing his brutalised throat as he timidly got to his feet. For a second, the room tilted, but he steadied himself, looking away from the fresh corpse before him.

'There goes our questioning,' he said weakly, seeing the young man's brown eyes deepen in shame.

'I panicked. It all happened so quickly and...' Marcellus' voice trailed off.

Your eyes are definitely not the cold steel of a revolver.

'It's okay,' the detective whispered, making sure the lad would not get lost in his thoughts. 'I understand what happened. You saved my life.'

'What do we do?' Marcellus quickly asked.

'We do what we can,' Melling said, turning his eyes back to the book on the desk, whilst easing the tension from his neck. His windpipe still seemed shrunken in fear, like a startled animal who cowers away in the corner. Robora had almost killed him. Where the hell Dunfield was... well that was another painful mystery.

Robora almost killed you.

No. He had stopped breathing. Robora had succeeded in killing him, but Marcellus had saved him. 'Do you really think I was dead?' Melling whispered slowly, and Marcellus gave him a concerned frown.

'Your pulse was as good as gone.'

'You saved me,' Melling said, voice coming out halfway between a whisper and a croak.

'It was nothing,' Marcellus replied, waving away the gratitude. If he hadn't been there however, the detective would really have been... he didn't want to finish that sentence, and he hated himself for not exercising more caution. 'You were caught off guard, is all,' his saviour remarked, seemingly reading his thoughts. Melling nodded, turning over the names which meant nothing to him for the moment. A corpse lay bleeding, but both men did their best not to look at it. It was the unaddressed slaughtered elephant in the room.

'This book was open when I entered.'

'Try and talk less,' Marcellus said, but Melling shook his head. The symbols were still there: a small circle with a line through it, the other: a 'v' shape which was underlined. Circling back to the beginning of the heavy book, he found hundreds of pages on eastern philosophies. The writing was printed and seemed to be an encyclopaedia of sorts; this was perhaps a disguise, as, all of a sudden, the information was replaced by handwriting. Scribbles and personal notes pieced together the further along he moved through the book. There were dates with long stretches of prose – then there were the symbols from before, matched with names he didn't recognise.

'If these are the names of initiated students,' he said, realising that the names of the deceased must be present: 'then...' He raced to where the writing stopped, rewinding pages until he found the last entry. 'It's today's date!'

He trailed his thumb over just one name as his heart quickened.

'Lea Algrin,' Marcellus read, beside him now.

'I've heard that name before.'

He turned back a few more pages of entries until he saw a name he recognised outright: Judy Collier. 'The girl I told you of: Judy Collier, here dated the day of her death. She has both symbols, with the first crossed out. It's a key!' He read aloud what was written beneath: 'Courtier Collier left us today out of necessity. Apollonia's Bridge will mark her final moments. She is with truth now.'

Melling felt understanding try and burn his way through his mind as he glossed over some prior names. He poured back the pages until he found the name he was looking for: Samuel Cadence. He too, was marked with an underlined 'v'.

V

'Samuel jumped to his death, so I'm willing to bet anything that sign right there means an impact fall.'

Marcellus gave him an unsure look as Melling rolled the pages over to Alexander Dawn.

'Same symbol, but a question mark,' the young lad noted.

V ?

'Right. He jumped too, but he's still alive, hence the question mark, which must mean that the death was incomplete.' He turned over to Judy's name again as Robora's blood began to curdle. 'Judy has her original symbol removed for the same as Alexander's and well, I saw her jump to her death. Clearly, she was meant to do something else, but it doesn't say!' His throat was getting drier by the second and he paused to cough away the rusty feeling that was making his windpipe throb.

'Are you alright, Detective?' Marcellus asked, but his eyes widened in horror upon seeing just how his body had chosen to reveal its damage. 'Bloody hell, you're entirely blue!'

'I'm alright, truly,' Melling defended, but Marcellus cast him a doubtful glance, turning away.

'I'm sure there's something around here we can use to cover it.'

Melling froze, stone dead.

'Wait,' he whispered, searching his mind for the reason those words had shocked him. The timeline of the past few days was like a difficult horizon to stare into, but as he focused, sentences slowly rose into view.

Detective Melling, allow me to introduce Miss Lea Algrin, the best female physicist we have the pleasure of housing here...

Of course! The master had introduced her! That's why her name was so familiar. They had been in the library, and she had offered a well-rehearsed greeting to the detective. But why was she so relevant to this very moment? He felt the heat of the room and the odour of pages. She had been ill-dressed for the atmosphere.

I would personally feel close to death in that scarf of yours.

I, I – I'm not sure what you mean, Detective?
He found Lea's entry and symbol: a circle pierced by a line.

The guillotine blade of understanding fell. 'Oh my God. She's going to…'
Understanding was then followed by rationality, the latter finally pushing him to read what followed from the girl's name. The detective did not need to wait long to be disgusted. Clearly, the girl's sacrifice had long been awaited, for the text plunged the reader right into the final preparations for her demise. Melling devoured the sentences until he reached a smudged entry: the ink was still dark.
… Now that the season has been interrupted, Courtier Algrin has been urged to take the final step, sooner than anticipated. The season will have to close abruptly. Courtier Algrin is ready for liberation.
Horror, cold and pure, stole control of Melling. Robora's stealthy attack coupled painfully with the chiming clause: *Now that the season has been interrupted.* They knew that Melling knew. They were tying all loose ends. His actions had hastened theirs. That Robora had been waiting for him stung for all that it revealed. He was once again behind. He recalled the intoned phrasing of the chanting, robed figures at Huxley Castle.
We are in the season.
Lea Algrin was ready for her liberation. Melling looked at Marcellus in alarm. 'We need to get to the porters now! Right now!'
They left the body, Marcellus taking the book as they sprinted back the way they had come. It was not long before the detective was overwhelmed, heaving for oxygen through his thinned airways. He waved Marcellus on, repeating Lea's name so that there could be no mistake. Melling panted like a dehydrated animal, hugging himself in comfort as the air grazed against his windpipe. As he soothed his injury, his mind fell back into its habitual pattern of inquisitions. Robora was dead. Why had he been there and where was Dunfield?
So, you figured us out in the end, did you?
He had, but why was Robora the one waiting for him? Dunfield's voice relayed through his thoughts again.
Our detective didn't mean anything by it, Lea… nothing at all.

Nothing at all? How had he overlooked the peculiarity of the situation? It made so much sense now, for taking drastic actions often took some slow inuring. Convincing a student to hang herself? It would be insane to think she could do it immediately. The scarf was a testament to that, guarding the horrors of practice. With a pang in his heart, he recalled how Judy Collier had dressed in the warm room of Ferrum Court, also with a scarf tightly wound about her throat. Now that Melling considered this, the original circle with a line symbol by her name suggested a similar ending. It was Melling who had chased her to the bridge, and a different symbol now represented her death. If he had just paid attention, he could have saved this girl's life!

'No,' he corrected aloud to himself. There was still time for Lea Algrin.

As if to echo that premonition, Marcellus came bounding round the trees towards him, a map flapping in the wind.

'Come on!' he yelled, and Melling, with a renewed grunt, trailed beside him, lungs straining to match the younger man's rhythm. The runner turned, shouting that he had seen Frederick and Sebastian milling by the entrance, their search for Robora obviously having turned up empty. 'I told them to see who goes in and out!'

They arrived before another medieval structure which housed many rooms, evident with the modern windows built into its stony layers. They passed inside, and Marcellus, all business under adrenaline, stopped the first student he saw: a red-haired lad with confused eyes and a plump expression.

'Do you know Lea Algrin?'

The lad shook his head and Marcellus waved him on. Seconds later a trio of girls passed through the corridor, and he yelled after them. 'Excuse me ladies, do any of you happen to know a Miss Lea Algrin?' Two of the girls shook their heads save one, a brunette in spectacles, who nodded but seemed unwilling to answer, half-turning to walk away. 'Your leisure time can wait,' Marcellus said aggressively, flashing his identification. 'Take me to her room, *right* now.'

Nervous, she led both men up the darkened stairway until they were outside her chamber.

'Leave us,' Melling told the girl, and she hurried off in fear. Marcellus knocked on the door loudly.

'Lea!'

There was no reply. 'Lea open up!'

'Lea, it's Detective Robert Melling from the London Metropolitan Police Service. I'm here to help you.'

They strained their ears to the door, hearing nothing save their own breathing. Then there was a thud, like the sound of something hitting the floor. 'Oh my God! Open it now!'

Marcellus wrestled with the handle furiously, but the door remained closed. 'Now Marcellus!' Melling wailed, voice sounding foreign to himself. In angst, the younger man pulled the service revolver from inside his jacket pocket and aimed it at the door's lock. He fired three rounds which cracked through the empty silence of the hallway, splintering wood onto the floor. Stepping back, Marcellus crunched a heavy right boot into the door, and it swung open, causing him to fall backwards.

Melling was horrified to find a girl with rusted, copper hair dangling by her neck in the middle of the room; a chair was toppled onto its side beneath her. She writhed like a caught fish, and Melling raced into her, wrapping his tired arms around her waist, and hoisting her up as much as he could. She coughed and spluttered, legs trembling violently in his embrace.

'The rope's tied to the lamp!' Marcellus yelled, now beside him. He corrected the chair, then standing on it, began to unfasten the knot. The girl was still alive, meaning that her neck was not broken; the damage to her throat came out as incoherent sputters.

'Quickly!' the detective groaned.

'It's too tight, I can't untie it!'

'Well, do something!'

As Melling felt himself growing weaker, he heard Marcellus pull against the lamp, and as his jolts shook through the poor body that Melling was holding, he realised that his partner was going to try and pull her down. It took five unbearable yanks until Melling realised that he was no longer only half-supporting the girl's weight, and she crashed down onto him, winding him in the fall. Melling spluttered for air, coughing in exertion.

'She's silent!' Marcellus shouted, rushing to her side. Melling watched in helplessness as the man checked for her breathing. Her chest was barely rising, timidly pushing air through a painfully restricted air space.

Master Dunfield's evil grin played through the detective's mind as Marcellus tried to aid the body. 'Come on, come on,' he repeated between feeding her his own air. The lad's brown eyes were full of growing despair and the final embers of dwindling hope struggled to remain fierce.

'I'll support her,' Melling said, pushing him aside. 'You get an ambulance here and you do it fast.'

Marcellus cast him a doubtful look.

'You're hardly getting enough air on your own.'

'Let me save her. I can't run like you can.'

XXIX

Volta

'How did you know?' Marcellus asked him as the twitching girl was carried away by medics into the back of an open ambulance. It would struggle to drive through the cobbled roads without jolting her around. Melling remembered her squirming as she dangled from the lamp inside her room. 'Detective?'

'Sorry. Well, you see, intuition really. I'd met her before. Master Dunfield, who we were after, had the audacity of introducing her. It was so warm in the library that day and she had the thickest scarf around her neck. When you wanted to cover up my neck, I realised what the scarf maybe signified.'

'You made that connection well then,' Marcellus said, shaking his head at the chance of it.

'I realise now that Judy Collier, the girl who jumped when I chased her. She had both symbols. She had also worn a thick scarf when we'd interviewed her, and it was a warm indoor classroom.'

'Bloody ironic that it happened to you too. Doesn't all this imply some sort of rehearsal? We're assuming that they'd practiced with a rope before?'

'Right, you are. I had wondered how the indoctrination process worked. It cannot be easy to convince budding academics to tie their own noose. An adjusting process *does* make sense.'

'We were lucky. Very lucky that you made us act so quickly.'

'You saved her, as you did me, Marcellus. You said it yourself: I wasn't breathing. In the excitement of it all, I didn't have the chance to properly thank you. If I can ever return even half the debt, you let me know.'

'We'll see,' Marcellus said, brushing aside the gratitude. It was clear he was still wrestling with the demons of the day. 'What was her name again?' he asked Melling, and the detective nodded his head approvingly at the question.

'Lea Algrin.'

'I don't think I'll be able to forget seeing her like that,' he said, deliberately avoiding the topic of the dead Robora. 'Sebastian should be arriving at the hospital in time with the ambulance. Are you sure it's necessary?'

'If she isn't watched by someone in the hospital, then she may try again. Besides, this way we can also be updated.'

'Any news with the book?'

'It's strange. The first chunk seems an ancient encyclopaedia of sorts, but there are so many philosophies to sift through, one can't find a unifying theme.'

'Does it belong to them? The details that is? Does it explain who they are?'

'No. It was probably a disguise.' He turned to the last written page, thumbing Lea's name.

'Anyone after her?'

Melling shook his head, turning the pages over to highlight their emptiness. The sheer size of the volume probably added to the book's stealth – it was easily confusable for a painstaking thesaurus or encyclopaedia, doomed to a shelf-life of forever, part of the shelf itself. 'The writing explains the progress of initiates, but thankfully, it stops with Lea.'

'Mr Melling?' an elderly porter asked him from outside the lodge. 'Phone for you.'

The detective gave Marcellus the weighty book, then walked inside to where a phone call was waiting.

'Robert?' Starling's excited voice called into the phone. 'Calmet told me to call here.'

'What is it, what happened?'

'We've got him!'

'Who?'

'Dunfield!'

Dunfield?

'God… that's… that's brilliant, but how?'

'We were passing through town, and I saw him! He was talking with that man by the station! The one you noticed earlier, and I recognised him!'

So, his paranoia had been justified. 'We would probably have missed it all, but a part of me latched onto his presence. Isn't that incredible? I saw him! We arrested him!'

Finally, some luck on our side!

'I just can't believe the bloody luck of that,' Melling said. It was difficult to process, especially considering how scared he'd been that they'd been discovered, their plans foiled. Their objective returned to him, and his heart quickened. 'But what about the rest, did you take the station?'

'You won't believe how we did! Harry realised that we needed to act fast about things, and we were right on time!'

Melling laughed triumphantly then coughed.

'Are you alright?' Starling asked with concern.

'Just fine,' he said, coughing away the rasp. 'Tell me more!'

'Harry was switched on as usual. I needed to get the cars to him, but by the time I was there, he already had Dunfield pinned to the cobblestones. At the station, when Sergeant Lynne saw the master in handcuffs, he tried to stop us, but Harry! My God, how Harry put a stop to him!'

'Is he alright?'

'More than alright!' Starling shouted. 'Buried his muzzle into the Sergeant's throat before anyone could think twice.'

'And the officers?' he asked, growing giddier with every detail.

'They folded when the others flashed their identification. Your chief, Artegal, even called in to assert his jurisdiction!'

'I am speechless! I… I… don't even know how to feel!'

They had bloody well done it. And his body hardly knew how to respond. He felt elated, but possibly too airy, as though he wasn't quite there in the present moment.

'We've done it, Robert! By God, we've done it! Caspar… the inspector was in the mail room when it happened. I had the pleasure of arresting him myself!'

Melling had to smile at the thought of the corrupt inspector behind bars, and he could tell Starling felt a deep satisfaction in being the man to do it. There was certainly a betrayal there which Starling had needed to avenge.

'Seems it's all over then,' he said, feelings floating strangely in indecision. It seemed that fortune had decided to favour them in a sudden moment, after days of taunting despair. Nevertheless, the last time he had felt this way, Sergeant Lynne had told them how he would take things off their hands. Distrust was clearly deeply embedded in any of Melling's Huxley-related reasoning.

'You have Robora, then?' Starling asked in excitement. Melling's soul soured at the question, thinking again of the bloodied body that was currently guarded by Frederick, Marcellus' other henchman. 'Robert?'

'He's dead.'

'What? How?'

'Well, I'll explain all when I see you. He was waiting for me in Dunfield's office. They knew we were coming.'

'I wanted to call in and –'

'Don't,' Melling said, killing Starling's apology whilst shaking his head. 'You were right to act fast; we didn't have time for that. Plans change. Regardless, he almost killed me, but here I am.'

'Robert are you –'

'It's fine. Marcellus took care of it. But that's not really what ails me.'

'What then?'

'There was another one. Another girl.'

'No,' Starling said, his voice landing hollow.

'She barely made it. We got to her just in time but she's damaged… badly.'

'What did she do?'

'She hanged herself. If we had been seconds later…'

'You saved her Robert, you saved her.'

Melling swallowed, trying to deny himself tears.

'Hopefully. Listen, we'll come over to the station now, just do me one favour, would you?'

'Anything.'

'Tell Dunfield that I'm coming for him.'

XXX

Is Our Cell Elysium?

'He's here,' Harry said, having taken Melling to the final cell of a cold corridor in Huxshire's police station. Sitting on the shallow bench at the back, the master was waiting. His gown was neatly folded beside him, and he was dressed in a sharp French suit.

'Evening, Detective,' he greeted with a grin. Again, Melling was surprised by the melodic sound of his voice and the handsome youth that had clung to his expression despite his age. Melling looked at his watch.

'Not just yet. It's only five.'

'That means you're too late.'

Melling glared at his smiling eyes.

'For what?'

The master said nothing in response. 'For Miss Lea Algrin?' Melling asked, noting how the corners of the man's smile died. 'Ahh. Seems I'm a step ahead then, and I guess, late for nothing.'

'Not sure what you mean, Mr Melling,' the master said politely.

'You can spare me the rhetorical angle. You want to know if she's alive, don't you?'

Dunfield remained silent. 'She is, you'll be displeased to know. But I can assure you, her parents won't share in your displeasure.'

Harry opened the cell and Melling dragged a steel chair inside, taking a seat before the culprit. 'They'll also be happy to learn that the man responsible is in the four-walled comfort of a prison cell.'

'You've only delayed the inevitable,' the man corrected with a yawn. Then the master's lips curled up slightly, reminding Melling of a jackal or hyena. 'If anything, you've cursed her. Hanging, wasn't it? Wonder if her windpipe will ever recover?'

Melling could hardly comprehend these words.

'You really are evil,' he said in a low growl.

'Well, I would argue that the crueller man sits before me, letting a young woman suffer like that.'

'Well, you may argue what you like,' Melling said flatly. 'Just know for that the remainder of your lonely days, you'll be arguing with yourself.'

'I didn't hear Professor Robora make his way down here,' the man replied with his intrinsically musical timbre, a small smile still playing on his lips. He stared powerfully at the scarf around Melling's neck. The detective grinned in return.

'That's because he's lying in a pile of his own blood. In *your* office, actually.'

That murdered the master's smile and his eyes parted in sorrow. 'Oh, don't tell me you're upset? Here I was thinking that death was the end-goal?'

'Still no closer to the truth, Mr Melling,' the master muttered, anger dripping into his lips.

'Regale me, Mr Dunfield.'

'That's master.'

'Of nothing.'

'Very well,' the man said, crossing his arms, clearly no longer in a mood to entertain the detective. Luckily Melling had a suspicion on how to stir a response.

'The murderer is murdered. I'm *almost* upset that it wasn't you in his place. At least this way, you get to suffer for the remainder of your pathetic life.'

'Don't call him a murderer!' the master growled, raising his voice.

'Well, how else should I name him? Student slaughterer? Professor of death? Scholar of suicide?'

'We are not killers.'

'Well, you do a very good job of forcing parents to bury their children.'

'They wouldn't be upset if they understood!'

That's it. Tell me what's behind the evil in your eyes.

'Understand what, exactly? Because from over here, in the land of the *sane*, you appear nothing more than an evil man with a god complex.'

'God has nothing to do with it,' the man replied, able to chuckle.

'There we can both agree.'

'Look at you. You actually believe that you've cornered evil, don't you? You sit here, confronting and labelling as though you've delved us to the root. Well, let me assure you *Detective* Melling, that you have understood nothing. Even outside of these affairs. I know more than you ever will. Even about yourself. Perhaps I should prove it to you.'

In that moment, the master seemed to stare right through the detective, and it took a moment to shake the sickly feeling away.

'You saw yourself as a father figure to your students. I noted how passionate you were about your position when you walked around the college. Do explain to me how you can smile at the prospect of their deaths because I am finding it taxing to come to terms with.'

Again, the prisoner chuckled.

'As though of Hemlock I had drunk...'

'You are not Socrates,' Melling spat, noting a look of surprise in the man's eyes. 'Yes, I understood that reference. Socrates was condemned to death for misguiding the children of Athens – something we now see as a tragedy. But where the Greek jury may have falsely accused and made him drink hemlock, I think the label suits you rather well. So don't sit here and make yourself out to be some sort of great man who your condemners don't understand, because let me tell you, history will *not* look kindly on you.'

'Until the day those historians die.'

'I'm sorry?'

'You see, Mr Melling, our courtiers are always given a choice. We never force their hand.'

'But you guide it.'

'As a guiding hand should. We instruct.' As he spoke, Dunfield seemed overly assured of his own innocence. It was mystifying.

'The fact that you cannot draw the same parallels that I can, bewilders me.'

'I am sure much bewilders you. What do you know of Iamblichus, Mr Melling?'

'Not much.'

'He was a Syrian Neoplatonist. Though I can see by your expression that someone has already explained that to you.'

'They tried to, although I must confess that I was never a philosopher.'

'Well,' Dunfield said with a smile. 'He is notable for his defence of Egyptian occult rituals. You see, he felt that an embrace of such practices could lead a human closer to the divine.'

'I believe it's called Theurgy?'

'You've done your reading,' the prisoner observed with an eerie grin. 'And what of Hermes Trismegistus?'

Melling cleared his throat.

'The Egyptian demi-god?'

'The mystical scribe of the Hermetica,' Dunfield corrected. Melling wanted to step in with Calmet's conclusions but was too experienced in interrogation to steer the master away from his admissions.

'I must admit that I am rather ignorant on the topic.'

'Well, in the Ptolemaic times, when the Greek and Egyptian cultures merged, Hermes Trismegistus was the best way they could explain the sacred nature of the magic they knew was so linked to the divine. They credit to him the spells in the Corpus Hermeticum. A Greek manuscript of this arrived in Florence in 1462, translated by the Italian scholar, Marsilio Ficino.'

'I see.'

'History owes much more than they dare to realise to this Corpus Hermeticum. It single-handedly shaped the Renaissance.'

'Surely you don't mean single-handedly?' Melling asked, and Dunfield chuckled.

'This is why you will never understand us, Mr Melling. That scripture held the secrets of the ancients. Secrets that one is required to believe in before their mysteries can be revealed.'

'Well, I won't insult you by pretending to be a believer,' Melling said flatly. 'I don't even believe in the accepted deities, let alone yours.'

'Who said anything about deities?' Dunfield asked, smiling at his look of surprise. 'We do share your dislike of institution though.'

'We share nothing except Huxley and this cell.'

'We share our entire History, Mr Melling, for as I said, the Enlightenment could not have occurred without Hermeticism.'

'Forgive me, Master Dunfield,' Melling said evenly. 'Though my knowledge on the subject is, as I said, limited, I am quite certain that ritual suicide didn't shape the Renaissance.'

Again, Dunfield's lips played into a smile. It rounded his agate eyes, making them glow slightly in the darkened shadow he was cast in.

'Ficino went down in history as one of the most influential Neoplatonists. He translated the Hermetica because its Christian-like undertones were patent: a purity and a final destination. These are highly Catholic ideas. Ficino thus became famous throughout history for translating the supposed mysteries Hermeticism could offer, but his context for doing so was not heretical. It was decidedly Catholic. He also translated much else of ancient philosophy. Nevertheless, he also had a grandson, someone who became a highly devoted disciple, Marco Ronanti. He, however, has managed to escape our timeline. You've, no doubt, never heard his name?'

'Should I know of him?'

'The rare occasion when he does venture into scholarship is to reference his journals. You see, he was obsessed with Henosis.'

'Henosis?' Already the detective was getting lost in terminology, and he felt he needed Calmet.

'Henosis,' Dunfield repeated, almost as a whisper. 'The mental pursuit of reaching the Neoplatonists' ideal of the one – the divine.'

'The one. That's called the monad, correct?'

'Yes, the monad. A sense of wholeness and divine purity. Ronanti was a devout monist – a believer in the one, that is. He believed that the architect of life as well as its final truth was destined to remain apart from our understanding. He didn't believe in a divine God like his Catholic relatives, but he was too intelligent to dismiss the fact that something was governing his existence. The idea of the one appealed to him.'

'Surely any embrace of hermetic ritual may have displeased those Catholic relatives you mentioned?' Melling asked, realising further still how spot-on Calmet had been.

'He conjured a far more discordant philosophy but kept it secret in his journals. He believed that in the same way that the magic of the ancients required a sense of belief, it was a belief in the one that would lead him to it.'

'I think I follow, though I don't see why students have to die.'

'Neoplatonists still believe in a soul, as did Ronanti, and it doesn't take a Catholic to believe in sin.'

'Nor to see a sinner,' Melling concluded flatly, but Dunfield shook his head at the label.

'View me how you will, Mr Melling, it won't affect my soul.'

Melling had seen many wild and absurd things in his life, but to be hearing such storytelling as this, from a master of such a renowned institution, it was a sobering reality for just how dangerously bizarre life could be.

'So, you are a follower of this, Marco Ronanti?'

Dunfield shook his head again.

'Ronanti felt that life was a danger, and that with every year of age, the soul became more vulnerable to corruption and sin. He ended his life ritually, stressing in his journals that his belief in the one, as well as a desire to understand it, would save his soul, guiding him towards life's realms of truth.'

'Wait, just so I understand,' Melling interrupted. 'He thought that life's ultimate truth could only be answered by death, and that to save his soul from sin, the sooner he ventured towards the one, the better.'

'Correct.'

'And you have to *want* to see this ultimate truth for your soul to reach it?'

Dunfield nodded.

'*Credo ut intelligam*,' Dunfield said, casting Melling back to when he had heard those words at Huxley castle. Belief came before knowledge. 'He was a pioneer,' the master continued. 'After his death, his father, upon finding his journals, kept them a secret. As you can imagine, a man of such sharp insights was bound to be condemned. The journals were thus lost for many years. Until they resurfaced in the same family, though the name had changed, in the early nineteenth century. Sergio Robora, the descendant of Ficino and Ronanti, became enamoured by his ancestors' journals.'

'I'm assuming Professor Robora's family name is of little coincidence?'

'It was actually me who showed him his past.'

'So, this... Sergio?'

'He took his family to England to study archaeology at Cambridge, where Richard Lepsius was a visiting professor.'

'Who published the Book of the Dead, right?' Melling said, earning a look of surprise in the agate eyes of Dunfield. 'Those spells to get into the underworld? That's about all I know of him.'

How different would things have been if I had not visited Calmet, Melling thought.

'Well,' Dunfield mused slowly, 'the Egyptian title is actually: the Book of Going Forth into the Light, not the Book of the Dead.'

'*In lucem*,' Melling said. Finally piercing the truth. 'Into the light. That's why you say it, isn't it?'

Dunfield offered a questioning look, and it was clear to Melling that the man was surprised at how much the detective had interpreted so far. He didn't want to be overconfident, determined to let the man speak for himself. Melling also did not wish to reveal that he had seen Dunfield chant those same words at his castle initiation. 'You must remember that Inspector Todd was all too happy to tell me of the chanting at Lucy Rosewood's service?'

The master's eyes darkened as he recalled Melling telling him that information all those days ago when they first met at Dunfield College. 'I wonder why the inspector was so forthcoming?'

'He can't help himself,' Dunfield said, brows sliding in irritation. 'Exclusion breeds admiration.'

'Exclusion? Wait, you're telling me that he isn't a part of…'

'No. He has not earned the title of courtier.'

'Then what is he to you?'

'A lover of Huxley, willing to look the other way as long as his beloved town remains peaceful.'

'I find that a difficult motivation.'

'Well, that and his duties to the sergeant and captain, who yes, are courtiers. But as you have arrested them, you know this already.'

'And who *are* you exactly?' Melling asked, feeling the truth's revelation arriving on the man's lips.

'Well, Sergio Robora drew ancient parallels with Lepsius' translations on the Egyptian death guides. He thought it was his duty to give life to Ronanti's work, and so, he established the *Custodes Veritatis*, imbuing its Hermeticism with Lepsius' findings.'

'The Keepers of Truth,' Melling translated aloud.

'Your Latin was always strong,' Dunfield said with a distant smile.

'What does that mean?'

'If you must know, Robert, we had our eyes on you whilst you were here. Dr Farway always deemed you a protégé. He felt obligated to open your eyes.'

The blood drained from Melling's face as he tried to comprehend what he was hearing. 'Oh, don't look so shocked. You were awfully bright, and, I might add, awfully susceptible to Farway's praises. He thought we could make you so much more. Perhaps if I had been a professor at the time.'

Melling tried to move his lips, and it was some moments before he managed a weak utterance.

'He was going to kill me?'

Dunfield shook his head.

'He thought you deserved the path to truth.'

'You would have killed me,' Melling said in a pained whisper, soul retreating into the darkest depths of his body. Dr Alfred Farway, a man who had been so influential on the young Melling – a man who had almost swayed Melling from becoming a detective. A man who still wrote to him, whom he would have turned to for help had Starling not met him at the station.

'It was no matter. No consequence. You shifted your academic pursuits towards crime, and he didn't want to risk your moral compass preventing hundreds more from taking your place.'

Hearing that horrible notion, no matter how remote it was from his line of thinking, he began to feel guilty. The man had a powerful way of eliciting certain feelings, and he evidently knew it. 'I must say it is comical to watch you try and process this,' Dunfield murmured.

Melling shook the angst from his mind, determined to switch the power around. His disillusionment of who his superiors had been, was at first appalling, now angering.

'Thank you for revealing Farway's malpractice. That's one face under the hood.'

'Oh, he's long gone. We all are. You won't find any of us. We've disbanded.'

'It won't be difficult to trace those who go missing. Soon, you will all be in cells.'

'Perhaps,' Dunfield said with a playfully arrogant smile. 'But we live on in other ways.'

Melling felt as though he had heard enough, and he was beginning to feel sick. The damage to his throat was still fresh, and the long conversation had tired him. The man had revealed the truth of this organisation: the *Custodes Veritatis*. But there were still so many unanswered questions.

'There's something I would like some clarity on.'

Dunfield smiled.

'What is it, Detective?'

'The feathers. It's about weighing the heart to test virtue. I know that, but how does it factor into what you believe?'

'So, I *did* see someone that night.'

'*Tenebris in lucem*,' Melling said flatly, proving that yes, he had found the man and his followers at the castle. Dunfield decided to answer the initial question.

'The Egyptians thought that only the virtuous would go to paradise. We feel that only the virtuous deserve truth. Sergio Robora used Lepsius' translations to help solidify our beliefs with new rituals.'

This notion of what one deserved made Melling's anger rise even more. It abhorred him to the highest degree to hear a murderer judge his victims.

'Virtuous how?'

'Ambitious is perhaps another translation. Not everyone can see beyond the lies of existence. Of those who can, their desire for truth must also coincide with a desire to liberate their fellow prisoners. There is a very specific person we are after. Do not forget, they must be willing to believe before they can know, which is almost impossible for most. The longer one is alive, the less likely their souls can think to embrace such things. People are too focused on the material, they become sinners.' Hence why students were so perfect. They were at such a transitional time in life, still mouldable. Melling disliked the 'ambitious' element to this immensely, and recalled how people had used the word to describe Samuel and Lucy and…

It cannot be.

The master cocked his head to the side like a caged parrot, searching into Melling's lost eyes. The latter was no longer looking at the prisoner; his mind's eye was too imaginative in recreating the past. Its chosen memory?

Dockery.

His and Harry's friend, someone so particular, bright, and loved by all. Dockery was close to being the perfect student: studious, eager and, as

Melling's own father had announced: an ambitious boy. His death had stunned and sickened Melling, especially upon learning that the note he had left his mother had raised more questions than it had answered. The *Custodes Veritatis* had certainly existed in Melling's student days. They had killed his friend.

'How do you manage it?' he finally asked, watering eyes readjusting to the prisoner before him.

'Manage what?' the man asked with a honeyed smile. Melling refused to dignify the master by even bringing up Dockery's name. The detective did not need his affirmation. Learning that Dr Farway had sought the same end for him meant that Dockery's demise was finally answered.

'Clearly if you sought my death back when I was but a boy here, then others were beside me on the rungs of your ladder. But how could it have taken so long for justice to reach this place?'

'By justice I assume you mean the spoiling of our purpose. Well, that few are able to transcend into our eyeline of potential means that the enlightened few never raise enough brows. We are naturally, however, in the business to free as many souls as we can but... you *are* right. We cannot succeed for long if we are reckless in numbers.'

Melling disliked how the man avoided terms such as death and slaughter.

'What you mean is: it wasn't feasible to leave a string of student corpses for people to investigate?'

'Such venom,' the man said in disapproval. 'But the logic is there, yes. What you *might* appreciate knowing is that we have never been an annual affair, or at least, we did not begin as one. Purely for logistics alone, we have always needed time between each student's courageous step.'

'There is a ritual component to that, I assume?' the detective pondered, and the man nodded.

'Not every student is as willing to leave false knowledge behind the year they initiate. Fortunately, their courses are hardly ever one year. There is a correlation to those with deep, academic yearnings and their time with us. We thus provide them the time to inure themselves to their future. Some, such as Judy, become useful mediators between us and fellow courtiers. They also help to persuade those would-be initiates.'

Melling swallowed his revulsion at the cavalier simplicity of the speech. 'So, you *are* an annual affair, to use your words. But you mean to say that people are not dying all at once.'

'Indeed. We usually say farewell once a year to at least one or two during the season of rebirth. At least, we used to do our best to have it so. Sometimes, if things caught too much attention, we would have to wait a season, maybe even a few.'

The season.

Melling finally appreciated what was meant by this. Their philosophy, so connected to this notion of rebirth, was well-suited to Spring and all its floral, sunlit allusions.

'So, if I were to catalogue the morgue from March to say, June?'

Dunfield acquiesced his affirmation with a slow nod.

'We are concerned with sunrises as opposed to sunsets. Our attention to detail means that no one would ever start to notice. Besides, student suicide is a natural phenomenon outside of our influence. Despair-induced demise happens everywhere, and to think, you might even find misery a more acceptable reason to end life than the pursuit of liberation.' The man chuckled. 'A heartless notion if you ask me: death out of pain. We choose death out of darkness.'

'Give me a moment,' the wearying detective interrupted. 'Why did you speak in the past tense, just now?'

Dunfield raised an expectant brow, waiting for him to... 'Oh I see. Lucy, Samuel, Alexander, Judy. You *used* to aim for one a year, but you've started aiming for more.'

'Everything was carefully orchestrated. You see, we've expanded our influence, especially amongst the Huxshire Police,' he added, motioning around him. 'We were able to make it so that people went quietly, and mourning was localised. Unfortunately for us, there has been a new coroner in town.'

'Michael Crown? He seemed a Huxley local.'

'He is, but he only began working for the town last year. He asks many questions that one. He also discusses death too much with other locals. You see, Crown was your friend in discovery long before you arrived; he makes student demise more of a common conversation. Before

Crown, we managed to keep things well, as I said: localised. It is also a blessing that many locals do not wish to acknowledge the death of students. It goes against their blissful psyches. Sometimes though, I confess, a student makes a rather grander exit than we intended. As with Samuel, who chose Apollonia's Bridge as his terminal of departure. Such behaviour is usually not recommended. Courtiers know they need to preserve our ideology for future courtiers. That is what usually forces us to miss a season.'

Melling was struggling to remain passive. The master was revealing all that he longed to know. Things were beginning to become explainable. Ludicrously heinous, yes, but answerable.

'So, if Crown was making matters worse for you, and Samuel's death such a spectacle for the town, why not pause until things blow over? Why not, as you would phrase it, miss a season? Especially when you knew I was pursuing you?'

'Your thinking is valid,' the man acknowledged. 'Judy was not meant to leave us so soon, but your chase made her reason with emotion rather than reason itself. She chose to leave us, and I cannot fault her for that. Indeed, she is most certainly in touch with true knowledge at this moment. As for Alexander, well, Judy knew it was the perfect time for him, and we thought we could make it so that you would never hear of it. Inconvenient perhaps, but we do appreciate the need for flexibility. Things were completely out of your eyeline except, well...'

'Starling's wife knew the family.'

'Not intimately, but her friend is godmother to Samuel, I believe. That was a painful misfortune for us to swallow. With more deaths comes more connections to deal with which, well, which would usually not be so much of an issue.'

'Unless Starling's guest is someone like me,' Melling said flatly, lips curling. 'I bet you weren't expecting me to go to Alexander's room either?'

Dunfield decided to dismiss the matter.

'That Starling's wife was connected was simple chance. One we could not have seen coming, for believe me, we know much. If anything, it just shows how behind you truly were. After Crown showed you the amenta, another stroke of chance for you I might add, we realised that

Inspector Todd was not equipped to handle things from then on, and Sergeant Lynne stepped in so as to close matters with you.'

'Wouldn't have worked. I wouldn't have been satisfied until full understanding reached me.'

'So, you think.'.

'It seems I owe more to fortune than I realised,' Melling allowed himself to say.

'And to what gain?' Dunfield posed disgustedly. Melling was shocked by the earnest pain in the man's alluring eyes.

'Is that a joke? Some perverse version of gallows humour?'

'We send the virtuous straight to the divine realm of pure truth, and you seek to prevent us from doing so,' Dunfield said, spitting the final few words out. Melling at first, was not sure how to respond, again nauseated by this notion of virtue. Then, with a long exhale, he slowly unwound the scarf around his neck. He saw Dunfield inhale quietly at the sight of his bruises. He walked over and lowered his voice.

'Your man, Professor Robora, did this to me. You can say whatever you want about the souls of the innocent students who have died because of you, but Robora,' he paused, lowering his voice further. 'Robora was trying to kill me in cold blood. So, he was shot in cold blood. His soul is stained. If your beliefs are true, well, Robora is as far from the divine as possible, and you know what? That'll put a smile on my face whenever I remember it.'

'We are setting them free!' Dunfield maintained in a raised voice, but Melling could hear that it had cracked slightly. 'It is our duty to show them the light! We are saving their souls!'

Melling pondered a reply, but language was failing him. He wanted to leave in silence. He finally had his answers. All expect one, however.

'I have a final question.'

The man's agate eyes, though angered, glowed with curiosity.

'Yes?' he said in a slow, seething hiss.

'Calmet Traum,' Melling said, staring into the man's face for recognition. 'He had his heart broken by the *Custodes Veritatis* about fifteen years ago, right?'

Dunfield nodded slowly.

'Artful genius on our part that he persecutes himself to this day,' the master responded with a smile. 'He was too naïve for his own protégé.

Too cowardly for her brilliance. It was *she* who warned us about approaching him. He would never have understood. She left him behind some instructions, I believe.'

'Wait,' Melling reasoned with a broken heart. 'You wanted him to focus on that. On his own potential role?'

'It needed to be *his* fault. Then we could offer to placate him. Once he left the university, we knew he would victimise himself, disgusted that she would even feel able to ask for him to dissect her dead brain.'

'You ruined a man's life by doing that!'

Dunfield just scoffed.

'Larger goals at stake.'

'You know,' Melling said, looking to kill the master's smile. 'If we were in different times, I'd give Calmet my Smith & Wesson, and look the other way whilst he blew your skull wide open. Send your brain all over the floor and your soul straight to hell. Sadly, hell isn't a guarantee to me, but a living hell is.'

With that he really was finished talking. Taking his chair from the cell, he watched Harry lock the door, leaving Dunfield in darkness.

As they left however, Melling didn't realise that the master was still grinning, grinning as though he still had the upper hand. The man listened to the decrescending taps of the detective's disappearing footsteps. 'Robert... *Melling*,' he said to himself with a giggle. 'Soon enough you will know how little you pierce the truth.'

XXXI

Todestrieb

Melling gazed into the obscurity of Apollonia's Bridge below him, reliving the sensation he had felt when his love had beckoned him from below. Lighting a Gitanes, he exhaled his melancholy, and peered now at the few passers-by who were making their way home in the cooling light of the dying horizon. He walked to where he had last seen Judy alive. The last twenty-four hours had revealed many of life's mysteries to him, but Judy's case was still unresolved.

Inspector Todd had broken down after Dunfield's interview, revealing detail after detail of what he knew. Part of the *Custodes Veritatis'* efficiency was utilising the police to smother any discussions or issues. You could avoid justice when justice as an institution was on your side. The inspector may not have been a courtier, but he knew who was initiated. He had revealed all. He had no other choice. Starling kept saying that he had seen the error of his ways and was trying to do the right thing. Melling wasn't as sure.

Those initiated students had been placed under police protection as Melling refused to sleep without them being watched. The next day, Melling, alongside Huxley officers, had tried to deal with those students calmly, attempting to relate to their version of events, exposing their doctrines as sinister rather than benevolent. The authorities would continue a process of careful protection without Melling, and the students would soon be back home with their families and loved ones. That was that. Melling had even watched the blonde boy from the ceremony at the castle break down before his eyes. The detective had held him for what seemed an eternity. These new initiates rapidly realised how they had been deceived, and it was harrowing to watch them come to terms with this fact.

It was not all good news however, for Melling had been late in finally considering what the inspector had told him on his first night: that a classmate of Lucy Rosewood, who had given a speech in her honour, had gone home to her parents due to mourning. Getting the relevant information had allowed him to call the parents; clearly, she had been part of the *Custodes Veritatis*. Yet the conversation with her loved ones was all too brief. The pain and disgust he had felt after this experience was so great that he had almost released his anger on the inspector. Harry Saturn had pulled him back before he could assault a prisoner.

If only the man had told them…

Melling had been so preoccupied with everything else that he had forgotten. Again, here in Huxley, he realised how much his detective skills had waned. How much he had aged. He hated that he was now pointing the finger at himself, and so he repressed the phone call and all it signified. He didn't want to mentally rehash the experience as the day continued, focusing instead on the rest of the day's seamlessness.

Nevertheless, the seamlessness of this new day only felt peculiar. In Huxley he had felt as in a darkened cave, struggling to find his way out. The sudden ability to be saving Huxley's misguided youth was almost unbelievable. He was too accustomed to conflict and mystery to truly relish in this victory. Indeed, he hardly felt victorious. For not the first time in the last few days, his mind was struggling to decipher just which emotions to feel. Melling was also immensely altered by his first full night's sleep in a year, and his companions had remarked on his change in expression. He hadn't dreamed of Lorelei, and as the day began to end, the fact that he hadn't been haunted began to gnaw away at him. He was puzzled by the sudden retreat of his deadly subconscious. Having thus uprooted Huxley's evil, the detective decided he would turn to Calmet Traum for answers.

He was thus paused on Apollonia's Bridge, caught in the memory of Judy's last moments. He still wondered how she had managed to cry such real tears for the man she loved: Samuel Cadence. Samuel had wanted to jump, and she had seen it, yet she had also claimed to love him. Somehow, she was probably responsible for persuading him to seek suicide in the first place. It didn't make sense. If she loved Samuel, surely, she would have wanted to save him? Had she loved their philosophy more?

It was like that a lot in his career: a giant truth would solve the paperwork of his case, but many divergent pathways which had been unearthed along the way still needed addressing. Sometimes solving a case was a fallacious idea, like thinking you had beaten a country simply because you had occupied its capital, forgetting that thousands of insurgents could fight to a bitter end. Judy was one such unresolved riddle. As much as he had interviewed students, no one had offered him much more than he already knew.

He shivered in the nascent cold, shaking his head. Perhaps, this mystery would remain unresolved now that both lovers were dead. But, as he walked to the other side of the medieval structure, he noted a small young woman bundled under a patchy blanket, quaking in the cooling evening. Her feet were exposed, and he recalled their bruises. This was the homeless girl with red hair he had seen upon his arrival. He walked slowly towards her. Her grey eyes stood out aggressively against her dirtied features, and her lips were quivering into a wounded blue. She couldn't have been older than seventeen. She had been there the day Judy had died, red hair hanging over gaunt, sleepless sockets. Had this poor soul been forced to witness the horrors like the rest of the crowd? Then it struck him.

Of course, she had!

For she inhabited the walkway.

Crouching by her side, he took off his scarf and placed it before her. Her untrusting eyes glared at the object, until, as she looked at the donor, a flash of recognition glowed from within.

'Why?' a cold voice whispered.

'You need it, I believe, more than I do,' Melling said evenly. She gazed at him unreadably, and her lips twitched into a sinister smile.

'Have been subjected to worse,' she said in a slight northern accent. He looked about him with a grimace. There was something absurd in this young and shoeless character; there was a strangeness to her that didn't quite seem real – a pull in her eye that appalled. He took off his coat and extended this as an offering too. She cocked her head, paling eyes narrowing in distrust. Slowly, she leaned forward and allowed Melling to hang it over her bruised shoulders.

'You've seen what I had to witness… and more?'

She nodded in reply. 'Would you share your memories a moment?' he asked softly. She didn't respond, so he continued. 'How long have you been here?'

'How long any of us is here makes no difference. Alone since birth, me, anyway.'

'No one looks out for you?'

'Tourists keep me going. Huxley would rather they didn't.'

Melling grunted as he sat down crossed legged before her.

'How old are you?'

'It isn't just me, you know?' she said somewhat aggressively. 'Ain't one of me, but many. Bridge is mine.'

'Not sure why I'm telling you this,' Melling sighed, 'but the only thing my father hated about Huxley was the fact that the streets were littered with those such as yourself. How could it be, he thought, that such a desired destination would have so much poverty?'

'A hero,' she said with a scoff then a scowl.

'Words won't help you,' Melling muttered back. She did not reply for a long moment.

'People step over us. Always. Feet and money always missing us. Words we get plenty. Bucket full of words we got. Huxley got colder. We got more words. More bruises, less toes, but always more words.' She pulled her blanket up to reveal a mangled foot; a smudged stump replaced where her two smallest toes would have been. Melling winced. He already felt an idea forming as to where a portion of his father's inheritance would be going next.

'Huxley was colder than I ever realised,' he said, moving onto a different track. Her keen eyes followed his thread easily, and she sneered.

'All wrapped up, but cold inside.'

'That girl… I was chasing her. Had you seen her before?'

She remained silent, dropping her head so that her eyes were shielded by her auburn hair. He stared at her in earnest until her smile quietened. At last, she raised her head and answered.

'I seen her, sure. Seen her with that boy too.'

'The boy who jumped in the night a few weeks ago?'

She nodded and her smile returned.

'The same. Singing about bread – no, bakers! Bakers, that was it.'

Melling exhaled uncontrollably and her smile grew with his tension.

'Seen you too,' she added, almost with a touch of childish malevolence.

Melling shuddered under her curious stare.

'I suppose you would have,' he allowed. She seemed as though she desired to hear more but he murdered her intrigue in favour of his own. 'What happened?'

Her eyes became uncertain. 'To the boy, I mean?'

She slouched under the question, but with a sigh, answered him plainly. 'Girl was crying; she was talking him down. He wouldn't listen though. No, he would not.'

'My God. You're sure she wanted him to come down?'

'Saw it with my own eyes. He said she was weak. Yep. Too weak.'

'Weak how?'

'Said she'd lost her ways. Then he jumped. Couldn't sleep much with her crying. Crows were up before she left. Lost a lot of money I did, sleeping through the day.'

Melling winced at her callousness and her smile returned. So that was another riddle solved. Judy had loved Samuel, but he had loved their philosophy more.

Exhaling his despondence, Melling left all the notes he had in her dirtied hands. 'Thank you,' he managed, before grinding his molars and getting to his feet.

'*In lucem,*' she called as he walked off, and he turned back to her with a heavy heart. He stared blankly at her for some moments, and she answered with a look almost like bewilderment. At this point he was not even sure he had heard her correctly, but then she finally repeated the chant of the *Custodes Veritatis*. '*In lucem* is what he said. Said it before the drop.'

He paused at the additional information and the wretch sneered. With that, Melling could properly imagine Samuel's departure in his mind's eye. Those parting words made things all too real, and he stubbornly attempted to whiten his mind. He nodded his goodbye, then walked in the direction of the new town.

Judy Collier had lost the man she loved to her own religion. She had wanted others to submit to her seductive suggestions of suicide, and somehow her own romantic attachments to another had provided a tragic irony. In a way, Judy was perhaps with Samuel now.

*

'I suppose I should buy you a drink then?' Harry Saturn said to Louis Starling as he pushed open the dated door of the *Abenborg*. As they entered the fog of cigarette smoke and leathery air, Starling wasn't sure what Harry meant.

'How so?'

'Well,' Harry said, finding a table and hanging his coat over the back of a chair. 'I asked you to lodge a friend of mine, and you end up discovering a suicide cult where you live.'

Starling laughed.

'I suppose you *do* owe me.'

'Not only that,' Harry said, eyes wandering over the mass of bodies who were cramped inside the musky room. 'But you end up saving Robert's life, joining him in solving the case, and arresting the local inspector.'

'Well, when you put it like that,' Starling acknowledged with an awkward smile, watching Harry move away and meander through the crowd. As the visitor bought two pints, the Huxley local bit his thumb nervously, letting the words sink in.

It was true that he could never have expected such a week in his darkest dreams. Harry, an old friend, had asked him a favour. He'd been happy to help. In the process he'd learned that his home and former university had been housing an evil so absurd and intellectualised, it refused acceptance. The man to bring the truth to light had almost hurled himself from a bridge whilst sleepwalking, something a disgraced pseudo-doctor had tried to explain to Starling who, well, had decided it was best to just be grateful Melling's condition was somehow improving. This week had altered Starling's mental paradigms completely, and he tutted to himself as he considered this, Harry returning with a Guinness.

'Nothing stronger?'

'The night is young, though we are ancient.'

That made Starling smile. They drank the cold, irony stout, listening to the burly voices of the gentlemen around them. 'You know,' Harry eventually said. 'Robert and I used to pick up girls here as students?'

'Oh, us too,' Starling replied, smiling under the nostalgia.

'And yet there are neither women nor students in this bar anymore, hey? This seems the pub for the forgotten.'

'Too right,' Starling agreed. 'Aging is quite a sad story, I must say. I used to look at my mum and wonder if she had ever been young. You know, you sort of forget they used to be our age? Now I'm as old as her when she died. It's strange. I feel like my sense of self is under threat.'

'Thanks for keeping the mood nice and light,' Harry said with a dramatic eyebrow raise, and they both laughed. 'You're right though. About age that is. Running my father's tailors initially felt like the chance to thank him, or to continue his work in a new way, and now, even I realise I'm becoming exactly who he was. The idea of being a second him was an outrageous concept and still, here I am, as cantankerous, stubborn, and old-fashioned as the man who raised me. My uncle was even worse, and I remind Robert of him, apparently.'

'Your boys may one day be the same.'

'God, I hope not. I hope they keep doing things I never liked, and things I never knew were possible.'

'Cheers to that,' Starling said, and they clinked glasses.

'Speaking of matters I don't much like nor understand. You want to explain to me again just exactly that Calmet fellow's prognosis?'

'Well,' Starling began. 'I'm afraid I don't much understand it either. You have to imagine, I mean, I deal in real medicine. Calmet has always tried to justify what I would deem fanciful. That is: most of us want to explain away magic through science, but he uses science to validate the strange. I mean, stuff well beyond Freud. And yet...'

'And yet...'

'It seems to work. You must realise: I saw Robert try and throw himself from Apollonia's Bridge! He was muttering to himself. Then he sees spectres in the night! There wasn't anything I could have given him that his own doctors wouldn't have already tried. I'm still not fully sure as to why I thought of Calmet, but well, there was something in the air that seemed to whisper his name.'

'Hmm.'

'It just seemed the right thing to do.'

'And here we are.'

There were some moments of silence as they drank, Starling eventually lighting a cigar.

'You know something else I've not fully understood?' the Huxley local asked his old friend.

'What's that, old boy?'

'This whole suicide thing.' His voice was guarded as he asked, as though the timbre was tiptoeing around the truth. Harry seemed to interpret that Louis wasn't referring to the *Custodes Veritatis*.

'As a student Robert was always very empathetic. He was good with literature because he could conjure another's perspective so well. He could get himself inside the prose, if that makes sense? Strangely, it made him a good detective. He could live inside other people's worlds.'

'But why suicide? I know it's noble of him to look out for families who have gone through such things, and well, to see if people need to be held accountable for the misery of another but...'

'The idea of Scotland Yard having someone to focus on suicide sounds bizarre?'

'Well yes. And I don't mean to doubt Robert but...'

'You're right to find it bizarre, because well, it would be. See, Robert doesn't specialise in suicide at all. As if they'd pay him for that. It's a personal preference and has become his epithet in the industry. His superiors have always found this strange and made sure he solves actual crimes. He's bloody good at solving them, by the by. But he always manages to involve himself in suicide whenever he can.'

'But *why?*' Starling's voice was far surer of itself now.

'He would tell you if you asked,' Harry said, eyes becoming poignant. 'And I do mean *you*. But it is best that you asked me instead. You see the answer he gives is enough to make you move on, make you accept.'

'The answer he gives?'

'What he tells people: that he has seen enough horrors in life. That he would rather help those whose only crime was against themselves. It's enough to make you understand, but then you keep thinking on it and demand another reason.'

'Exactly. I mean, it's very particular. Somehow, I felt I shouldn't ask.'

'He has enough torture happening in his head right now, so I think it best *I* tell you.' With that, he lit his own Dominican, and exhaled slowly, as if bracing himself. Starling's palms were wet.

'Robert spent a lot of time in Paris after Huxley,' Harry eventually began, voice soft, almost unsure of which pitch to conjure.

'He was a good boy at heart, very empathetic, but very misunderstood. He had the curse of an overread mind. He longed for an artistic life, not fully understanding what that could mean, nor how that would work. That reality was *real*, and that you needed to exist then and there, not in books. He chased a lot of beautiful women, blurring their beauty with apparent truths. He was very lost.'

'He would make a complicated character,' Starling said.

'That he would. He certainly played one. Bill, his father, William Melling that is, indulged him, understanding that the lad just needed some life experience. Bill was a really good father. He came from pretty much nothing, and his life was far from easy. Then there's the Great War – all our fathers know of that.'

'Too right,' Starling said in a whisper, somewhat guessing where this tale may be heading.

'Bill was always telling Robert to work, and to use those skills, but after a while I think he sometimes regretted paying for those schools and all those tutors. In his mind it had burdened such a delicate boy with too much philosophy.' He cleared his throat. 'I really wish he could have seen how strong Robert really is. That he was just as stubborn an ox as his father. I'm sure Bill would have also really liked that his son wanted to work for Scotland Yard, but alas, he never got to hear of it.' Harry paused for a moment to finish his Guinness. It hurt him a lot to recount the story. His left hand twitched and he took a long, slow drag before he began again. 'Robert was going to come home with Lorelei. Surprise his father. He was beyond in love. It was when Hitler took the rest of the Czechs, actually. War was in the air and well… it seemed Bill had already decided that history was to repeat itself and, the stubborn ox had decided he didn't want to see that happen to his boy.'

'You mean he…'

Harry just nodded. 'I don't believe it,' Starling managed to say, voice a heavy whisper, practically inaudible in such a loud room. The smokers and drinkers about him morphed into an irrelevant, singular crowd.

'They found him in his study,' Harry said flatly. 'He'd used his gun. Letters his wife had sent him while he was away fighting were on the table. That seemed to explain it. I mean: there wasn't a note, or anything.'

Starling released an unsteady breath.

'So, all this time, Robert has been trying to... well... he's been...'

'Consoling his dad's spirit? Yes. He blames himself. He thinks he failed him. It broke him, and he had little time to process it because, well, like most of us, soon he was becoming a soldier. In any case,' he paused again. 'Every suicide he handles provides some sort of step towards, well, I'm not sure there's a verb to describe just what he's doing. But it is almost like the prayers people say for those in purgatory. Whenever he handles a suicide, he does it for Bill Melling. I think in his mind his father's suffering is still ongoing. He chips away at it with every condolence he offers, every suicide note he reads, every mother he hugs.'

'That's... that's...' Starling couldn't find the words. Eventually he settled for sorrow: 'that poor man.'

'Robert is carrying many worlds on his shoulders,' Harry said. 'But I believe this is the biggest burden of them all.'

*

Robert and Calmet wandered out into the darkened cold of Huxley, meandering up the pathways which led to Dunfield College. The detective was quiet on the way. Only the sound of the wind was audible as it tickled past his ears. Calmet was just as silent, seemingly engrossed in his own thoughts and smoking away the seconds with his cigarette. The castle beckoned from above them, and the waning moon only half-managed to illuminate the Gothic spires which clung to the sky like falling ivy cast in dark ivory. Melling's cheekbones grew colder. He had given his coat to the girl with auburn hair and had forgotten to ask Calmet to borrow a new one; he had been anxious to leave the emotions of the house behind. The rehashing of Dunfield's so-called 'genius' was a particularly morose moment. The anguish in Calmet's eyes when he was told of how the *Custodes Veritatis* had made it so that the German would persecute himself for his student's suicide – Melling would do his best to block that from his mind. But something stranger still, unsettled him more.

'Last night I slept soundly,' he had said to Calmet. 'I have spent every night of every month of this year unsatisfied. Either woken or disturbed, and since arriving in Huxley, I have almost died. Well in fact, I did actually…'

'Die,' Calmet finished for him. 'Yes. Your neck looks slightly better, Detective. As for the death, well, I'm sure you yourself must have some idea why the nightmares stopped?'

'You told me to yield to my subconscious desire, and well, I realise now that a night ago when I saw Lorelei, I still did not.'

'What did you do?'

'She approached me, but I was afraid. I begged her to leave me in peace.'

'Despite his evils, Professor Robora has perhaps lifted your curse.'

'I don't really go in for that sort of thing, Calmet. I have followed the rationalities of your science, but the more mystic it becomes the less I believe.'

'The subconscious is a reality whether one agrees or not. It is the realm of repressed desire.'

Melling had been sweating under his overworn clothes. 'And as you stopped breathing, you satisfied your desire.'

'That cannot be true.'

'My professor in Munich would argue that every human being has what's called a *todestrieb*. It is a death-drive. A desire for a conclusion.'

'But the very essence of being human is striving to exist and procreate. I'm afraid I don't agree.'

'How easy it was for professors to convince students to seek death. So much for this myth of procreation. They must have appealed to something?'

Melling had been chewing nervously on his cigar. Reason had left the room.

'That's not the same,' he had managed to say.

'Ahh, well. In any case, that your death-drive was amplified was already clear to both of us. You longed to be with your wife, and though your rational brain would never think to follow through on such a thing: let us say that the subconscious is not rational. Perhaps it is even too rational, willing to act without hesitation.'

'So, denying the truth?'

'By resisting your desire, it was only repressed deeper into the subconscious. If it had continued, it would have manifested itself impulsively, racing past the guards of reason. But, whether fortunately or unfortunately, this Robora played the part of your subconscious and brought you to the brink of death.'

Melling had needed to revisit his death: the echoing call of Lorelei as he drifted under. Then Marcellus had resuscitated him.

'So, the desire's been satisfied?'

'*Auf Wiedersehen*,' Calmet had said with a laugh.

Robert shivered under the memory, but Calmet thought he now shivered under the cruel wind.

'It is especially cold tonight,' he said as the market road that led to Dunfield College revealed itself. They were Dunfield-bound because Melling still felt as though the *Custodes Veritatis* were not quite in his grasp. For such a detailed philosophy, Melling wanted something tangible. The master's study beckoned him, and the detective knew who he would want beside him should he need to decode the occult. Calmet knew well beyond what Melling could hardly comprehend, and this understanding showed him once more that perhaps he was near the end of his tenure. How much had he missed this week which he would have threaded together in hours had he been his younger self?

In Huxley he had hardly detected, merely observed. The truth had fallen awkwardly around him from the mouths of others. He had just been stubborn enough to search for it. The case might read as a success on paper, but Melling considered it a great failure.

'You know, Calmet. I should thank you on behalf of London, really.'

'It was fated. I had already been hurt by Huxley.'

'Maybe.'

'You have done many a service by coming here, Robert.'

'Are you in my thoughts?'

That made Calmet laugh.

'I do not swing my pocket watch now,' he said, earning a half-smile.

'Usually, I am the one with the answers. Not the random doctor who I paid to help me sleep.'

Calmet said nothing in response. 'I think my days are done. Think about that poor girl from Lucy's funeral service. Her death. How could I have forgotten what the inspector had said about her? I was sleeping last night.'

'Her death isn't your fault.'

'The day Olivia Rosewood called me she mentioned that her daughter had been reading things out of character. Ten years ago, I would have made that connection far quicker. Maybe Alexander Dawn wouldn't be in a coma. Maybe Lea Algrin wouldn't have hanged herself… then…'

'Perhaps you simply could never have imagined such a horrible thing from Huxley?'

'Perhaps,' Melling said, breath rising towards the silhouette of Huxley Castle. 'Nonetheless, it is my job to realise the perverse.' His voice now found the pitch of rueful futility. 'No, Calmet, my days are done. There was my flustered nature, my dreams, my personal goings on. Too much has happened. Maybe with my wife, it was all too recent for me to get back into my work.'

'You solved the case,' Calmet said, offering a warm smile despite the cold air.

'And children are still dead. You don't understand. I used to be brilliant. *Brilliant.* Even the young lads had heard of me. This isn't about my pride, I just feel perhaps it is time for fresh eyes, fresh legs. I was bloody good at solving. I could feel what others couldn't. I wouldn't take things as they seemed. Here in Huxley, I let things remain as appeared. I have floated along the cobbles until the truth arrived. I used to meet it halfway at least. My days are spent. I've been chewed up by the world, and it might cost someone their life… it *has* cost some their lives. It's time for those younger lads to fill my shoes.'

'I do not really have an answer to that, Robert. Simply that I understand what you have said, and that it takes a strong man to know when it is time to hang up his coat. But please, it is not you who is responsible for Judy, or that girl from the service. Any of them. You are the one who came to save them.'

'Thank you,' Melling said. He couldn't say much else.

They walked past the emptied market stalls that guarded the wooden gate of Dunfield College. As his breath danced away in fog, the detective knocked on the ancient entrance, but only the wind answered. He knocked again, more loudly this time, hurriedly putting his hand back into his pocket to avoid exposure. It *was* almost unbearably cold, just as Calmet had said. Minutes exhaled by, and the detective had all but given up by the time a rough male voice called from behind the door.

'Who's there?'

'It's Detective Robert Melling from the Metropolitan Police. I need to see Master Dunfield's study. It's about the students who died.'

There was no reply, and Melling wondered if the man had even heard him. Then, the heavy wooden gate groaned in protest, half-opening for the men, who stepped through to meet a froglike man, hunched over under nature's cruelty.

'You'll be needing a lamp, Detective,' he said with a haggard croak. 'We've killed the electricity.'

'Has anyone been there since the body of the professor was removed?' The man shook his head, disappearing into his lodge. Returning with two lamps, one for both Calmet and Melling, he handed them a grey key.

Thus, Calmet and Melling navigated through the pathways that carved along the black lawns until they were walking through the invasive branches of the flourishing evergreens. It felt strange for Melling, walking back to the place which could have marked his death.

He wondered if his subconscious was perhaps guiding him, disguising itself behind a desire to investigate.

'I've never seen that before,' Calmet said in appreciation of the library's clock tower. The darkened lapiz was coloured a gloomy, pacific blue. The golden hands seemed to disappear into a murky sea, and Melling too, had to admire the beauty. 'German design,' the hypnotist added as they walked between the shrubbery that lined the pathway of the master's lodge. Melling eyed the wooden cabin in suspicion and paused at the golden letters by the door. 'It's awfully cold out here, Mr Melling,' Calmet murmured.

'Right! Apologies.'

He took the grey key from his pocket and inserted it into the keyhole. It wouldn't unlock. 'Wait a moment.'

He turned the handle in suspicion and the door opened easily.

'It was already unlocked,' Calmet whispered. Melling grabbed the cold handle of the Smith & Wesson in his pocket. They slowly stepped into the shadowy study, their lamps glowing onto the wooden floors and bouncing off the velvet-bound books which lined the shelves. Melling looked behind the door, swallowing nervously. No one. 'Maybe the last person forgot to lock it?' Calmet offered, but then they were interrupted by the melancholic chimes of the library tower bell. Neither gentleman said anything as the dooming rings resounded eleven times. Then, when they were once again in silence, Melling decided to shake off his ill-feeling.

'Come on,' he said, 'let's see what we can find.'

They began by dissecting the contents of the master's mahogany desk, which bore fruitless results. They scoured the room, leaving nothing uninspected. Eventually, in frustration, Melling poured through every single book around him. Noting his efforts, Calmet chuckled.

'There isn't enough time in the night for *that* exercise.'

'I have to try,' Melling said in frustration, replacing yet another book of unrelated details.

Soon, the library bell instructed them that it was half past the hour, and Melling was no closer to finding anything.

'You won't be leaving until you're finished, will you?' Calmet asked, lamp glowing against the soft brown of the wood beside him. 'Maybe we should call Louis.' But as Calmet wanted to turn, he saw something in Melling's eyes that made him shudder.

'What is it?' the detective asked, but Calmet shook his head with a cough, unwilling to acknowledge his concern.

'I, well, it's nothing.'

'You sure?' Melling asked, unsettled by the man's stare. He was blatantly disturbed, looking at the detective as though he was afraid of him.

'Just the shadows playing with me,' Calmet reassured. Melling was going to push the matter, but he too was spooked by shadows: in the lamplight he thought he saw Lucy's symbol beside Calmet. He rubbed his eyes for clarity. The shadow remained. He walked over to Calmet's side and traced his hand over the symbol. Yes! He was not mistaken. It was the very same inverted sunset which the German had first explained to him. Calmet peered at the lines Melling traced with his finger. '*Mein Gott*,' he whispered. 'Is that what I think it is?'

'Yes! But what does it signify?'

Melling pulled out the books to either side, discarding each one as their revelations showed him nothing of value. He traced his hand slowly around the shelf, reaching for some sort of opening or suggestion of a hidden compartment. His nail grazed a small gap at the back of the shelf; grinning, he slid his finger back along the wooden panel. 'Hold on.' He pushed the panel to the side, and it moved with a definitive click. A creaking sound was heard from under the master's desk, and the gentlemen turned around in surprise, believing an intruder to be standing behind them. They were alone.

'My, my,' Calmet said with a grin. 'That is clever.'

'Let's see,' Melling replied, crouching under the desk to learn that two floorboards had risen by an inch at their edges. Pulse quickening its propagation, he managed to dig his finger underneath and lift the boards up until a safe-like space was revealed. An iron chest was buried within. 'Aha!' he shouted in delight, retrieving the chest. He was instantly disappointed when it turned out, only naturally, to be locked. Not just locked. A hammer looked like it would struggle to crack open the metal which surrounded the keyhole, and a sledgehammer would clearly be required to smash through the heavy iron of the chest itself.

He placed it on the desk, holding his lamp to the deeply embedded lock, seeing how the same inverted hieroglyph was painted above it.

'That seems ship sturdy,' Calmet said. 'I wonder if there is anything which we can use to break it.' He stepped away from the desk to survey what objects he might use, eyes falling on the fireplace. However, as his hand found the poker, the door to the study opened with a groan. Calmet raised the poker in defence and Melling jumped before the desk.

'Who's there?'

The hunch-backed porter waddled into the study. 'Oh'.

The man eyed the poker.

'I hope you don't intend to use that, boy,' he said to Calmet in suspicion, who lowered the instrument in apologies.

'Is anything the matter?' Melling asked.

'Well,' the man grumbled. 'I've received a phone call asking you both return to the police station as soon as possible.'

Melling and Calmet looked at one another in fear.

'Why?' Melling asked. The man looked at him carefully before he spoke.

'Said that the master escaped.'

Melling's blood felt as though it had curdled around his heart.

'We need to get there now.'

The detective hoisted the chest into his arms, following Calmet and the porter from the room. They immediately left the man behind however, hurrying through the dark undergrowth and out into the air. Melling paused to readjust the chest, trying to spy the path back towards the gate. The college was painted a ghostly hue. 'This way,' he said to Calmet, but the latter didn't respond. 'Calmet?' he asked, turning around to where his companion was waiting. 'What's the matt –'

And then he saw it.

In the light of the waning moon, the library's grey stone was pallored a sickly white. The wind whipped up behind Melling, blowing onto his neck and singeing his skin. His eyes rested on the lapiz face of the oceanic clock, hands minutes away from the midnight strike. In the darkened shadows beneath, it was almost difficult to spot. But in the movements of the wind, the rope was visible. It swung to the side, standing out against the backdrop of the lighter stones. At the bottom of the rope, swinging like the pendulum of a grandfather clock, was the silhouetted figure of the master. Melling couldn't see his face, but his tingling goosebumps could affirm that it was Gabriel Dunfield. The body swayed to and fro like ticking seconds, and Melling could just about hear the stretching fibres of the cord that bore his weight. In his mind's eye he saw the smiling agate eyes, closed though they must be under the grip of death. So that was why the office had already been unlocked. Clearly the man had not just escaped from prison but had decided to escape into the unknowns of *his* certain truth.

Seeing the swinging man, lifeless in the chiaroscuro, Melling did not feel vindicated. Hell was an attractive idea because it promised punishment to those who deserved it, even when they escaped our clutches. But Master Dunfield did not believe in hell. Truthfully, Melling did not believe in hell either. There was just no saying where it all ended, how one was judged, if they were even judged at all, or if the body truly did just return to dust, the soul a mere piece of human handiwork to help us sleep at night, or to correct our wrongs, tossing and turning under a guilt of our own make believe. From the Egyptians to Melling's own era, no one had ever come back from that final destination, at least properly, not as someone's ghost. Nor without attaching a religion to them supposedly doing so, and that, for the detective, diluted the veracity of such claims. The only return of the dead Melling knew of was his own wife's midnight hauntings, and they were of his own creation. There seemed to be too much ego in death.

Shuddering under the spectacle of the dangling corpse, Melling again appreciated that in many ways Dunfield had been right: life's ultimate truth could only be found in death. To be, stealing Hamlet's most famous two words, was to be in ignorance of the *whys* behind existence, but death, death was our final confirmation of what it had all been for. The detective decided that he would not remember the man for his evil. Dunfield had spent his profession behaving as a culprit, but in these final moments, he had become a self-oppressor: a victim of his own hand, and Melling could never fail to pity the victim of suicide. In some ways, stretched though they be, Melling hoped that there might at last be some sort of peace for such a man. Now that the gentleman lay swinging from the clock tower of Dunfield library, the detective began to realise what Nietzsche had meant when he had suggested looking at life beyond good and evil. Beyond morality. Suicide had shown that Master Gabriel Dunfield must truly have believed in the innocence of his own philosophy, like the Aztec priest who sacrificed a child for the sake of the sun. In a mixture of disgust, wonder, and something ineffable, Melling turned around, leaving the dangling corpse to slither across the moonbeams.

'*In lucem*,' he murmured.

XXXII

But That I Would Not Lose Her

Sight for So Long

1947

It was still a strange feeling for Robert Melling to lie against a cushioned mattress, safely guarded by silken sheets. It was a stranger feeling still, to be lying against the warm, olive-skinned goddess who now shared his bed. He traced a curious finger along her collar bone, still enraptured by an intense newfangleness. The motion woke the sleeping beauty, and she rolled over to face him, raven curls dangling into lazy, cinnamon eyes.

Lorelei's morning face was, for Melling, like drinking a sugary coffee after a day of sweat and labour; like shutting the door of a hearth-warmed log cabin after trekking in a blizzard; like the promise of a clean bed. There was a homeliness in her eyes that an author will always struggle to illustrate, especially since this homeliness was idiosyncratic for the lover. Melling himself tried to conjure a metaphor that would justify her immanent promise of security, but, well, language cannot always convey our feelings. Especially the feelings of one who has spent the past few years lying awake, dreaming of *her*, the enemy's shells raining relentlessly overhead.

'*Arrête de te torturer l'esprit ainsi, mon mari,*' she whispered, wrapping warm fingers around his left cheek.

Stop torturing yourself, my husband.

That noun would take some even greater getting used to than the bedsheets, but he was overjoyed by the possibility of growing accustomed to hearing it on her lips. It eclipsed the sound of muddy shrapnel in an instant. She grinned. 'I like calling you my husband,' she said in an indolent murmur, giving him a long, purposeful kiss. Then she stared at the curtained window of their beachside hotel room, sunlight forcing its way through heavy, white curtains.

'*Merde!* What time is it?'

'Who cares?' Melling answered, snaking an arm around her fleeing waist. She snuggled against him with a laugh.

'We have things to do today, *mon amour.*'

'Says who?'

'*Ton amour…*'

'What's the point of a honeymoon if I can't have you all to myself?'

'But that is the point, Robert,' she said, running sincere fingers over his arm. 'You have me all to yourself now.'

'It isn't enough,' he whispered, and she laughed, slapping his forearm then wriggling free of his embrace.

'*Allons-y!* We have things to do.'

Melling was reminded of a poem by John Donne, *The Sun Rising*, but he had only now felt its true significance.

'Busy old fool, unruly sun,' he muttered, 'why dost thou thus through windows and through curtains, call on us?'

Lorelei turned to him, naked frame pausing before the closed curtains. '*Qu'est-ce que tu as dit?*' she asked with a smile. He jumped up from bed and ran towards her, she, laughingly, pushing him away.

'I was cursing the sun, my dear!' he yelled, she in return giggling at his liveliness.

Thus, laughing and holding one another, their lazy morning managed to remain lazy for a little longer, the curtains remaining closed for the two lovers to enjoy the miracle of being together. The cushioned mattress and silken sheets became their cosy den once again, despite the sun rising.

Robert Melling rejoiced in knowing that just as daybreak was a certainty, so too, now, was Lorelei. Despite the ephemerality of life, this morning moment hinted at an immortality; one which claimed that passion could master time. As many writers have often stressed, being nestled in a lover's arms, despite the inevitable parting, was an opiate against that future distance. Head in the sand, eyes closed, body to body. There *was* an imperishability in that. It didn't matter if one day they would be parted. They had loved. They had loved properly. They had shared in one another. The familiar scent of her shoulder. The scar on her right hip. The warm goosebumps of your lover's thigh against your own – *that* was immortality.

Limbs renewedly entangled, sweat beads gliding down one another's skin, Melling closed his eyes to the sun, pulling his Lorelei closer against him. So it would be, he promised himself. Especially after all that he had been through. No moment wasted was an ubiquitous claim for any lover. But for a man who had seen what he had seen, he felt determined to live up to the promise more so than any man had yet been able. As Donne had so poetically predicted, whenever time would get in the way, Melling could eclipse the sun by shutting out the world, crushing its demands with his eyelids…

But that I would not lose her sight for so long.

XXXIII

The Platform's End?

In the aggressive iridescence of the evidence room, Melling opened the soft pages of Gabriel Dunfield's journal to discover a detailed diary. It had been inside the iron chest from the master's study. Louis Starling, Harry Saturn and Calmet Traum watched the detective read in painful silence.

'It's him writing about students,' Melling said, voice dripping distaste.

'Don't look to me for a second opinion,' Starling said in disgust.

'Prospective students are evidently documented extensively before indoctrination is considered.' He wondered if one of these journals might house his past. A sharp ache pushed between his eyes and he winced; it goaded with the thumb print of a cruel sadist. Calmet's eyes widened in worry.

'Everything alright?'

'Yes, fine,' Melling said, waving his hand dismissively. He didn't like the confused look the German doctor was giving him – it reminded him of how he had stared at him in Dunfield's study.

He skipped ahead to the most recent weeks of the master's writing, and with his erratic movement, an envelope fell from the pages. It was addressed to Dunfield himself and dated just over half a year ago. Inhaling to calm his nerves, the detective opened it slowly, running his uneasy fingers over the folded card. It too, was addressed to the master, and Melling read carefully. His headache was potent now.

Courtier Dunfield,

I write to you with new developments.

Your man, Courtier Robora, has been most helpful in instructing us in our pursuits. His guidance will allow us to work more effectively and secretively, as our duty demands.

I am writing now with an enormous feeling of excitement, for my beloved pupil has shown some intrigue to our ways. He is of the brightest minds that I have witnessed in my career as a professor of law, and he is brighter still in appreciating what the Custodes Veritatis can do for him. He will allow more time for education with us. His name is Jacob Wenley, and I shall look forward to presenting him as Courtier Wenley soon enough. I suspect his step into liberation should commence very soon after. He is desperate to know more than he yet can.

Tenebris in lucem,

Courtier Michaels

The letter dropped from Melling's hands in a gasp, and he stumbled backwards. Harry's hands were the only thing steadying him. 'What is it, Robert?' his friend asked, voice a whisper. The detective was silent.

'What is it?' Starling repeated, *his* voice wavering with drops of fear. Still Melling could not reply. He slowly walked back to the table and his hands trembled as he re-read the name.

Jacob Wenley.

Yes. It was the same boy. His lips quivered as the voice of Constable Whaites jumped out of his memories.

Boy, Detective? He was almost twenty-three. Hardly a lad by any means.

Yes. Jacob Wenley. The law graduate who had stepped in front of the twenty-seven past two train, as it raced past Horsham station in Sussex. 'Platform one,' Melling murmured in recollection, Calmet again staring at him in a manner altogether different to the way Starling watched in fear.

But the lad, Wenley, was not a Huxley graduate? The detective's stomach upturned in nausea, and he drummed his worried fingers on the evidence table, reliving the corporeal carnage that had splattered Jacob across the tracks. Starling and Harry were speaking; Harry had taken the letter now. Melling hardly noticed them. His conversation with Constable Whaites further returned to him.

Jacob was such a smart boy too – such a dreadful shame. Where is it you went to, Detective? Somewhere posh, wasn't it? He was at somewhere similar.

Had this truly been the work of the *Custodes Veritatis*? He closed his eyes in intense concentration until Dunfield's agate irises forced their way into his vision, and he was once again, back inside a Huxley cell.

'It won't be difficult to trace those who go missing,' Melling had said in triumph. But the master had smiled that sinister smile.

Perhaps… But we live on in other ways.

'My God,' Melling groaned to himself, heart straining inside his constricted chest. 'It isn't just here. They aren't just at Huxley,' he whispered. 'Wenley… I was at his death.'

He ran anxious hands through his aging hair, until Harry's inhale of breath seemed to confirm just how much Melling had failed. He felt his control fall away, and he slammed a fist onto the table. 'I haven't bloody stopped anything!' he shouted. Who knew how many institutions

Dunfield's colleagues had infected? They may have saved Huxley's initiates, but there would be more, currently nameless to Melling, who would fill their suicidal shoes. Melling could not believe it. He had stopped nothing. That thought reprimanded him over and over as an invisible taunter pressed a sharp thumb between his eyes. Rage gave way to melancholy. All he could see was the master's all-knowing agate glare.

It is our duty to show them the light!

It often seemed like Melling's entire life was cruelly connected, destined to keep him a step behind with every step he took. He pulled a cigarette from his case and lit it shakily, inhaling deeply before throwing his lighter onto the table like a stone. His headache was unbearable now. The others were speaking to him. It didn't matter what they had to say.

'Robert we should –' Harry tried again, but before he could finish his sentence, Melling had flipped the table and chest onto the floor. He screamed like a mother who had lost her child. The pitch brought tears to the listeners. No one dared to move. In fact, behind him, Harry and Louis were too afraid to say anything. They watched in horror as Melling rubbed his face over and over, frantically smoking as he thought and rethought all of the implications.

'Everyone shut up,' Melling said, staring into the floor. 'Just… silence.' Calmet stood to the side, shaking his head in sadness. He had seen something in the detective's eyes the night before in the master's study, and what it had betokened scared him greatly. He saw it more clearly now that Melling was manic. The German doctor knew that the final strands of Robert Melling's reason were at risk of slipping away. He understood that the detective, after a lifetime of heartbreak, might finally see his mental faculties break entirely.

It seemed an eternity passed before anyone said anything. Melling had forgotten they were even there.

'Robert?' Harry asked, tentatively putting a hand on his shoulder.

'What is it?' Melling snapped, rudely, shrugging the hand away.

'You're muttering to yourself,' Calmet said flatly. The detective did not respond, for he had not even heard the reply. All he could see was Jacob Wenley's corpse and the master's agate eyes.

It took an unbearably long time before the others could eventually console him and bring him into the present reality. It all ended with the detective shedding seemingly an endless supply of tears. There were too many 'whys' inside his head; they tumbled out as sobs. Someone had to be the man to face the evils on behalf of the wronged. Melling was exhausted by how often that someone had to be him. He was unravelling under the truth of how horrible life could be and would continue to be. Darkness persisted.

Bertie, a friend in Paris, had once said: Huxley's ghosts always meet. The speaker and the recipient had been all smiles back then, but Melling recalled the words now under the disgusting weight of broken necks, falling bodies, carved symbols, dark puppets, comas, absurd philosophies. He believed he had stopped it. That he had buried Huxley's wrongs. But Huxley had returned, meeting the living as ghosts always do. He had stopped nothing. Dunfield's death did not betoken an end. Huxley's ghosts haunted the living still, still cooing dark philosophies into the ears of students, who knew where, or how many. What's more: Melling wasn't sure he was the man to stop it anymore. He didn't feel he had the strength left inside of him. It was someone else's turn to pick up the pieces. It might not be the end for the *Custodes Veritatis*, but it was beginning to feel like end of Detective Robert Melling.

*

Mrs Gladys Dryad was humming patriotic melodies when the post fell through the letterbox of 13, Thurloe Place in South Kensington. She had been dusting the library when the clang of the metal guard startled her. She found the small pile and began sifting through; it was her custom to remove any advertisements before leaving the post on Melling's desk. Two items she immediately knew she could throw away. One letter, however, demanded a second glance. It had the house address and Melling's full title, but there was a strange wax symbol which sealed the envelope. Gladys had never seen such a symbol before. It reminded her of a hieroglyph.

'Most strange,' she muttered; then she realised that the return address was in Huxley. The detective himself was due to return from Huxley tomorrow, and she found it peculiar that this letter should beat him to the door. She read the addressee's name: Master Gabriel Dunfield of Dunfield College. 'Most strange,' she repeated with a shrug.

She carried the post to Melling's study, then returned to her chores. She wondered what she would prepare for his homecoming meal.

Fin

About the Author

Julian Kitsz began writing as a hobby at 16, but, after a first draft of *In Lucem* during the pandemic, decided this novel was to be his debut. He read English at the University of Cambridge, where, during his second year, the notion of Huxley College began to take shape. The writer's heroes are the likes of Keats and Wilde, and Kitsz intends to bridge the gap between classic styles and a modern audience. All enquiries can be made via the author's website: juliankitsz.com.

About the Artist

This book's cover is the work of Harry Carley, an artist, illustrator and printmaker from Kent, England. His main practice revolves around drawing and print making, as well as producing monotypes from his photography. Commonly working with an achromatic palette, he relies on experimental mark making and tonal variation to generate form and depth. All enquiries can be directed to: Harryoliverart@gmail.com.

Printed in Great Britain
by Amazon

32192544R00179